A FISH
IN MEMISON

Also by E. R. Eddison

The Poems, Letters and Memoirs of Philip Sidney Nairn
Styrbiorn the Strong
Egil's Saga
The Worm Ouroboros
Mistress of Mistresses
The Mezentian Gate

A FISH DINNER IN MEMISON

by

E. R. Eddison

HarperCollins*Publishers*

HarperCollins*Publishers*
77-85 Fulham Palace Road
Hammersmith, London W6 8JB
www.harpercollins.co.uk

This edition 2014
1

978-0-00-757815-3

Typeset by Palimpsest Book Production Limited, Falkirk, Stirlingshire

Printed and bound in Great Britain by
Clays Ltd, St Ives plc

MIX
Paper from
responsible sources
FSC™ C007454

Contents

INTRODUCTION

BY JAMES STEPHENS

THIS is a terrific book.

It is not much use asking, whether a given writer is great or not. The future will decide as to that, and will take only proper account of our considerations on the matter. But we may enquire as to whether the given writer does or does not differ from other writers: from, that is, those that went before, and, in especial, from those who are his and our contemporaries.

In some sense Mr Eddison can be thought of as the most difficult writer of our day, for behind and beyond all that which we cannot avoid or refuse – the switching as from a past to something that may be a future – he is writing with a mind fixed upon ideas which we may call ancient but which are, in effect, eternal: aristocracy, courage, and a 'hell of a cheek'. It must seem lunatic to say of any man that always, as a guide of his inspiration, is an idea of the Infinite. Even so, when the proper question is asked, *wherein does Mr Eddison differ from his fellows?* that is one answer which may be advanced. Here he does differ, and that so greatly that he may seem as a pretty lonely writer.

There is a something, exceedingly rare in English fiction, although everywhere to be found in English poetry – this may be called the aristocratic attitude and accent. The aristocrat can be as brutal as ever gangster was, but, and in whatever brutality, he preserves a bearing, a grace, a charm, which our fiction in general does not care, or dare, to attempt.

Good breeding and devastating brutality have never been strangers to each other. You may get in the pages of, say, *The Mahabharata* – the most aristocratic work of all literature – more sheer brutality than all our gangster fictionists put together could dream of. So, in these pages, there are villanies and violences and slaughterings that are, to one reader, simply devilish. But they are devilish with an accent – as Milton's devil is; for it is instantly observable in him, the most English personage of our record and the finest of our 'gentlemen', that he was educated at Cambridge. So the colossal gentlemen of Mr Eddison have, perhaps, the Oxford accent. They are certainly not accented as of Balham or Hoboken.

All Mr Eddison's personages are of a 'breeding' which, be it hellish or heavenish, never lets its fathers down, and never lets its underlings up. So, again, he is a different writer, and difficult.

There is yet a distinction, as between him and the rest of us. He is, although strictly within the terms of his art, a philosopher. The ten or so pages of his letter (to that good poet, George Rostrevor Hamilton) which introduces this book form a rapid conspectus of philosophy. (They should be read after the book is read, whereupon the book should be read again.)

It is, however, another aspect of being that now claims the main of his attention, and is the true and strange subject of this book, as it is the subject of his earlier novels, *Mistress of Mistresses* and *The Worm Ouroboros*, to which this book is organically related. (The reader who likes this book should read those others.)

This subject, seen in one aspect, we call Time, in another we call it Eternity. In both of these there is a somewhat which is timeless and tireless and infinite – that something is you and me and E. R. Eddison. It delights in, and knows nothing of, and cares less about, its own seeming evolution in time, or its own actions and reactions, howsoever or wheresoever, in eternity. It just (whatever and wherever it is) wills to be, and to be powerful and beautiful and violent and in love. It enjoys birth and death, as they seem to come with insatiable appetite and with unconquerable lust for more.

The personages of this book are living at the one moment in several dimensions of time, and they will continue to do so for ever. They are in love and in hate simultaneously in these several dimensions, and will continue to be so for ever – or perhaps until they remember, as Brahma did, that they had done this thing before.

This shift of time is very oddly, very simply, handled by Mr Eddison. A lady, the astounding Fiorinda, leaves a gentleman, the even more (if possible) astounding Lessingham, after a cocktail in some Florence or Mentone. She walks down a garden path until she is precisely out of his sight: then she takes a step to the left, right out of this dimension and completely into that other which is her own – although one doubts that fifty dimensions could quite contain this lady. Whereupon that which is curious and curiously satisfying, Mr Eddison's prose takes the same step to the left and is no more the easy English of the moment before, but is a tremendous sixteenth- or fifteenth-century English which no writer but he can handle.

His return from there and then to here and now is just as simple and as exquisitely perfect in time-phrasing as could be wished for. There is no jolt for the reader as he moves or removes from dimension to dimension, or from our present excellent speech to our memorable great prose. Mr Eddison differs from all in his ability to suit his prose to his occasion and to please the reader in his anywhere.

This writer describes men who are beautiful and powerful and violent – even his varlets are tremendous. Here, in so far as they can be conjured into modern speech, are the heroes. Their valour and lust is endless as is that of tigers: and, like these, they take life or death with a purr or a snarl, just as it is appropriate and just as they are inclined to. But it is to his ladies that the affection of Mr Eddison's great and strange talent is given.

Women in many modern novels are not really females, accompanied or pursued by appropriate belligerent males – they are mainly excellent aunts, escorted by trustworthy uncles, and, when they marry, they don't reproduce sons and daughters, they produce nephews and nieces.

Every woman Mr Eddison writes of is a Queen. Even the maids of these, at their servicings, are Princesses. Mr Eddison is the only modern man who likes women. The idea *woman* in these pages is most quaint, most lovely, most disturbing. She is delicious and aloof: delighted with all, partial to everything (*ça m'amuse*, she says). She is greedy and treacherous and imperturbable: the mistress of man and the empress of life: wearing merely as a dress the mouse, the lynx, the wren or the hero: she is the goddess as she pleases, or the god; and is much less afraid of the god than a miserable woman of our dreadful bungalows is afraid of a mouse. And she is all else that is high or low or even obscene, just as the fancy takes her: she falls never (in anything, nor anywhere) below the greatness that is all creator, all creation, and all delight in her own abundant variety. *Je m'amuse*, she says, and that seems to her, and to her lover, to be right and all right.

The vitality of the recording of all this is astonishing: and in this part of his work Mr Eddison is again doing something which no other writer has the daring or the talent for.

He is also trying to do the oddest something for our time – he is trying to write prose. 'Tis a neglected, almost a lost, art, but he is not only trying, he is actually doing it. His pages are living and vivid and noble, and are these in a sense that belongs to no other writer I know of.

His *Fish Dinner* is a banquet such as, long ago, Plato sat at. As to how Mr Eddison's philosophy stands let the philosophers decide: but as to his novel, his story-telling, his heroical magnificence of prose, and his sense of the splendid, the voluptuous, the illimitable, the reader may judge of these things by himself and be at peace or at war with Mr Eddison as he pleases.

This is the largest, the most abundant, the most magnificent book of our time. Heaven send us another dozen such from Mr Eddison,

JAMES STEPHENS
15th December 1940

To my son-in-law
Flying Officer KENNETH HESKETH HIGSON
who in an air fight over Italy
saved his four companions' lives
at cost of his own
I DEDICATE THIS BOOK
which he had twice read.

Proper names the reader will no doubt pronounce as he chooses. But perhaps, to please me, he will let *Memison* echo 'denizen' except for the *m*: pronounce the first syllable of *Reisma* 'rays': keep the *i*'s short in *Zimiamvia* and accent the third syllable: accent the second syllable in *Zayana*, give it a broad *a* (as in 'Guiana'), and pronouce the *ay* in the first syllable (and also the *ai* in *Laimak*, *Kaima*, etc., and the *ay* in *Krestenaya*) like the *ai* in 'aisle': accent the first syllable in *Rerek* and make it rhyme with 'year': keep the *g* soft in *Fingiswold*: remember that *Fiorinda* is an Italian name, *Beroald* (and, for this particular case, *Amalie*) French, and *Zenianthe*, and several others, Greek: last, regard the *sz* in *Meszria* as ornamental, and not be deterred from pronouncing it as plain 'Mezria'.

This divine beauty is evident, fugitive, impalpable, and homeless in a world of material fact; yet it is unmistakably individual and sufficient unto itself, and although perhaps soon eclipsed is never really extinguished: for it visits time and belongs to eternity.

GEORGE SANTAYANA

χρόνια μὲν τὰ τῶν θεῶν πως, ἐς τέλος δ᾽ οὐκ ἀσθενῆ.
EURIPIDES, *ION*, 1615

. . . though what if Earth
Be but the shaddow of Heav'n, and therein
Each to other like, more than on earth is thought?
MILTON, *PARADISE LOST*, V. 571

Ces serments, ces parfums, ces baisers infinis,
Renaîtront-ils d'un gouffre interdit à nos sondes,
Comme montent au ciel les soleils rajeunis
Après s'être lavés au fond des mers profondes?
—O serments! ô parfums! ô baisers infinis!
BAUDELAIRE, *LE BALCON*

ἔλθε μοι καὶ νῦν, χαλεπᾶν δὲ λῦσον
ἐκ μερίμναν, ὄσσα δέ μοι τέλεσσαι
θῦμοσ ἰμμέρρει τέλεσον· σὺ δ᾽ αὔτα
        σύμμαχοσ ἔσσο.
SAPPHO, *ODE TO APHRODITE*

A LETTER OF INTRODUCTION

To George Rostrevor Hamilton

My dear George,

You have, for both my Zimiamvian books, so played Pallas
Athene – sometimes to my Achilles sometimes to my Odysseus
– counselling, inciting, or restraining, and always with so foster-
brotherly an eye on the object we are both in love with, that it is
to you sooner than to anyone else that this letter should be
addressed. To you, a poet and a philosopher: from me, who am
no poet (for my form is dramatic narrative in prose), nor philosopher either. Unless to be a humble lover of wisdom earns that
name, and to concern myself as a storyteller not so much with
things not of this world as with those things of this world which
I take to be, because pre-eminently valuable, therefore pre-eminently
real.

The plain 'daylight' parts of my story cover the years from April
1908 to October 1933; while, as for the month that runs contem-
poraneously in Zimiamvia (from Midsummer's Day, Anno Zayanae
Conditae 775, when the Duke first clapped eyes on his Dark Lady,
to the 25th July, when his mother, the Duchess of Memison, gave
that singular supper-party), it is sufficient to reflect that the main
difference between earth and heaven may lie in this: that here we
are slaves of Time, but there the Gods are masters.

There are no hidden meanings: no studied symbols or allegories.
It is the defect of allegory and symbolism to set up the general

above the individual, the abstract above the concrete, the idea above the person. I hold the contrary: to me the value of the sunset is not that it suggests to me ideas of eternity; rather, eternity itself acquires value to me only because I have seen it (and other matters besides) in the sunset and (shall we say) in the proud pallour of Fiorinda's brow and cheeks – even in your friend, that brutal ferocious and lionlike fox, the Vicar of Rerek – and so have foretasted its perfections.

Personality is a mystery: a mystery that darkens as we suffer our imagination to speculate upon the penetration of human personality by Divine, and vice versa. Perhaps my three pairs of lovers are, ultimately, but one pair. Perhaps you could as truly say that Lessingham, Barganax, and the King (on the one hand), Mary, the Duchess, and Fiorinda (on the other), are but two persons, each at three several stages of 'awakeness', as call them six separate persons.

And there are other teasing mysteries besides this of personality. For example: Who am I? Who are you? Where did we come from? Where are we going? How did we get here? What is 'here'? Were we ever not 'here', and, if so, where were we? Shall we someday go elsewhere? If so, where? If not, and yet we die, what is Death? What is Time, and why? Did it have a beginning, and will it have an end? Whatever the answer to the last two questions (i.e., that time had a beginning or that it had not: or an end) is either alternative conceivable? Are not both equally inconceivable? What of Space (on which very similar riddles arise)? Further, *Why* are we here? What is the good of it all? What do people mean when they speak of Eternity, Omnipotence, God? What do they mean by the True, the Good, the Beautiful? Do these 'great and thumping words' relate to any objective truth, or are they empty rhetoric invented to cheer or impress ourselves and others: the vague expressions of vague needs, wishes, fears, appetites of us, weak children of a day, who know little of (and matter less to) the vast, blind, indifferent, unintelligible, inscrutable, machine or power or flux or nothingness, on the skirts of whose darkness our brief lives flicker for a moment and are gone?

And if this is the true case of us and our lives and loves and all that we care for, then Why is it?

> Ah, Love! Could you and I with Him conspire
> To grasp this sorry Scheme of Things entire,
> Would not we shatter it to bits – and then
> Re-mould it nearer to the Heart's Desire!

Why not? Why is there Evil in the world?

Such, in rapid and superficial survey, are the ultimate problems of existence; 'riddles of the Sphinx' which, in one shape or another, have puzzled men's minds and remained without any final answer since history began, and will doubtless continue to puzzle and elude so long as mankind continues upon this planet.

But though it is true that (as contrasted with the special sciences) little progress has been made in philosophy: that we have not today superseded Plato and Aristotle in the sense in which modern medicine has superseded Hippokrates and Galen: yet, on the negative side and particularly in metaphysics, definite progress has been made.

Descartes' *Cogito ergo sum* – 'I think; therefore I exist' – has been criticized not because its assumptions are too modest, but because they are too large. Logically it can be reduced to *cogito*, and even that has been shorn of the implied *ego*. That is to say, the momentary fact of consciousness is the only reality that cannot logically be doubted; for the mere act of doubting, being an act of consciousness, is of itself immediate proof of the existence of that which was to be the object of doubt.

Consciousness is therefore the fundamental reality, and all metaphysical systems or dogmas which found themselves on any other basis are demonstrably fantastic. In particular, materialistic philosophies of every kind and degree are fantastic.

But, because demonstrably fantastic, they are not therefore demonstrably false. We cannot, for instance, be reasonably driven to admit that some external substance called 'matter' is prior to or condition of consciousness; but just as little can we reasonably deny the *possibility* of such a state of things. For, logically, denial is as inadmissible as assertion, when we face the ultimate problems of existence outside the strait moment of consciousness which is all that certainly remains to us after the Cartesian analysis. Descartes, it is true, did not leave it at that. But he had cleared the way for Hume and Kant to show that, briefly, every assumption which he himself or any other metaphysician might produce like a rabbit from the hat must have been put into the hat before being brought out. In other words, the scientific method, applied to these problems and pressed to its logical implications, leads to an agnosticism which must go to the whole of experience, as Pyrrho's did, and not arbitrarily stop short at selected limits, as did the agnosticism of the nineteenth century. It leads, therefore, to an attitude of complete and speechless scepticism.

If we think this conclusion a *reductio ad absurdum*, and would seek yet some touchstone for the false and the true, we must seek it elsewhere than in pure reason. That is to say (confining the argument to serious attitudes of speculation on the ultimate problems of existence), we must at that stage abandon the scientific attitude and adopt the poet's. By the poet's I mean that attitude which says that ultimate truths are to be attained, if at all, in some immediate way: by vision rather than by ratiocination.

How, then, is the poet to go to work, voyaging now in alternate peril of the Scylla and Charybdis which the Cartesian–Kantian criticism has laid bare – the dumb impotence of pure reason on the one hand, and on the other a welter of disorganized fantasy through which reason of itself is powerless to choose a way, since to reason (in these problems) 'all things are possible' and no fantasy likelier than another to be true?

Reason, as we have seen, reached a certain bed-rock, exiguous but unshakable, by means of a criticism based on credibility: it cleared away vast superfluities of baseless system and dogma by divesting itself of all beliefs that it was possible to doubt. In the same way, may it not be possible to reach a certain bed-rock among the chaos of fantasy by means of a criticism based not on credibility but on value?

No conscious being, we may suppose, is without desire; and if certain philosophies and religions have set up as their ideal of salvation and beatitude a condition of desirelessness, to be attained by an asceticism that stifles and starves every desire, this is no more than to say that those systems have in fact applied a criticism of values to dethrone all minor values, leaving only this state of blessedness which (notwithstanding their repudiation of desire) remains as (for their imagination at least) the one thing desirable. And in general, it can be said that no religion, no philosophy, no considered view of the world and human life and destiny, has ever been formulated without some affirmation, express or implied, of what is or is not to be desired: and it is this star, for ever unattained yet for ever sought, that shines through all great poetry, through all great music, painting, building, and works of men, through all noble deeds, loves, speculations, endurings and endeavours, and all the splendours of 'earth and the deep sky's ornament' since history began, and that gives (at moments, shining through) divine perfection to some little living thing, some dolomite wall lighted as from within by the low red sunbeams, some skyscape, some woman's eyes.

This then, whatever we name it – the thing desirable not as a means to something else, be that good or bad, high or low (as food is desirable for nourishment; money, for power; power, as a means either to tyrannize over other men or to benefit them; long life, as a means to achievement of great undertaking, or to cheat your heirs; judgement, for success in business; debauchery, for the 'bliss proposed'; wind on the hills, for inspiration; temperance, for a fine and balanced life), but for itself alone – this, it would seem, is the one ultimate and infinite *Value*. By a procedure corresponding to that of Descartes when, by doubting all else, he reached through process of elimination something that he could not doubt, we have, after rejecting all things whose desirableness depends on their utility as instruments to ends beyond themselves, reached something desirable as an end in itself. What it is in concrete detail, is a question that may have as many answers as there are minds to frame them ('In my Father's house are many mansions'). But to deny its existence, while not a self-contradictory error palpable to reason (as is the denial of the Cartesian *cogito*), is to affirm the complete futility and worthlessness of the whole of Being and Becoming.

It is not to be gainsaid that a position of complete scepticism and complete nihilism in regard to objective truth and objective value is, logically, unassailable. But since, logically, he who takes up that position must remain speechless (for nothing, *ex hypothesi*, can be affirmed, nor does anybody exist to listen to the affirmation), must desire nothing (for there is nothing to be desired), and do nothing (for nothing is worth doing), therefore 'the rest is silence'.

Proceeding, then, on the alternative supposition – that is to say, accepting the fact of consciousness as our fundamental reality and this undefined but unelimineable 'one thing desirable' as the fundamental value – we are free to speculate on the ultimate problems of metaphysics, using as instrument of investigation our mind at large, which includes (but is not restricted to) the analytic reason. Such speculation is what, for want of a better word, I have called *poetic*. It might (with some danger of misconception) also be called the kind of speculation appropriate to the lunatic, or to the lover! for—

> The lunatic, the lover, and the poet,
> Are of imagination all compact.

Three broad considerations may here be touched on:

(1) It does not seem necessary to postulate a plurality of ultimate values. Truth, Beauty, Goodness, are commonly so postulated. The claim of Truth, however, can hardly survive examination. On the one hand, the empirical truths of science or the abstract

truths of mathematics are 'values' either as a means to power, or else for a kind of rightness or perfection which they seem to possess: a perfection which seems to owe its value to a kind of Beauty. On the other hand, Truth in the abstract (the quite neutral judgement, 'That which is, is') can have no value whatsoever: it acquires value only in so far as 'that which is' is desirable in itself, and not merely on account of its 'truth'. If Schopenhauer's *The World as Will and Idea* is a statement of the truth, then truth has, ultimately, a negative value and we are better off without it (except as a means to power, etc.). Truth, therefore, is only an ultimate value if it is good. But the 'Good', again, is ambiguous, meaning both (a) good as an end to be desired, and (b) moral good. In sense (a) it is surely tautologous to speak of the 'good' as distinct from the beautiful; in sense (b) it is arguable (and, as I myself hold, true) that acts are morally 'good' only in so far as, in the last analysis, they tend to create, serve, or safeguard, Beauty. The trinity of so-called 'ultimate values' is thus reduced to one.

(2) No sane theory of values will ultimately square with the facts of this world as we know it 'here and now.' But ultimate value, as we have seen, is one of the 'bed-rocks': not so, however, this world, which we know only empirically and as a particular phase of our other 'bed-rock' (*viz.* consciousness). Accordingly, the test of any metaphysic is not that it should square with the world as we know it, but that it should square with the ultimate value. (Cf. Vandermast's words in *Mistress of Mistresses*: 'In this supermundal science concerning the Gods, determination of what Is proceedeth inconfutably and only by argument from what Ought to be.')

(3) Concrete reality, whether as consciousness or as value, has two aspects which are never in fact separated or separable: the One and the Many: the Universal and the Particular: the Eternal and the Temporal: the Never Changing and the Ever Changing. It is the inseparability of these modes of Being that makes it

idle to seek abstract Beauty, Truth, Goodness, apart from their particular manifestations, and equally idle (conversely) to try to isolate the particulars. The Many are understandable only as manifestations of the One: the One, only as incarnate in the Many. Abstract statements, therefore, such as have been occupying our attention in the proceedings pages, can bear no nearer relation to the concrete truths which they describe than (for example) the system of latitude and longitude bears to the solid earth we live on.

It is on these terms only, then (as an explanation of our 'latitude and longitude'), that it is possible to sum up in a few lines the conception which underlies *Mistresses of Mistresses* and *A Fish Dinner in Memison*.

In that conception, ultimate reality rests in a Masculine-Feminine dualism, in which the old trinity of Truth, Beauty, Goodness, is extended to embrace the whole of Being and Becoming; Truth consisting in this – That Infinite and Omnipotent Love creates, preserves, and delights in, Infinite and Perfect Beauty (*Infinitus Amor potestate infinitâ Pulchritudinem infinitam in infinitâ perfectione creatur et conservatur*). Love and Beauty are, in this duality, coequal and coeternal; and, by a violent antinomy, Love, owing his mere being to this strengthless perfection which he holds at his mercy, adores and is enslaved by her, while Beauty (by a like antinomy) queens it over the very omnipotence which both created her and is her only safeguard.

Ultimate reality, as was said above, must be concrete; and an infinite power, creating and enjoying an infinite value, cannot be cribbed or frozen in a single manifestation. It must, on the contrary, be capable of presenting itself in an infinite number of aspects to different minds and at different moments; and every one of these aspects must be true and (paradoxically) complete, whereas no abstract statement, however profound in its analysis, can ever be either complete or true. This protean character of truth is the philosophical justification for religious toleration; for it is almost inconceivable that truth, realized in the richness of its concrete actuality, should ever present itself to two minds alike. Churches, creeds, schools of thought, or systems of philosophy, are expedient, useful or harmful, as the case may fall out. But the ultimate Vision – the 'flesh and blood' actuality behind these symbols and formulas – is to them as the living body is to apparel which conceals, disguises, suggests, or adorns, that body's perfections.

This 'flesh and blood', then, so far as it shapes itself in *Mistress of Mistresses* and is on the way to further definition in the *Fish Dinner*, shows this ultimate dualism as subsisting in the two supreme Persons, the divine and perfect and eternal He and She, *Zeus* and *Aphrodite*, 'more real than living man'. All men and women, all living creatures, the whole phemonenal world material and spiritual, even the very forms of Being – time, space, eternity – do but subsist in or by the pleasure of these Two, partaking (every individual soul, we may think, in its degree), of Their divine nature—

'The Lord possessed Me in the beginning of His way, before
His works of old. I was set up from everlasting, from the
beginning, or ever the earth was . . . When He prepared the
Heavens I was there: when he set a compass on the face of
the depth: when He established the clouds above: when He
strengthened the fountains of the deep: when He gave to the
sea His decree, that the waters should not pass His command-
ment: when He appointed the foundations of the earth: then
I was by Him, as one brought up with Him, and I was daily
His delight, rejoicing always before Him . . . Whoso findeth
Me findeth life, and shall obtain favour of the Lord. But he
that sinneth against me wrongeth his own soul: all they that
hate Me love death.'

(*Proverbs*, VIII: there spoken by *Wisdom*; but it is truer of a less mundane matter. For wisdom can never be an ultimate value but a means only to something beyond itself, e.g. a guide to action; whereas She [*l'inutile Beauté*] is not a means but the end and mistress of all action, the sole thing desirable for Herself alone, the *causa immanens* of the world and of very Being and Becoming: 'Before the day was, I am She'.)

Mundane experience, it must be admitted, goes, broadly, against all this: it affords little evidence of omnipotent love, but much of feeble, transient, foolish loves: much of powerful hatreds, pain, fear, cruelty. *'Tout passe, tout casse, tout lasse'*: death, disease, deformity, come to mortals indiscriminately. 'And captive good attending captain ill' – this and all the accusations of Shakespeare's LXVIth sonnet are true of 'this vain world', and always have been true. This world, to say the best of it, has always been both good and bad; to say the best of it, it is a flux, in which, on the whole, the changes compensate each other.

But (standing upon the rock – the Zeus–Aphrodite dualism), we are faced, in this imperfection of mundane experience, with the problem of Evil; and (standing upon that rock) the only solution we can accept is one that shall concede to Evil something less than reality. Lame excuses for the impotence, unskilfulness, inattentiveness, callousness, or plain malevolence of God Almighty, to which all other solutions of the problem reduce themselves, are incompatible with the omnipotence of Love, which can hardly be supposed to possess, in action, the attributes of an idiot or a devil. (It may be said, no doubt, that Love is *not* omnipotent but subject to some dark Ἀνάγκη or necessity that binds even a God. Obviously this can neither be proved nor disproved, but it is repugnant to my judgement. For, if true, it means that the Scheme is indeed rotten at the core.)

Sub specie aeternitatis, therefore, this present world is understandable only on the assumption that its reality is not final but partial. On two alternative hypotheses might it thus be credible—

(i) as something *in the making*, which in future aeons will become perfect;

(ii) as an instrument of ἄσκησις, a training-ground or testing place.

Both hypotheses, however, present difficulties: (i) Why need omnipotence wait for future aeons to arrive? why have imperfections at all? (ii) (The same difficulty in a different aspect) If perfection were available – and, to omnipotence, what is not? – why need omnipotence arrange for tests or trainings?

We are forced back, therefore, on the question: if illusion, *why is there this illusion?*

There seems to be no clear answer to this question; and no certain test (short of experience) of the truth of any particular experience. This world has got to be lived through, and the best way of living through it is a question for *ethics*: the science of the Good in action. A 'good' action is an action of Love, i.e. (see above) an action which serves *Beauty*. The 'good' man in action is therefore doing, so far as his action is good, and so far as his power goes, what the divine eternal Masculine is doing: creating, serving, worshipping, enjoying and loving Her, the divine eternal Feminine. And, by complement, the 'good' woman in action is doing, so far as in her lies, what the divine eternal Feminine is doing; completing and making up, that is to say, in her unique person, by and in her action and by and in her passivity, 'whatsoever is or has been or shall be desirable, were it in earth or heaven'. In action therefore, this is 'All ye know on earth, and all ye need to know.'

But man is not πρακτίκος only, but θεωρητικός – concerned not with action only but with contemplation – and the unanswered questions in the third preceding paragraph remain. May there possibly be one answer to both? *viz.* that there is no *necessity* for these peculiar and (to us) inconvenient arrangements, but that – for the moment – they are amusing?

That they are far from '*amusing*' to *us*, here and now – that they daily, for some or other of their helpless victims, produce woes and agonies too horrible for man to endure or even think of – is perhaps because we do not, in the bottom of our hearts, believe in our own immortality and the immortality of those we love. If, for you and me as individuals, this world is the sum, then much of it in detail (and the whole in general plan) is certainly not amusing. But to a mind developed on the lines of the Mahometan fanatic's, the Thug's, the Christian martyr's, is it not conceivable that (short, perhaps, of acute physical torture) the 'slings and arrows of outrageous fortune' should be no more painful than the imagined ills of a tragic drama, and could be experienced and appraised with a like detachment? The death of your nearest and dearest, e.g., would be but a deepening of experience for you, if you could believe and know (beyond peradventure and with that immediacy which belongs to sense experience) that there *is* no death, except of the body in this transient and unsatisfactory life; that Truth rests indeed in that eternal duality whereby the One Value is created and tendered by the One Power; that the Truth is not abstract and bodiless, but concrete in all imaginable richness of spirit and sense; that the parting is therefore but for a while; and, last, that the whole of human history, and the material cosmos known to science, are but trivial occurrences – episodes invented perhaps, and then laid aside, as we ourselves might conceive and in a few minutes reject again some theory of the universe, in conversation after supper.

It may be asked, Why not suicide, then, as a way out? Is not that the logic of such an other-worldly philosophy? The answer surely is that there is a beauty of action (as the Northmen knew), and only seldom is suicide a fine act. Unless it is time to 'do it in the high Roman fashion': unless we stand where Othello stood, or Cleopatra, suicide is an ignoble act, and (as such) little to Her liking. The surer we are of Her, therefore, the less we are likely to take, in despair, that dark leap which (though not, as is vulgarly said, an act of cowardice: it demands much courage if done deliberately) is essentially a shirking of the game She sets us. And that game (as no one will doubt, who has looked in the eyes of 'sparkling-thronèd heavenly Aphrodite, child of God, beguiler of guiles') is a game which, to please Her, we must play 'according to its strict rules'.

This book can be read as well before as after *Mistress of*

Mistresses. The chief persons appear in both books, but each is a self-contained work complete in itself.

Yours affectionately,

E. R. E.

Dark Lane
Marlborough
Wiltshire
29th July 1940

A Fish Dinner in Memison

PRINCIPAL PERSONS

THE KING
BARGANAX, DUKE OF ZAYANA
EDWARD LESSINGHAM
LADY MARY LESSINGHAM
THE DUCHESS OF MEMISON
FIORINDA

I

APHRODITE IN VERONA

'ÇA M'AMUSE.' The words, indolent, indolently fallen along the slowness of a lovely lazy voice, yet seemed to strike night, no, Time itself, with a sudden division; like as when that bare arrow-like three-octave E, high on the first violin, deep on the cello, stabs suddenly the witched quietude of the *andante* in the third Rasoumoffsky Quartet. A strange trick, indeed, in a woman's voice: able so, with a chance phrase overheard, to snatch the mind from its voyaging in this skiff between sightless banks: snatch and translate it so, to some stance of rock, archaean, gripping the boot-nails, high upon mountains; whence, as gathering your senses out of sleep, you should seem to discern the true nature of the stream of things. And here, tonight, in Verona—

Lessingham looked round, quickly enough to catch the half mocking, half listening, inclination of her head as her lips closed upon the lingering last syllable of that private 'm'amuse'. The words had been addressed, it was clear, to nobody, for she was alone at her table: certainly not to him: not even (curiously) to herself: to velvet-bosomed Night, possibly, sister to sister: to the bats, the inattentive stars, this buzz of Latin night-life; little white tables with their coffee, *vino rosso*, *vino bianco*, carafe and wine-glass, the music and the talk; wreaths of cigar-smoke and cigarette-smoke that hung and dissipated themselves on airs that carried from the flower-beds of the mid piazza a spring fragrancy and, from the breathing presences of women, wafts of a more exotic and a deeper stirring sweetness. Over all, the tremendous curved façade of Diocletian's amphitheatre, ruined deep in time, stood desolate in the glare of electric arclights. In Lessingham's hand arrested on the table-top, the cigar went out. Into the stillness all these things – amphitheatre, electric lights, the Old and the New, this simple art of living, the bat-winged night, the open face of the dark – seemed to gather and, with the slow upsurging might of their rise, to reach to some timeless moment which seemed her; and which seemed as fixed, while beyond it life and the hours streamed unseizable as the unseizable down-streaming spray-motes into which water is dissipated when it falls clear over a great height – *Ça m'amuse.*

Then, even as in the *andante* the processional secular throb of the arpeggios, so Time seemed now to recover balance: catch breath: resume its inexplicable unseizable irreversible way. Not to be explained, yet upon that echo illuminated: not to be caught, yet (for that sudden) unprecedentedly submitting itself within hand-reach: not to be turned back, yet suddenly self-confessed as perhaps not worth the turning. She looked up, and their eyes met.

'Vous parlez français, madame?'

'O, depende dello soggetto: depende con cui si parla. To an Englishman, English.'

'Mixed with Italian?'

'Addressed to a person so mixed. Or do I not guess aright?'

Lessingham smiled and replied: 'You pay me a doubtful compliment, signora. Is it not a saying: "Inglese Italianato e Diavolo incarnato"? And as for the subject,' he said, 'if the signora will permit a question: is there then a special fitness to be amused, in French?'

'Simply to be amused – perhaps, No. But to be amused at *this* – Yes.'

'And *this* is?—'

Her hand, crimson-gloved, on which till now her cheek had been resting, traced, palm-upwards, a little half circle of disdain indicative of the totality of things. 'There is a something logical:

a something of precision, about the French, which very well fits this affair. To be polite to it, you must speak of it in French: it is the only language.'

'There is in Latin, equally, a precision.'

'O but certainly: and in a steam roller: but not altogether *spirituel*. Il faut de l'esprit pour savourer nettement cette affaire-là'; and again her hand delicately acknowledged it: 'this clockwork world, this mockshow, operated by Time and the endless chain of cause and effect. Time, if you consider it,' she said, 'works with so ingenious a simplicity: so perfect a machine. Like a clock. Say you are God: you need but wind it up, and it proceeds with its business: no trouble at all.'

'Until,' said Lessingham, 'you have to wind it up again?'

The lady shrugged her shoulders.

'Signora,' he said, 'do you remember M. d'Anquetil, at that enjoyable unrestrained supper-party in *La Rôtisserie de la Reine Pédauque*? "Je vous confierai que je ne crois pas en Dieu."'

'And permit me, sir,' said she, 'to continue the quotation from that entertaining book: "Pour le coup, dit l'abbé, je vous blâme, monsieur." And yet I am glad; for indeed it is a regrettable defect of character in a young man, to believe in God. But suppose, sir, that you in fact were – shall I say? – endowed with that authority: would you wind it up again?'

He paused before answering, held by the look of her: the passivity of her lips, that was like the swept silences of the sky expectant of dawn, or like the sea's innumerable rippled stillness expectant of the dark after sunset: an assuredness, as native to some power that should so far transcend omnipotence as that it needs no more but merely to be and continue in that passivity, and omnipotence in action must serve it.

Like the oblique wide circle of a swift's flight, down and round and up again, between earth and sky, the winged moment swung: now twenty years backwards into earliest childhood: the tennis lawn, of a June evening, of the old peelhouse where he was born, youngest of seven, of a great border family, between the Solway

and the Cumberland hills: church bells, long shadows, Rose of
Sharon with its sticky scent: Eton: then, at eighteen (getting on
for eight years ago now), Heidelberg, and that unlucky episode
that cut his studies short there. Then the Paris years, the Sorbonne,
the obsessed concentration of his work in Montmartre studios,
ending with the duel with knives with that unsavoury musician
to whose Spanish mistress Lessingham, with the inexperienced
ardour and quixotism of youth, had injudiciously offered his
protection. And so, narrowly escaping imprisonment, to Provence
and his Estremaduran Amaryllis: in a few weeks their parting by
mutual consent, and his decision (having overspent his allowance,
and in case his late adversary, again in hospital, should die, and
that be laid at his door) to enlist in the *Légion Etrangère* under
an assumed name. His desertion after some months (disillusioned
with such a school but pleased with the experience for the power
it gave him), and escape through Morocco in Egypt. Arrival penni-
less at the British Agency: news that his father, enraged at these
proceedings, had stopped allowances and cut him out of his will.
So, work his passage home as a stoker on a P. & O.: upon his
twenty-first birthday, the twenty-fourth of November, 1903, land
at Tilbury, and (by his mother's means, that queen of women,
seconding friendship and strong argument of flesh and blood) at
one again with his father before Christmas; and so a year in
England, his own master and with enough money to be trusted to
do what money is meant for: look after itself, and leave its owner
free. Then east, mainly India: two seasons exploring and climbing,
Eastern Himalaya, Karakoram. Journey home, against official advice
and without official countenance, dangerously through Afghanistan
and Persia: then nearly the whole year 1906 in Greece, on horseback, sailing among the islands, studying in Athens. Then – the
nineteenth of December, 1906. Sixteen months ago.

The nineteenth of December: Betelgeuze on the meridian at
midnight, his particular star. The beginning: dinner at his sister
Anne's, and on with her party to that historic ball at the Spanish
Embassy. Queer composition, to let the theme enter *pianissimo*,
on muted strings, as it were; inaudible under such a blaring of

trumpets. Curious to think of: towards the end of the evening, puzzling over his own scribble on his programme, 'Dijon-Fiammetta', against the next waltz, and recalling at last what it stood for: 'Fiammetta' – *flame*: red-gold hair, the tea-rose she wore in it, and a creamy dress like the rose's petals. Their dancing: then, afterwards, sitting out on the stairs: then (as in mutual unspoken agreement to leave deserted partners to their devices in the glitter and heat of the ballroom, and themselves to savour a little longer this quiet), their sitting on, and so through two dances following. Whether Mary was tired, or whether minded to leave the ball of conversation to him, they had talked little. Dark girls were the trumpets in that symphony; and he had throughout the evening neither lacked nor neglected opportunity to store his mind with images of allures, Circean splendours, unstudied witty charms, manifested in several partners of that preferred complexion. The mockery! that on such hushed strings, and thus unremarked, should have been the entry of so imperial a theme. So much so, that the next morning, in idle waking recollection casting up the memories of the night before, he had forgotten her.

And yet, a week later, Christmassing with Anne and Charles at Taverford Manor, he had forgot the others but begun to remember her: first, her talking of *Wuthering Heights*, a very special book of his: then a saying of her own here and there: the very phrase and manner. She had been of few words that night, but those few singularly as if her own yet not self-regarding: pure Maryisms: daffodils or stars of the blackthorn looking on green earth or out to the sun. As for instance this (comparing Highlanders and the Tyrolese): 'Mountain people seem all rather the same – vague and butterflyish. If they lose something – well, there it is. All ups and downs. I should think.' Or this (of the smallness of human beings in an Alpine valley): 'What weasels we look!' Also, there had been near the corner of her mouth, a 'somewhat', that sometimes slept, sometimes stirred. He had wondered idly who she was, and whether these things took place as well by daylight. And then, next week, at the meet of the West Norfolk, his fresh introduction to her, and satisfying himself on both questions; and, as for the second, that they did.

Then, six months afterwards. Twenty-fourth of June. That river-party: that well planned, well timed, confident proposal: its rejection (a discomfiture in which he had not been singular; rather ninth or tenth; if talk were to be trusted). And, most devastating, something in the manner of her refusal: an Artemisian quality, quiver of startled hind, which stripped scales from his eyes to let him see her as never before: as the sole thing, suddenly, which as condition absolute of continuing he must have, let the world else go hang; and, in the same thunderclap, the one sole thing denied him. And so, that feverish fortnight, ending (thank heaven) with the best terms he might make (her cousin Jim Scarnside playing honest broker): burial of that black No, upon condition he should himself leave the country and not before fifteen months come back for his answer: eighteen months, as first propounded; which he would have shortened to August year (that is harvest time); but Mary would not give ground beyond Michaelmas: 'An omen too, if you were wise – Vintage.'

Vintage. *Vindemiatrix*: she who harvests the grape: the delicate star in whose house the sun sits at autumn, and with her mild beams moderates his own to a more golden and more tranquil and more procreative radiance.

Nine months gone: Dahomey, Spain, Corsica. And April now: the twenty-second of April. A hundred and fifty-nine days to go.

The back arrowed swoop of the moment swung high into the unceilinged future, ten, fifty, sixty years, may be: then, past seeing, up to that warmthless unconsidered mock-time when nothing shall be left but the memorial that fits all (except, if there be, the most unhappiest) of human kind: *I was not. I lived and loved. I am not.* Then (or was it a bat, of the bats that hawked there between the piazza lamps and the stars?) it swung near, flashing darkly past that Dark Lady's still mouth, at whose corner flickered a something: miraculously that which, asleep or awake, resided near the corner of Mary's mouth.

Queen of Hearts: Queen of Spades: 'Inglese Italianato': the conflict of north and south in his blood; the blessing of that – of all – conflict. And yet, so easily degraded. As woman's beauty, so easily degraded. The twoness in the heart of things: that rock that so many painters split on. Loathsome Renoir, with his sheep-like slack-mouthed simian-browed superfluities of female flesh: their stunted tapered fingers, puffy little hands, breasts and buttocks of a pneumatic doll, to frustrate all his magic of colour and glowing air. Toulouse-Lautrec, with his imagination fed from the stews, and his canvases all hot sweat and dead beer. Etty's fine sensuality coarsely bitted and bridled by a convention from without, and starved so of the spirit that should have fed it to beauty from within. Burne-Jones's beauties, nipped by some frost: Rossetti's weighted with undigested matter: Beardsley, a whore-master, prostituting his lovely line to unlovely canker-buds. Even the great: even Titian in his *Sacred and Profane Love*, even Botticelli in his supreme Venus, were (he said in himself), by some meddling from within or without, restrained from the ultimate which I would have, and which as a painter I (Kapaneus's θεῶν θελόνιτων ἐκπέρσειν πόλιν, ἡ μὴ θελόνιων φησι – with God's will, or if not, against it) will attain. Did the Greeks, with their painted statues, Apelles with Phryne for his model, attempt it? Did they, attempting, succeed? We can never know. Do such things die, then? Things of the spirit? Sappho's burnt poems? Botticelli's pictures of 'beautiful naked women' of like quality, perhaps, with his Venus and his nymphs of spring? – poor consolation that he was burnt that burnt them.

Yes. They die ὃ δ' ἐν στροφάλιγγι κονίης κεῖτο μέγας μεγαλωστί, λελασμένος ἱπποσυνάων – half brother to man-slaying Hector, and his charioteer; under the dusty battle-din before Ilios, 'mighty, mightily fallen: forgetful of his horsemanship'. All time past, the conflict and the heartbreak (he looked at the amphitheatre, a skeleton lifted up to witness): frozen. He looked at her: her eyes were more still than the waiting instant between the flash and the thunder. No. Not frozen; for that is death. No death here: rather the tenseness of sinew that is in the panther before the leap: Can Grande's tomb, as this morning, in broad sunshine. Below, under the Gothic canopy carved in stone, the robed figure, lying in state, of the great condottiere, submissive, supine, with pious hands clasped upon his breast as in prayer, *'requiescat in pace'*, *'Domine, in manus tuas'*, etc., weak childhood come back like a song's refrain, sightless eyes facing upwards. But above, high upon that canopy, the demonic equestrian figure of him in the April sap of his furious youth, helmed and harnessed, sword aloft, laughing on his caparisoned horse that seems itself to be informed with a secret kindred laughter, to say *ha! ha!* among the trumpets: a stirring together of the warring mights and glories, prides, overthrowings, and swiftnesses, of all worlds, to one flame; which takes on, of its mere eternity and only substantiality, as ice will scorch or fire freeze, the semblance of a death-like stillness.

All this in a few seconds of time: apocalyptically.

Lessingham answered her: 'Signora, if I were God Omnipotent, I should be master of it. And, being master, I would not be carried by it like a tripper who takes a ticket for a cruise. I would land where I would; put in to what ports I liked, and out again when I would; speed it up where I would, or slow it down. I would wind it to my turn.'

'That,' she said, 'would be a very complicated arrangement. One cannot deny it would be a pleasure. But the French precision, I fear, would scarcely apply itself so fitly, were that the state of things.'

'You would hardly have me do otherwise?'

Slowly drawing off her right-hand glove, she smiled her secular smile. 'I think, sir (in my present mood), that I would desire you, even so, to play the game according to its strict rules.'

'O,' said Lessingham. 'And that (if it is permissible to enquire), in order to judge my skill? or my patience?'

Her fingers were busied about her little gold-meshed bag, finding a lira for her wine: Lessingham brought out a handful of coins, but she gracefully put aside his offer to pay for it. 'I wonder?' she said, looking down as she drew on her crimson glove again: 'I wonder? Perhaps my answer is sufficient, sir, if I say – Because it amuses me.' She rose. Lessingham rose too. 'Is that sufficient?' she said.

Lessingham made no reply. She was tall: Mary's height to an

inch as he looked down at her: incredible likenesses to Mary: little turns of neck or hand, certain looks of the eye, that matter of the mouth (a thing surely unknown before a living woman). Unlike Mary, she was dark: jet-black hair and a fair clear skin. 'Good night, sir,' she said, and held out her hand. As if bred up in that gracious foreign courtesy, he bowed: raised it to his lips. Strangely, be made no motion to follow her; only as she turned away, watched her gait and carriage, inhumanly beautiful, till she was vanished among the crowd. Then he put on his hat again and slowly sat down again at his table.

So he sat, half an hour more, may be: a spectator: looking at faces, imagining, playing with his imaginations: a feeling of freedom in his veins: that strange glitter of a town at night, offering boundless possibilities. In that inward-dreaming mood he was unconscious of the clouding over of the stars and the closeness of the air, until rain had begun in big drops and the whole sky was split with lightning which unleashed the loud pealing thunder. Hastening back drenched to his hotel with collar turned up and with the downpour splashing again in a million jets from the flooded pavement, he, as in a sudden intolerable hunger, said in himself: 'It is long enough: I will not wait five months. Home tomorrow.'

She, in the mean while (if, indeed, as between World and World it is legitimate to speak of 'before' and 'after'), had, in a dozen paces after Lessingham's far-drawn gaze had lost her, stepped from natural present April into natural present June – from that night-life of Verona out by a colonnade of cool purple sandstone onto a daisied lawn, under the reverberant white splendour of midsummer noonday.

II

MEMISON: KING MEZENTIUS

COMING now beyond the lawn, that lady paused at the lily-pond under a shade of poplar-trees: paused to look down for a minute into depths out of which, framed between the crimson lilies and the golden, looked up at her, her own mirrored face. The curves of her nostrils hardened: some primal antiquity seemed suddenly to inform the whole presence of her, as if this youth and high summer-season of her girlhood were, in her, no season at all: not a condition, bearing in its own self its own destiny to depart and make place for future ripenesses, of full bloom, fading and decay; but a state unchanging and eternal. Her throat: her arm: the line of her hair, strained back from the temples to that interweaving of darkness with sleek-limbed darkness, coiled, locked, and over-laid, in the nape of her neck: the upward growth there, daintily ordered as black pencillings on the white wings of a flower-delice, of tiny silken hairs shading the white skin; her lips, crystal-cold of aspect, clear cut, red like blood, showing the merest thread-like glint of teeth between; these things seemed to take on a perfection terrible, because timeless.

The lord Chancellor Beroald, from his seat beneath an arbour of honeysuckle leftwards some distance from where she stood, watched her unseen. In his look was nothing of that worship, which in dumb nature seemed: rather an appraising irony which, setting profession beside performance, fact beside seeming, sucks from their antic steps not present entertainment only, but knowledge that settles to power.

'Is your husband in the palace?' he said presently.

'How should I know?'

'I had thought you had come that way.'

'Yes. But scarcely from taking an inventory.'

'Ha, so there the wind sits?'

He stood up as she came towards him, and they faced each other in silence. Then, light as the stirring of air in the overarching roof of poplar leaves above them, she laughed: held out a hand to him, which he after a pause dutifully, and with some faint spice of irony to sauce the motion, kissed;

'Your ladyship has some private jest?'

She sat down, elegantly settling herself on the rose-coloured marble bench, and elegantly drawing down, to smell to, a spray of honeysuckle. The black lashes veiled her eyes, as she inhaled from eight little branching horns of crimson, apricot-gold, and creamy colour, the honeysuckle's sweetness. Then, letting go the trailing flower, she looked round at him sitting now beside her. 'I was diverted,' she said, 'by your look, my noble brother. That look you had, I remember, when you enveigled me to fall in with your pretty plan touching my former husband.'

'As we mount the hill,' said the Chancellor, 'the prospect opens more large. That was beginnings.'

'O, I spoke not of beginnings: not with that Borgian look. Piazza steps in Krestenaya.'

'Leave this talk,' said the Chancellor.

'Having yourself, before, fobbed him off on me like a base coin, to serve your own turn,' said she; 'and, soon as well rid of him, teased me to taking of this Morville: so much the better alliance for you, as being by some distant removes able to claim kinship with the Parrys. You think, I suppose, that, holding in me the Queen of Spades, you shall always be able to command the Ace to take knaves with?'

'Fie, sister!'

'Fie, brother! And you shall see, I'll play cards for love, not for policy. And next time you shall need to play me the King of Hearts, to be worth my Ace to trump him.'

'What's this?' said the King behind them: 'chancellors with kings i' their hands? That was ever ruin, sure, whether to him that held or him that was holden.'

'Serene highness,' said the Chancellor, rising and turning about to face his master: 'you do know me: I ne'er play cards.'

The King laughed. 'Nor I: save now and then with the Devil; and that's now and then both good and needful.' Well six foot tall stood the Chancellor, clean of build and soldier-like; but the King, in black-bearded majesty, with eagle eyes, from under his black bonnet plumed with black eagle's feathers, looked down to him. The Duchess of Memison on the King's arm was as the beauty of an autumn evening leaning on night: a beauty of clouds and fire, of red-gold effulgence of sunset shining low through pine-tops and fern-fronds, when a little mist steals along the hillside and homing wild-duck stream high against the west. That Dark Lady, still seated, still with her back towards them, had but reached a jewelled hand to the honeysuckle to draw it down again to smell to.

'My Lady Fiorinda.'

She turned, saw, and rose, all duty and obedience, yet with the self-ordered unhasting haste of a foam-footed wave of the sea in calm June weather. 'Your gentle pardon, not to have known your highness' voice. Madam, your grace's humble servant.'

'I have pardoned worse than that,' said the King, 'in a Valkyrie.'

'In a Valkyrie? Am I that?'

'Answer her, madam.'

'O,' said the Duchess, 'she is none of mine. Let her answer for herself.'

'None of yours? and in lovely Memison? where the very birds do fly to you at your becking? By whose doing but by yours should I have met her this morning, on a white horse, galloping, at the first spring of day as I rode up through your oak-groves.'

'As to speak of Valkyries,' said Fiorinda: 'I had supposed rather

that your highness thought my horse had ta'en command of me:
so swift as you rode me down and had him by the bridle.'

The King met her eyes, green and hard. 'It is best way,' he said,
'with a Valkyrie: safer treat Goddess as woman than woman as
Goddess. And, as to speak of pardon: tell me not, mistress! You
knew. And studied so to sit on: note whether I'd call you.'

She stood silent, looking down, as a statue unconcerned save
that from the faint lifting, like the wings of a sea-swallow in flight,
of her slender black eye-brows and from some subtle change about
her mouth, there seemed to be shed about her a coldness as of
the waste between the worlds.

'I have procured a place for you,' said the King: 'lady of the
bedchamber to the Duchess. Will you thank me for it?'

She looked up, and first at the Duchess. 'I'll thank both, and offend
none. And, so please your serenity, I'll ask my husband's leave first.'

'No need,' said the King. 'That's asked and given this hour since.
And now attend me, Beroald.' He said apart to the Duchess,
looking into her green eyes across her fingers as he raised her hand
to his lips, 'You see, madonna: I will do your way.'

'The Chancellor? O I am glad,' said she, and it was as if some
benediction came and went like a breath of honeysuckle among
common garden sweetnesses.

'Then, ladies, give us leave for an hour. 'Fore God, matters of
state, here in Memison, serve as salt pilchards and fumadoes 'twixt
the wines, lest too much sweetness quite cloy us. Even as lovely
Memison and your dear acquaintance, madam, are my noonday
shadow and greenery in the desert of great action.'

'And yourself,' said the Duchess, 'Lord of us and all; and yet
slave yourself to that same desert.'

'Of one thing only, in earth or heaven, am I slave.'

'And 'tis?'

'Of my own self will,' said the King, laughing at her. 'Come
Chancellor.'

They two walked away slowly, over the lawn and through under
that colonnade to another lawn, a hundred and fifty paces in

length, may be, and forty across, with the long eastward-facing wall of the castle to bound it on the further side. Fair in the midst of that lawn they now began to pace the full length of it back and forth with slow and deliberate strides; and whiles they talked, whiles they seemed, falling silent, to weigh the matter. Low was their talk, and in that open sun-smitten place no danger of eaves-dropping; unless the blackbird that hopped before them, jerking his tail, should listen and understand their discourse; or the martin, skimming to and fro in flashes of black and silver, still coming and returning again to her nest in the colonnade.

'I have eggs on the spit, Beroald.'

'I know,' said the Chancellor, very soberly.

'How should you know? I never told you.'

'I can smell them, even through this air of lilies.'

'Beroald, I have resolved to employ you in a matter I did mean, until this morning, none should have hand in but myself only. Am I well advised, think you?'

'If your serenity mean, well advised in undertaking of the thing, how can I answer, knowing not for certain what it is?'

'I mean,' said the King, and there was a tartness in his voice, 'is it well advised to open, even to you, a business of so much peril and import?'

The Chancellor paused. Then, 'That is a question,' he said, 'my Lord the King, that neither you nor I can answer. The event only can answer it.'

'You say, then, the event must show whether I be a fool to trust you? Whether you be, as I think, a man of mettle, and a man of judgement, and my man?'

'Your highness hath spoke my thought with your own mouth.'

'As cold as that?'

'Well, there is this besides,' said the Chancellor: 'that you were always my furtherer; and I, having looked on this world for five times seven years, have learnt this much of wisdom, to "bow to the bush I get bield frae".'

'A fair-weather friend could say that,' said the King, searching his face. 'But we are to put into a sea we cannot sound.'

The Chancellor replied, 'I can say no more; save that, if this be action indeed, as your highness (as I have ever known you) counteth action, then, choosing me or any other man, you have but a weak staff to lean unto.'

'Enough. Beroald, my eye is on the Parry.'

'So are lesser eyes.'

'These four years.'

'Since his crushing for you of Valero's rebellion in the March of Ulba. You have taken your time.'

'I would let him run on in his course of spending.'

'Yet remember,' said the Chancellor, 'his policy is that of the duck: above water, idle and scarce seen to stir; but under water, secretly and speedily swimming towards his purpose.'

The King said, 'I know an otter shall pluck down yonder duck by the foot when least she doubts it.'

'It will need civil war now to bring him in.'

'He is my Vicar in Rerek. Will it not argue a feeble statecraft if I, that have reigned twenty-five years in troubles and disquietudes, cannot now command my own officer without I make war against him?'

'Your serenity may have information we know not of. But most certain it is that, ever since the overthrow of those attempts in the Marches made him higher crested, he hath used your royal commission as his grappling-iron to grapple to his private allegiance the whole mid kingdom 'twixt Megra and the Zenner. I say not he meaneth openly to outbeard the sovereign himself. I think not so. But waiteth his time.'

They took a turn in silence. Then said the King, letting his right fore-arm, that had lain loosely about the Lord Beroald's neck, slip back till the hand shut strong upon his shoulder: 'You remember we lately found a league in hand 'mongst some discontented spirits in Rerek and the Marches, which practice, though the branches on't were easily cut off, yet was it thought to have a more dangerous and secret root. I myself have since, by divers ways, as many lines meet in the dial's centre, come nearer to the truth. There be five or six, instruments of his: names, were I to name 'em you'd ne'er believe me: so many showing friends, so many unshowing enemies. I have letters, enough to satisfy me. Advise me: what shall I do?'

'Summon them before you, himself and all, and let them answer the matter. If their answer be not sufficient, take off their heads.'

'What? When the cry "Puss, puss, where art thou?" were next way to fright 'em to open rebellion? Mend your counsel, my lord Chancellor: this serves not.'

'Serene highness, I am a man of law, and should meddle no further than my commission. Yet is it the platform and understanding of all law that the King, just cause arising, may lawfully act without the law? You are our great pilot, on whom all we cast our eyes and seek our safety. For security of your person, it were good this Vicar were made away. This then is my counsel: assure yourself well of your forces, and, that done, strike: and at unawares.'

The King laughed in his great black beard. 'You have confirmed my very resolve, and so shall it be. But with two provisoes. First, I'll not, like an unskilful boor, kill my good hawk 'cause she turns haggard: I'll tame my Horius Parry, not end him.'

'I'm sorry, then,' said the Chancellor. 'He is a buzzard: he is of bad carry: you can make him do nothing.'

'Who are you, to prescribe and measure my ability?'

'It should not be for my honesty to flatter you. Moreover, your highness hath proved him a man that neither believeth anything that another man speaketh, nor speaketh anything himself worthy to be believed.'

'I say to you,' said the King, 'I'll bring him to lure. As some reclaim ravens, kestrels, pies, what not, and man them for their pleasure, have I not so used him as my own these years and years? I would not lose him for twice the purchase of that dominion he holdeth for me.'

Beroald said, 'If my words be too thin to carry so tough a matter, let your serene highness be advised further: require of my lord Admiral, or Earl Roder, or old Bodenay, your knight marshall in Rialmar, their opinions; or your tributary princes in north Rerek: they'll say the same.'

But the King answered him, 'Not all of you, Beroald, on your bended knees, nor all my liege subjects up and down the Three Kingdoms, might move me in this. Besides,' he said, halting and turning to look Beroald in the eye, '(and here's second proviso): to be King, as I have ever opinioned and ever set my course according, should be by competency, not by privilege. If I of myself be not competent of this thing to perform it, better goodnight then and a new king i' the land.

'Hearken, therefore, and note it well. 'Twas not by chance I guested with him in Laimak two weeks since in such loving-kindness, in my progress, and well forced; nor by chance that I removed thence with great show of pomp south hither into Meszria. It was to lull them. For all this I did, knowing secretly that he is to meet one night, in some convenient place remote among the upper waters of the Zenner, with five or six (the same I spoke on), there to complete and make up their plot for seizing of Rerek to be a kingdom of itself, with him king thereof. Of time, place, and other particulars of this meeting set, I expect information hourly. You and I, we two alone, will keep that tryst with 'em: wherein if I bring not the rest to destruction and him to his obedience, at least I'll die attempting it.

'Well? Will you go, or bide behind?'

The Chancellor very pale and proud of mien, gazing as if into some distance, said after a minute: 'I'll go, my Lord the King.' The King took him by both hands and kissed him. 'And yet,' said the Chancellor, facing him now squarely, 'I would, with your serene highness' leave, say one word.'

'Say on, what thee lust.'

'This, then: I think you are stark mad. And yet,' he said and drew up his lip, 'I may well humour my master in this, to suffer myself to be murdered along with him; for I am not afraid of my death.'

The King looked strangely at him: so might some eagle-baffling mountain look upon its own steadfastness imagined dim in some lake where rufflings of the water mar the reflection: so, it may be, might Zeus the cloud-gatherer look down, watching out of Ida. 'If such fate expect my life, then better so. This must be for us a master-hour, an hour that judgeth all others. I'll not turn back, Beroald.'

III

A MATCH AND SOME LOOKERS ON

'TIME, you know, is a curious business', said Lord Anmering, tilting his head forward a little to let the brim of his panama hat shade his eyes; for it was teatime, and the afternoon sun, from beyond the cricket field below, blazed out of cloudless blue full in their faces. 'Love of money, we're told – root of all evil. Gad! I think otherwise. I think Time strikes deeper.'

Lady Southmere replenished the vacuum with one of the more long-drawn, contemplative, and non-committal varieties of the inimitable transatlantic 'Aha'.

'Look at Mary,' he said. 'Look at me. If I wasn't her father: wasn't thirty-two years her senior. Wouldn't I know what to do with her?'

'Well, I dare say you would.'

'Easy enough when they're not your own,' he said, as they walked on slowly, coming to a halt at the top of two flights of shallow steps that led down to the field from the gardens. 'But when they are – By Jove, that's the style!' The ball, from a magnificent forward drive, sailed clean over the far fence, amid shouts of applause, for six. 'If you let your boy go and smash my melon-houses, knocking the bowling about like that, I'll tell you, I'll have no more to do with him. We mustn't forget,' he said, lower again: 'she's very young. Never force the pace.'

'O but don't I just agree? And the very dearest, sweetest—'

'You know her, well as I do. No, you don't, though. Look there,' putting up his eye-glass to examine the telegraph board: 'Eighty. Eighty: a hundred and sixty-three: that's eighty-four to win. Not so bad, with only three wickets down. It's that boy of yours is doing it: wonderful steady play: nice style too: like to see him make his century. You know our two best bats, Chedisford and that young Macnaghten, didn't add up to double figures between 'em: Hugh's got his work cut out for him. Look at that! Pretty warm bowling. A strong team old Playter's brought us over this time from Hyrnbastwick: Jove, I'd like to give 'em a whacking for a change. Well, Hugh and Jim seem settled to it. Would you like to come down over there: get a bit of shade?'

'I would like to do anything anybody tells me to. This is just too perfect.' She turned, before coming down the steps, to look back for a minute to the great west front of Anmering Blunds, where it ranged beyond green lawns and flower-beds and trim deep-hued hedges of clipped box and barberry and yew: long rows of mullioned windows taking the sun, whose beams seemed to have fired the very substance of the ancient brickwork to some cool-burning airy essence of gold. This wing, by Inigo Jones, was the newest part, masking from this side the original flint-built house that had been old Sir Robert Scarnside's whom Henry VIII made first Earl of Anmering. Round to the right, in the home park, stood up, square and grey, Anmering church tower. A sheltering wood of oak, ash, beech and sycamore was a screen for hall and church and garden against the east; and all the midsummer leafage of these trees seemed, at this hour, impregnate with that golden light. Northwards, all lay open, the ground falling sharply to the creek, salt marshes and sand-dunes and thence-away, to the North Pole, the sea. Southwards and landwards, park and wood and meadow and arable rose gently to the heaths and commons: Bestarton, Sprowswood, Toftrising. Lady Southmere, waiting on the silence a minute, might hear as under-tones to the voices of the cricket field (of players and lookers on, click of wood against leather as the batsman played) the faint far-off rumour of tide-washed shingle, and, from trees, the woodpigeon's rustic, slumbrous, suddenly started and suddenly checked, discourse: *Two coos, tak' two coos, Taffy, tak' two coos, Taffy tak*— From golden rose to larkspur a swallowtail butterfly fluttered in the heat. 'Just too perfect for words,' she said, turning at last.

They came down the steps and began walking, first north, and so round by the top end of the cricket field towards the tents. 'I'll make a clean breast of it,' she said: 'twenty-six years now I have been English and lived in the Shires; and yet, Blunds in summer, well, it gets me here: sends me downright home-sick.' Just as, underneath all immediate sounds or voices, those distant sea-sounds were there for the listening, so in Lady Southmere's speech there survived some pleasant native intonations of the southern States.

'Home-sick?' said Lord Anmering. 'Virginia?'

'No, no, no: just for Norfolk. Aren't I English? And isn't your Norfolk pure England as England ought to be?'

'Better get Southmere to do an exchange: give me the place in Leicestershire and you take Blunds.'

'Well and would you consent to that? Can you break the entail?'

'My dear lady,' he said, 'there are many things I would do for you—'

'But hardly that?'

'I'm afraid, not that.'

'O isn't that just too bad!' she said, as Jim Scarnside, playing forward to a yorker, was bowled middle stump.

Fifty or sixty people, may be, watched the game from this western side where the tents were and garden chairs and benches, all in a cool shade of beech and chestnut and lime and sycamore that began to throw shadows far out upon the cricket field: a pleasant summer scene as any could wish, of mingled sound and silence, stir and repose: white hats and white flannels and coloured caps and blazers contrasting here and there with more formal or darker clothes: a gaiety of muslin frocks, coloured silks, gauzes and ribbons, silken parasols and picture hats: the young, the old, the middle-aged: girls, boys, men, women: some being of the house-party; some, the belongings of the eleven that had driven over with Colonel Playter from Hyrnbastwick; some, neighbours and acquaintance from the countryside: wives, friends, parents, sisters, cousins, aunts. Among these their host, with Lady Southmere, now threaded his way, having for each, as he passed, the just greeting, were it word, smile, formal salutation or private joke: the Playter girls, Norah and Sybil, fresh from school: old Lady Dilstead, Sir Oliver's mother, and his sister Lucy (engaged to Nigel Howard): young Mrs Margesson, a niece of Lord Anmering's by marriage: Romer, the bursar of Trinity: Limpenfield of All Souls': General Macnaghten and his wife and son: Trowsley of the Life Guards: Tom and Fanny Chedisford: Mr and Mrs Dagworth from Semmering: Sir Roderick Bailey, the Admiral, whose unpredictable son Jack had made top score (fifty) for the visiting eleven that morning: the Rector and his wife: the Denmore-Benthams: Mr and Mrs Everard Scarnside (Jim's parents) and Princess Mitzmesczinsky (his sister): the Bremmerdales from Taverford: the Sterramores from Burnham Overy: Janet Rustham and her two little boys: Captain Feveringhay; and dozens besides.

'Sorry, uncle,' said Jim Scarnside, as their paths met: he on his way to the pavilion. 'Ingloriously out for three.'

'I was always told,' Lady Southmere said, 'you ought to block a yorker.'

'My dear Lady Southmere, don't I know it? But (I know you won't believe this), it was all your fault.'

'That's very very interesting.'

'It was.'

'And please, why?'

'Well. Just as that chap Howard was walking back the way he does to get properly wound up for one of those charging-buffalo runs that terrify the life out of a poor little batsman like me—'

'Poor little six foot two!' she said.

'Just at that instant, there, on the horizon, your black and white parasol! And I remembered: Heavens! Didn't Mary make me promise that Lady Southmere should have the first brew of straw-berries and cream, because they're so much the best? and isn't it long past tea-time, and here she comes, so late, and they'll all be gone? So there: and Nigel Howard sends down his beastly yorker. Is it fair? Really, Uncle Robert, you ought not to allow ladies to look on at serious cricket like ours. All very well at Lord's and places like that; but here, it's too much of a distraction.'

'But dreadfully awkward,' said she, laughing up at him, 'not to have us to put the blame on? Jim!' she called after him as they parted: he turned. 'It was real noble and kind of you to think about the strawberries.'

'I'm off to rescue them.' And, using his bat like a walking-stick, he disappeared with long galloping strides in the direction of the tea-tent.

St John, next man in, was out first ball. This made an excitement, in expectation that Howard should do the hat-trick; but Denmore-Bentham, who followed, batted with extreme circumspection and entire success (in keeping his wicket up, though not indeed in scoring).

'Who's this young fellow that's been putting up all the runs? Radford? Bradford? I couldn't catch the name?' said an old gentleman with white whiskers, white waistcoat, and that guinea-gold complexion that comes of long living east of Suez. His wife answered: 'Lord Glanford, Lord Southmere's son. They're staying here at the house, I think. And that's his sister: the pretty girl in pink, with brown hair, talking now to Lady Mary.'

His glance, following where hers gave him the direction, suddenly came to rest; but not upon Lady Rosamund Kirstead. For Mary, chancing at that instant to rise and, in her going, look back with some laughing rejoinder to her friends, stood, for that instant, singled; as if, sudden in a vista between trees, a white sail drawing to the wind should lean, pause, and so righting itself pass on its airy way. A most strange and singular look there was, for any perceiving eye to have read, in the eyes of that old colonial governor: as though, through these ordinary haphazard eyes, generations of men crowded to look forth as from a window.

Glanford, with a new partner, seemed to settle down now to

win the match by cautious steady play, never taking a risk, never giving a chance. When, after a solid half hour of this, a hundred at last went up on the board, the more cavalierly minded among the onlookers began to give rein to their feelings. 'Darling Anne,' Fanny Chedisford said, arm in arm with Lady Bremmerdale, 'I simply can't stick it any longer: poke, poke, poke: as soon look on at a game of draughts. For heaven's sake, let's go and drown our sorrows in croquet.'

'Croquet? I thought you agreed with Mary—'

'I always do. But when?'

'When she said it was only fit for curates and dowagers, and then only if they'd first done a course in a criminal lunatic asylum.'

'O we're all qualified after this. Try a foursome: here's Jim and Mr Margesson: ask them to join in.'

'Did I hear someone pronounce my name disrespectfully?' said Jim Scarnside. Fanny laughed beneath her white parasol. 'Ah, it was my much esteemed and never sufficiently to be redoubted Miss Chedisford. You know,' he said to Cuthbert Margesson, 'Miss Chedisford hasn't forgiven us for not making it a mixed match.'

'Broom-sticks for the men?' said Margesson.

'Not at all,' said Fanny.

Jim said, 'I should think not! Come on: Margesson's in next wicket down. It does seem rather cheek, when he's captain, but after all it's his demon bowling made him that, and his noted diplomacy. Let's take him on and coach him a bit: teach him to slog.'

Anne Bremmerdale smiled: 'Better than croquet.' They moved off towards the nets.

'Are you a bat, Miss Chedisford? Or a bowler?' said Margesson.

'Well, I can bat more amusingly than this.' Fanny cast a disparaging glance at the game. 'My brothers taught me.'

'All the same,' Margesson said, 'Glanford's playing a fine game. We shall beat you yet, Lady Bremmerdale. How is it you didn't bring your brother over to play for Hyrnbastwick?'

'Which one? I've five.'

'I've only met one. The youngest. Your brother Edward, isn't it?'

'She couldn't bring him because she hasn't got him.'

Fanny said, 'I thought he was staying with you now at Taverford?'

'Not since early May.'

'He's the kind of man,' said Jim, 'you never know where he is.'

Fanny looked surprised. 'I'd have sworn,' she said, 'it was Edward Lessingham I saw this morning. Must have been his double.'

'Antipholus of Ephesus,' said Jim: 'Antipholus of Syracuse.'

'About eight o'clock,' said Fanny. 'It was such a dream of a morning, all sopping with dew. I'd got up with the lark and walked the dogs right up onto Kelling Heath before breakfast. I'd swear no one in these parts had that marvellous seat on a horse that he has. So careless. My dear, I'll bet you anything you like it was he: galloping south, towards Holt!'

'Really, Fanny, it couldn't have been,' said Anne.

'There are not many young men you'd mistake for him,' said Fanny.

Jim said to them, 'Talking of Kelling Heath, I'll tell you an idea of mine; why can't we get up a point-to-point there this autumn? What do you say, Cuthbert?'

'I'm all for it.'

'I tackled Colonel Playter about it today at lunch: very important to get him, as M.F.H., to bless it: in fact, he really ought to take it over himself, if it's to be a real good show. He likes the idea. Did you sound Charles, Anne?'

'Yes I did: he's awfully keen on it, and means to get a word with you this evening. Of course you could have a magnificent run right over from Weybourne Heath to Salthouse Common, and back the other way; pretty rough and steep, though, in places.'

Fanny accepted the change of subject. May be she thought the more.

Bentham was out: caught at the wicket: six wickets down for a hundred and nine, of which Glanford had made sixty off his own bat. Margesson now went in, and (not because of any eggings on of impatient young ladies – unless, indeed, telepathy was at work – for Glanford it was who did the scoring), the play began to be brisk. Major Rustham, the Hyrnbastwick captain, now took Howard off and tried Sir Charles Bremmerdale, whose delivery, slowish, erratic, deceptively easy in appearance, yet concealed (as dangerous currents in the body of smooth-seeming water) a puzzling variety of pace and length and now and again an unexpected and most disconcerting check or spin. But Glanford had plainly got his eye in: Margesson too. 'We're winning, Nell,' said Lord Anmering to his niece, Mrs Margesson. 'A dashed fine stand!' said Sybil Playter. 'Shut up swearing,' said her sister. 'Shut up yourself: I'm not.' People clapped and cheered Glanford's strokes. Charles Bremmerdale now could do nothing with him: to mid-off, two: to mid-on, two: a wide: a strong drive, over cover's head, to the boundary, four: to long-leg in the deep field, two – no – three, while Jack Bailey bungles it with a long shot at the wicket: point runs after it: 'Come on!' Four: the fieldsman is on it, turns to throw in: 'No!' says Margesson, but Glanford, 'Yes! come on!' They run: Bremmerdale is crouched at the wicket: a fine throw, into his hands, bails off and Glanford run out. 'Bad luck!' said Jim Scarnside, standing with Tom and Fanny Chedisford at the scoring table: Glanford had made ninety-one. 'But why the devil will he always try and bag the bowling?'

Glanford walked from the field, bat under his arm, shaking his head mournfully as he undid his batting-gloves. He went straight to the pavilion to put on his blazer, and thence, with little devia-tion from the direct road, to Mary. 'I am most frightfully sorry,' he said, sitting down by her. 'I did so want to bring you a century for a birthday present.'

'But it was a marvellous innings,' she said. 'Good heavens, "What's centuries to me or me to centuries?" It was splendid.'

'Jolly decent of you to say so. I was an ass, though, to get run out.'

Mary's answering smile was one to smoothe the worst-ruffled feathers; then she resumed her conversation with Lucy Dilstead:

'You can read them over and over again, just as you can Jane Austen. I suppose it's because there's no padding.'

'I've only read *Shagpat*, so far,' said Lucy.

'O that's different from the rest. But isn't it delicious? So serious. Comedy's always ruined, don't you think, when it's buffooned? You want to live in it: something you can laugh with, not laugh at.'

'Mary has gone completely and irretrievably cracked over George Meredith,' Jim said, joining them.

'And who's to blame for that?' said she. 'Who put what book into whose hand? and bet what, that who would not be able to understand what-the-what it was all driving at until she had read the first how many chapters how many times over?'

Jim clutched his temples, histrionically distraught. Hugh was not amused. The match proceeded, the score creeping up now very slowly with Margesson's careful play. General Macnaghten was saying to Mr Romer, 'No, no, she's only twenty. It is: yes: quite extraordinary; but being only daughter, you see, and no mother, she's been doing hostess and so on for her father two years now, here and in London: two London seasons. Makes a lot of difference.'

Down went another wicket: score, a hundred and fifty-three. 'Now for some fun,' people said as Tom Appleyard came on the field; but Margesson spoke a winged word in his ear: 'Look here, old chap: none of the Jessop business. It's too damned serious now.' 'Ay, ay, sir.' Margesson, in perfect style, sent back the last ball of the over. Appleyard obediently blocked and blocked. But in vain. For one of Bremmerdale's master-creations of innocent outward show and inward guile sneaked round Margesson's defence and took his leg stump. Nine wickets down: total a hundred and fifty-seven: last man, nine. Hyrnbastwick, in some elation, were throwing high catches round the field while Dilstead, Anmering's next (and last) man in, walked to the wicket. Margesson said to Tom Appleyard, 'It's up to you now, my lad. Let 'em have it, damn slam and all if you like. But, by Jingo, we must pull it off now. Only seven to win.' Appleyard laughed and rubbed his hands.

There was no more desultory talk: all tense expectancy. 'If Sir Oliver gets the bowling, that puts the lid on it: never hit a ball yet.' 'Why do they play him then?' 'Why, you silly ass, because he's such a thundering good wicket-keeper.' George Chedisford, about sixteen, home from Winchester because of the measles, maintained a mature self-possession at Lord Anmering's elbow: 'I wish my frater – wish my brother was in again, sir. He'd do the trick.' 'You watch Mr Appleyard: he's a hitter.' By good luck, that ball that had beaten Margesson was last of the over, so that Appleyard, not Dilstead, faced the bowling: Howard once more, a Polyphemus refreshed. His first ball was a yorker, but Appleyard stopped it. The second, Appleyard, all prudent checks abandoned, stepped out and swiped. Boundary: four. Great applaudings: the parson's children and the two little Rustham boys, with the frenzy of Guelph and Ghibelline, jumped up and down jostling each other. The next ball, a very fierce one, pitched short and rose at the batsman's head. Appleyard smashed it with a terrific over-hand stroke: four again – 'Done it!' 'Match!'

Then, at the fourth ball, Appleyard slogged, missed, and was caught in the slips. And so amid great merriment, chaff and mutual congratulations, the game came to an end.

'Come into the Refuge,' said Jim Scarnside, overtaking Mary as they went in to dress for dinner: 'just for two twos. I left my humble birthday offering in there, and I want to give it to you.'

'O, but,' she said, pausing and looking back, one foot on the threshold of the big French window: 'I thought it was a bargain, no more birthday presents. I can't have you spending all those pennies on me.' Her right hand was lifted to a loose hanger of wistaria bloom, shoulder-high beside the doorway: in her left she carried her hat, which she had taken off walking up from the garden. The slant evening sun kindled so deep a Venetian glory in her hair that every smooth-wound coil, each braid, each fine straying little curl or tendril, had its particular fire-colour, of chestnut, tongued flame, inward glow of the brown-red zircon, burnished copper, realgar, sun-bleached gold: not self-coloured, but all in a shimmer and interchange of hues, as she moved her head or the air stirred them.

'Twenty pennies precisely,' said Jim. 'Can't call that breaking a bargain. Come. Please.'

'All right,' she smiled, and went before him through the small tea-room and its scents of pot-pourri, and through the great skin-strewn hall with its portraits and armour and trophies and old oak and old leather and Persian rugs and huge open fire-place filled at this season with roses and summer greenery, and so by a long soft-carpeted passage to the room they called the Refuge: a cosy sunny room, not belonging to Mary specially or to her father, but to both, and free besides to all dogs (those at least that were allowed in the house) that lived at Blunds, and to all deserving friends and relations. Those parts of the walls that were not masked by bookcases or by pictures showed the pale reddish paper of Morris's willow pattern; a frieze of his rich dark night-blue design of fruit, with its enrichments of orange, lemon, and pomegranate and their crimson and pallid blooms, ran around below the ceiling. There was a square table with dark green cloth and upon it a silver bowl of roses: writing things on the table and chairs about it, and big easy chairs before the fire-place: a bag of tools (saws, hammers, screw-drivers, pliers and such-like) behind the door, a leather gun-case and fishing-rods in this corner, walking-sticks and hunting-crops in that, a pair of field-glasses on the shelf, some dog-medicines: pipes and cigar-boxes on the mantel-piece: on a bureau a large mahogany musical-box: an early Victorian work-table, a rack full of newspapers, a Cotman above the mantel, an ancient brass-bound chest covered with an oriental rug or foot-cloth of silk: a Swiss cuckoo-clock: a whole red row of Baedekers on one of the bookshelves, yellowbacks on another: *Wuthering Heights* open on a side-table, Kipling's *Many Inventions* open on a chair, and a text of Homer on the top of it: a box of tin soldiers and a small boy's cricket bat beside them: over there a doll or two and a toy theatre, with a whole mass of woolly monkeys, some in silver-paper armour and holding pins for swords: a cocker spaniel asleep on the hearth-rug, and a little dark grey hairy dog, a kind of Skye terrier with big bat-like ears and of beguiling appearance, asleep in an armchair. There pervaded this room, not to be expelled for all the fresh garden air that came and went through its wide windows and door which opened on the garden, a scent curiously complex and curiously agreeable, as of a savoury stew compounded of this varied apparatus of the humanities. Plainly a Refuge it was, and by no empty right of name: a refuge from tidiness and from all engines, correctitudes, and impositions of the world: in this great household, a little abbey of Thélème, with its sufficient law, '*Fay ce que vouldras*'.

Mary sat on the table while Jim unearthed from somewhere a little parcel and presented it to her, with scissors from the work-table to cut the string. 'Twenty, you see, for the birthday cake,' he said, as she emptied out on the green baize a handful of little coloured candles.

'You are so absurd.'

'We ought to have the cake,' he said. 'No time for it now, though. Look: there are heaps of colours, you see. Do you know what they mean?'

'How should I know?'

'I'll show you': he began to arrange them side by side. 'They're highly symbolical. Nine white. Those are your nine first years: *tabula rasa*, from my point of view. Then, you see, a red one: a red-letter day for you when you first met me.'

'Was I ten then? I'd forgotten.'

'La Belle Dame sans Merci, always forgets. Now, look: violet, blue, green, yellow, orange, pink.'

'The rainbow?'

'Haven't I charming thoughts?'

'Then three goldy ones. Gold dust in them,' said she, touching them with one finger.

'Because of the presents,' Jim said, 'that I'd like to have given you these last three years, had I been Midas or John D. Rockefeller. Last, you observe: Black. For my own sake, because you're going to be married.'

'My dear Jim, what awful nonsense! Who told you so?'

'That would be telling. Isn't it true?' He backed to the fireplace and stood looking at her.

The sudden colour in her cheek, spreading yet lower as she faced him, made her seem (if that could be) yet lovelier. 'It is not so,' answered she. 'Nor it was not so. And, indeed, God forbid it ever should be so.'

'O dangerous resolution. But I really think it's uncommon nice of you, Mary. Of course, for myself, I gave up hope long ago; and you'll have noticed I've even given up asking you these last – two years, is it? No, since your last birthday:' Mary gave a little start. He moved to the window, and stood not to look direct at her: 'that was really when I decided, better give it up. But it does help my self-esteem to know there's no one else in the offing,' he said, lightly as before, playing with the scissors. 'May I tell people the good news?'

'Certainly not. Why should you go meddling with my affairs? I think it's most insolent of you.'

'Well, I thought you might like me to tell – well, Glanford: just to break the news to the pore fella.'

There was dead silence. He looked round. Mary's head was turned away: she seemed to be counting the little candles with her finger. Suddenly she stood up: went over to the fire-place. 'Sheila's a naughty little thing,' she said: the form curled up on the chair moved the tip of a feathery tail and, with a pricking and apologetic laying again of bat-like ears, cast up at Mary a most melting glance. 'Ate a quarter of a pound of butter in the larder this morning; and yet now, what a little jewel she looks: as if butter wouldn't melt.' She bent and kissed the little creature between the eyes, a kind of butterfly kiss, then, erect again, confronted Jim.

'It was infernal cheek on my part,' he said, 'to say that. Still: between old friends—'

Mary swept up the candles. 'I must fly and change.' Then, over her shoulder from the doorway, where she turned for an instant, tall, light of carriage in her white dress, like a nymph of Artemis: 'Thanks for a word fitly spoken, *mon ami*!

IV

LADY MARY SCARNSIDE

THAT something which, asleep or awake, resided near the corner of Mary's mouth peeked at itself in the looking-glass: a private interchange of intelligence between it and its reflection there, not for her to read. She turned from the dressing-table to the window. It was slack-water, and the tide in. Under the sun the surface of the creek was liquid gold. The point, with its coastguard cottage, showed misty in the distance. Landscape and waterscape departed, horizon beyond horizon, to that meeting of earth and heaven which, perhaps because of the so many more and finer gradations of air made visible, seemed far further remote in this beginning of midsummer evening than in the height of day. Mary stood for a minute looking from the window, where the airs stirred with honeysuckle scents and rose scents and salt and pungent scents of the marsh and sea.

Suddenly she moved and came back to the looking-glass. '"Then that's settled, Señorita Maria. I carry you off tonight." – And that,' she said aloud, looking at herself with that sideways incisive mocking look that she inherited from her father, 'was a piece of damned impertinence.'

There was a knock at the door. 'Come in. O Angier, I'll ring when I'm ready for you: ten minutes or so.'

'Yes, my lady. I thought your ladyship would want me to do your hair tonight.'

'Yes I'll ring,' Mary said, giving her maid a smile in the looking-glass. She retired, saying, 'It's nearly half past seven, my lady.'

Half past seven. And half past seven this morning. Twelve hours ago. Thrown from her ring, where the sun took it, a rainbow streak of colour appeared on the carpet: her white kitten made a pounce to seize the mysterious dancing presence, now there, now gone. And then, half past seven tomorrow. Always on the go, by the look of it: everything. Nothing stays. She moved her finger, to draw the iridescent phantom again along the carpet and so up the wall, out of reach from velvet paws that pounced. And yet, you can't believe that. The whole point about a thing like this morning is that it does stay: somewhere it stays. What you want to find out how to get back to it: or forward? for it is forward, too. Or perhaps back and forward don't belong to it at all: it just is. Perhaps back and forward just aren't. Perhaps, perhaps, perhaps.

To ride her down like that: if anyone had seen them. 'Unpardonable,' Mary said, as she took her seat at the mirror and began to let down her hair. And Tessa is a pretty good little mare: showed him a clean pair of heels for a mile or so. Something in the shadowy backgrounds of the mirror surprisingly assumed a neat little black thoroughbred horse's face, and shockingly said to Mary: 'Haven't I a perfect mouth? to have understood and slowed down the least little bit in the world just at the—'

The north-westerly sun made it hot in the dressing-room. The door was shut between this and her bedroom, to keep that cool for the night: bedroom with windows that opened north and east to let in the mornings. She was in a kind of kimono of pale blue silk after her bath, and now, for this heat, while she sat to brush her hair, she untied the sash, and with a shake of her shoulders, let the soft garment fall open and down about her hips. 'Carry you off tonight.' It really was a bit much. The extraordinary cool-ness of it all, after that dreadful scene they had had at the end of April, when he had turned up five months before his time, and she had said – well, said enough to end it for most men, one would think. And yet now, this morning, after six weeks of obedient absence and silence— She had ridden to hounds often enough;

but to be hunted like a hare! True, she had started the thing, in a way, by turning to ride off in the other direction as soon as she saw him. But still. Her bosom rose and fell with the memory of it: as if all the wide universe had suddenly run hunting-mad, and she the quarry: she and poor little Tessa with her flying feet: an excitement like darkness with sudden rollings in it like distant drums; and the trees, the solid ground, the waking buttercups and meadowsweet with the dew on them, the peggy-whitethroat on the thorn, the brier-rose at the edge of the wood, larks trilling invisible in the blue, the very upland newness of the summer air of this birthday morning, all had seemed as if caught up into that frenzy of flight to join in the hunt, multiplying the galloping music of Lessingham's horse-hooves, now loud, now dim, now loud again, to a hue and cry and a gallop of all these things. And then the coolness of him, after this wild horse-race: the astounding assurance of this proposition, put to her so easily and as if it were the simplest thing in the world: and his having a motorcar, so that they shouldn't be caught. Most monstrous of all, about the luggage: that he had luggage for her as well, every possible thing she could want, every kind of clothes.

How did he know? Mary laid down her brush and leaned back, staring into her own eyes for a minute in the looking-glass. Then, after a minute, some comical matter stirred in her eyes' inward corners. 'How did you know?' she said, addressing not her own image but the mirrored door over its shoulder, as if somone had come in there and stood in the doorway. Then, with eyes resting on herself again, she said suddenly in herself: 'This is how I should— If we were to be— If we are to be— But no, my friend. Not to be swept up like – like a bunch of candles.'

She and her looking-glass self surveyed one another for a while, coolly, in detail, not looking any more into each other's eyes nor over each other's shoulders to the door beyond. At length the looking-glass image said, not audibly, but to Mary's inward ear: I suppose a man sees it differently. I think I understand, partly, how he might see it: something very delicate, easily hurt, easily broken, but so gentle that you couldn't bear to. Like a field-mouse or some such: or like a baby. No, for what matters about a baby is what it is going to be; but this – here it is, full-fledged: what it is and what it ought to be, in one: doesn't want to change: just to be. That is enough for anybody. And its power, what all power ought to be: not to overpower the weak, but overpower the powerful. Really it hasn't any power: except that it need only lift a finger, and every power there is or ever could be must rise to protect it.

But that isn't true (said the looking-glass image, going over with musing untroubled eyes the thing before it: chin, throat: gleam of a shoulder betwixt fallen masses of flame-coloured hair: arms whose curves had the motion of swans in them and the swan's whiteness: breasts of a Greek mould and firmness, dove-like, silver-pure, pointing their rose-flowers in a Greek pride: and those wild delicate little perfections, of the like flame colour, beneath her arms): that isn't true. And with that (perhaps for two seconds) something happened in the mirror: a two-seconds' glimpse as of some menace that rushed upwards, like the smoke of some explosion, to yawning immensities bleak, unmeaning, unmindful of the worm that is man; into which void there seemed, for that moment, to be sucked up all comfort of cosy room, home, dear ones, gaiety of youthful blood, the sweet nostalgia of childhood born of the peace of that June evening, its scents, its inwardness and whispered promise: the familiar countryside that made a lap for all these: the sea, island-girdling of England: the kindly natural earth: the very backgrounds and foundations of historic time: sucked up, swallowed, brought to nought. And, naked to this roofless and universal Nothing, she: immeasurably alone, a little feminine living being, and these 'little decaying beauties of the body'.

But two seconds only, and blood danced again. Mary jumped to her feet: put on some clothes: rang the bell.

She was nearly ready when her father's knock came on the door: his voice, 'Can I come in?'

'Come in, Father.' She swam towards him with the style of a du Maurier duchess and shook hands in the most extreme high-handed affectation of the moment. 'So charmed you could come, Lord Anmering. So charmin' of you to spare us the time, with so much huntin' and shootin' this time of year, and the foxes eatin' up all the pear-blossom and all.'

He played up; then stood back to admire her, theatrically posed for him, with sweeping of her train and manage of her point-lace fan. Her eyes danced with his. 'Looking very bonnie,' he said, and kissed her on the forehead. 'Table arranged? I suppose you've given me Lady Southmere? And Hugh on your right?'

'O yes. Duty at dinner: pleasure afterwards.'

He caught the look on her face as she turned to the dressing-table for her gloves: this and a strained something in her voice. 'Not a very nice way,' he said, 'to talk about our friends.'

Mary said nothing, busy at her looking-glass.

Lord Anmering stood at the window, trimming his nails, his back towards her. Presently he said quietly, 'I'm getting a bit tired of this attitude towards Glanford.'

Mary was unclasping her pearl necklace to change it for the sapphire pendant: it slipped and fell on the dressing-table. 'Damn!' she said, and was silent.

'Do you understand what I said?'

'Attitude? I've none, that I'm aware of. Certainly not "towards".' She fastened the clasp at the back of her neck, turned and came to where he stood, still turned away from her in the window: slipped her arm in his. 'And I'm not going to be bullied on my birthday.' His arm tightened on hers, a large reassuring pressure, as to say: Of course she shan't.

He looked at his watch. 'Five past eight. We ought to be going down.'

'O and, Father,' she said, turning back to him half way to the door, 'I don't think I told you (such a rush all day): whom do you think I met out riding this morning? and asked him to come to dinner tonight? Edward Lessingham. Only back from Italy, and I don't know where, last month.'

Lord Anmering had stopped short 'You asked him to dinner?'

'Yes.'

'What did you do that for?'

'Ordinary civility. Very lucky, too: we'd have been three thirteens otherwise, with Lady Dilstead turning up.'

'Pah! We'd have been three thirteens with him, then, when you asked him. And it isn't so: we were thirty-eight.'

'Thirty-nine with Madame de Rosas.'

'My dear girl, you can't have that dancer woman sit down with us.'

'Why not? She's very nice. Perfectly respectable. I think it would be unkind not to. Anybody else would do it.'

'It's monstrous, and you're old enough to know better.'

'Well, I've asked her, and I've asked him. You can order them both out if you want to make a scene.'

'Don't talk to me like that,' said her father. She shrugged her shoulders and stood looking away, very rebellious and angry. 'And I thought you knew perfectly well,' he said, 'that I don't care for that young Lessingham about the place.'

'I don't understand what you mean, "about the place".'

'I don't care about him.'

'I can't think why. You've always liked Anne Bremmerdale. Isn't his family good enough for you? As old as ours. Older, I should think. You've hardly seen him.'

'I don't propose to discuss him,' said Lord Anmering, looking at her piercingly through his eye-glass: then fell silent, as if in debate whether or not to speak his mind. 'Look here, my darling,' he said, at last, with an upward flick of the eyebrow letting the eye-glass fall: 'It's just as well to have cards on the table. It has been my serious hope that you would one day marry Hugh Glanford. I'm not going to force it or say any more. But, things being as they are, it is as well to be plain about it.'

'I should have thought it had been plain enough for some time. Hanging about us all the season: most of last winter, too. People beginning to talk, I should think.'

'What rubbish.'

'All the same, it was nice of you to tell me, Father. Have you been plain about it to him too?'

'He approached me some time ago.'

'And you gave him your—?'

'I wished him luck. But naturally he understands that my girl must decide for herself in a thing like that.'

'How very kind of him.' Mary began laughing. 'This is delightful: like the ballad:

> He's told her father and mither baith,
> As I hear sindry say,
> But he has nae teld the lass her sell,
> Till on her wedding day.'

Her voice hardened: 'I wish I was twenty-one. Do as I liked, then. Marry the next man that asked me—'

'Mary, Mary—'

'—So long as it wasn't Hugh.' Mary gave a little gulp and disappeared into her bedroom, slamming the door behind her. Her father, feet planted wide apart in the middle of her dressing room floor, waited, moodily polishing his eye-glass with a white silk pocket-handkerchief scented with eau de Cologne. In three minutes she was back again, radiantly mistress of herself, with a presence of mischief dimpling so elusively about mouth and eyes in her swimming towards him, that it were easier tell black from green in the rifle-bird's glinting neck, than tell whether in this peace-making she charmingly dispensed pardon or as charmingly sought it. 'Happy birthday?' she said, inclining her brow demurely for him to kiss. 'Must go down now, or people will be arriving.'

Among the guests now assembling in the drawing-room Lessingham's arrival was with some such unnoted yet precise effect as follows the passing of a light cloud across the sun, or the coming of the sun full out again as the cloud shifts. Mary said, as they shook hands, 'You know Mr Lessingham, Father? You remember he and Jim were at Eton together.'

There was frost in Lord Anmering's greeting. 'I had forgotten that,' he said. 'When was it I met you last?'

'About a year ago, sir,' said Lessingham. 'I've been out of England.'

'I think I remember. You've lived abroad a good deal?'

'Yes, sir: on and off, these last seven years.'

'What did you come home for?'

Lessingham's eyes were grey: straight of gaze, but not easily read, and with a smoulder in the depths of them. He answered, 'To settle up some affairs.'

'And so abroad again?'

'I've not decided yet.'

'A rolling stone?'

Lessingham smiled. 'Afraid I am, sir.'

Jim joined them: 'Did I tell you, uncle, about Lessingham's running across some of your Gurkha porters when he was in India two or three years ago? that had climbed with you and Mr Freshfield in Sikkim?'

'You're a climber, then?' Lord Anmering said to Lessingham, looking him up and down: very tall, perhaps six foot three, black-haired, sunburnt but, as his forehead showed, naturally white and clear of skin, and with the look of one able to command both himself and others, as is not often seen at that age of five and twenty.

'I've done a little.'

'A lot,' said Jim. Lessingham shook his head. 'In the Himalaya?' said Lord Anmering.

'A little, sir.'

'A little!' said Jim: 'just listen how these mountaineers talk to each other! Twenty-two thousand feet he did once, on – what's the name of it? – one of the cubs of Nanga Parbat. A terrific thing; and pages about it at the time in the *Alpine Journal*. Come,' he said, taking Lessingham's arm, 'I want to introduce you to my sister. She married a Russian: we can never pronounce the name, none of us; so please don't mind, and please don't try. You're taking her in to dinner: that's right, Mary?'

Mary smiled assent. For a flash, as she turned to welcome the Denmore-Benthams who had just come in, her glance met

Lessingham's. And, unless seen by him and by her, then to every living eye invisible, something (for that flash) danced in the air between them: 'But, after dinner—'

Dinner was in the picture gallery (where later they were also to dance), the only room big enough and long enough to take forty people comfortably at one table. A fine room it was, eighty feet perhaps by twenty-five, with a row of tall low-silled windows going the whole length of its western wall. These, left uncurtained when dinner began, and with their lower sashes thrown up to admit the evening air, were filled with the sunset. Dozens of candles, each from under its rose-coloured little prim hat of pleated silk, beamed down clear upon the white of the table-cloth, the glass, the silver and the china and the flowers of Mary's choosing and delicate trailers of greenery; imbuing besides with a softer, a widelier diffused and a warmer glow the evening dresses, the jewels, the masculine black and white, the faces, hosts' or guests': faces which, young, old or of doubtful date, were yet all by this unity of candle-light brought into one picture, and by the yet airier but deeper unity that is in pleasant English blood, secure, easy, gay, fancy-free. And (as for proof that England were to wrong her own nature did she fail to absorb the exotic), even the Spanish woman, midway down the table between Jim Scarnside and Hesper Dagworth, was assimilated by that solvent, as the sovereign alkahest will subdue and swallow up all refractory elements and gold itself.

Conversation, like a ballet of little animals (guests at Queen Alice's looking-glass party when things began to happen), tripped, paused, footed it in and out, pirouetted, crossed and returned, back and forth among the faces and the glasses and the dresses and the lights. For a while, about the head of the table, the more classic figures revolved under the direction of Lord Anmering, Mr Romer, General Macnaghten and Mr Everard Scarnside. Lady Rosamund Kirstead, on the skirts of this Parnassus, her back to the windows, tempered its airs with visions of skiing-slopes above Villars that February (her first taste of winter sports), and so succeeded at last in enveigling Anne and Margesson and Mr

Scarnside from those more intellectual scintillations (which Anne excelled in but Rosamund found boring) down to congenial common ground of Ascot, Henley, Lord's, the Franco-British Exhibition, in prospect and retrospect: what to wear, what not to wear: August, September, grouse-moors and stalkers' paths of Invernesshire and Sutherland.

Lessingham, further down on the same side of the table, held a three-cornered conversation with Amabel Mitzmesczinsky on his right and Fanny on his left: here the talk danced to merrier and stranger tunes, decking itself out as if the five continents and all past and present were its wardrobe. Into its vortex were drawn Tom Chedisford and Mrs Bentham from across the table, till Jack Bailey sat marooned; for, while Mrs Bentham, his rightful partner, who had hitherto displayed a most comforting interest in things within the grasp of his understanding, unfeelingly began to ignore him for the quattrocento, Lucy Dilstead on his other side conducted an esoteric conversation, not very vocal, with her fiancé. Jack, hearing at last in this loneliness a name he knew (of Botticelli's *Primavera*), took advantage of a lull in the talk to say, with honest philistine conviction, 'And *that's* a *nasty* picture.' Jim and Hesper Dagworth experimented by turns, Hesper with his own Spanish, Jim with the lady's English, on Madame de Rosas, who thus became a distraction in the more serious discussions carried on by Bremmerdale, Colonel Playter, and Jim, on the subject of point-to-points. Appleyard with his funny stories kept the Playter girls in fits of boisterous laughter, till finally they took to bombarding him with bread-pills: an enterprise as suddenly ended as suddenly begun, under the horrified reproof of the parson's wife and the more quelling glare of the paternal eye upon them.

At the foot of the table Mary, as hostess, seemed at first to have her hands full: with Hugh on her right, rather sulky, scenting (may be) an unfavorable climate for his intended proposal, and becoming more and more nervous as time went by; and, on her left, the breezy Admiral, flirting outrageously with Mrs Dagworth who seemed, however, a little distrait, with her eye on Hesper and the de Rosas woman. But Mary's witty talk and the mere presence of her worked as lovely weather in spring, that can set sap and blood and the whole world in tune.

Lessingham and Mary, breaking off from the dance as it brought them alongside the door, went out quickly and through the tea-room and so out from the music and the stir and the glitter to the free air of the terrace, and there stood a minute to taste it, her arm still in his, looking both into the same enbowered remoteness of the dark and the star-shine: the fragrant body of night, wakeful but still.

Mary withdrew her arm.

Lessingham said, 'Do you mean to make a practice of this? For the future, I mean?'

'Of what?'

'What you've been doing to me tonight?'

'I don't know. Probably.'

'Good.'

Mary was fanning herself. Presently he took the fan and plied it for her. The music sounded, rhythmic and sweet, from the picture gallery. 'That was rather charming of you,' she said: 'to say "good".'

'Extremely charming of me, if I was a free agent But you may have noticed, that I'm not.'

Mary said, 'Do you think I am?'

'Completely, I should say. Completely free, and remarkably elusive.'

'Elusive? Sometimes people speak truer than they guess.'

'You've eluded me pretty successfully all the evening,' Lessingham said, as she took back the fan. The music stopped. Mary said, 'We must go in.'

'Need we? You're not cold?'

'I want to.' She turned to go.

'But, please,' he said at her elbow. 'What have I done? The only dance we've had, and the evening half over—'

'I'm feeling – ratty.'

Lessingham said no more, but followed her between the sleeping flower-borders to the house. In the doorway they encountered, among others, Glanford coming out. He reddened and looked awkward. Mary reddened too, but passed in, aloof, unperturbed. She and Lessingham came now, through the tea-room and the great galleried hall, to the drawing-room, where, since dinner, at the far end a kind of platform or stage had been put up, with footlights along the front of it, and in all the main floor of the room chairs and sofas arranged as for an audience. Shaded lamps on standards or on tables at the sides and corners of the room made a restful, uncertain, golden light.

'You've heard the castanets before, I suppose?' said Mary.

'Yes. Only once properly: in Burgos.'

'Castanets and cathedrals go rather well together, I should think.'

'Yes,' he said. 'I never thought of that before; but they do. A curious mix up of opposites: the feeling of Time, clicking and clicking endlessly away; and the other − well, as if there were something that did persist.'

'Like mountains,' Mary said; 'and the funny little noise of streams, day after day, month after month, running down their sides.'

Lessingham said, under his breath, 'And sometimes, an avalanche.'

They were standing now before the fireplace, which was filled with masses of white madonna lilies. Over the mantelpiece, lighted from above by a hidden electric lamp, hung an oil painting, the head-and-shoulders portrait of a lady with smooth black hair, very pale of complexion, taken nearly full-face, with sloping shoulders under her gauzy dress and a delicate slender neck (ἁπαλή δειρή, as Homer has it in the hymn). Her forehead was high: face long and oval: eyebrows arched and slender: nose rather long, very straight, and with the faintest disposition to turn up at the end, which gave it a certain air of insolent but not unkindly disdainfulness. Her eyes were large, and the space wide between them and between lid and eyebrow: the lid of each, curving swiftly up from the inner corner, ended at the outer corner with another sudden upward twist: a slightly eastern cast of countenance, with a touch perhaps of the Japanese and a touch of the harsh Tartar.

'Reynolds,' said Lessingham, after a minute's looking at it in silence.

'Yes.'

'An ancestress?'

'No. No relation. Look at the name.'

He leaned near to look, in the corner of the canvas: *Anne Horton 1766.*

'Done when she was about nineteen,' said Mary. There seemed to come, as she looked at that portrait, a subtle alteration in her whole demeanour, as when, some gay inward stirrings of the sympathies, friend looks on friend. 'Do you like it?'

On Lessingham's face, still studying the picture, a like alteration came. 'I love it.'

'She went in for fatty degeneration later on, and became Duchess of Cumberland. Gainsborough painted her as that, several times, later.'

'I don't believe it,' he said. He looked round at Mary. 'Neither the fat,' he said, 'nor the degeneration. I think I know those later paintings, and now I don't believe them.'

'They're not interesting,' Mary said. 'But in this one, she's certainly not very eighteenth-century. Curiously outside all dates, I should say.'

'Or inside.'

'Yes: or inside all dates.'

Lessingham looked again at Mrs Anne Horton – the sideways inclination of the eyes: the completely serene, completely aware, impenetrable, weighing, look: lips as if new-closed, as in Verona, upon that private *ça m'amuse.* He looked quickly back again at Mary. And, plain for him to see, the something that inhabited near Mary's mouth seemed to start awake or deliciously to recognize, in the picture, its own likeness.

It recognized also (one may guess) a present justification for the *ça m'amuse.* Perhaps the lady in the picture had divined Mary's annoyance at Glanford's insistent, unduly possessive, proposal, at her own rather summary rejection of it, and at Lessingham's methods that seemed to tar him incongruously with the same brush (and her father, too, not without a touch of that tar): divined, moreover, the exasperation in Mary's consciousness that she overwhelmingly belonged to Lessingham, that she was being swept on to a choice she did not want to make, and that Lessingham unpardonably (but scarcely unnaturally, not being in these secrets) did not seem to understand the situation.

Mary laughed. It was as if all the face of the night was cleared again.

The room was filling now. Madame de Rosas, in shawl and black mantilla, took her place on the platform, while below, on her right, the musicians began to tune up. Lessingham and Mary had easy chairs at the back, near the door. The lamps were switched out, all except those that lighted the pictures, and the footlights were switched on. 'And my Cyprus picture over there?' Lessingham said in Mary's ear. 'Do you know why I sent it you?'

Mary shook her head.

'You know what it is?'

'Yes: you told me in your letter. Sunrise from Olympus. It is marvellous. The sense of height. Windy sky. The sun leaping up behind you. The cold shadows on the mountains, and goldy light on them. Silver light of dawn. And that tremendous thrown shadow of Olympus himself and the kind of fringe of red fire along its edges: I've seen that in the Alps.'

'Do you know what that is, there: where you get a tiny bit of sea, away on the left, far away over the ranges?'

'What is it?'

'Paphos. Where Aphrodite is supposed to have risen from the sea. I camped up there, above Troodos, for a fortnight: go up with my things about four o'clock every morning to catch the sunrise and paint it. I'll tell you something,' he said, very low: 'I actually almost came to believe that story, the whole business, Homeric hymn, Botticelli's picture in the Uffizi, everything: almost, in a queer way, when I was looking across there, alone, at daybreak. But—' he said. The strings burst into the rhythm of an old seguidilla of Andalusia: the Spanish woman took the centre of the stage, swept her shawl about her shoulders and stood, statuesque, motionless, in the up-thrown brilliance of the footlights. Lessingham looked up at her for a moment, then back at Mary. Mary's eyes had left picture for stage; but his, through the half-light, fed only upon Mary: the profile of her face, the gleam of the sapphired pendant that in so restful a sweet unrest breathed with her breathing. 'But,' he said, 'it was you.' The dusky sapphire stood still for an instant, then, like a ship from the trough of the sea, rose and, upon the surge, down again.

'It would be a foolish myth if it could have been anyone else but you,' he whispered. And the castanets began softly upon a flutter or rumour of sound, scarce heard.

An Andalusian dance, done by a hired woman to please the guests at an English country house in this year of Our Lord 1908. And yet, through some handfasting of music with landscape and portrait painted and their embarking so, under the breath of secular deep memories in the blood, upon that warmed sapphire rocked on so dear a sea, the rhythms of the dance seemed to take to themselves words:

Αἰδοίην χρυσοστέφανον καλὴν Ἀφροδίτην—

Awful, gold-crowned, beautiful, Aphrodite—

and so to the ending:

Hail, You of the flickering eyelids, honey-sweet! And vouch-safe me in this contest to bear victory; and do You attune my song. Surely so will I too yet remember me of another song to sing You.

The castanets, on a long-drawn thinness of sound, as of grass-hoppers on a hot hillside in summer, trembled down to silence. Then a burst of clapping: smiles and curtseys of acknowledgement from the platform: talk let loose again in a buzz and chatter, cleft with the tuning of the strings: under cover of which, Mary said softly, with her eye on the Cyprus picture, 'You didn't really believe it?'

'No. Of course I didn't.'

'And yet perhaps, for a moment,' she said: 'with that burning on the edge of the shadow? For a moment, in the hurry to paint it?'

Lessingham seemed to answer not her but the mystery, in the half-light, of her face that was turned towards his. In mid speech, as if for the sweet smell of her, the living nearness of her, his breath caught and his words stumbled. 'I think there's part of one,' he said, 'believes a lot of queer things, when one is actually painting or writing.'

'Part? And then, afterwards, not believe it any more?'

In a mist, under his eyes the sapphire woke and slept again as, with the slight shifting of her posture, the musk-rose milk-white valley narrowed and deepened.

She said, very softly, 'Is that how it works? With everything?'

'I don't know. Wish I did.'

V

QUEEN OF HEARTS AND
QUEEN OF SPADES

A HALF mile north-east from the summer palace at Memison, out along the backbone of the hill, a level place, of the bigness of a tennis-court, overhangs like a kestrel's nest the steeps that on that side fall abruptly to the river-mouth of Zeshmarra, its water-meadows and bird-haunted marshlands. Here, years ago, when King Mezentius made an end of the work of raising about the little old spy-fortalice of Memison halls and chambers of audience, and lodging for twenty-score soldiers and for the folk of all degree proper to a princely court besides, and brought to completion the great low-built summer palace, with groves and walks and hanging gardens and herb-gardens and water-gardens and colonnades, so that there should be no season of the year nor no extreme of weather but, for each hour of the day, some corner or nook of these garden pleasances should be found to fit it, and gave it all, with patent of the ducal name and dignity, to Amalie, his best-beloved; here, on this grassy shelf, turning to that use a spring of clear water, he had devised for her her bath, as the divine Huntress's, in a shade of trees. A rib of rock, grown over with rock roses and creeping juniper, shut it from sight from the castle and gardens, and a gate and stairs through the rock led down to it. Upon the other side oaks and walnut-trees and mimosa-trees and great evergreen magnolias made a screen along the parapet with vistas between of Reisma Mere and, away leftwards, of the even valley floor, all cut into fields with hedgerows and rounded shapes of trees, clustering here and there to a billowy mass of coppice or woodland. And there were farmsteads here and there, and here and there wreathings of smoke, and all the long valley blue with the midsummer dusk, the sun being settled to rest, and the mountains east and north-east dark blue against a quiet sky. All winds had fallen to sleep, and yet no closeness was on the air; for in this gentle climate of the Meszrian highlands, as there is no day of winter but keeps some spice of June in it, so is no summer's day so sun-scorched but some tang of winter sharpens it, from mountain or sea. No leaf moved. Only, from the inner side of that pool, the bubbling up of the well from below sent across the surface ring after widening ring: a motion not to be seen save as a faint stirring, as mirrored in the water, of things which themselves stood motionless: pale roses, and queenly flower-delices of dark and sumptuous hues of purple and rust of gold. In that perfect hour all shadows had left earth and sky, and but form and colour remained: form, as a differing of colour from colour, rather than as a matter of line and edge (which indeed were departed with the shadows); and colour differing from colour not in tone but in colour's self, rich, self-sufficing, undisturbed: the olive hue of the holm-oak, the green-black bosky obscurities of the pine, cool white of the onyx bench above the water, the delicate blues of the Duchess's bathing-mantle of netted silk; incarnadine purities, bared or half-veiled, of arm, shoulder, thigh; her unbound hair full of the red-gold harmonies of beechwoods in strong spring sunshine; and (hard to discern in this uncertain luminosity or gloam of cockshut time) her face. Her old nurse, white-haired, with cheeks wrinkled like a pippin and eyes that seemed to hold some sparkles blown from her mistress's beauty, was busy about drying of the Duchess's feet, while she herself, resting her cheek on her right hand with elbow propped upon cushions of dove-grey velvet, looked southward across the near water to the distant gleam of the mere, seen beyond the parapet, and to woods and hills through which runs the road south to Zayana.

'The sun is down. Your grace will not feel the cold?'

'Cold tonight?' said the Duchess, and something crossed her face like the dance, tiny feathered bodies upright hovering, wings a-flutter, downward-pointing tails flirting fan-like, of a pair of yellow wagtails that crossed the pool. 'Wait till tomorrow: then, perhaps, cold indeed.'

'His highness but goeth to come again, as ever was.'

'To come again? So does summer. But, as we grow old, we learn the trick to be jealous of each summer departing; as if that were end indeed, and no summer after.'

'In twenty years' time I'll give your beauteous excellence leave to begin such talk, not now: I that had you in cradle in your side-coats, and nor kings nor dukes to trouble us then.'

'In twenty years?' said the Duchess. 'And I today with a son of two and twenty.'

'Will his grace of Zayana be here tonight?' Myrrha said, sitting on the grass at the Duchess's feet with Violante, ladies of honour.

'Who can foretell the will-o'-the-wisp?'

'Your grace, if any,' said the old woman; 'seeing he is as like your grace as you had spit him.'

'Hath his father in him, too,' said the Duchess: 'for masterfulness, at least, pride, opinion and disdain, and ne'er sit still: turn day in night and night in day. And you, my love-birds, be not too meddling in these matters. I am informed what mad tricks have been played of late in Zayana. Remember, a spaniel puts up many a fowl. Brush my hair,' she said to the nurse: 'so. It is not we, nurse, that grow old. We but sit: look on. And birth, and youth, the full bloom, the fading and the falling, are as pictures borne by to please or tease us; or as seasons to the earth. Earth changes not: no more do we. And death but the leading on to another summer.'

'Sad thoughts for a sweet evening,' the old nurse said, brushing.

'Why not? Unless (and I fear 'tis true) shades are coveted in summer, but with me 'tis fall of the leaf. Nay, I am young, surely, if sad thoughts please me. Yet, no; for there's a taint of hope sweetens the biting of this sad sauce of mine; I can no more love it unalloyed, as right youth will do. Grow old is worse than but be old,' she said, after a pause. 'Growing-pains, I think.'

'I love your hair in summer,' the nurse said, lifting the shining tresses as it had been something too fair and too fine for common hand to touch. 'The sun fetches out the gold in it, where in winter was left but red-hot fire-colours.'

'Gold is good,' said the Duchess. 'And fire is good. But pluck out the silver.'

'I ne'er found one yet,' said she. 'So the Lady Fiorinda shall have the Countess's place in the bedchamber? I had thought your grace could never abide her?'

The Duchess smiled, reaching for her hand-glass of emerald and gold. 'Today, just upon the placing of the breakfasting-covers, I took a resolve to choose my women as I choose gowns. And black most takingly becomes me. Myrrha, what scent have you brought me?'

'The rose-flower of Armash.'

'It is too ordinary. Tonight I will have something more strange, something unseasonable; something springlike to confound midsummer. Wood-lilies: that were good: in the golden perfume-sprinkler. But no,' she said, as Myrrha arose to go for these: 'they are earthy. Something heaven-like for tonight. Bring me wood gentians: those that grow many along one stem, so as you would swear it had first been Solomon's seal but, with leaving to hang its pale bells earthward, and with looking skywards instead through a roof of mountain pines, had turned blue at last: colour of the heaven it looked to.'

'Madam, they have no scent.'

'How can you know? What is not possible, tonight? Find me some. But see: no need,' she said. 'Fiorinda! This is take to your duties as an eagle's child to the wind.'

'I am long used to waiting on myself,' said that lady, coming down the steps out of an archway of leafy darknesses, stone pine upon the left and thick-woven traceries of an old gnarled strawberry-tree on the right, her arms full of blue wood gentians, and with two little boys in green coats, one bearing upon a tray

hippocras in a flagon and golden globlets, and the other apricots
and nectarines on dishes of silver.

'Have they scent indeed?' said the Duchess, taking the gentians.

'Please your grace to smell them.'

The Duchess gathered them to her face. 'This is magic.'

'No. It is the night,' said Fiorinda, bidding the boys set down
and begone. The shadow of a smile passed across her lips in the
meeting of green eye-glances, hers and the Duchess's, over the barrier
of sky-blue flowers. 'Your grace ought to kiss them.'

The Duchess did so. Again their glances met. The scent of those
woodland flowers, subtle and elusive, spoke a private word as into
the inward and secretest ear of her who inhaled that perfume: as
to say, privately, 'I have ended the war. Five months sooner than
I said, my foot is on their necks. And so, five months before the
time appointed – I will have you, Amalie.' She caught her breath;
and that perfume lying so delicate on the air that no sense but
hers might savour it, said privately again to Amalie's blood, 'And
that was in that room in the tower, high upon Acrozayana, with
great windows that take the sunset, facing west over Ambremerine,
but the bedchamber looks east over the sea: the rooms where
today Barganax your son has his private lodging. And that was
this very night, of midsummer's day, three-and-twenty years ago.'
She dismissed her girls, Myrrha and Violante, with a sign of the
hand, and, while the nurse braided, coiled and put up her hair,
kissed the flowers again, smoothed her cheek against them as a
beautiful cat will do, gathered them to her throat. 'Dear Gods!'
she said, 'were it not blasphemy, I could suppose myself the Queen
of Heaven in Her incense-sweet temple in Cyprus, as in the holy
hymn, choosing out there My ornaments of gold and sweet-smelling
soft raiment, and so upon the wind to Ida, to that princely herdsman,

Ὃς τότ᾽ ἐν κροπόλοις ὄρεσιν πολυπιδάκου Ἴδης,
Βουνκολέεσκεν βούς, δέμας ἀθανάτοισιν ἐοικώς

Who, on the high-running ranges of many-fountain'd Ida,
Neat-herd was of neat, but a God in frame and seeming.'

'Blasphemy?' said Fiorinda. 'Will you say the Gods were e'er angered at blasphemy? I had thought it was but false gods that could take hurt from that.'

'Even say they be not angered, I would yet fear the sin in it,' said the Duchess: 'the old son of ὕβρις – man to make himself equal with God.'

Fiorinda said, 'I question whether there be in truth any such matter as sin.'

The Duchess, looking up at her, abode an instant as if bedazzled and put out of her reckonings by some character, alien and cruel and unregarding; that seemed to settle with the dusk on the cold features of that lady's face. 'Give me my cloak,' she said then to the nurse, and standing up and putting it about her, 'go before and see all fit in my robing-room. Then return with lights. We'll come thither shortly.' Then, the nurse being gone, 'I will tell you an example,' she said. 'It is a crying and hellish sin, as I conceive it, to have one's husband butchered with bodkins on the piazza steps in Krestenaya.'

Fiorinda raised her eyebrow in a most innocent undisturbed surprise. 'That? I scarce think Gods would fret much at that. Besides, it was not my doing. Though, truly,' she said, very equably, and upon a lazy self-preening cadence of her voice, ''twas no more than the quit-claim due to him for unhandsome usage of me.'

'It was done about the turn of the year,' said the Duchess; 'and but now, in May, we see letters patent conferring upon your husband the lieutenancy of Reisma: the Lord Morville, your present, second, husband, I mean. What qualification fitted Morville for that office?'

'I'll not disappoint your grace of your answer. His qualification was, being husband of mine; albeit then but of three weeks' standing.'

'You are wisely bent, I find. Tell me: is he a good husband of his own honour?'

'Truly,' answered she, 'I have not given much thought to that. But, now I think on't, I judge him to be one of those bull-calves that have it by nature to sprout horns within the first year.'

'A notable impudency in you to say so. But it is rifely reported you were early schooled in these matters.'

Fiorinda shrugged her shoulders. 'The common people,' she said, 'were ever eager to credit the worst.'

'Common? Is that aimed at me?'

'O no. I never heard but that your grace's father was a gentleman by birth.'

'How old are you?' said the Duchess.

'Nineteen. It is my birthday.'

'Strange: and mine. Nineteen: so young, and yet so very—'

'Your grace will scarcely set down my youth against me as a vice, I hope: youth, and no stomach for fools—'

'O I concern not myself with your ladyship's vices. Enough with your virtues: murder, and (shall we say?) *poudre agrippine*.'

Fiorinda smoothed her white dress. 'The greater wonder,' she said, with a delicate air, 'that your grace should go out of your way to assign me a place at court, then.'

'You think it a wonder?' the Duchess said. 'It is needful, then, that you understand the matter. It is not in me to grudge a friend's pleasures. Rather do I study to retain a dozen or so women of your leaven about me, both as foils to my own qualities and in case ever, in an idle hour, he should have a mind for such highly seasoned sweetmeats.'

The Lady Fiorinda abode silent, looking down into the water at her feet. The full moon was rising behind a hill on the far side of the valley, and two trees upon the sky-line stood out clear like some little creature's feet held up against the moon's face. A bat flittered across the open above the pool, to and again. High in the air a heron went over, swiftly on slow wing-beats, uttering three or four times his wild harsh cry. There was a pallour of moonlight on that lady's face, thus seen sideways, downward-gazing, and on her arm, bare to the shoulder, and on the white of her gown that took life from every virginal sweet line of her body, standing so, poised in that tranquillity; and the black of her hair made all the awakening darknesses of the summer night seem luminous. And now, with the lifting of her arm to settle the pins in her back hair, there was a flash of black lightning that opened from amid those pallours and in a flash was hidden, leaving upon the air a breathlessness and a shudder like the shudder of the world's desire. At length, still side-face to the Duchess, still gazing into that quiet water, she spoke: 'A dozen? Of my leaven? Must they be like me to look upon? or is it enough that they be—? but I will not borrow your grace's words.'

Something seemed to stir in the warm air, with the falling tones of her voice: a languorous opening, rising and falling and closing again, of some Olympian fan. As it should have been sunset beholding the going up of Night, the Duchess stood and beheld her: as to say – You and I are one: the same common sky: one air: beauty, colour, fire. Night is young, rising in her ascendant while sunset dies: Night, kirtled with blackness and a steely glitter of stars: bat-wings; owl-wings soundless as the feathered wings of sleep; and, coming and going in unplumbed pools of gloom, pairs of eyes, bodiless, like green moons, and the soft breathing of snakes that glide by invisible. So Night enters on her own, bitter-sweet with a passion of nightingales; and all presences of earth and air and water cover their faces before her: young (young enough, the Duchess said in herself, to have been my daughter), yet far older than all these: older than light: older than the Gods. But sunset, too, has her climacteric, renewed at every down-going: flowering into unimagined fire-shadows, as of some conflagration of the under-skies where all dead splendours and lovelinesses past and gone are burnt up with their own inward fire, and the red smoke of it is thrown upward in rays among incandescent mists, and overhead heaven is mottled like a kingfisher's wings, turquoise and gold and greenish chrysolite more transparent than air; and the sea spreads to a vast duskiness of purple on which, as on the dear native bosom of their rest, all winds fall asleep.

Fiorinda looked suddenly in the Duchess's face, through the deepening dusk, with eyes that seemed washed to the very hue of that chrysolite of the sky. 'Words!' she said. 'Will your noble grace abdicate your sovereignty to words: tonight, of all nights? Have words so much power? In Memison? O open your eyes, and wake.'

For an instant the Duchess seemed to hold her breath. Then, with a high and noble look, 'Put away your displeasure,' she said, 'and pardon me. The mistress of a great house hath many melancholies, and so it fareth with me tonight: not for aught concerns you. I bit the hand was nearest.'

'Your grace has done me that honour to be open with me. I will be open too. I am not a commodity, not for any man.'

'No,' said the Duchess, searching Fiorinda's face. 'I think that is true.' She paused: then, 'What are you?' she said. The dusk seemed to deepen.

'That is a question your grace must ask yourself.'

'How? ask myself what am I myself? Or ask what you are?'

'Which you will. The answer fits.'

'Well,' said the Duchess: 'as for myself, I am a woman.'

'I have been told the same. And will that content you?'

'And with some beauty?'

'That is most certain.'

'Yet it answers me not.'

'No,' said Fiorinda. 'It is words.'

The Duchess said, 'I will search lower.'

'Do, as the lady said to her gallant. You shall find a thing worth the finding.'

'We are both, to say, in love.'

'O unhandsomest and most unrevealing word of all. And of me – to say, in love!'

'Shall I tell you, then,' said the Duchess, 'who it is you are taken in love with?'

'I dearly wish your grace will do so.'

'With your own self.'

Whether for the failing light that veiled their faces, or because the thought behind each withdrew as a bird behind leafage until the intermittent flutter only and the song remains, their faces were become harder to read now and the beauty of each less a thing of itself and more a thing of like substance with the beauty (so unagreeable and contrarious to itself) which it looked upon. Of all their unlikes, unlikest were the mouths of those ladies: Amalie's with clear clean Grecian lines which gave strength and a certain inner heat of pride and resolution to what had else been over-sweetness: but Fiorinda's settling itself, when at rest, to a quality more hard and kinless than is in stone, or in the grey dawn at sea in winter, or in the lip of a glacier seen at a great height against frozen airs under the moon. And yet, near the corner of each mouth, bringing a deep likeness to these unlikes, dwelt a some-what: a thing now still, now trailing a glitter of scales along the contours of lips that were its nesting-place and secret intricate playground of its choice. This thing, alert suddenly at the corner of the Duchess's mouth, beheld now as in a mirror, its second self in the curl of Fiorinda's lip, as, with a little luxurious silent laugh, she threw up her head, saying, 'And with whom else indeed should one be in love?'

'Why, with all else,' replied the Duchess, 'sooner than with that.'

Fiorinda drew nearer. 'Let me consider your grace, then, and try: suppose you skin-changed to the purpose: rid away the she in you: more bone in the cheekbones: harder about the forehead: this dryad cast of your eyebrows masculated to a faun: up-curled mustachios: more of the wolf about the mouth – no, truly, I think there is something in a woman's mouth is lost in a man's. Kiss me.'

The Duchess, freeing herself from that embrace, stood half dazed and trembling, as one who, caught up and set on some pinnacle without the limits of the world, has thence taken one eye-sweep, one inward catch of the breath, and a headlong stoop back again to the common voices of earth: the thrush's note and the wren's, the talking of running water beneath alder and sallow, faint tinkle of cow-bells from hill pastures about Memison.

There was a sound of footsteps: the guard's challenge: opening of the gate beyond the trees: a swinging of lights among the leaves. Six little boys came with torches and took their station in a half circle above the pool; so that those ladies stood in the torches' pulsing glow, but the shadows, rushing together on the confines of that warmth and brightness, made darkness where before had been but translucent ultramarines and purples of the chambered dusk. And now, down those steps from the arched shade of pine-tree and strawberry-tree, came the King. 'Leave us the lights, and begone,' he said. The boys set the torches on their stands and retired, the way they came. Fiorinda, with an obeisance, took her leave, departing up the steps in a mingled light of the torchlight which is never at rest and the silver-footed still radiance of the moon.

'Word is come,' said the King, as they turned from watching her: '"The foxen be at play."'

'That is the word you waited on?'

The King nodded, Ay.

'We have not even tonight, then?'

'The horses are saddled.'

'But will you not stay supper?'

He shook his head. 'Too much hangeth on it. The foil must be in their bosom when they thought it a yard off.'

'Well,' she said, and took hands with him; her grip less like a love-mate's than a fellow commander's: 'your right hand find out all that you have hated, my friend.'

The King sat down now on the deep-cushioned bench of onyx-stone, she standing beside him, her hand still in his, too close held to have escaped, even and it would. Presently she raised her eyes from their sidelong downward gazing and met the King's eyes, dark, looking up at her. 'How chance you go not?' she said.

'Because I stand upon a just order in all things.' With that, he drew her down to him on the bench, saying behind her ear, on a breath that came starry as the alighting of thistle-down, yet, as his hands possessed her, resistless as the rising tide of the sea: 'Amalie, I chose you and loved you in my happiest times.'

The Duchess spoke: 'This be farewell. I'll not bring you on your way. Better fall from this than, i' the manner of the world, walk down again. And tell me,' she said, after a pause, as they stood now, her cheek against his, for she was tall, and his head bent to hers as he held her yet in his arms: 'If we were Gods, able to make worlds as we chose, then fling 'em away like out-of-fashion garments, and renew them when we pleased: what world would we have, my friend?'

And the King answered her and said: 'This world, and none other: as a curst beast, brought by me to hand; with lovely Memison, for a jewel of mine about its neck; and you, my love, my dove, my beautiful, for its rose, there set in adamant.'

VI

CASTANETS BETWIXT THE WORLDS

LESSINGHAM sat iron-still. The music started once more: a bolero. Madame de Rosas, with bare arms braceletted with garnets above the elbow, bare-headed, and with one scarlet camellia in her hair, began upon an extremely slow, extremely smooth, swaying and rolling of the hips. Not to look at the sapphire, he looked at her: the red of her mouth, the whites of her black eyes. But immediately it was not she but the sapphire that, on the platform there, moved to these swaying rhythms; while the air of Mary's presence, fining gross flesh to the pure spirit of sense, raised it to some estate where flesh and spirit put on one another.

Slowly, and upon disparate faint clicks of wood with wood, scarce distinguishable even through the pale texture of the now muted strings, the castanets awoke again; then, softlier still, quickened their beat, and in a most tense graduality began to gather strength, as if horse-hooves should begin to draw nearer and nearer at a gallop from very far away. Here, no doubt, in this present drawing-room of Anmering Blunds, was the physical sound of them: the production, in natural air, of certain undulations which struck upon the tympanum of this ear or of that with varied effect, noted or ignored by this brain or that, winding strange horns, letting loose swift hunting-dogs, wild huntsmen, in as many shadowy fields as minds there were to take the infection of this old clicking music dear to the goat-footed wood-god. But the inward springs or being of that music took a further reach; even as the being of some deep-eddying river-spate shapes and steers (not is shaped or steered by) these motions of leaf, twig, drowned flower-petal, water-fly, bubble, streak of foam, purling ripple, uprooted floating water-weed, which, borne by on its surface, swirling to its swirl, do but dimly portend the nature of the power that bears them.

Northward twenty miles beyond Memison, in the low valleys of the Ruyar, King Mezentius rode with the Chancellor, knee to knee. Now they breathed their horses: now put them to a walking-pace, breasting the long upward training of meadowland north of Mavia: now quickened to a hand-gallop in the dewy pastures of Terainsht. Iron-still was the King's countenance under the moon, and with a look upon it as if he had some hammers working in his head. But his seat in saddle was free and jaunting, as if he and the great black horse he bestrode shared but one body between them. So rode the King and Beroald, without word spoken; and in the beat of their horsehooves, irking the soft summer night, was the beat of the castanets, dear to goat-footed Pan.

But in lovely Memison, where, seated with her women about her, the Duchess looked upon the revels held under the sky that night, this inside secret music touched the sense less unpeaceably, as it had been the purr of some great sleepy cat that rested as she rested.

And now that same peace, quiet as summer star-shine in a night without wind, settled too about Mary, whether through the music, or through the opening, like night-flowers when the sun is down, of the innermost heart and mind within her, or through some safety that came of Lessingham's nearness: of his coat-sleeve touching, light as a moth, her bare arm between shoulder and elbow.

'Go, my Violante,' said the Duchess: 'bid them lay a little table for his grace here beside me and bring a light collation, caviar, and then what you will, and framboises to finish with; and Rian wine. For that is royal wine, and best fits tonight: red wine of the Rian.'

Violante went, lightly in both hands gathering her gown, down the half-dozen steps which, wide, shallow, made of panteron stone and carpeted in the midst with a deep-piled carpet of a holly-leaf green, led from this gallery down to the level where the dancing was. The summer palace in Memison is in plan like the letter T, and all along the main limb of it (which faces south) and along the shorter limb (which faces west) this gallery runs, with doors giving upon it and great windows, and with columns of some smooth white stone with silvery sparkles in it: these, set at fifteen-foot intervals, carry the roof above, and the upper rooms of the palace. A grass-plat, a hundred paces or more in length by sixty broad, lies below the gallery, with a formal garden of clipped ancient yew to bound it on the southern side, and a tall thick hedge of the same dark growth upon the western; and on the grass, in the north-west corner of this quadrangle, was an oaken floor laid down on purpose that night to dance on, with hanging lamps and flamboys and swinging lanterns round about on every side of it to give light to the dancers. Fifty or sixty couples now footed the coranto, in such a shifting splendour of jewels and colour of tissue in doublet, kirtle, lady's gown, rich-wrought fan and ornament, as is seen in some cascade that comes down a wide wall of rock in steep woods facing the evening sun, and every several fringe of freshet as it falls becomes a fall of precious stones: amethyst, golden topaz, ruby, sapphire, emerald, changing and interchanging with every slightest shifting of the eye that looks on them.

But as when, with the altering of the light, some watered surface or some column of falling water among the rest suddenly throws back the radiance of the great sun itself, and these lesser jewels are dimmed, so was the coming of the Duke of Zayana among this company. He came without all ceremony, with great easy strides, so that Medor and Melates, who alone attended him, had some ado to keep up with him: without all ceremony, save that, at word gone before him, the music stopped and the dancers; and two trumpeters, standing forward from their place behind the Duchess's chair, sounded a fanfare.

Duke Barganax halted upon the steps and, with a sweep of his purple cloak, stood a moment to salute the guests; then upon one knee, kissed the Duchess's hand. She raised him and, for her turn, kissed him on the forehead.

'You are late,' said she, as, letting a boy take his cloak, the Duke seated himself beside her in a golden chair.

'I am sorry, my lady mother. The King, I am told, was here today?'

'Yes.'

'And gone again? Why was that?'

She shook her head.

'Thunder in the air?'

Amalie shrugged her shoulders gracefully. 'And why late?' she said. Like they seemed, she and he, one to the other, as the she-lion and her son.

'Only that I had set myself to finish a head I was painting of for a new piece I am upon, of a mural painting of Hippokleides' betrothal feast. And so, third hour past noon ere I took saddle.'

'"Hippokleides, you have danced away . . . your marriage." A subject needing some delicacy of treatment! And whose head that you painted?'

'Why, a late lady of your own: Bellafront's.'

'Bellafront? She is red: Titian: of our colour. Could you not have left it till another day, this painting?'

'She might have been dead when I came home again.'

'Dead? Is she sick then?'

'No!' said the Duke, laughing. ''Tis no more but follow my father's good maxim; when I was little, and the best strawberry saved up at the side of my plate to eat it last: told me, eat it now, since I might not live to eat it later.'

'You are absurd,' said Amalie: 'you and your teacher both. Is it true, Count Medor?'

'I were a bad servant, to call my master absurd,' replied Medor; 'and a worse courtier, to contradict your beauteous excellency in your own house. Well, it is true. He is absurd. But always by choice, never upon compulsion.'

'O perfect courtier! But, truly, men are absurd by nature; and were you, my noble son, less than absurd, then were you less than man. And that – faugh! It was naught of mine: whether to have bred it, or to truckle withal.'

Supper being done, they sat on now (Barganax, with those Lords Melates and Medor, the Duchess, with her Myrrha, Violante and others), looking on the scene, in a contented silence which awoke ever and again into some lazy bandying of contented humorous talk. Lamps above and about them shed a slumbrously inconstant light. From great stone jars, ranged along the terrace edge, orchids laid out their strange and luxurious shapes, dusky-petalled, streaked or spotted, haired, smooth-lipped, velvet-skinned, exhaling upon the warm air their heady heavy sweetness.

'Will not your grace dance tonight?' Medor said at length to the Duke.

Barganax shook his head.

'Why not?' said the Duchess. 'But no: it were unkind to ask you. You are in love.'

'I was never in love yet,' said Barganax.

'Then all these tales are but false?'

'The Duke,' said Medor, 'has never been out of love: to my certain knowledge, these seven years.'

'What will you say to that?' said the Duchess. 'As captain of your bodyguard, he should know.'

'It is a prime error in these matters,' said Barganax, 'to fall in love. Women are like habits: if good, they stick fast, and that becomes tedious: if bad, and you love 'em, the love will stick like a leech though the woman go. No, I have taken a leaf out of their book: treat 'em as they treat fashions: enjoy for a season, then next season cast about for a new one.'

Amalie fanned herself. 'This is terrible good doctrine. To hear you, one might imagine some old practitioner, bald before his time with o'er-acting of the game, spoke with your lips. If you be not secretly already in love, take care; for I think you are in a dangerous aptness to be so.'

The Duke laughed. 'I was never sadly in love but with you, my lady mother': he took her hand in his and kissed it. 'Nor need you to blame me, neither. Surely 'tis the part of a good son to look to's parents for example? and here's example of the highest in the land for me to point to, when I will not overmuch fret myself for aught that's second best.' He was leaned back in his chair, legs crossed at full stretch before him, silent now for a minute. His fingers, of the one hand, played absently with the Duchess's, while through half-closed lips his eyes rested on the bright maze of the dance and night's blue curtain beyond. 'And, for your old masters of the game, madam: no. I am too hard to please. I am a painter. But pity of it is, nothing lasts. All passes away, or changes.'

'Your grace,' said Medor, 'is a painter. Well, a picture painted will not change.'

'Give it time, dear Medor, it will rot. And long ere that, you shall find the painter has changed. That, I suppose, is why pictures are so good, soon as painted.'

'And no good, certainly, before they are painted,' said the Duchess. 'For is it not but in the painting that a picture takes being?'

'That is certain.'

Medor said, 'I have long begun to think, my lord Duke, that you are an atheist.'

'By no means.'

'You blaspheme, at least,' said Amalie, 'violet-crowned Kythereia, the blessed Goddess and Queen of All.'

'God forbid! Only I will not flatter Her, mistake Her drifts. She changes, like the sea. She is not to be caught. We needs must believe Her fixed and eternal, for how should perfection suffer change? Yet, to mock us, She ever changes. All men in love, She mocks; and were I in love (which thanks to Her, I am not, nor will not be), I know it in my bones, She should mock me past bearing. Why, the very frame and condition of our loving, here upon earth, what is it but an instrument of Hers to mock us?'

'Is this the profundities your learned tutor taught you, the old grey-beard doctor?'

'No, madam. In this, myself taught myself.'

Medor smiled:

> 'Tho' wisdom oft hath sought me,
> I scorn'd the lore she brought me,
>   My only books
>   Were women's looks,
> And folly's all they taught me.'

'Well, Medor? And what of your young lady of the north, Prince Ercles' daughter, you told me of? What has she taught you?'

Medor answered soberly: 'To keep her out of such discussions.'

'Forgive me,' said the Duke. 'I know not what pert and pricking spirit leadeth me by the sleeve tonight.' He leaned forward to pluck a pallid bloom of the orchid. 'Flowers,' he said, slowly examining the elegant wings and falls, domed and spreading sleeknesses: raising it to his nostrils to take the perfume. 'As if it had lips,' he said, considering it again. He dropped it: stood up now, leaning lightly against one of those silvery-sparkled pillars, the easier to overlook the company.

'You have out-Memisoned Memison tonight, madam,' he said presently. 'And the half of them I ne'er saw till now. Tell me, who is she in the black gown, sequins of silver, dancing with that fox Zapheles?'

The Duchess answered, 'That is Ninetta, Ibian's younger daughter, newly come to court. I had thought you had known her.'

'Not I,' said the Duke. 'Look, Melates: for dancing: as if all from the hips downward she had never a joint, but all supple and sinuous as a mermaid. I said I will not dance tonight; but, by heavens,' he said, 'I am in two minds, whether not to try, in this next dance following, which will she the rather, me or Zapheles. But that were 'gainst present policy. I am taming that dog-fox now by kindness: to do him that annoyance now were the next way to spoil all.'

'Well, there is Pantasilea,' said the Duchess, as there now passed by in the dance a languorous sleepy beauty, heavy eyelids and mouth like a heavy crimson rose: 'a friend of yours.'

But the Duke's gaze (which, never so idle-seeming, not the littlest thing escaped) noted how, upon that word, Melates reddened and bit his lip.

'I retired long since,' said the Duke, 'in favour of a friend. Now there,' he said, after a little, 'is a lady, I should guess, madam, of your own choosing. There: with hair coloured like pale moonshine, done in plaits crown-wise round her head: one that I could paint in a green dress for Queen of Elfland. Is she maid or wife?'

'She is indeed of my choosing: Lydia, wife to a chamberlain of mine.'

'Does he use her well?'

'It is to be hoped so. I think he loves her.'

The Duke sat down again. 'Enough. Go, Melates. I shall not dance: I am looker-on tonight. No, in sober sadness, I mean it. But I would have you dance. Medor too.'

'I had liever keep your grace company,' said Medor. Melates with a low leg departed.

'There is no hope for Medor,' said the Duke. 'As good as wedded already.'

Amalia smiled at the Count over her peacock fan. 'And looks,' she said, 'as who should say, "God send it were so."'

Their talk drifted idly on.

Below, in a pause between the dances, Mistress Pantasilea waited, on Melates's arm, for the music to begin again. 'You came this evening with the Duke?'

'Yes.'

'He and his father: very unlike.'

Melates raised his eyebrows. 'Very like, I think.'

'One red: t'other black.'

'Well?'

'One all for love: t'other all for doing.'

'I have two spears,' said Melates: 'each of gold and iron: the one with main show of iron, t'other of gold. Yet are both fair to look on, and each fit for the business at need.'

'This one hath a more speeding trick, I would warrant, to lay down ladies than to govern a kingdom.'

'You do belie him,' said Melates. 'Say rather, he grounds himself thus early in a wide apprenticeship to both these noble arts.'

'Come,' said she: 'while you defend and I accuse, mischief is we both needs must love him.'

Now began, stately and slow, a pavane. Barganax, on his feet again, still idly watching, bent over now and then to his mother's ear or to Medor's or to one of her girls', to ask or answer somewhat or let fall some jest. But now, at a sudden, upon one such motion, he stopped short, hand flat-palmed against the pillar, bending forwards a little, following very intently with his eye one couple amongst the dancers. The Duchess spoke. He made no reply. She looked round: saw that he had not heard: saw the fashion of his gaze, tense, like a bowstring at stretch: saw the direction of it: followed it. For well two minutes, very discreetly not to be observed, she watched him, and (hidden behind her eyes that watched), with a smile of the mind.

'Do you remember,' Mary said, 'that dance at the Spanish Embassy?'

'Do I remember!' said Lessingham, while, under his gaze, the quiver of velvet darkness within the sapphire deepened to the shadow or rumour of some profounder and living presence: as of all eyes and lips that have been man's since the world began: blinding themselves there, swept down there, drowned there to a kiss.

'It was curious,' Mary said, very low: 'our first meeting: not to have known.'

The Duke spoke, suddenly down into Medor's ear, that was nearest: 'What is she?'

Medor looked where the Duke gave him the direction. Something blenched in his eye. 'I cannot tell. Till now, I have never seen her.'

'Find out, and tell me,' said the Duke, head erect, feeding his eyes. Under the upward curl of his mustachios the lamplight rested upon the Olympian curve of lips which, unlike other men's, the hotlier blown upon in the fires of luxury the finer ever and more delicate became their contours, and the subtler and the more adamantine their masterful lines of strength and self-domain. 'Go,' he said. 'I would be informed of name and quality of everyone here tonight: 'tis as well, that the Duchess be not put upon by outsiders and so forth. Get me particulars.'

The Duchess Amalie, in the mean time, very slowly and equably fanning herself, abode (in all beseeming) utterly remote and unaware.

It was after midnight now, and between the last dances. The Duchess and her ladies were, the most of them, now retired, and most of the guests departed. The full moon, riding in her meridian but low down in Capricorn, flooded the out-terraces westwards above the moat with a still radiance of silver. The Duke with slow, measured paces came and went with Melates the length of the terrace to and fro, two hundred paces, may be, to every turn. Eastward, the lights about the summer palace glimmered beyond the yew-trees: there was no music: no sound, save the crunch of the gravel as they walked, little night-sounds in the leaves, and, from below beyond the moat, a loud singing of nightingales. The path was white under the moon: the shaven grass of the borders on either hand wet with dew: the clumps of giant pink asphodel that, at spaces of ten feet or so, rearing their lovely spikes taller than a tall man, lined the length of that terrace on either hand, were blanched too to an indeterminate immateriality of whiteness.

And now as they walked, they became ware of two other persons come upon the terrace at the further end: a man and a woman, she on his arm, moving now slowly towards them. Midway, they met and passed. That lady's smile, as she acknowledged Barganax's lifted bonnet, came like the flashing, in a vista parted between blood-red lilies, of the deadly whiteness of some uncharted sea-strait.

'Do you know that lady?' said the Duke as they walked on.

Melates answered, 'I know her. But name her I cannot.'

'I can tell you who she is,' said the Duke. 'She is young sister to my lord High Chancellor.'

'Why, then, I know where 'twas I saw her. He has kept her exceeding close: never till now at court, I think: certainly I ne'er saw nor heard of her at your presences, my lord Duke, in Zayana.'

'Myself,' said the Duke, 'I ne'er saw her till tonight I saw her dance the pavane, with this man that is, I am told, her new husband.'

'Your grace will remember, there was a notorious murder. True, it was never brought home where it belonged.'

The Duke was silent for a minute. Then, 'Your great men, Melates, have commodity for bringing to pass suchlike a needful thing, when need is, without all undecent show or scandal.'

'There was show enough here,' said Melates: 'six hired cutters to make sure of him in broad daylight, in Krestenaya marketplace. And yet none durst name my lord Chancellor in it, nor her, save in a whisper and curtains drawn: and then, as your grace knows, there were pretty tales told.'

'I've heard 'em.'

'And yet,' said Melates, 'for less matter, himself hath ere this headed or hanged, in this time, scores of common men.'

'The way of the world,' Barganax said. 'And some will say, best way too: better a hundred such should die, than one great man's hand to be hampered.'

'But, too cruelly practised,' said Melates, 'may breed such discontent as should pluck us down, as history hath ere now remembered.'

'There was never yet great men plucked down by the common riff-raff,' said the Duke, 'but they had first of their own selves begun to fall from their greatness. Never in this world, Melates: nor yet in any world. For that is a condition of all possible worlds.'

'Your grace speaks wisely. Did your secretary (and late your tutor) learn you this? Doctor Vandermast?'

'I have learned much from the learned doctor: as this, for

example – whenever you seem to speak wisdom, never to tell who taught you. Observing which, I shall doubtless in time have got a white beard and reputation of a great wise man. Unless indeed, which is likelier, cold steel—' the Duke waited as they met and passed, now the second time, that lady on her husband's arm: the green glint of her eyes in the moonlight, looking steadily before her: the glint of the moon on her teeth as she spoke some answering word to her lord: the carriage which, lily in crystal, became itself the more for the gown that veiled it, less like to natural woman's walk than to the swaying on languid stem of some undreamed-of flower, beside those curled and sweet-smelling darknesses those orchids upon the inner terrace should seem work-a-day hedgerow weeds. 'Or unless the bite of a she-puss,' said the Duke, when they were out of hearing, 'should first be cause of my death.'

They walked on, silent, till they came to the south end of the terrace. Here, in the shadow of a holm-oak, the Duke stood a minute, watching the moon through the leaves. 'The King my father it was,' he said, watching the moon, 'that would needs have this woman in Memison. The Duchess would not have her at first.'

Melates held his peace.

'He likes it that beautiful woman should be here,' said the Duke. 'I grant, he has an eye for them. Well,' he said, looking round at Melates: 'is it not fit that he should? Answer me. It is not for me to talk always and you stand mum.'

'It is not for me, my lord Duke, to judge of these high matters.'

'So? I think there is some devil of folly in you I must exorcize. Out with it: will you say the Duchess my mother were wiser make 'em all pack, show them the door?'

'I beseech your grace: this is not my business.'

'By God,' said the Duke, 'I can smell your thought, Melates; and hath the stink of a common horse-boy's. I say to you, her grace, my lady mother, is a queen rose; a goddess among them. By heavens, it were give small regard to her own quality or to the King's highness' discerning judgement, were she with timorous jealous misdoubts to let overcloud the sweet weather we have here. This that I tell you is truth. Will you believe it? Study your answer: for, by God, if you will not, you are friend of mine no more.'

But Melates, as who would please one that is out of his princely wits, answered and said, 'Your grace hath most unjustly mistook me. I believe, and did ever believe it. How else?'

They turned to walk north again between the dewy grasses and the uncertain whispering darknesses. Before them as they walked, their cast shadows flitted, hard-edged and black against the moon-flooded pallour of the path.

'Were you ever in love, Melates?'

'I have tried to follow the fashions your grace sets us.'

'Fashions in love?'

'I know not.'

'Fashions to keep out of it.'

Slower and slower they walked, step with step. And now, forty or fifty paces ahead, they saw those others coming towards them: saw him suddenly break from his lady, run to the parapet on the left above the moat, clap hand upon the balustrade and make as if to vault over. Then back to her, and so again arm in arm.

Encountering now once more in mid-terrace, both parties, as upon a mutual impulse, stopped. Some puckish spirit danced in Barganax's eye. 'I am glad, sir,' he said, 'that you thought better of it: resolved after all not to drown yourself.'

The lady abode silent: motionless too, save that, upon some slow, exquisite, half amused, half in derision, little condescensions of her head, she seemed to note the words: as if here were some strayed divinity, elegantly indifferent, noting these things from above. The fingers of her hand, in the crook of her lord's arm, lay out silver-white under their shimmer of jewels: a sensitive, beautiful hand, able (by the look of it) as an artist's, with sure and erudite touch, to set deep notes a-throb, attemper them, weave them to unimagined harmonies. So she stood, leaning sideways on that man, quiet and still in the unclouded serenity of the moon: virginal-sweet to look on as a wood-lily; yet with a secret air as if, like Melusine in the old story, she could at seasons be snake from the waist down.

The man smiled, meeting the Duke's bantering gaze. 'If you did but know, my lord Duke,' he said, 'what I was in truth a-thinking on in that moment!'

And Barganax was ware suddenly of that lady's eyes resting on himself, in a weighing look, completely serene, completely impenetrable. Deeper than blood or the raging sense, it seemed to touch his face: first his cheek below the cheekbone; then from head to foot the touch of that look seemed to go over him, till at last it mounted again to his face and so to his eye, and came to rest there with the same sphinxian unalterableness of green fires that slept.

'Curious our first meeting: and not to have known.' Very low Mary had said it at first; and now, this second time, so low, so withinward, that the words, like a kestrel's nestlings that flutter at the nest, unready yet to trust themselves to wings and the untried air, rested unuttered within the closure of her lips. But, 'Yes,' it was said now, as if by some deeper abiding self that had lain asleep till now within her: 'I knew. I singled you out then, my friend, as I now remember, though at the time it was almost unconsciously: yes, completely unconsciously. I knew, my friend. And knew, too, that you did not yet know.' And about the words was a shimmer like the shimmer of the sun upon the tide off Paphos, the unnumbered laughter of ocean waves.

They were departed, two and two again, on their several ways. When at last the Duke spoke, it was as a man who would obliterate and put out of memory the flaming semblant, and grapple himself safe to common waking fact. 'Shall I tell you, Melates, what was in truth in the man's mind, then when like a jackanapes he ran and skipped upon the parapet? It was the thought that this instant night, within this half hour maybe, he should have that woman where he wished.'

They walked on in silence. At length, 'What will you call her?' said the Duke.

'Call whom?'

'Whom else do we talk on? That woman.'

Melates said uncourteously, 'I should call her a dog-fly.'

'A dog-fly!' With the moon behind them, the Duke's face was unreadable. 'Well, Goddess hath borne that word from Goddess ere this.' And he began to laugh, as it were privately to himself.

They looked round and saw that the terrace was empty now, save for themselves only. 'Leave me,' said Barganax. 'I have a business to consider with myself. I will study it here awhile alone.'

But that Lady Fiorinda, walking now in an obscurity of yew-trees, with that unconsidered arm to lean upon, turned Her mind to other thoughts. At Morville's third or fourth asking, What was she meditating upon so quiet? she answered at last, 'Upon certain dresses of mine.'

'Dresses. Of what material? Of what colour?'

'O, of the most delicatest finest material.' The man saw snicker in her mouth's corner that little thing that neither now nor ever would heed nor look at him, but seemed always as if playing devilishly apart with some secret, boding no good. 'And for colour,' said she (noting, from above that mantelpiece perhaps, through Anne Horton's side-bended eyes, these lovers): 'of a red-gold fire-colour, as the extreme outermost tongue-tip of a flame.'

'It is a colour should most excellent well become you.'

'Better than this black, you think?' And that little thing, in a pretty irony not for his sharing, twinkled its eye (comparing, perhaps, two dresses of that fire-colour, so much alike: one, near of her own age, there beside Lessingham: the other here, in Memison, older by twenty years: dresses wherein She walked as it were asleep, humble, innocent, forgetful of Her Olympian home).

'Black?' said he, laughing. 'You are dreaming! You are in yellow and cloth of gold tonight.'

'O most just and discerning eye! How all-knowing an estate is matrimony!' And this time, the upward curl of the corner of her lip was as a twisting of tiny scaly limbs (as the thing said perhaps, in her secret ear, that a deadly sorrow it was if such a dull owl must much longer go uncuckolded).

But presently when, with those lips which hold the world's
desire, She began to speak again, it was Her own poetess's words,
and in the sweet Aeolian tongue: the ageless, fadeless, lilied numbers
rising again in their undead youth: not as sound, not as movement
or succession: rather as some subtlety of the air, some silvered
showering of darkness: that shudder of the sense which, like
meteors, runs near to heaven:

'φαίνεταί μοι κῆνος ἴσος Θέοισιν
ἔμμεν ὤνηρ ὄστις ἐναντίος τοι
ἰζάνει, καί πλασίον ἄδυ φωνεύ-
σας ὑπακούει

καί γελαίσας ἱμερόεν, . . .

Like is he, I think, to a God immortal,
That man, whosoever he be, that near you
Sits and thus to you and to your sweet talking
Privately listens,

And lilt of your dear laughter: a thing to send the
Heart within my bosom a-leap; for barely
So can I this brief little while behold you,
—Speech quite forsakes me.

Ah, my tongue is broken: a sudden subtle
Fire beneath my skin in an instant courses;
Eyesight none remains to mine eyes: mine ears roar,
Drown'd under thunder.

And the sweat breaks forth, and a trembling seizes
All my body: paler than grass in summer
I: in all else, scarce to be told, I think, from
One that lay lifeless.

Yet, to dare all—'

All the leaves in that Memison garden trembled. Lessingham, too, trembled, leaning towards his dear. And Mary, lost and trembling, felt her inmost being dissolve and fail within her, under his eyes and under those self-seeing immortal eyes of Hers that, for the instant, borrowed his.

Midnight sounded, grave, deep-tongued, from Anmering church tower. Mary, on Lessingham's arm, stood quite still, here at the far seaward end of the garden terrace, listening: listening now to Lessingham's whispered 'Time to go.'

'Don't go. Not yet,' she said.

'I don't mean to: not without you.'

'O don't let's – all over again. I've told you, and told you: I can't.'

'You said you would.'

'I know, but I oughtn't to have said it. I can't. I can't.'

'You can. I'll look after "can", my darling: that's my job.'

Mary shook her head. They turned and began to walk, very slowly.

'You know my trouble,' said Lessingham, after a silence. 'I can't do without you. Can't live, without you. You know that.'

She shook her head again, saying, almost inaudibly, 'No. I don't.'

'I don't mean shoot myself, or any tom-foolery like that. Simply, shan't live: my dead body walking about, if I haven't you.'

Her face remained unreadable.

'The devilish thing about you,' he said, 'is that, before, I used to think of all sorts of things I might do, and do damned well. I knew it. But since you – all that's changed. There isn't a hard thing in the world I could not do, standing on my head, with you caring about it; but without you, not a thing of them worth the doing. You don't understand,' he said. 'How could you understand? But will you believe it?'

She said, like the sound of a moth's fluttered wing, 'Yes.'

'O my beloved,' he caught the hand on his arm and kissed it: a cold little hand for a June night. 'Then come. Everything ready: change of shoes if it's wet crossing the paddock: a new fur coat (we can give it away tomorrow if you don't like it)—'

Mary stopped: took away her arm: stood looking down, face averted, her breath coming and going, her hands tight shut. 'How dare you do these things?' she said, in a kind of whisper. 'How dare you tell me about them? Why did you come? Why? I told you not to. How dare you?'

Lessingham watched her. 'It's been pretty difficult,' he said after a while, without moving: 'waiting: all this patience and obedience.' For a minute they stood so; then she took his arm, and once more they began slowly walking. 'We should never forgive ourselves,' he said presently: 'you and I, to turn back.'

'Don't ask me this, my friend. For I mustn't.'

'You're mine,' he said, his lips touching her hair above the ear: then very softly, 'you must.'

'Yes: I am yours. But I mustn't.'

'You must. Why not?'

'I'm someone else's too,' she said, looking towards the house and its dark upper windows.

They walked on. The silence became frightening: the stiffening of Lessingham's arm under her hand: and now, when she looked up, his face, staring down at his own feet as they moved step by step.

'Be kind?'

'You're not being very kind to me,' he said. 'I'm not sure I've not been a fool: not been too patient and obedient:' Mary made a little sound of incredulous dissent: 'not sure,' he said, 'that I'm not too late.'

'What on earth do you mean?'

'Don't let's be absurd.'

'You mean, when I said "somebody else's"—'

The whole night seemed to turn suddenly sultry and sullen and unfriendly.

'Can't you give me too,' Mary said, 'a little credit, for being patient? Being obedient?'

'Obedient! A dangerous virtue.'

Again she stopped, and they stood off from one another.

'Don't let us play hide-and-seek. I'm frightened when you think I would— You thought—?' Lessingham gave no sign.

'O, good heavens!' She held out both hands to him, laughing as if he and she should enjoy a private joke together. 'Shall I tell you then? I refused – why, nearly two hours ago I should think. But why should you need telling?' she said.

He took the hands in his: lifted them up and up, to bring her nearer: a tremulous and starry propinquity, in which spirit to spirit drew so close that the bodied senses of sight, touch, smell, seemed (as dragon-flies newly uncased from their prisons of the pupa) to hang faint and lost in the mid condition between two modes of being. Only that little thing, to all modes acclimatized and self-conditioned, and now very impertinently awake and active, regarded him from near her lip's corners. Answering which, something laughed in Lessingham's eyes. 'So that's what made him look like— By heavens, I'd like to—'

'What?'

'Break the fellow's neck,' he said tartly, 'for daring— But it shows: there's pressure. And you're alone.'

'If people should say: if he should think: O of course, that girl: we didn't hit it off, and now, you see, on the rebound—'

'Tsh! *They say, Quhat say they? They haif said. Let thame say.*' But the moon, shining down in her classic serenity on Mary's white evening dress and on those upper windows of Anmering Blunds, seemed to discover in these thumping words a sudden and most disconcerting insufficiency: at least as applied to Mary, and by him.

He let go her hands and stood, not irresolute but as if withdrawn for the moment into some inside privateness of deliberation: a silence that began to gather danger, as if one should listen for the muffled sound of bulls horning and wrestling behind closed doors. Then Mary watched the unconscious pose of him settle to lines such as, bound to an earthly permanency of bronze or marble, are sometimes seen in a masterwork of Donatello. He looked up. 'May I pick one?' They were standing near the stone pillar of a pergola grown over with Gloire de Dijon roses. Mary nodded, yes. 'May I give it to you?' She took it, very gentle and quiet. 'Let's walk along a little,' he said. 'Let me think.

'Well,' he said, at last: 'what's to be done?'

There was no answer, unless in the presence of her hand on his arm.

'Will you marry me?'

'I've promised to.'

'How can you? What if they won't let you?'

'Give me two months: perhaps three.'

'O these months. What then?'

'I'll have got things right by then. And if not—'

'If not?'

'If not – well: I've promised.'

'You promised to come away with me tonight,' he said.

He was suddenly kneeled down, his arms about her knees, his cheek pressed against her side. Presently he felt how her hand, very gently, began to stroke, the wrong way, the short cropped hair at the back of his neck: heard her voice, very gentle and trembling: 'Dear. We mustn't go tonight. I didn't realize: it's too big, this of ours: it is All. How can we say, "Let the rest go: take this"? The rest? it's part of this. That would mean spoil this for its own sake. It would be hateful. We can't do that. Shouldn't deserve each other if we could.' It was as if those moon-trod spaces of lawn and cricket field were tuned to a music bearing as under-song some life to which this is but exordial. He heard her say, 'Nothing can take it from us: not if we died, I think.'

'We shall die someday. What then?'

'I don't know,' Mary said. 'Perhaps this is only the shadow of it.'

'I don't believe it. This is all.' His clasp tightened: his eyes now, not his cheek, buried themselves against her side.

Suddenly Mary, so standing, very still, began to say rather breathlessly, rather brokenly: 'You could, you could make me go tonight. But you won't. It would spoil everything. It would hurt me. I'd always thought you were too fond of me to do that:

thought you would never want to hurt me: you, of all people.'
Through the hammerings of his own veins he felt the trembling
of her and the failing, like the yielded body of a bird in his encir-
cling arms: felt the touch of her hand again, on his neck: heard
her voice, nearer, lower: "But I'm not going to turn back. I don't
doubt you, my friend. Here I am. Your very own Mary.' The
summer night seemed, upon that silence, to be suddenly frozen.
'All of me. Do what you like with me.'

But Lessingham, in this new worst wrestling behind those doors,
held fast: remained as if himself, too, were frozen: then did but
this: still on his knees, catch her two hands and kiss them: kiss
the Gloire de Dijon, still held in one of them: then, rising to his
feet, take her in his arms. 'Good night, my dear, my love, my
beautiful. Too good and perfect for me, but my own. You make
me ashamed. Kiss me goodnight: I'm going.'

And, for last goodnight, Mary, mistress of the situation, touching
with the tip of her nose the most sensitive part of his ear, whispered
in it: 'Didn't I say: An omen, if you were wise? Michaelmas
– Vintage.'

VII

SEVEN AGAINST THE KING

KING Mezentius and my lord Chancellor Beroald, having refreshed them with a few hours' sleep at Rumala, rode down from the Curtain into Rubalnardale: taking thus the easternmost, the directest, and the roughest-wayed and so most unfrequented pass over the mountains out of South Meszria northwards to the marches of the Zenner. They rode armed at all points, but cloaked and hooded. They were alone, even as alone they had set forth the evening before from Memison. A little beside Ilkis they began to bear away more northerly, leaving the beaten way and giving a wide berth to Kutarmish town; meaning to strike the river ten miles or more upstream and come over it by an unfrequented ford, and thence up by forest ways to the neighbourhood of Gilgash and the place intended. The sun had topped the far snow ridges of the range of Ramosh Arkab, and flooded all the vale of the Zenner with its fresh and unclouded glory of summer morning. They came on without haste now, and with time in hand.

'Beroald,' said the King, reining in his horse at the top of a slope where the moorish champaign began to fall away northwards before them in fold upon fold of heather and silver birch down to the green flats, purpled with distance, of water-meadow and woodland and winding river, 'I have changed my mind concerning this undertaking.'

The Chancellor, with his most saturnine smile, said, 'I am glad to hear it.'

'Glad? Why you know not yet what it is.' The King threw back the hood of his cloak: put off his helm: suffered for a minute the wild delicate morning breeze to play about his forehead and ruffle the ambrosial curls above his brow. Clear and smooth his brow was as the polished ivory; but the rest of his countenance, down to the beginning of the great black beard and mustachios, was weather-bitten and passion-worn with the tracings of iron resolution and of a highness of heart beyond the nature of man, and of humour and a most eagly suddenness of thought and act. And now, as he laughed, it was as if the infection of some unsmotherable superfluity within that King, ever rash, ever headlong, like lightning, or like the rut and furious rage of love, fed the cold light's flame in the watching eyes of the Chancellor that watched him. 'For the life of me,' he said, 'I cannot bring myself to permit even you, Beroald, now that I come to the pinch, to have share with me in the grand main act.'

The Chancellor shook his head. 'I have long given over seeking to compass your serene highness or learn your drifts. You will go alone, then?'

'Alone.'

Beroald was silent.

'Come,' said the King, putting on his helm and drawing the hood over it once more: 'you are a politician, and yet see not reason in that?'

'I see unreason in going at all. If I had your authority, I would be so bold to unvicar him, and be done. But that case I argue no longer. Your serenity over-ruled me there.'

'Remember,' said the King, 'I go tonight to reclaim an outrageous unstaid hawk. If I go accompanied, he may think he has high cause to fear lest this wild worm of ambition wavering in his head shall be uncased and laid open to the view of the world. That may alarm him to some unadvised violence: fall upon us then and there, and so spill all. For if he do so, then one of two things, and both evil: the worse, me and you to be slain, fighting alone against too much odds; or else (the lesser evil) slay him – as I had resolved not to do, but to reduce him.'

He paused. The Chancellor but tightened his lips, thinking it folly, no doubt, to spurn against the hard wall. 'You shall therefore,' said the King, 'await me in a place I will show you, under a wood's side, a little this side of Gilgash. If I be come not again before midnight, then must you doubt not but that the worst is befallen, and so, haste haste post haste, back to Sestola, and do thus and thus,' (instructing him at large in the whole manage of affairs).

Mean time, forty miles or more north-away, in the hold of Laimak, that grey eyrie by strength insuperable upon its little hill, which had been to the Parrys since generations both refuge from the storm and seat key and sustainment of that power whereby, through long vicissitudes and whether by open means or dissembled, they swayed the middle kingdom and fattened on the land of Rerek, the Lord Horius Parry, upon this sweet morning of the twenty-fifth of June, stood a minute at his window of his private chamber: gazed south. There was a tranquillity in his gaze: a tranquillity on his unfurrowed brow. Close-sprouting as a pile of velvet, the cropped hair ran up and back over the round head of him to the large bull neck: red hair, stiff like hog's bristles, growing far down the chine. His beard, clipped short too, came to a blunt point on the chin. His light hazel-hued eyes were small, set near, like a bear's: the sharpness of their glance as the flashing of diamonds. There was about his nostrils a mobility, an expansion, a bestial eagerness, so that, to look at him, one had sworn he lashed a tail. And yet, over all, that tranquillity, as of a mind at peace with its own self: all the great frame of him reposeful as a falcon hooded, or as quiet waters above some under-suck of the sea. Broad and heavy he was of body, may be nearly fifty years of age, yet knit to that hardness that comes of the soldier's life and the hunting-field, turning to brawn all over-grossness which might else proceed from overmuch pleasuring of table or bed. He scarce reached the middle stature; and yet, for some native majesty of glance and bearing, seemed a man that could be tall without walking on tip-toe.

'For's health, a were best be gone,' he said without looking round. 'Have you summoned me out that squadron of horse?'

Gabriel Flores answered him, seated at the broad oak table among papers and ink and seats: 'Below the main gate, half-hour from now, your highness. As for him, a will hear no reason.'

'Here's a villain that would face me down. Is he mad?'

'Like enough.'

'Bring him in.'

'If your highness pleased, I could send two lads to souse him in the moat. That might learn him.'

'Bring him in, you sucking-pig.'

Gabriel went and returned. 'The Lord Sorms,' he said loudly, falling behind to let him precede. But the room was empty. Sorms, much too aback, turned in anger upon Gabriel.

'You must have patience, my lord. His highness will certain be here anon.'

'You villain, I am tired out with patience. Where is the money I gave you?'

'Your lordship hath had money's worth, and three times told, in my wise advice.'

'What? That I must spend yet a week waiting on my right in Laimak? Arquez hath done me wrong. 'Tis now six months since, with leave under seal vicarial and in your hand delivered to me, I have by suit of the King's peace and in all due forms took course to right me. But in vain. There's some works strings against me. I am not grounded in lands, and the faculty is very bare. At great charges I came south. I sent three days since to the Vicar for audience, but he would not be spoken with. I spoke with Rossillion: yesterday again with you: one might as well try to collect milk from a he-goat with a sieve. I sent after to the Vicar but he could not attend it for hunting. Or I will have it this morning, or I will hunt with him, by God's leave.'

He strode up and down the room. Gabriel at the table fiddled about his papers: presently looked up. 'I will yet, saving your worship, say a word of wisdom to you. 'Tis clean out of the ordinary, unbidden guests in Laimak. The Vicar's highness hath matter enough in hand without you and your private differences. He is wrath already with these importunings. Were I in your lordship's shoes, out of Laimak I would go while commodity yet is for departing. Till the fury of his highness settle, come not before him.'

'I'll have my right,' said Lord Sorms. 'If not, I am resolved to hold you all such play as you shall be weary of. And you, master secretary, I do begin to discern for as honest a man as any is in the cards if the kings were out. You and your lord too.' His jaw fell as, turning to a sound behind him, he faced the Parry in person, come secretly in at a little hidden door.

'Well, my Lord Sorms,' said he, with much sweetness of words and amiable countenance, 'I have read your lordship's depositions. And well have I in mind the painfulness it must have been to you, abiding here so long, desirous to know whether your matter be in any wise compounded, or like to be shortly compounded, or no.'

'I thank your excellency. These concerns, be they but a trifle unto you, are to me a thing of good moment and importance. The pleadings, six months now, lie before your court signorial in Leveringay. Your secretary here, since April, hath notice of appeal unto your excellency's person as Vicar General in Rerek of the King. Nought moves. And now, marvelling not a little of the very frosty coldness and slack remissness shown me, I cannot but, joining words and deeds together, thereby see that all is but finesse. I cannot but think there be practices which—'.

'Ay, practices,' said the Vicar gently, gently drawing near to Sorms: Gabriel's ferret eye watched his master's. 'And herein is lapped up a very great secret, which 'tis but fair, perhaps, I should now make plain unto your lordship, why I have had small leisure for your domestical concerns. Well, thus it standeth: I, of my envious covetous and vengeable disposition, do now enterprise shortly no less than to usurp and seize, wrongfully and against all right, the whole sovereign power of the King in Rerek. Which to keep safe in your mouth, take this:' and, leaping like unkennelled Cerberus, stabbed him in with a dagger from his belt, first by the ear, next in the ribs, last down by the collar-bone.

Gabriel, that was small and little of stature, leaned back against the table, watching this business; his teeth, jagged and uneven, showed yellowish betwixt dark beard and mustachios.

'I'll teach these little lords,' said the Vicar, throwing the bloodied dagger on the floor. 'Come muling to me with their ails and plainings,' he said, his breath coming and going with the exertion: 'and me so grieved with so great causes. Come hither, my mopsy.' Gabriel came: his face grey, his eyes wide with apprehension. The Vicar grabbed his two wrists in a handful, while with the other hand, broad as a dried haddock, freckled, shimmering in the sunlight with reddish growth of hairs, he fingered Gabriel's weasand. 'You heard what I said to the scum?'

'Yes.'

'You credit it?' His eyes, searchful as needles, looked down into Gabriel's.

'Not till your highness shall say it again to me.'

'How dare you imagine it other than a lie?'

'Your highness need scarce be so rabious against me. I daren't.'

'And yet, weren't very so? What then? Speak, filth, or I'll end you.'

'Whom have I but your highness? I am yours. You can work me like wax.'

The Vicar's eyes searched his, as a knife should search a wound. Gabriel held his breath. Suddenly the Vicar drew him to him, like a woman: kissed him. 'Even you, my little pigsnye, should find it dangerous too surely to know my drifts. I find close habours of discontentment: matters that may be uncunningly and indiscreetly handled: foolish and furious designs. Go, I'll mell me with no flirtations but them as end in bed. They shall see my back-parts, but my face shall not be seen. And so, walk you eared for attention in my foot-steps, if you hope to live through these next dangerous days. So,' he said, letting go of him, 'it is a careful life. Wipe up the mess. Feed that carrion to the dogs. Then attend me at the main gate. We must be by sun-go-down at the place you wot of.'

The sun was of that same day now near upon setting when Count Mandricard drew rein, coming out of the wood onto the northern edge of the clearing before a certain old waste and broken house desolate among pine-forests a mile above the little village of Gilgash, that lies just within the limes of Rerek. He was a big man, dull-eyed, horse-faced, with brown leathery wrinkled skin and long straggly beard with never a curl in it. There seemed a great stillness in the clearing. Westwards, gleams of the sunset pierced here and there the purplish-greenish obscurity of pine-frondage and close-set upright trunks. Presently he walked his horse up to the house door. Nettle-beds crowded up to the walls on either side. The windows were shuttered. He edged his horse round, and so, leaning sideways from the saddle, reached to give the door a great thump with the pommel of his sword. The still-ness settled yet deeper after the sound of that blow and of the scutter of little feet (rats, may be) that followed it. Mandricard waited a minute, then, growling some obscenity, swung from the saddle, tried the latch, went in. The house was empty, of a displeasant odour of dry-rot and of spiders: odour of grave-mould. He spat and came out again: swung up again into saddle. Dusk was gathering swiftly and the last embers of the sunset dying between the boles: blood among gallows-trees. 'Some and some is honest play,' he said in himself. 'Snick up. If I take heed to come to the Devil's banquet pat o' the hour appointed, why not they?' He spat. 'Clavius,' he said in himself: 'a young sly whoreson. In all abomination of life, brisk as a body-louse, but I'd ne'er trust him unless held by the ears. Why he will use him's a wonder: having took his father's head, too, for letting himself be so bedid-dered in the Ulba enterprise, and he Lord President of the Marches. Then Gilmanes. Well, a man that could betray his own brother-german to him, to be cut in pieces in Laimak dungeons, I suppose a may trust him after that. Fellow's jealous as a kite, too, of Ercles and Aramond: knows that, long as the Parry sits firm in Rerek and favours him, himself'll be left in peace to keep his claws on Veiring and Tella which else must straight fly back to allegiance to Prince Ercles. Knows, too, should a been unlorded long since, outed of all his hopes, for's misgovernment, but the Vicar pled for him: rubbed it off. Well, a may count on Gilmanes.

Stathmar – well: albeit I'd fear his goodness. No moving, though, without him. Who hath's buttocks firm in Argyanna may with one finger sway the march-lands. Olpman: I count him but a daw. He's no starter. Arquez: I hate Arquez: what's he but a common ruffian or thief, grown fat with the usurping of others' rights? He hath used him afore, true enough; and meaneth (it is in every man's mouth) to uncastle Sorms for him. – And there's the sum. I think he hath need of better tools to make such a frame perfect.'

He let the reins hang loose on the pommel. The soft measured noise of champing of grass carried in that ugly stillness a threat, as of Time's sands running out. As if it were said: How if all this were but to feel our affection to his person? Not meaning to strike, but first – having summoned us together here, in this outest corner of the realm – to choose out, snap in two, throw on the midden, any blades of meaner mettle? Strange how all we cannot but entirely love and cleave unto him, like unreasoned beasts, that himself is evermore false and double. May be there's a design in these chance delays: heaven's design or his. Perilous, too, to be unobedient to the sovereign – 'Howsoever, I'll think so,' said Mandricard suddenly. 'Pack while we may.' And so, giving the reins a shake, rode away through the woods northwards.

He was departed but a few minutes when the others began to come in: Prince Gilmanes first, on a white horse: overtaking him, Count Olpman.

'Your excellence rides well armed, I see.'

'You too,' said the Prince.

'Whom must we meet tonight?'

'Yon can answer that as well as I can.'

'Our host, our two selves, and four besides of his picking. How like you of those four?'

'Tell me their names first.'

Olpman smiled craftily. 'With your excellency's leave, I'll see 'em afore I name them.'

'God's death!' said the Prince, 'are we children, to beat about the bush when each knows, and each knows t'other knows? No matter: 'tis safest may be. How like you of them?'

'Trust him to pick sound.'

'Trust? Sounds strangely after such talk; and in the mouth of a man of law.'

'When time comes for action, no moving save upon some hazard.'

'I'll tell you, Olpman, wherein I'll put my trust. In hate sooner than in love, and ambition than loyalty, and commodity than either. 'Tis therefore I trust the Vicar.'

'Why? Because of commodity?'

'Yes. Commodity: to me in him, to him in me. You I'll trust, 'cause of the hate you bear to Beroald.'

'Well, your excellency too, I think, hath small reason to love that one.'

'For respect of what?'

'Yonder lecherous and bloody woman. Your nephew sticked with daggers at Krestenaya.'

The Prince gave a little shrug of the shoulders. A haughty unkind cold melancholy man he seemed, not without charm of manner. 'O as for that, I know not. The like occasion had egged us to the like cruelty. Yours, my lord, is the more unfallible ground: beholding this Beroald, your sometime pupil, ten years your younger, preferred, 'gainst all justice and reason, to this high place, of great Chancellor of Fingiswold. They ought not to think it strange if we shall otherwise provide for ourselves, and join with other, when we find no conformity nor towardness with them. – Here's Arquez and Clavius. 'Tis fear holds those two.'

'Fear, 'cause the matter he knows against 'em?'

'Aye. And 'cause he can break them in pieces when he will. – Here's Stathmar. Good. I smell comfort in Stathmar.'

In the failing light it was barely possible to know faces now, the moon yet unrisen. The Vicar himself on a great chestnut stallion rode in last: Gabriel at his elbow on a brown jennet and with a led horse in his hand laden with saddle-bags and two hogsheads of wine. 'God give you good e'en,' said the Vicar, leaping from horseback and passing the reins to Gabriel. 'Five. Well, go we in. Every man his own horse-boy tonight. Turn 'em into the yard behind the house: we'll take no chances where unreadiness might undo all. Gabriel, shutter the windows i' yon chamber: darken the chinks with cloaks: then light candles, set the wine on the table and the meat pies. We'll confer whiles we sup.' Then, under his breath, unobserved, to Gabriel, 'And forget not,' he said, 'the word I gave you: in case.' Gabriel answered with a little swift weasel-glance, secret, gone the next instant, sufficient.

They sat about a bare trestle table: the Vicar at the near end by the door, Olpman upon his right, armoured to the throat, and Stathmar upon his left, with bold honest brown eyes, square brown beard and shaven head, a big man and a strong, may be forty years of age. Huge in bulk, upon Olpman's right, sat Arquez, with tiny piglike eyes buried in rolls of flesh; then, at the table's end facing the Vicar, Gilmanes, with Clavius on his right, and so again Stathmar. Youngest of them by much seemed this Clavius, of a malapert and insolent carriage, fluffy yellow beard, and pale fish-like eyes. Gabriel by the Vicar's command was ever in and out, to keep watch: held his meat in one hand, his sword ready in the other, and took his sup of wine between-whiles.

The Vicar sat uncloaked now, in tanned leather jerkin armed all over with scales or sequins of polished iron and with golden buckles at neck and waist and a gorget of iron plate damascened with gold and silver. Bolt upright, his hands flat-palmed before him on the table, he went over his company man by man. 'You have begun ill with me, Prince,' he said for first word, thrusting out his jaw at him: 'broke faith ere we be set at table.'

Gilmanes changed colour. 'I know not what your excellency means.'

'Bring a train of soldiers with you, when I made it condition all should come alone. I saw 'em myself in Gilgash.'

'I'm sorry. 'Twas but three or four only, for safety of my person.'

'I can care for your person, my lord. Robbers and reivers walk not here at liberty uncorrected, in South Rerek, as in your northern parts they do use. If I am to trust a man, a shall trust me, tit for tat. Who else hath done like that? Olpman, I noted your badge on half a dozen buff jackets as I came through the village.'

'Your noble excellence will pardon me, I hope,' said the Count, 'if I mistook the condition.'

'If me no ifs. All this is against you, and shall be, till you make it good.'

'I thought we were free to bring 'em up to Gilgash so we came alone hither to Middlemead.'

'The Devil dirt in your beard. You deal like the fish sepia, you lawyers: ever smother your traces in voidance of too much ink. Stathmar?'

'Not an one, my lord.'

'There speaks a man. Clavius?'

'I dare not venture myself unmanned on the Meszrian border: by cause of Ibian.'

'Your old kind Meszrian host? Go, I think you've reason.' The Vicar laughed, a single crack betwixt a snarl and a bark. If I'd been so unkind as give you bound to Ibian when he asked me, go, I'd wager five firkins of muscatel 'gainst a couple of peasen you'd ne'er gone gulling again. – Arquez?'

Arquez sullenly answered, 'No.'

'What's no? I say you brought men, contrary to troth plighted 'twixt us. Answer me directly without colour whether it be so or not.'

'I say directly, your highness, it is not so.'

A combust black choler seemed to darken the Vicar's eyes glaring upon him. There was silence a minute. Then the Vicar spoke again, sitting back in his chair with folded arms. 'By the ear-feathers of Sathanas! I'm heartily minded to a done with you all. My Lord Stathmar and I come hither alone, as articled:' (here Gabriel, passing in his hithers and thithers out of the door, with none to mark him, laughed in his sleeve): 'the rest break faith, e'en in so slight a matter, quick as a dog will eat a pudding.' Like rabbits under the menace of the stoat, those great lords sat mum, meeting one after the other the eye of him upon them. 'Where's Mandricard?'

None could tell. 'If he hath turned tricksome – go, they say kings have long hands: a shall find that I have longer. I'll have him caboshed like a stag and bub my wine from's brain-pan. Look you,' he said, and a sudden great clattering blow of his fist on the board made all leap in their seats, 'If there be any here doubteth to confide himself to me in this business, let him go home now. I'll take it upon my honour I'll bear him neither grudge nor disfavour. So only it be now o' the instant; for, after this business be opened, to turn back then shall cost a man nothing but his life.'

But they, as with one mouth, with most vehement heat of oaths and promises, pledged him their fealty.

'Then,' said he, 'to proceed with frankness to the matter. There's not a man here but of Rerek born and bred. In this land of our fathers hath changes come about, these ten years or more. We be loyal liege subjects all unto our sovereign Lord the King (Gods send he live for ever). For all that, we feel the changes: feel the foreign hand upon us. Instance myself: Laimak since thirty generations her own mistress, but now fief royal: we must do suits and services. For the lesser fish i' the pond, where were they today if I had not stood 'twixt them and forfeit of their privileges? Where were Mandricard? County Olpman, where were you? With the headsman's hands already fumbling at your neckband, whose mercy, say, save mine could have availed to keep that head of yours upon your shoulders? Ay, and a dozen more i' the like despaired condition, attainted after Valero's treason? You, and you too, my Lord Stathmar, are witness to the sharpness of my correction of that traitor: to the sharpness too of my dealing with some that, seeing the realm fallen in a roar, thought it time to oppress their neighbours. But I shaved their beards right smooth and clean – insolents, o' the kidney of yonder office nobility we see puffed up now, Jeronimy, Beroald, Roder, and their kind: crammed till they belch again with the rightful sustenance of better men. So help me, I'll pluck down some or another of them too, ere I come to my grey hairs. Then you, Gilmanes. Be you remembered the King took Kaima from you, the most rich and precious stone out of your princely coronal, 'cause of this matter of your brother

Valero; but by my procurement, was given you back again. I helped you 'gainst your neighbour Princes, Ercles and Aramond, that, of their long accustomed malice many years rooted, so vexed you in your borders. 'Twas thanks only to my speedy intelligence but last winter, in your little beggarly town of Veiring, that you 'scaped there unmurdered. I have still helped and upholden you in correcting of the mutiny of certain cities in your parts, which were dread in time to allure and stir the more part of the other cities to the like. To you, Arquez and Clavius, I say but this: I have in a casket matter against you enough (should you displease me) to send you to them that shall cut out the head, gammon, and flitches, and hang up the rest *pro bono publico*.

'Broach some more wine, good pug,' he said to Gabriel. 'So much friendly exhortation marvellously dries the throat.' He thrummed a morris dance on the table with his fingers while the wine was pouring. When he looked up, the thunder-clouds had left his face. 'We be loyal liege subjects all,' he said. 'But sad 'tis and true 'tis, no King lives for ever; and 'tis mere prudence to ponder what waits us round the next turning. 'Twere no great wonder if some that have well and truly served King Mezentius should boggle if it were to come to King Styllis.'

'As, by law, come it must,' said Count Olpman: 'to the son born in wedlock and undubitate heir.'

'An untried boy,' said Stathmar.

'Proud, insolent, jealous of all true merit,' said Gilmanes.

'God abolish his name under heaven,' said Clavius.

Arquez ground his teeth.

'Such inconveniences,' said the Vicar, 'are lightly by wise policy to be turned to advantage. But mischief is in his tutors. Be sure of this, my lords: come that day, you shall see a triumvirate of court sycophants, under colour of young Styllis, take power i' the Three Kingdoms: Roder, 'cause the boy clings yet to him as to's wet-nurse; the fat Admiral, 'cause of legitimacy and what has been must be; and Beroald, 'cause in the sheep's-heads o' the other two is not brains sufficient betwixt the pair of 'em to keep 'em from disaster not a sennight's space, nor resolution enough to hold to any course resolved on, but still must run to him.'

'And besides all this,' Stathmar said, 'your excellency has to reckon with Zayana.'

'Aye, I was coming to that.'

'O, I redoubt not him,' said Olpman. 'So he have his pretty pussy to huggle withal, it forceth not. A do-little, a—'

'There your judgement, my Lord Olpman, so needle-eyed as I have known it, turns blind as a beetle,' said the Vicar. 'Five years now he hath shown himself, in conduct of his dukedom, high-thoughted like to's father. Because in his underage and jollity he will eat and drink and have dalliance with women, be not you so bedoted as think that the sum. Bastard blood is very bold and hurtful: the more so, come of the loins of King Mezentius. And we manage not this young Duke, he may yet prove a main part of our undoing. Styllis, Barganax, and yonder three unite and joined against us, our matter were like to go evil. But feed we but their factions and hold 'em apart (as, with him, we may use the offences Styllis hath unbrotherly committed and shall likely yet commit against him) – why, with such a policy, I dare pawn down my life, Rerek shall still find her a cloak for every rain.'

There fell a silence. Under the Vicar's careless-seeming yet most discomfortably mind-searching glance, men's eyes shifted, as though each looked for other first to unrip the seals and show what underlay these unresty hints and half-spoken loose suggestions. 'Let me put in your minds, if you forget,' said the Vicar, 'that you, not I, first sought such a conference as this is, when each severally in writing you put yourselves to my protection. And, that you may see how merely for the common weal I take hand in the thing, I'll tell you: if there be any man living you think likelier than me to help you in such perilous circumstances as but now we spoke on – show him to me. I'll give place to him, swear him fealty and upholding.'

Every man of them sat mute as a fish.

'You, Prince Gilmanes: will you undertake, say?'

Amid angry murmurs, Gilmanes made haste to disclaim so ungrateful an eminence.

'Shall's let this stand adjourned, then? How if we send to Ercles in Eldir, bid him our following?'

'God strike him dead first!'

'The old keen tiger that in a wait hath lain for us so long?'

Clavius began to hum a ditty sung by Gilmanes's faction in the street of Veiring:

> The elder from Eldir
> God sent him here selder!

When he might have hearing again, Gilmanes said, 'Shall Rerek speak with one man's voice, with whose if not with the Parry's?'

Gabriel Flores, eyed and footed like a weasel, went betwixt bench and wall filling first for his great master then for the rest. All drank deep. Then the Vicar spoke. 'If I have given you,' he said, 'any sour words tonight, be satisfied 'twas but in consideration of the secret knowledge I had of my own will, and being resolved to make some difference between tried just and false friends ere I would strip off all farthingales to the bare nature of these high purposes. Let's confess it was never merry world in Rerek since Fingiswold came up. Which thing, though it be coloured *per jus regale*, yet it is tyranny. Which tyranny – considering the straiter amity between me and you concluded, and considering your several private promises in writing (which, as I shall satisfy you, import an army of well five thousand men, veterans all, to be had abroad in a readiness at any time now upon ten days' notice given, resting upon Kutarmish) – why, 'twere abomination irremissible and everlasting scorn upon us if we overtopple it not.' He paused. All they as they listened seemed but more and more to fan their feathers in his lime. 'That is to say,' he added, 'occasion arising.'

For a minute none spoke, man watching man. Then Gilmanes, making a cast about the table with his long pale eyes and running his tongue along his thin and bloodless lips, said, 'I question but one thing, my lords. His highness said "occasion arising". But is not occasion instant upon us? Seeing the greatness of our adversary and his infinite dominion in Rerek, that already hath gone far to work us all from princes into pages. Thinks, too, that he knoweth, I ween, some hollow hearts in Rerek; and is himself one that keepeth his displeasure in close, then, like God's severe judgement, dallieth not where to strike he doth purpose.'

The air in that room seemed suddenly to have grown closer. Again man eyed man. Then, 'God send him here,' said Arquez with a thick gluttonish laugh, 'and give me the unbowelling of him.'

The Vicar looked at Arquez then sidelong at Gilmanes, through half-closed lids. 'Argument: ergo, dally not we, but strike first?'

'Ay,' said Clavius, 'and strike him into the centre.'

'Who speaks against it?' said the Vicar. 'In so extreme jeopardous a work as you now propound to me, needs must each stand by all or else all go down *in solido*.'

'Better that,' said Gilmanes, 'than be still kept under like beasts and slaves.'

'Who speaks against it?'

But in a confusion of high and clamorous words they cried out saying, 'Strike, for Parry and Rerek!' 'Death to Mezentius!' 'Throw the crooked tyrant to the Devil!' 'Chop him into steaks!'

'You, Stathmar?' said the Vicar, seeing him sit silent amid this rant.

''Tis but that I will not,' answered he, 'be one of those who rashly before a great man enter into talk unrequired. To my thinking, it is better the sword be sheathed than unsheathed. Howsomever—'

The Vicar stroked his beard thrice. Huge as a lion he seemed, high seated in that great chair; and red as a fox; and untrusty to handle as a quick eel by the tail; and a king *in potentia*, wanting but the regal crown and sceptre; and wicked out and out. In the nick of time, ere he should speak again, the door flew open in Gabriel's face, and before them in his majesty stood the King.

All leapt to their feet, and, save the Vicar's and Gilmanes's, every man's hand to his sword-hilt. It was as if the instant moment itself leapt and hung tip-toed on an instability of movelessness, while men's minds, violently unseated, waited on direction. Only the Lord Horius Parry, as in lightning-swift apprehension of the posture of affairs, and of the choices, deeply ravelled of good and bad, of known and unknown, not to be eluded nor long put off, fateful of life and death, which it imported, seemed to face it with a mind intact and unremoved. Like the snapping of a string wound to extreme tension, Gabriel heard the silence break with the King's 'Good evening, cousin': heard in the deep cadence of the King's voice, careless and secure, an almost imperceptible over-tone of irony that thrilled less upon the ear than upon the marrow that runs within the neck-bones: saw the Vicar's obeisance: saw, for one breath, their mingling of eyes together, his and the King's, as if each would craftily undergrope the other's policies.

All saluted the King now, with an unhearty greeting but yet with due humble show of allegiance, drinking to him peace, health, joy, and victory upon his enemies. The Vicar made place for him at the table's head, seating himself at the King's right, betwixt the King and Count Olpman. 'Bare a fortnight since I tasted your noble entertainment, cousin, in Laimak,' said the King, raising to his lips the goblet from which the Vicar had but just drunk his health, and pledging them all in turn. 'And now, benighted in these woods, what luckier find than this hospitable room? or what luckier choice of loving friends and subjects to be met withal?' His eye seemed merry, as of a man set among them of his household, nothing earthly mistrusting.

''Lack,' said the Vicar, 'this should seem to your serene highness a strange dog-hole, I'd a thought. And, truth to say, we be assembled here 'pon a strange business.'

Wise men started, and light men laughed in themselves, at these words. But the King said, unconcerned, 'I had supposed yours was, as ours, a hunting party.'

'It might be named so. Your serenity has had good sport, I hope?'

'Tracked the big bear to his hole,' replied the King: 'but as yet not killed.'

The Vicar met his eye without quinching. 'As for our hunting,' he said, 'your serene highness will laugh at us. You have heard, may be, stories of this same farmstead: that there was of old a man dwelt alone in this place, a bonder, rich in goods and in cattle, alone save for's thralls. And these thralls, uncontented, it seems, with his hard and evil usage of 'em, one night, 'pon agreement had together, took and murdered him.' Glancing round the table while he talked, he saw them sit like dumb beasts, as if afeared to meet some eye upon them were they to look up, his or another's. Only the King, idly fingering his wine-goblet, gave him look for look: idly, as one who rolls on his tongue the wine of some secret jest, the delightfuller to him because hid from all men else. The Vicar proceeded: 'Since when, to this day, none durst live in the place for dread of the dead sprite which, as is said, rideth the roof a-nights, breaketh the necks of man and beast, and so forth. And is neglected so, some three generations and all fallen to ruin. Now the Prince here and my Lord Olpman, they laid me a wager, a thousand ducats, that these tales were sooth and that something bad resorteth indeed to the house; but I tell 'em is but old wives' foolishness and fiddle-faddle. Which to determine, we mean to sit out the night here, drinking and discoursing, with these four lords besides to witness whether aught beyond ordinary shall befall us.'

The King smiled. 'I'd a sworn there were things in this house worth the finding out. Coming but now, supposing it empty, and finding, 'pon opening of the door, this jolly company within, put me in mind of the old tale of the shepherdman's coming by night beside Holyfell in Iceland. He saw that the fell was opened on the north side, and in the fell he saw mighty fires and heard huge clamour there and the clank of drinking-horns; and he heard that there was welcomed Thorstein Codbiter and his crew. He and his crew. You remember?'

'That had, that same night, as was known later, been drowned in the fishing?'

'Yes: dead men,' said the King: 'feasting that night in Holyfell. There's the difference: that here, at present, are all yet alive.'

Furtively, as though some strange unwonted horror began to invade them, men's eyes sought the Vicar's. Gabriel Flores, watching there apart, bethought him how most things have two handles. How if one of these comates of mischief had blabbed out all to the King beforehand? How if his master, sitting so thoughtful, had the like inkling? Gabriel waited for his eye. But the Vicar, smiling to himself, played softly with the great seal-ring on his left thumb and gave eye to no man. 'Your highness sees some danger, then?'

'A certain danger,' replied the King lightly, yet not a man there sat at ease under the look he now swept round the table, 'in meddling with such business as brought you here tonight.'

The Vicar still smiling, nodded his head: still intent upon his ring. Men watched him as if they knew, how smooth soever his looks were, there was a devil in his bosom.

'In some serene highness' school well brought up,' said Gilmanes, after a pause, and his teeth flashed, 'we are inured to dangers.'

'And yet,' said the King, 'there is measure in all things. Courage of the wise: courage of the fool.'

'The second we know,' said the Vicar. 'What is the first?'

'Is it not a native part of wisdom? A wise King, for instance, that will trust his person unguarded amongst his loyal loving subjects.'

Men began to shift in their seats a little, as unballasted ships are rocked and tossed. Clavius, being high with wine, shouted out, 'Yes: and a hundred swords ready behind the door to secure him.'

'That,' replied the King, 'were an unwise mistrust of them that were loyal. And yet for a jest: instance the extreme of improbability: say you were of that rank sort, here met to devise my ruin. Then I, having some wisdom, and knowing as a King should know, might come indeed, as I am come, but with a force of men without prepared to seize upon you; 'stead of (as 'tis) secure in my friends, and not so much as a man-at-arms to guard me.'

Olpman whispered privately to the Vicar, 'This be set forth to blear our eyes. He hath men at call. Our only safety, strike and strike suddenly.'

'Quiet, fool, and wait my word,' said the Vicar. He paused a moment, smiling, playing with his ring: then made sign to Gabriel to fill round the wine again. A look of intelligence passed between him and Gabriel, slight and fleeting as, at slack-water, is the beginning of the turning, this way and no longer that, of the great tide unresistable of the sea. Gabriel, when he had filled round, went out by the door. The Vicar found means to say to Olpman under cover of the general talk, 'I had prepared this beforehand. We will a little play for time. When you shall hear me say to Gabriel, "Why not the wine of Armash?" that is a sign to him to admit those that shall dispatch the King's business for him right suddenly. Pass round the word. This too: that no man, on his life, stir afore my bidding.'

While Olpman was cautiously in this sense instructing Arquez, the Vicar said covertly to the King, 'I entreat your highness, let's manage your faces so as none shall doubt we speak on aught but trivial matters. And if I speak improbably, yet believe it—'

'No more,' said the King, with a like secrecy and a like outward carelessness. 'I'll tell it you myself. You have stumbled tonight upon a wasps'-nest. But I am come on purpose to take it. All present, you alone excepted, play underboard against my royal estate and person. I have proof: I have letters. Your charge it shall be that not a man of them escape.'

'A squadron of horse, my own, distant from the farm some half mile,' said the Vicar. 'And these, I well guess, have twice as many against us. What profit in men-at-arms, though, when the head is off?'

The King laughed. 'I am glad you are not a fool, cousin.'

The Vicar, playing as before with the great ring on his thumb, said, 'Go, I think there's not one here, I alone excepted, believes your serene highness is in truth come alone here and unattended.'

'But you, cousin, are not a fool,' said the King.

'I know now. I have put my life in your highness's hand.'

'How so?'

'Sitting thus at your right hand. Your hand next my heart. And your dagger, I see, ready to your hand.'

'We are neither of us slow of understanding,' said the King. 'And I think either would be sorry to lose the other.'

They had means to speak some word or two more thus privately. Then came Gabriel Flores in again with a flesh flagon of wine. 'I shall in a moment,' said the Vicar, 'give your serene highness proof of my love and fidelity plain and perfect.' Gabriel filled first to the King, then to the Vicar, who whispered him some instruction in his ear. 'And you shall see too I can play at shuttlecock with two hands,' said the Vicar, under his breath to the King. 'Which oft cometh well.'

As Gabriel passed now behind Count Olpman's chair, his eyes met his master's, and he paused. Gilmanes, Clavius, and Stathmar were in talk, heads together, at the far end of the table. Olpman, biting his lip, had secretly, under cover of the table-top, bared his sword. The Vicar rapped out suddenly to Gabriel, 'Why not the wine of Armash?' and, the word scarce out of his mouth, hurled his heavy goblet in Gilmanes's face, throwing at the same time with his other hand his dagger, which pinned Clavius's right hand (put up to save him) to his cheek. Gabriel, bringing down the wine-flagon with all his might upon the bald pate of Olpman from behind, dashed out his brains. The King was sprung to his feet, sword drawn: the Vicar beside him. Amid this broilery and fury, leaping shadows on wall and ceiling, knives thrown, chairs and benches overset, the King crossed blades with Stathmar: both notable swordsmen. Arquez threw a pie-dish at the King: grazed his cheekbone: then a chair, but it fell short, sweeping (save one) every candle from the table. At fifth or sixth pass now in that uncertain light, Stathmar fell, run through the heart. Arquez, seeing this: seeing Olpman lie sprawled over the board, his head in a pool of blood: seeing Gilmanes stretched senseless, and Clavius wounded and in a mammering whether to fly or fight: threw another chair, that tripped up the Vicar rushing bloodily upon him: then yet another at the King. It missed. Arquez jumped for the window. The King caught the chair in mid-air, hurled it again, took him on the backside, well nigh broke his tail-bone. Down from the window he dropped, and Gabriel, with skilfully aimed kicks and with strampling on his face and belly, soon stopped his noise.

Clavius, casting himself prostrate now under the King's feet, cried out that, might but his life be spared, he would declare all: 'I was neither author nor actor: only persuaded and drawn in by Olpman and Gilmanes and by—' His speech dried up in his throat as, gazing wildly round, he saw how the Vicar beheld him with a look as fell, as venomous, and as cruel as is in the face of the death-adder.

'Tie them all up,' said the King: 'these three that be left alive.' Gabriel tied them hand and foot with rope from the pack-saddles: set them on a bench against the wall: gathered some candles from the floor to make a better light. Gilmanes and Arquez were by now come to themselves again. Little content they seemed with their lot; seeing moreover how the King drew a sheaf of papers from his bosom. But never a word they uttered.

The King's countenance seemed as a pouring down of black darkness from the sky, where all else becomes undiscernable, even to the stars whose operations make the fortunes and the destinies of men. 'Some things,' he said, 'be provable, some unprovable. I know not how many principal members there be and how many unprincipal. I say (and that not without sufficient evidence of your own letters) that you came hither confederated to work an utter mischief against my estate, that am your King and Lord. What reason had you for such ingratitudes and undeserved unkindness? – You, Gilmanes? That four years ago I spared your life at the suit of your grey beard, and ever since have too patiently borne with your harsh government and cruelties used against my liege-men? But your ungracious and unheard wickedness shall come down upon your own pate. – You, Arquez? In hope that, if the realm were but turmoiled and shaken, your oppressing of your neighbours might have easy scope? It will come to fifty thousand ducats that you have robbed of my good subjects; but now is your audit near. – You, Qavius? Because time and again my hand has opened bounty to you, but, for all that, you have remained our well proved evil willer, and, as we see, a fool besides and a dastard.

'I bid you, therefore,' he said to the Vicar, 'let me see the three heads off, of Clavius, Arquez, and Gilmanes, before either any man else go from this room or come into it. Olpman's too: should have been. Second bite, after I'd pardoned him his share in Valero's rebellion; it was too much. But the rat your secretary saved us that trouble. Stathmar I'd have spared. A good man, but unfit, after this, to be in the land, considering too he held the government and sway of so high a place. Him I'd have banished. But Fate, you see, hath banished him further than I could.'

For a minute there was dead silence. Then the Vicar motioned to Gabriel. 'Work for you to try your hand on. You have the King's warrant. Creep into them.' Gabriel took up his sword and stepped forward, trying the edge with his thumb. The Vicar said again, 'Creep into them, basset.'

But Clavius began to scream out against the Vicar: 'What of yonder cruel devil, that bred all our miseries? Setter on of all this, the arch-rebel himself—?'

'Hold!' said the Vicar like a thunder-crack, and Gabriel lowered his blade, swung hastily for the blow.

'—Spoke to us, King,' shouted Clavius, ''ere you came in: a seditious discourse farsed full of unfitting words, bordering on such strange designs that had made me haste forth, but that in the nick of time your serene highness fortunately coming in—'

The Vicar's face was scarlet: his regard inscrutable as stone. But in the King's eyes there but flickered an ironic smile. He snapped his fingers: 'Why are their heads not dealt with?' and Gabriel speedily dealt with them, having off the head first of Clavius, then of Arquez (at two strokes, for the fatness of his neck); last, of Gilmanes.

'Your secretary, I see,' said the King, taking the Lord Horius Parry by the arm now and causing him to go with him out into the open air, 'hath some pretty fetches: beyond what commonly we look to a learned clerk to do. Well, a fair riddance,' he said, as they stood now alone under the starry sky, their eyes not yet used to the darkness. 'Such men, alive or dead, lack substantial being: are a kind of nothing. Except Stathmar (whom I slew for indeed he gave me no choice) I'll be sorry for none of them: discard 'em as not worth the holding.

'But now, as for you, cousin: procurer and speciallest contriver

– nay, deny it not – of all this horrible treason. What have these done to be destroyed if you go free?'

There was a strange stillness came upon the great muscles of the Parry's arm, locked in the strong arm of the King. Out of the masking darkness he answered and said, 'Your serene highness hath not a tittle of evidence there against me.'

'No. I said, you are not a fool.'

'And besides, it is something, I'd a thought, that I saved your highness's life.'

'And why?' said the King. 'Why did you that?'

They were pacing now, with slow deliberate steps, away from the house. It was as if, for a minute, under the undark summer darkness, blood talked to blood in the unquiet silence of their linked arms. Then the Vicar gave a strange awkwardish little laugh. 'This is scarce the moment,' he said, 'to ask your serene highness to swallow gudgeons. I could give you a dozen specious untrue reasons you'd disbelieve. Truth is, with the suddenness and unknownness of your coming, I know not why I did it. If I had but a little backed my hand—'

The King took him by either shoulder, and stood a minute staring down into his face. There was light enough, of starshine and that luminosity which lingers at this time of year in a kind of twilight all night long, to betray a most strange uncustomed look of the Vicar's eyes: almost such a look as himself was used to meet in the eyes of Gabriel Flores. The King began to laugh: the Vicar too. 'Truth is,' said the King, 'thinking of the matter unappassionately, there's something so glues me and you together as neither life nor death shall unglue us. Which you, my most wolvy and most foxy sergeant major general of all the Devil's engineers, are not able to forget when my eye is upon you (according to the old saying, *ex visu amor*). But when you are too much left to yourself, you are sometimes prone to forget it.'

'I'll swear to your serenity,' said the Vicar, 'by all the dreadfullest oaths you shall require me of—'

'Spare your oaths,' said the King, 'and your invention. I and you do well understand each other: let it rest at that. Indeed, and more of your lies might try my temper. Send that little jackal of yours to call up your men you told me of: explain the miscarriage of these five noble persons within there how you will. Take the credit of it to yourself if you like: I grudge it you not. Good night, cousin. And ponder you well the lesson I have read you this evening. There is my horse, tied by the gate there.'

'But your highness's men?' said the Vicar bringing the King's horse with his own hand.

'I told you already, I am alone.' He leapt into the saddle lightly as man of five and twenty.

'Alone?' said the Vicar and stood staring, 'Nay,' he said, 'but I thought—'

'Are you in truth, cousin,' said the King, gathering his reins, 'so universal a liar as you end by seeing a lie in truth herself, even presented to you stark naked? As the drunkard that swallowed the true live frog in his beer-mug, supposing it but such another fantasm as he was customed to? Good night.'

'Alone?' said the Vicar again, in himself, as the hoof-beats of the King's departing died away, leaving behind here only a great stillness and the night. 'Go, I believed it within there 'mong those timorous and unthankful vipers. As well, perhaps, that I did. And yet: truth unbusked and naked, considered another way – might a tickled me up to what I'd now a been sorry for. And now – thinking on't in cold blood – go, 'tis a thing not believable!'

VIII

LADY MARY LESSINGHAM

IT was now the twenty-fourth of June, nineteen hundred and fourteen, at Wolkenstein in the Grödner Dolomites, nine o'clock, and a morning without cloud. Up in the sky, beyond church-spire and river and meadow and chalet and rolling pasture and pine-forest and grass-smooth steep-going alp, hung the walls of the Sella. Seen through that haze of air and the down-shedding radiance of the sun, the millions upon millions of tons of living rock seemed as if refined away to an immateriality of aery outsides, luminous, turquoise-shadowed, paler and thinner than thin clouds, yet immovable and sharp-outlined like crystal. It was as if slab, gully, scree-slope, buttress, and mile-long train of precipice wall, cut off from all supports of earth and washed of all earthy superfluities which belong to appearances subject to secular change, stood revealed in their vast substantiality; the termless imperishable eidolon, laid up in Heaven, of all these things.

On the terrace before the inn, people were breakfasting at a dozen little tables. Here a lime-tree, there a wide umbrella striped white and scarlet, made its pool of shade upon green-and-white chequered table-cloth, gravel, and paved walk. Outside these shades, all was drenched with sunlight. Here and there, a glass ball, blue, yellow, or plain silver, the size of a man's fist and having a short bottle-neck to take the top of the bamboo stick that supported it, gleamed among the rose-trees to rebate the glance of witches. All the time, amid the clink of breakfast things, was the coming and going, strong and graceful upon their feet, of the inn-keeper's two daughters: capable, self-possessed, with a native ease of manner and an infectious laughter, charming to look at in their red petticoats, many-coloured aprons, Tyrolean blouses of white linen, and embroidered belts with clasps of silver. Underneath all the sounds and movements was an undersound of waters falling, and, closer at hand, a hum overhead of bees in the lime-trees which put out at this season their delicate sweet-smelling pendant flowers. And, an intoxication of lilies to make eddies of these simplicities, sat Mary: by herself at an outer table, part in sun part in shadow.

There seemed a morning coolness, dew upon an ungathered lily, to rest upon her sitting there, unconscious, to all appearance, of the many pairs of eyes that having once looked could not but look again, as bees drawn (fly where they can) still to the honey-dropping of Aganippe's fount. Unregarding these looks, she now ate a piece of bread and honey; now (as if the little girl awoke anew in her to usurp the woman) dipped sugar in her coffee, and sucked and dipped and sucked again; now shaded her eyes to look up to the pale tremendous outlines afar of those dolomite walls under the sun.

Upon the sound from indoors of a voice among the many voices, she looked up. To a careless eye's beholding, scarcely she seemed to move the least lineament of her face. Yet to Lessingham, making his way across to her table from the clematis-shadowed door of the coffee-room, there was in some hardly perceptible quickening of her body and its every seen or unseen half-suggested grace, a private welcome that thrilled upwards as the lark ascending welcomes day. He took a chair and sat down facing her, himself in the full glare of the sun. He was in his travelling-clothes. They both laughed. 'My dear Señorita, how extraordinary to run across you here, of all places!'

'Most extraordinary. And *most* embarrassing!'

'Of course I can understand that this is the last place in the world you'd expect to see me.'

'The last in the world. So metropolitan. Much more natural to meet you in that shocking Georgian village in Suanetia: years ago – you remember? The year after I was married.'

'You? married? How distressing! Did I know it at the time?'

'Behaved as if you didn't.'

'O I shall always do that. Do you mind?'

'I think I prefer it,' Mary said, and her foot touched his under the table. 'We must be careful what we say. (Don't look round) – the gentleman behind you, with not one blade of hair on him: I'm a great puzzle to him. I'm sure this will make him draw the worst conclusions. A German gentleman, I think. He was in the train two days ago, coming up from Bozen. Had a curious stammer, and every time he stammered he spat. His wife has quite decided I'm the scarlet woman: shameless English hussy gadding about like this alone.'

The elder of the girls brought Lessingham's coffee: '*And* a large cup,' she said, putting it down with a flourish.

'What a memory you have, Paula!'

'O well, but some things one remembers.'

'Are we to have the schuhplattler dance tonight?' said Mary. 'You and Andreas? I expect you've got all the steps now?'

The girl laughed. 'Tomorrow, it may be. Tonight, no, no. Tonight, some dancers from Vienna. We do not like them. But father say they can come once.'

'Why don't you like them?'

Paula screwed up her nose and shook herself. 'They are not as should be,' she said. 'Too saucy – I must get you some more butter: some more honey.' She went about it, direct as a water-hen hastens across a lawn to fetch food for its young.

'Herr Birkel is a pet,' said Mary. 'Tearful excitement when I arrived. Took my hand in both his. "Welcome, *My Lady*. You are taller, I think, than ever." – And then, ever so confidential and intense – "*And* prettier!"'

'Perfectly true. Even in ten days.'

'Ten days! It seems like ten months. Or – some ways – ten minutes. You look very spry and wide awake after your all-night journey.'

'Slept my berserk sleep out at Waidbruck: thirty-one hours solid. Hadn't had a wink for five nights. Woke up about midnight: dined, or rather breakfasted, on soup, an omelette, Wiener schnitzel, a bit of Hansl and Gretl cake, red wine, coffee: made them produce a chariot: and here I am.'

'I was so glad of your telegram,' said Mary. 'So all went well in Paris?'

'In the end. Only way – wear them down. Thing wanted tidying up: two years now since poor Fred went, and still hanging about with loose ends. So I just had to hold their noses to it till they signed what I wanted: just to get rid of me. Quite as amusing as fighting the Bulgarians. Much more amusing than Berlin in nineteen-twelve. – Hullo, who's this?' – as a tiny white kitten clambered up the wooden balustrade and so onto Mary's lap.

'Mitzi,' said she, handing it across the table to Lessingham. 'The fact is, you like to be in charge.'

'I wrote to your father from Paris as soon as the thing was through; and to Jim, as your trustee. Told him there's two sums of twelve hundred thousand to go into trust: one under our marriage settlement, the other for you personally. Together, about a third of the whole. That's in case some day I go crazy with all this money business: take to high finance and burn my fingers. Do you think it's some bad blood coming out?'

Mary smiled. 'There's never any telling! The Medici blood, reason enough, I should think.'

'Sounds nicer. Still, if it has the same effect? You know, I wouldn't really like to spend my life money-grubbing. Not really,' Lessingham said, holding up the kitten in his right hand where it sat as if in an armchair, and bringing it nearer and nearer to his face. 'Not really, really, really.' Mitzi, as if mesmerized, kept very still, staring at him out of eyes of that dawn-like blue that belongs to the eyes of little kittens; then, when he was near enough, put out a hesitating velvety paw to touch Lessingham on the cheek. 'Have we the same room as then?'

'Haven't you been to look?'

'Do you think I'd waste time on that, when they told me you were on the terrace?'

'Well, we have,' she said. 'And your dressing-room next door.'

'Do they blow the horn still at half past six, for them to open the doors for the beasts to go out to pasture?'

'Yes. And one microscopic child to drive them!'

'Want your wuzz again?'

She held out both hands: took the little creature. Lessingham lighted a cigar. They said no more for a few minutes; using perhaps the mountains, and the village life about them, and the bodily sight of each other sitting there, as a directer medium than overt speech. After a while, he spoke. 'Have you ever felt double inside?'

'No,' she answered, upon a note part mocking part caressing in her voice, as though 'No' were washed with honey-water.

'One half all *Ambitioso*: set the whole world to rights and enslave mankind. The other half, all *Lussurioso* and *Supervacuo*: makes me want to abduct you to some undiscovered south sea-island of the blest, and there, paint, write, live on sweetmeats: spend the whole course of everlasting time in the moving and melancholy meditation that man's life is as unlasting as a flower. Instead of either of which,' he said, getting up from the table, 'how about taking our lunch up to the Sella Pass?'

Doctor Vandermast, a learned man, present secretary and foretime tutor to the Duke of Zayana, was walking at break of day under Memison, by a trodden path south-eastward along the lake's edge, a mile or so on the way toward Reisma. It was between three and four o'clock: the twentieth morning after that secret master-stroke of the King's in Rerek. Reisma Mere, smooth like polished steel, spread to cool distances veiled in mist. Water, meadow-land, oakwood and beechwood and birch and far-off mountain ranges showed as but varying depths of that indeterminate grey, having a tremulousness within it as of awakening blue, which filled the whole sky. Only in the north-east the great peaks began to shape themselves to a gradual crystalline sharpness and to take on a more cold and azured tinge as the sky behind them became streaked with saffron, and at length, above the saffron, one or two little clouds (invisible till now) began to show purple, and to burn underneath with fire of gold. A delicate primrose-coloured light began to infuse all the east and to mirror itself in the still lake; and now, for first voice of day, the cuckoo replied to the owl's last hoot. The learned doctor, alone with the moment while other mortals slept, stayed it by his art: made it, as he walked, tarry for him awhile to his more perfect satisfaction and enjoyment.

He had years on his back four score. And yet, being spare of build as a dragonfly, all eyes and leanness, he carried himself erect and without old age's infirmity. Hollowed with thought were his eye-sockets under their bristling eaves, and wan and lanked with thought was his cheek, but not to take away the fire-edge of that spirit which burned in his eyes. His white beard fell to his girdle. He was clad in a flowing gaberdine, ginger colour, and upon his head a scarlet bonnet of linsey-woolsey. Suffering, by his art, time to resume its course, he paused at a footbridge across a stream that, grown up with waterweeds, barely trickled toward the lake. Under the further bank, where a thicket of alder overhung that stream, was a water-rat, sitting in a ball, holding in her little hands a bit of weed and eating it prettily, like a squirrel. The doctor bade her 'Good morrow, mouse'; and she, with a shy glance of beady black eyes set in her round head between small short rounded ears, greeted him again, in a tiny reed-like voice but with human speech.

'Where is Madam Anthea?' said the doctor.

'She passed by this way, reverend sir, about midnight on her way to the snows. Frighted me, me being in this dress and she in her teeth and claws.'

'What, frighted of your sister? How shall we call this, but the most gross unknowing of God? She could not hurt you, my Campaspe, even if she would.'

'It is not fit she should come in her dresses when I am in mine. Hers are too rough: mine, so easily torn.'

'You can take your true shape.'

'I like my little dresses. One must play and be merry a little: not duty and service all the time.' She whisked across from the weedy raft she had rested on and so up the bank, and sat there washing her face and ears. 'O we are all in our humours: grown a little restless, as you may conceive, sir, with all these doings.'

Under Vandermast's nose the little nymphish creature changed in the twinkling of an eye her fur dress for feathers: for the silk-smooth brownish green dress, creaming to greenish buff in the under-parts, of a peggy-whitethroat: fluttered her wings, and was gone. From a hiding-place among the branches she ran him a descant, sweet falling notes of her woodland warble. His eye followed the sound to a flicker in the alderleaves; and there she was with her eyebrows. 'There's been double-dealings of late,' she said; 'where neither of them had seen the other, nor none of them knew other's person, nor knew of other's coming.' She hopped from twig to twig; daintily picked an insect or two. 'Tell me, who is this King then? And this son of his, this Duke?'

'That question', said Vandermast, 'raiseth problems of high dubitation: a problem *de natura substantiarum*; a problem of self-ness. Lieth not in man to resolve it, save so far as to peradventures, and by guess-work.'

'And what is your guess?' She perched now in the tip-most leaves of the alder, bobbing and flirting her tail, looking down at him.

'You must be content with your own guesses, my little lovebird: I with mine.'

'Why?'

She paused on the spray a moment; then flew down into the grass before his feet. 'Well, I will tell you my guess so far,' she said: 'that they are one and the same, even as She in Her shapes is one and the same; and yet other. And this world his world: even as it is the King's. And by Her giving.'

All the whole arch of day above them widened and rose moment by moment to new infinitudes of dawn-washed golden light. That old man resumed his walk, slowly onward.

She flew after him: settled on his finger. 'Shall I take my true shape?'

'As you please. But you are very well suited thus.'

'But I long to do as shall please you. You are so strange in your likes and dislikes. Why are you so?'

'Well,' said Vandermast smiling, 'you must remember, for one thing, I am very orderly in years.'

'Do you choose, then.'

'Your little dresses? there's none prettier, I think, than my water-rat.'

She ran along his sleeve to the crook of his elbow and sat there eyeing him, while she washed her face with her paws. 'Why?'

'In these matters, is but one answer why.'

'Our Lady? She likes me thus?'

'Surely.'

'She likes me all ways. We are part of Her empiredom. Is it not so?'

'Please Her,' said the learned doctor, 'it is so.'

'There was a word in your mouth the other day: *deificatio*. What is that?'

'It is,' answered the doctor, 'a term of art, signifying a condition we can sooner imagine than understand: the fusing and merging of God and the soul into each other,'

'Why?' The mouse-like hand and arm of Campaspe, suddenly in her own shape now, gloved to the elbow with soft brown leather that gave out a sharp odour of water-plants under a hot sun, rested light as air on his sleeve. Her grown of pale satin wrought all over with carnation silk made, as she walked, little summer-noises as of wind coming and going among reeds and willows. 'Why?'

Vandermast smiled and shook his head. 'Naiad: dryad,' he began to say, slowly: 'hamadryad: oread: nymphs of the woods and of gentle waters and of the kinless mountain, what can you learn by me? For you know all that is needful to know: know it as to the knowing born, without knowing that you know it: knowing it from within. Whereas I, that am but a looker on from withoutward—'

Campaspe looked up into his face with her bead-like eyes. 'But who are you, then?' she said, and her hand tightened on his arm.

As from a window in the clouds a shaft of sunlight passes over the cold sea, so seemed for a moment the thought-furrowed lean countenance of Vandermast. 'I am, I suppose,' answered he, 'an old man that am yet in love with youth.'

'I had not thought of youth. Why with youth?' she said. 'What is youth?'

But that learned philosopher, armed with so questionable a she-disciple, but came his way in silence.

Mary, walking ahead up the pass (a practice grounded, by tacit agreement, in two sufficient reasons: to feed the eyes behind her, and to leave it to her to set the pace), paused now in the shortening shadow of a pine. They were by this time come up a thousand feet from the floor of the valley, to where the hollow mountain side is a maze of hills and dells, with wide turfy stretches starred all over with flowers, and on every hand little watercourses: some alive with beck or waterfall, some but dry beds where water comes down after rain. And at every turn, with the winding upwards of that intermittent and stony path, the cliffs of the Sella constantly changed their aspect, lying back in ever more and more forced distortions of perspective as the way led nearer their roots, and thrusting up in succession ever a fresh spur of foot-stool to eclipse by its nearness the loftier summits behind it, and, in a vast illusion of instability, lean out from the body of the mountain. Under the gathering power of the sun the whole hillside was alive with grass-hoppers both great and small, taking hither and thither their low criss-cross flights, some with scarlet wings some with orange some with blue, and filling the air with the hot metallic thrill of their chirping. Lessingham, halting a few paces below her in the open, shaded his eyes to see her where she stood looking upwards to the thin roof made by the pine-tree fronds. Air stirred in the branches, sending ever changing tesselated patterns of white sunshine and amethystine luminous shadow across Mary's upturned face: her beautiful fire-red hair, done in the beautiful Austrian way, gleamed where the sun caught it, like polished metal; and every loose tendril floating on the air was at one instant invisible, the next instant a trembling of flame.

'The stillness of the trunk,' she said, 'Incessant little movements in the top branches. Do you think the world has its roots in heaven, and its branches spread out earthwards?'

Lessingham sat himself down on a rock at her feet.

'What a blessing,' she said, 'to have you real lazy, for once. The first proper lazy holiday we shall have had, for over three years. Never since Egypt, that last winter before Janet was born.'

'We've not done badly. Honeymoon in Greece, nineteen hundred and eight Caucasus, nineteen-nine: pure laze—'

He looked up at her: the Grecian profile, sweet serene forehead, very slight depression between brow and nose: eyebrows sweeping upward from the nose, then levelling: nose finely modelled, straight, pointed, with an almost imperceptible tilt up rather than down: cheekbones just sufficiently showing their presence to bring strength to the dove-like contours of her cheek: chin firm, throat and neck lithe, tender and strong: lips like the lips of a Goddess, tranquil and cool, yet of a most quicksilver mobility to fit every thought, mood, and feeling, as now a kind of satirical merry luxury of self-pleasuring comedy that blesses where it strikes, as she said, 'The indolence of it, that Caucasus expedition! Nothing at all to show for it – except Ushba, of course, and about five virgin peaks!'

'Well and then next year, nineteen-ten,' he said, 'in the yacht to Lofoten in the early summer – true, I did dart across to Stockholm about those statues they wanted me to do for them. But, on the whole, pure lazes, both that and the month on the Italian lakes in the autumn. Still, I'll promise to be bone-lazy now for a bit. First instalment: I wrote and told brother Eric the other day (from Paris) to go to the devil, about the Parliament question. Too many jobs that want doing without that.'

'O I am so glad!' said she.

'And I didn't give him an address. I'm very fond of Eric, and very fond of Jacqueline; but really we don't want them butting in again like that on our voyage to Kythera, as they did at Avignon.'

They went on again, Mary ahead; maintaining for the best part of an hour a companionship of silence in which, the deeplier for no word spoken, presence quiveringly underfelt presence. From the top of the pass a ten minutes' pull up over steep grass and scree brought them to a shoulder of flowerclad alp, whence, out of sight of the path, you look east to the square-cut Towers of the Sella and west, further away beyond the hollow of the pass, to the rose-coloured wild fantastical spires and ridges of the Langkofel massif; Langkofel, Plattkofel, and Fünffingerspitze: a spectacle at first blush unbelievable, unveiling at that moment above breaking clouds in the broad unreached sky.

'Like nectar!' she said, taking in through eye and deep-drawn breath the thing before her. 'Don't you love to get up?'

'Up to a point.'

'Where would you stop?'

'Here.'

Mary drank the air again, standing tip-toe in an eagerness and poise liker to some creature of the woods and hills that is so fitted to its body that every changing motion expresses wholly and subtly, as music, the inward mood. Such a carriage, may be, had those swan maidens, king's daughters, flown from the south through Mirkwood to fulfil their fates; whom Weyland Smith and his brethren surprising at their upland bath, stole the swan-skin dresses of, and caught them so, and wedded them, and for a time sat in peace so. 'O I would not stop. I would go always higher. Wouldn't you come with me?'

'Would I, do you think?'

'Have to!'

'Well, but, say, twenty thousand feet: that might stop us. Heights above that, I've climbed at in the Himalaya. Can't breathe properly, lose your strength, can't sleep. And an awful depression: the sense of something watch, watch, watching you, always from behind. Like an oyster might feel, if it has an imagination, when the cook opens the shell with an oyster-knife and looks at it.'

'I know. But we'd choose to be creatures that can enjoy it. I'd like to be that,' she said, pointing, as a party of choughs, glossy black plumage and yellow beaks, glided, dived, and soared below the edge of the hill, balancing on air, uttering their soft rippling cries.

She came and sat beside him: began to investigate and spread out the lunch which Lessingham produced from his rucksack. 'Mass of eggs: I hope they've ducked them in cold water so that they'll peel properly. Rolls with ham in them. Chicken: I asked for that instead of veal today. All these snippety bits of sausage. Peaches. Plums – O you've squashed them! with your great coarse camera jabbing against them! A great wodge of butter. – Shall we ever grow old?' she said, as they began eating.

'No.'

'We shall. I'm twenty-six today. You'll be thirty-two in November. We'll have to start being middle-aged. Thirty-three is a generation.'

'You haven't given me my birthday present yet.' Lessingham said, when they had finished and buried the remains.

'Do you want it?'

'It's part of the bargain.'

'O stupid bargain.'

'I like to go on with it. I like outward and visible signs.'

'So do I. But this part of it – I mean the taking off – has lost its meaning. My dear, my dear, it has. The first time: even the second: but after that—'

'Well, you must think it a kind of exercise – a kind of ἄσκησις· – for me. Come. Only once a year.'

'Very well.' She took off her wedding-ring and gave it him.

'"Ours",' he said, examining it: reading the Greek cut deeply on the inside of the ring. 'HMETEPA. Feminine singular. Neuter plural. Mine, and yours.'

Their eyes, turned together, rested in each other a minute, grave, uncommunicative, as with the straining between them of some secret chain in nature.

'Suppose,' said Lessingham after a long pause, 'one of us were to die. Do you think then there could still be any question of "ours"?'

It was as if dogs howled on the shore. Mary looked away: across to the pale precipices of the Langkofel, rearing skyward above fans of scree that opened downward to the vast scatter of fallen boulders which fills the hollow below, called the Steinerne Stadt. 'What makes you say that?' she said.

'To hear you say Yes. I wish I could say *credo quia absurdum*, as you can.'

'I don't. I do believe. But not because it's absurd.'

Between Langkofel and Plattkofel, lower but more venomous to look at than either, with its knife-edged reddish pinnacles, stands the Fünffingerspitze. 'I climbed that thing twice; before I had a Mary,' he said. 'Alone, both times, like a lunatic. By the Schmidt Kamin. Deserved to be killed. No, it's not absurd,' he said: 'what we were talking about. But it's not believable. Not to me.' He ground his nailed boot into the earth. 'And the alternative,' he said, 'is, unfortunately, not asburd. And I find it unbearable: the mere thought, unbearable.'

She shivered a little, still looking at those mountains. 'I don't think we really know what we mean,' she said, very low, 'when we speak of Death.'

'I don't think we do,' said Lessingham. 'But all philosophizing on that subject comes back to an earth of wretchedness and of darkness. The Red King's dream in Alice. Go out – bang! – just like a candle.'

'I don't like it when you talk like that.'

'I used not to mind. Now I do.'

They sat silent. He began considering the ring once more, turning it about in the sun, fitting it on his little finger first of his right hand then of his left: it would not pass the second joint. At last, offering it to her with a grave courtliness of manner, 'Señorita,' he said, 'will you accept it back again?'

But Mary was stood up now, against the sky, looking down on him from above. And now, that minor diabolus twisting in its sleep there near her mouth's corner as if in the sweet unbusked luxury of some naughty dream, she replied, 'No. I shall not. By your own stubbornness you've unmarried yourself. I'll think it over in cooler blood: possibly answer your proposal tomorrow.'

'I'll come for the answer tonight,' he said.

'You'll find the door locked.'

'I'll get in at the window when you're asleep.'

'You won't. I'll scream: create an appalling scandalismos! No, I mean it.'

'You're a cruel wicked girl.'

'If you're not nice to me, it'll be the day after tomorrow.'

He stood up, safely pocketing the ring. 'Well. Couldn't I even have a kiss?'

Sideways, tentatively, as she was used to do in the days before the era of grace, Mary submitted a very sweet but very Artemisian cheek. His lips nearly cornered the little horned thing in its bed; but Mary jumped away. And now as they stood and laughed at each other, the thing said privately to Lessingham: 'Yes. A cruel wicked girl. Unpardonable. But what poverty of riches if she wasn't!'

It was ten of the clock in the forenoon, of Wednesday the fifteenth of July, in the lieutenant's house at Reisma. The master of the house was from home. The home-men and women were out in the fields along the lakeside, making hay. Under the sun's heat the house stood deserted, save only for its mistress, lazing herself on a bench of precious asterite stone under the cool of an open trellis of vines before the fore-court. Cushions made soft the bench for her reclining. Campaspe sat at her feet, holding up to her a mirror framed in pale mountain-gold garnished with sparks of small diamonds, sparks of aquamarines, and sparks of emeralds. Anthea, sitting sideways on the back of the bench, was fanning her mistress with a fan of white peacock-feathers which, at every to and fro, altered their sheen like a halo about the moon. The fingernails of Anthea tapered to claws: her hair seemed as lighted from within with a sun-like glory: white-skinned she was, of a classic cold perfection of form and feature, yet with eyes the pupils of which were upright slips opening to some inside hotness of fire, and with scarlet lips which disclosed, when she smiled, teeth of a mountain lynx. Behind Campaspe, there leaned against a pillar of the trellis-work that ancient doctor, resting, as in the contemplation of things of a higher strain than earth's, his regard upon the lady of the house.

'Signor Vandermast,' said she, 'it is now well onward in summer, and the days are hot and long. The Duke of Zayana, his eyes over-gazed in my excellencies, ceases not to solicit me in the unlawful purpose. My jealous husband sleeps dog-sleeps. Cool me a little, I pray you, with your unemptiable fountain of wisdom, and tell me why must I (being that I am) be teased with these inconveniences?'

'Why will your ladyship ask me such a question?' replied the doctor, 'to which You (being that you are) are Yourself the alonely one and unsoilable answer.'

'That answer,' said she, 'I could have had at any time this fort-night past, and without the asking: from his grace, who, as my true lover and humble servitor unguerdoned, is become to be as melancholy as a gib-cat. But I will not have lovers' answers, nor courtiers' answers, but an answer in philosophy.'

'Mine was an answer in philosophy, madam; not sustentable, indeed, in the very point of logic, but as by fingerly demonstration: as we term it, a probation ostensive. And it is the only answer.'

'Which, being unhooded, is to retort the whole upon poor me?' She reached an idle hand to pluck one of the moonlight-coloured feathers from Anthea's fan; considered curiously for a minute its shifting sheen. 'O wherefore hath nature made the lawful undelightful?'

'There,' replied the learned doctor, 'I can none otherways but reject your major premise, which is but the empiric's judgement of imperfect laws, imperfect delights. When we have justly conceived the infinite nature or being of the Godhead – *infinitam Die atque Deae existentiam* – conceived it, that is to say, *sub specie aeternitatis*, we see that it doth altogether transcend this nice and frivolous distinction of the good and the beautiful. In this world, the good is that which serves the beautiful. And if there be any world where it is not so, then that is a bad world.'

'I could imagine such a world,' she said, stroking the feather to and fro softly across her knees. 'You, signor, who are reputed perfect in your knowledge of all sciences and disciplines, able by your wisdom to unwrap the hid causes of things, and are besides a severe man, eschewing all sensual pleasures – can you unriddle me this: why must I, being that I am, have a body?' The silence hovered, listening to a bee's intermittent buzz and stillness among the jessamine blooms.

'I can answer but with the same answer again; desiring your ladyship but look yourself again in your self-loving glass. Some there be that have fantasied philosophical probabilities of a certain ὕλη, a *prima materia* or brute matter, wherein (as they feign) do all corporeal beings consist, and of a spirit able to inform or transhape that matter to significant being. But far be it such under-age arguments should intrude themselves into God's divine mysteries; the key whereunto, to shut and unshut, is in the blessed endless duality in onehead of substance and Godhead, whereby Beauty and Omnipotency are paired together.'

'Omnipotency: Beauty,' said she, turning the feather this way, that way, in her fingers, watching its coruscations of pallid many-coloured fires in an ever changing changelessness glimmer and fade and gleam again: 'Substance: Godhead: Duality: Matter: Spirit. A jargle of words to cast up dust betwixt us and things true and perfect, as the sun shines through white clouds, unclear. Signifying (I suppose, if you will come to the point), that God Himself is not self-perfect, and therefore He made Me?'

The doctor regarded her for a minute in silence. 'Yes,' he said. 'Schoolmen use these terms of generality as a kind of shorthand, to bear us in mind that large expression whereby it were partly possible the works of God might be comprehended in man's wit or reason. Your ladyship and that Other – He, the great Father of All – have so many countenances in Your variety that a man should as well seek to fit a garment to the moon as to set forth by enumeration of particularities the infinite nature of Gods. For instance, we speak of the Quesmodian Isles: say, "There be nine little islands on a row." "Islands": it is but a pointer only: a plucking of you by the sleeve, in order that you may consider them together and severally in their manifold, unique, and undividable verity: this birch-tree, this twig, this bird on the twig, this white cloud, this breath of wind that brushes the marrams like hair, this dew-snail, this bubble in this well-spring, this grain of sand, unlike all other, and yet bearing likeness to all other. Even so, in a more august generality, we speak of Beauty; comprehending under that style all that, on this orbicular ball, is affined with your ladyship, or derived from your ladyship, or conducing to your ladyship's pleasure.'

Fiorinda nodded: scarce discernible, the very shadow of a nod. 'And therefore He made Me?' Her voice, suffering itself to vanish down the silence as down slow irrevocable unpathed waters of Lethe, seemed to leave on the air a perfume, a breath, a deep assurance, redolent of all lost loved things since time began, or the stars of heaven were made and the constellations thereof. 'Me, created so consummately perfect that nought there is in earth or heaven that He thinks worthy to suit Me (being so superfine) but alone to reign? – Well, it was commendable!'

The stillness waited again on the bee in the jessamine flowers. 'I would dearly like,' she said, 'to be eavesdropper at some of your discourses with the Duke your master. Have you taught him the things a prince ought to eschew? As doting of women?'

'My Lady Fiorinda,' Vandermast replied very soberly, 'I have taught him this: to know the perfect when he shall see it.'

'So that his coming hither but yesterday, most peacockly strained to the height of your philosophy and at an undue hour of eleven o'clock in the night (my husband being from home), was with purpose, I suppose, to have grounded me in that same lesson? – Mew!' she said, 'I sent him away with no other book to read in than my unclasped side. Did I well so?'

'Everything that your ladyship does or ever shall do, is done well. You cannot, of your nature, do other.'

Her mouth sweetened and hardened again as she considered herself: first, reflected in Campaspe's looking-glass, the image of her face; next in the reposure of most soft content sweetly stretched along that couch, the rest. 'What a hell of witchcraft lies in woman's body,' she said. 'Body and head together, I mean. As aqua fortis by itself, nor vitriol by itself, hath no virtue against gold; but mix them, you have aqua regia. And that hath a virtue to consume and dissolve away even very gold itself.'

'Yet do I know a man,' said the doctor, 'compact of such metal as even Your alkahest, madam, shall not dissolve nor consume. As the ruby, which, when it cometh out of the fire uncorrupt, becometh and remaineth of the colour of a burning coal.'

'And I,' said that lady, and again in the honey-sweet cadence of each slowed word an echo sounded, faint, uncertain, full of danger, bitter-sweet: sea-sounds from a timeless shore: 'And I do begin to know him, I think, too: a man who is fingering for more of me than God allows him. And, I do almost begin to think,' said she, 'one who will gang till he gets it.'

Shadows were lengthening when Lessingham and Mary turned for home. It was the time of day when the sun, no longer using the things of earth as things to be trod under and confounded in a general down-beating of white light from above, inclines instead almost to a companionship with them. In that mood, the sun had now singled out, like treasures each by itself, each tree, each broad-eaved weather-browned chalet, each fold or wrinkle of the hillside, each bend of each goat-track, each stone, each littlest detail of the far-reared mountain faces, each up-turned flower; until each, washed in golden air, rested picked out as a thing both perfect in itself and making up with all things else in the landscape a more large perfection: perfection bearing but this spot, endemic in all perfections of earth, that in time they pass.

They came down by a track that kept high in the sunshine under the cliffs of the Sella, then dropped steeply through woods to join their path of the morning a few minutes above the inn at Plan. The barn where, on their way up, hearing the thud of wooden flails, they had seen a young man and a girl at work threshing, stood empty now; but the dusty smell hung yet about it of corn and husk. The white walls of the inn were gay with paintings of flower-shapes and shell-shapes and, between the windows above the porch, of the Virgin and Child and holy men. A fatal accident that morning, the girl at the inn told them, on the Fünffingerspitze: a herr and his guide: in the Schmidt Kamin. The bodies had been brought down to Canazei, the far side of the pass. She had heard

about it from Hansl Baumann, the chamois hunter. Herr Lessingham
would remember him: had they not hunted together, a year, two
years, since? Lessingham, as they went on again, felt Mary's arm
twine itself in his.

Evening drew on apace. Their path crossed the bridge and joined
the road, down which in a straggling slow procession cows were
coming back from the alp: a dwindling procession; for at each
house or turning, as they drew near the village, one or another
would drop out of line of her own accord and leisurely, of her
own accord, come home for milking. The goats too, undriven,
came taking each her own way home. Evening was sweet with the
breath of the cows, cool after the heat of the day, and full of
music: a many-pitched jangling music of cow-bell and goat-bell
in a hundred indeterminate drowsy rhythms. At one of the corners
a child, three years old perhaps, stood expectant. A goat stopped
came to him: paused while he gave her a hug with both arms
about her neck: then, still in that embrace, turned with him down
the path to a little poor house beside the river. Lessingham and
Mary, lingering to enjoy this idyll, saw how a girl, littler even than
the little boy, came from the house, staggering under the load of
an open wooden box or trough which she carried in her arms and
set down at last for the goat to eat. While she was eating, both
these children hugged and kissed her.

Urgently, like something lost, Mary's hand felt its way into his.

'What, my darling?'

'What you said this morning: about feeling double inside.'

'Yes?'

To change suits? I believe that's part of it, don't you think?'

'Change suits?'

'Colours. King of Hearts: Queen of Spades. How silly that we
can't, well – change dresses.'

'Queen of Spades? Good heavens, I would never change you!'

'O yes. You'd give your soul for it sometimes. Instead of *Le
Lys Rouge*, *La Tulipe Noire*. When you are in that frame of mind.'

'My darling, that is not me.'

'Don't be too sure. Somebody else in your skin, then. O yes;

and when I'm in the mood, indeed I prefer that somebody else to you, my friend!'

Lessingham was silent. Turning to go, they lingered yet a minute or two to watch the sunset on the Sella: a transformation at once more theatrical and more unearthly than that illusion of immaterial substantiality which the mountain had produced at breakfast-time. Hardly credible it seemed, that here was but, as in Alpine sunsets, an illumination of the rocks from without. Eyesight was witness against it, watching the whole vast train of storeyed precipices transformed to a single fire-opal, transparent, lighted from within by a quivering incandescence of red fire.

In a few minutes it was gone: swallowed up, as in the rising tide of a dead sea, by the rising shadow of night. Lessingham said, 'Do you remember sailing up to the Westfirth, past Halogaland, those sunsets on the Soundway? Not this burning inside. But they stayed.'

'For a time. But they went. They went at last.' The pallours that are between sunset and nightfall lay ashen on Mary's face, as on the face of the Sella. 'Even the Sella,' she said, 'must not even that go at last? Though we ourselves go too soon and too quickly to notice it.'

'Gods, I suppose, might notice it: see it, as we see the sunset go. If there were such a thing as Gods. Yes, it goes. All goes. And never comes back,' he said. Adding, with a sudden tang of waspish-headed discordous humour in his voice, 'How dull and savourless if it were otherwise!'

He looked round at her: saw, through the dusk, a faint lifting, like the wings of a sea-swallow in flight, of her eyebrows, and a faint mockery which, dragonflyish, here and away, darted across her lips. It was as if night and all the dark earth rose to her, upon a hunger of unassuageable desire.

Lessingham next morning opened his eyes to a greenish luminosity: spears of radiance and spears of shadowiness, all of a geometrical straightness, here vertical, there horizontal, there bent at obtuse angles and extending themselves away out of sight over his head:

all very still. And all very quiet; except for a continuous under-sound, like rain or like running water, saying to him, deliriously, lullingly, almost as with articulate speech: 'Do not think. Do not know in what bed and in what room you are waking, or in what country. Do not wake. Shut eyes again. Snuggle the bed-clothes up round your ears: burrow your cheek into the pillow. So, with all senses abandoned to the touch of the owl-feathered wings of sleep, which, moving hoverly about you, wake what thoughts will be wakened and lull the rest, your self may taste for a while, unstrung, inert, unattached, the pure sensual beatitude of its own slumber.

'Slumber of the spirit, green and still. From depths deeper than these light-beams can wade, every now and then a bubble is released, floats upward, distinct and perfect, touches the glasslike ceiling, bursts, and is gone. So: in irregular slow procession, like cows at evening. This Tyrolean dance, gay mountain-bred, dancing to the blood: danced, it is quite true, "to saucily" by these dancers from Vienna. Madame de Rosas rising through it, effacing it, Spanish and statuesque, upon a long tremolo of castanets: Mary listening, watching: Mary at Anmering: Mary under the pine-tree, and across her face, tesselated patterns weaving and unweaving of white sunshine and luminous jewelled shadows: grasshoppers on the hot slopes under the Sella, uttering – for whom if not for her? – their lily-like voice. Thunder-smoke of Troy burning:

ἔσσεται ἦμαρ ὅτ᾽ ἄν ποτ᾽ ὀλώλη Ἴλιος ἱρή
καί Πρίαμος καί λαός ἐϋμελίω Πριάμοιο·

The day shall come when holy Ilios shall fall,
    And Priam and the folk of Priam of the good ashen spear:

the slack weight in your arms beside the Struma: poor old Fred: like you, born for a fighter, beserk taint, brothers in blood: "Strike thunder and strike loud when I farewell": thud of shells bursting, whining of them in the air: but the thinness, the shrivelled lack of actuality – was it all for this? – of the actual fact: of the end:

trying to say something: bubbling of red froth between his front teeth: rattle of machine-guns – peas in a pig's bladder: no, castanets. Castanets, and the red camellia in that woman's hair: sense-maddening colubrine slow swaying and rolling of her hips: white of her eyes: smoothness of her hair: peace. Peace, in the velvet night of this single sapphire that carries in its dear unrest all these things and their swaying rhythms. It goes. All goes. All except Mary. Mary: always on the point to be caught, but never quite. Her galloping hoof-beats: like castanets. Kelling Heath and the awakening earth taking life from her life. The morning of life: the entry, upon pizzicato throbs, of that theme (which is Mary) of the Grand Variation in the C sharp minor quartet, Queen of Queens, unutterable treasure of all hearts: things deep in time crowding to her, forming new earths to take their arms about her, new earths to be born and gone again and forgotten again at each throb of her footsteps. "Perhaps my answer is sufficient, sir, if I say 'Because it amuses me'?" The crimson of her mouth: crimson gloves: her white skin: that same matter which, asleep or awake, resides near the corner of Mary's mouth: Mary, but with this blackness: Ninfea de Nerezza—'

So, of all these bubbles the slow last. At its touch, the glasslike ceiling trembled: tore like a garment: opened like a flower to a heaven unascended and unsullied of sunwarmed snows; and in the midst as it were a black flame to shine down the sun, and sweep up all senses in a moth-like wind-rushing blindness against that unspectable glory.

Wide awake, he leapt from his bed, flung open the green shutters, let in the white floods of sunshine. His watch on the chest of drawers said ten. He rang for his bath and, while it was getting ready, put the final touches to some lines he had written last thing before going to bed, on a half sheet of paper that lay on the top of a pile of manuscript and notes which he had been working over up till about three that morning.

Twenty minutes, and he had bathed and dressed. Then his eye fell for the first time on the envelope that lay on the bedside table. Her writing. He had slept late, and it was not his door that had been locked. Nether Wastdale paper: this morning's date, twenty-fifth of June:

Mon ami,

I've told Herr B. that we may or may not be back in a few days: meanwhile to keep the rooms. If you happened to be serious in the compliment you paid me yesterday on the Sella Pass, asking me to marry you, you know where to look for

Your Mary.

Lessingham, holding that letter in his hand, wore for one fleeting instant the aspect of a dog whose teasing mistress has made the motion to throw him the ball to run for, but has in fact teasingly retained it concealed in her hand. Next moment, in an up-bursting of volcanic mud-springs of black anger, his fist leapt up. He checked it in mid-air, and stood leaning his whole weight upon clenched hands on the table top: motionless, silent, only that once he growled like the Wolf fettered. The audience to whom alone these naked antics were uncurtained – the four walls of that room, clothed in their wallpaper of unaspiring design, the round-seated bentwood chairs, the harmless table, the floor-boards having in their faint smell of soap a certain redolence of conscious respectability, the plain green rug by the bed, the green and white striped one by the wash-stand, and the innocent morning sunshine that pleasantly companioned them all – looked on with comfortingly unseeing gaze.

He sprang erect, the look in his eye a boy's look on a hunting morning; locked away the writing materials in his portmanteau, and kicked it back under the bed: laughed silently at himself in the looking-glass: flung a few things together into a suitcase; and went leisurely down to breakfast. Within an hour he was driving down the valley to Waidbrück. And all the way, not to be shaken off, now dim, now loud, now lost for an instant, now near again, and wild hunting-music, winding and swelling in secret woods and heady-scented unpathed darknesses, led the hunt through

marrow and veins. He caught the train at Waidbruck; and about
five o'clock that evening, thanks to his native mastery in sweeping
away difficulties, to the inspired resourcefulness of Herr Birkel,
and to a reckless use of telegraph and telephone, took off from
Verona in a private aeroplane belonging to Jim's brother-in-law,
Nicholas Mitzmesczinsky.

With neither train nor boat connexions to hamper him, nor delays
of Sunday services, he landed, less than twenty-five hours after his
start from Verona. His man David, instructed by telegram, was
waiting with the car: coachman in the family like his father and
grandfather before him, with (of late, under protest and because
needs must) part-time transformations to chauffeur. Lessingham
took the wheel. It was – for a driver reckless and violent – two
hours' drive home.

Evening, as the car swung in at the drive gates, was beginning
with a spring-like freshness in the air after a showery day. The
Wastwater Screes, purplish black, stood against a confusion of
grey-brown rain-clouds which blundered pell-mell southeastwards
overhead. Riding higher than these and with a less precipitate
haste, billowy masses of a pale indigo hue swept over from the
west and north; and, like windows in heaven, rifts opened and
widened one after another to quiet sublimities of white cumulus
far above the turmoil and, above these again, of the ultimate sky
itself; rain-washed to a purity of most limpid and tender azure:
windless, immeasurably remote.

On the steps before the front door stood old Ruth: installed
now as housekeeper at this manor house of Nether Wastdale, but
still wearing cap and apron, as from years ago she had done, when
she had had charge, as nurse, of Lessingham and of all his brothers
and sisters before him.

'Well, Ruth,' giving her the key of his suitcase which had gone
round to the back door, 'you got my telegram?'

'Yes, sir.'

'Any news from her ladyship?'

'No, sir. Nothing so far.'

'She'll be here tomorrow. Miss Janet asleep?'

'Ay, she is: heavenly lamb. Jessie'll put out your things, in the dressing-room as soon as I just unlock the lobby door upstairs, sir. Everything's ready there according to standing orders.'

'No, I'll not sleep there tonight. The small room at the end of the west gallery tonight. O and, Ruth,' he called her back. 'You understand – they all understand, do they? Not a word to her ladyship when she arrives, about my being here first.'

'No, sir.'

'Don't let there be any mistake about it.'

'No, sir.'

'Right. I'll dine in the Refuge.'

'Yes, sir.' The old woman hesitated. Something, some obscure throbbing perhaps in the air about him of that gay hunting-music, obviously eased her mind. 'Please sir, if so happen her ladyship puts me the straight question, will you have me to tell her ladyship a falsehood, Mr Edward, sir?'

'What you've got to do, my dear Ruth, is not to let on and spoil the game. If you can't do that much, without telling a downright fib, you're not the woman I've known you for.'

'Mr Edward was always one to have his joke,' she said to David later.

'Ay, and her ladyship's a one too, bless her. But what beats me's his rampaging round with them there dang'd aeroplanes: hating and cursing 'em like he do, it's a caution. If he goes and breaks his neck one of these days, I'd be right sorry.'

'What'd you do then, David?'

'Reckon I'd have to find a new situation.'

'Like this?'

'Ay.'

'Is there one, think you?'

'May be not.'

'Back to Mr Eric's at Snittlegarth?'

'Not at my time of life! Mr Edward's a bit rough-like sometimes. But Mr Eric, when he's in his tantrums, they do say as these days he's nobbut a stark staring madman.'

'Where'd you go, then, David?'

'To that there Jackson Todd's.'

'That's good! Why, he's dead now, be'n't he?'

'Another like him, then. That's your gentleman nowadays. Got the brass, all right: but no better 'n a regular black card. I've see'd him at a shoot, over on them moors far side of Mungrisdale, afore Mr Eric took 'em over. Did himself main well over his lunch, he did: had about a quart of champagne, he did. And there he were, a-yawkening and a-bawkening like a regular black card.'

The same night Lessingham, in his way to bed, paused at the top of the wide staircase. With his master-key, that lived under the bezel of the ring on his left hand, he unlocked the lobby door on the right there, and went in. At the end of the lobby another doorway, doorless and heavily curtained, led into the Lotus Room: a room forty or fifty feet in length, newly built out upon the east wing of this old house. At the ends, west and east, were tall windows, and high-mantled open fire-places between them. Since its building, three years ago, few had set eyes on this bedchamber, or on the porphyry and onyx bathrooms or the dressing-room or Lessingham's great studio, upon which a door opened in the north wall, to the left of the bed: a four-posted bed, spread wide and of great magnificence, with hangings and coverlets of heavy bay-green figured silk and sweet-smelling pillars of sandalwood inlaid with gold. Candles, by scores, stood ready for lighting, upon tables and mantelshelves and in sconces on the walls; but at present the only light in the room was of electric bulbs, concealed in the chandeliers of crystal that, like clusters of gigantic globular fruits, hung from the ceiling.

Pausing in the doorway, he leisurely overwent the room with his eyes, as a man might some matter which he partly disbelieves. The ring, key exposed, was still in his hand: Mary's wedding-present, of massive gold having no alloy in it, in the shape of a scaled worm, tail in mouth, and the head of the worm the bezel of the ring, a ruby of great age and splendour: the worm Ouroboros, symbol of eternity, the beginning of which is also the end, and the end the beginning. And now, coming to the fire-place over against the bed, he unlocked with that key the doors of a cabinet set in the chimney-breast above the mantel and, gently, needfully, as an artist traces a curve, opened them left and right. Backing a few paces, he sat down on the sofa at the bed's foot and considered the picture thus disclosed.

And so it was presently, as if the picture spoke. As to say: In me, a portrait, constructed by you, upon canvas, with pigments ground in oil, some limited perduration is in a shorthand way, given to a fleeting moment. Looking at me, remember in your eye, in your ear, in your nostril, in your secret blood, what was present in that moment; and then, by all these senses under the might that is in you forced together, remember what was not present, nor shall be. Never present. Ever on the doorstep – *L'Absente de tous bouquets.*

To Lessingham now, sitting so in his contemplation, it was as if in the edge of his field of vision the carved lotuses of the frieze, under the hot flame of that picture bared, stirred slightly. The rude hunger of the flesh was become, as wind at night sets stars a-sparkle, the undistinguishable integument of some spiritually informing presence: of a presence which, so in the picture as in life, with a restful deep unrest underlay each perfection of the body. And in a strange violent antinomy, the alone personality of Mary, that, serene and unalterable, queened it in every feature of the face – more, in the whole deep indwelling music of body and limb – seemed, by some fiery intermarriage of incompatibles, to take into this particular self that universal, which unhorizoned as sea-spaces at morning or as the ocean of cloud-waves overseen from on high in the faint first incarnadine of a new dawn, rested its infinity in these nakednesses of breast, of flank, of somnolent exquisite supple thigh, and in these sudden mindblinding dazzlements of curled hair shadowing the white skin. All which unspeakable whole, out of the paint and out of the awaked remembrance, said: Would you have Me otherwise? Me, always here? given you without the sweat and the agony and the birth-pang of the mind? – No, my friend. Not in Elysium even.

For, said the picture (and said the painter, to himself, out of himself), passivity is not for you: not for any man. – For a woman? Well, a species of passivity: the illusion, perhaps, of stillness, as at the maelstrom's center. A passivity that rests in its own most deep assurance of queenship over all overt power. A queenship that subsists even in its vertiginous climacteric of self-surrender:

> A quiet woman
> Is a still water under a great bridge;
> A man may shoot her safely.

Mary, from her sleeping-carriage, arrived like day on the little lonely platform at Drigg about half past six the next morning: the sun in her eyes, sea-swallows' voices in her ears, and heady northern sea-smells salt in her nostrils. 'Leave it in the office, Tom. They'll come and fetch it this afternoon.'

'Yes, your ladyship,' said the porter, putting her things on his barrow. He, and in turn the station-master who took her ticket, and the girl doing the steps at the inn, for each of whom she had a happy familiar word as she passed, stood a moment to gaze after her with the estranged look of woodland creatures in whose faces a fire has been brandished suddenly out of the dark.

It was a sweet morning: fields still wet, and lanes smelling all the way of wild roses and honeysuckle, with now and then heavier luscious wafts from the meadowsweet and sometimes the pungent breath of the golden whin-flowers. So she walked home, seven or eight miles or so, swinging her hat in her hand for pleasure of the air.

Schooled, doubtless, to these ways, a well ordered household respectfully abstained from telling her that he was there first, and in fact now in his bath. And Mary for her part reading, doubtless, Ruth's too readable eyes, asked no questions. Only she remarked (falsely true) that the master had missed his train on Saturday morning, and would, it was to be feared, not be home till tomorrow. And so, resignedly, ordered her breakfast in the Refuge with Sheila. And was, resignedly, eating it when Lessingham came down.

And he, doubtless no less ready to take his cue, watched her for a minute, himself unseen, as, bending her white neck, she rested, chin in hand, in a beautifulness, so self-sufficing, a contemplation so remote and so chill, as it had been some corruptless and timeless divinity, having upon Her (since spirit must corporal be) the habit of woman's body, and for a small moment come down so.

IX

NINFEA DI NEREZZA

IT was high morning beside Reisma Mere, of Tuesday the twenty-first of July, with the shadows yet long, and with heavy dews that made lace shawls of the gossamer-spiders' weavings on hedge and wayside plant. Doctor Vandermast, walking his alone, came at unawares in a turn of the path upon the Duke his master. The Duke's back was towards him; he was in riding gear, and sat, facing away from Reisma, on a trunk of a fallen ash-tree, his horse grazing untethered in the brake near at hand. He was bare-headed, and the sun lighted a smoulder as of copper heating to redness in his short crisp-waved hair. Upon the doctor's good-morrow he turned with a black look that relented in the turning.

'Your grace is become since but one short month to be as lean and as melancholic as a stag in autumn.'

'Instance, then, of like effects worked by direct opposite causes.'

Vandermast sat him down on the trunk, not too close but so he might at ease observe Barganax when he would: countenance and bearing. 'It is but in the merest outwards and superficies that the effects are like. Inwardly, as is sufficiently demonstrated in the treatise *De Libertate Humana, Propositio XXX*, the mind, in so far as it understandeth itself and its body *sub specie aeternitatis*, to that extent hath it of necessity an understanding of God, *scitque se in Deo esse et per Deum concipi*: knoweth itself to exist in God, and to be conceived through God. And so, by how much the zenith standeth above the nadir, by so much more excellent is it to be a man unsatisfied than a four-footed beast satisfied.'

The Duke let out a bitter laugh. 'I must call you mad, doctor.'

'How so?'

'If you hope to reason with a madman. And, seeing you are mad, and safe so to talk nothings to, here's a piece of madman's wisdom came to me out of the suffocations that serve 'stead of air in these suburbs of hell, woman-infected watersides of Reisma, which 'cause I'm mad I turn from but still to return to, as the moth do the candleflame—

> Answere me this You Gods above:
> What's lecherie withouten Love?—
> A thinge less maym'd (They answer'd mee)
> Than maym'd were Love sans lecherie.'

'In a mad world,' said the doctor, 'that should be accounted madness indeed. For, albeit not so well declared as a great clerk can do, yet hath it the reach of unmutable truth; which is whole ever, and of that wholeness paradoxical, and of that paradoxicalness ever a thing that rides double. But the mad will ne'er content till he shall have patterned out to his own most mathematical likings the unpeerable inventions of God, which are the fundament and highest cornerstones of the world universal, both of the seen and of the unseen.'

'Invent some business shall make it needful I go home today to Zayana.'

Vandermast noted the proud and lovely face of him: haggard now and unspirited, as if he had watched some nights out without sleep. 'If your grace hath a will to go, what (short of the King's very command) shall stay or delay you?'

'My own will, which will not will it, unless forced by some outward urgence. I will yet will not. Unforced, I'll not go: not alone.'

They sat silent. Vandermast saw the Duke's nostril widen and a strained stillness of intention overtake the bended poise of his head and face. He looked where the Duke looked. Upon a head of lychnis, that flaming herb, a yard or more beyond Barganax's foot above a bed of meadowsweet, a butterfly rested, in a quivering soft unrest, now opening now closing again her delicate wings. White and smooth were her wings, as ivory; and ever and again at their spread-eagling set forth to the gaze panther-black splashes exquisitely shaped like hearts. It was as if into the sunshine stillness of morning a heat welled up, out of the half-uncased tremulous beauties of that creature and out of the flower's scarlet lip, open, amid leaves and so many frislets of tangled fragrancies.

'You in your time, I in mine,' said the doctor after a while, 'have wandered in the voluptuous broad way, the common labyrinth of love. We have approved by experiment the wise lesson of the Marchioness of Monferrato, when with a dinner of hens and certain sprightly words she curbed the extravagant passion of the King of France.'

'A dinner of hens?'

'Signifying *per allegoriam* that even as the so many divers and delectable dishes set before him were each one of them (save for variety of sauces and manner of presentation) nought but plain hen, so, in that commodity, all women are alike. It were well to be certified that it be not but that thing come up again. As the poet saith—

> Injoy'd no sooner but dispised straight,
>   Past reason hunted, and, no sooner had,
>   Past reason hated, as a swollow'd bayt
>   On purpose layd to make the taker mad;
>   Mad in pursuit and in possession so;
>   Had, having, and in quest to have, extreame;
>   A blisse in proofe, and, prov'd, a very wo;
>   Before, a joy proposed; behind, a dreame.'

Barganax, elbow on knee, chin in hand, lips compressed, sat on so when Vandermast had ended, as if weighing it, tasting it profoundly: all very still. When at length he spoke it was softly,

as to his own self retired into the secretary of his heart. 'Truth's
mintage,' he said: 'that's most certain. But that's but the reverse
side. Turn the coin, so: the obverse—

> Here, where all else is fair, I call thee fairest:
> Were the rest foul, foulest of all thou'dst be:
> So faithfully Love's livery thou wearest,
> Which art of all the rest the epitome.
> Virtues deifical, devils'-milk of wit,
> Eye-bite, maidenly innocence demure—
> No proud and lovely quality but it
> Jewels thine enchantments with its essence pure.
> O best of best, that else were worst of worst,
> Love's prelibation is to kiss thee first.

– And the obverse,' he said, rising to his feet to stand staring over
Vandermast, like a leopard at gaze, toward Reisma and the clear-
faced morning, 'is where the principal design is struck.' He looked
down: met the doctor's eye upon him. 'Well?'

Vandermast shook his head. 'Nay, I find I have trained up your
grace to be so good a metaphysician, there's no step further in the
argument. Thesis and antithesis, these be the leaved doors of truth.
Philosophy can but show us them: unlock them; may be, set them
open for us; but, that being done, it is for ourselves, each soul of
us alone, to pass through and see, each for himself, without all
guide or perspective-glass to clear the eye if it be purblind. What
should a man do with a weapon,' he said after a moment's pause,
'that knoweth not how to use it? There is a He and a She, and a
habitude of Them both, which we would have called the love, the
union, or the kindness of Them. As Their rule is infinite, Their
pleasures are unconfined.'

The Duke whistled his mare: she left feeding, whinnied, and
came to him, delicately over the dew-bedangled grass. In the saddle
he paused, then with some tormenting imp of self-mockery dancing
in his eye, 'You have done me no good,' he said holding out a
hand to the learned doctor: 'left me where I was. O Vandermast,'

he said, gripping the hand of that old man, 'I am plagued to bursting. To bursting, Vandermast.'

The aged doctor, looking up at him against the blue, beheld how the hot blood suffused all his face with crimson: beheld the hammering of it in his temples and in the great veins of his neck. 'And blackness,' said the Duke betwixt his teeth, 'is the badge of hell.'

He shook his reins and rode off, a kind of unresolved unwilling pace: not the road to Zayana.

My Lady Fiorinda was abroad too that morning a-horse-back. At the footbridge by the lake, where six days ago the learned doctor had talked with his water-rat, she came face to face with the Duke. She had walked her horse down to the edge of the stream to water it: he upon the western bank did the like. Three yards of stilled water parted them, and their horses drank at the same stream.

'Fortunately met. I was come to give your ladyship the farewell.'

'Farewell fieldfare?' said she upon a little eloquency of declension of her head. 'But is not this an odd up-tails-all procedure: farewell at meeting?'

'No: at parting.'

She rejoindered with but a satirical flicker of the nostrils.

'I purpose this day,' he said, 'to go home to Zayana.'

'I'm sorry to hear it.'

'Let's talk truth for a change.'

'Pray your grace begin, then. It will amuse me to mark a difference.'

'Truth is, I begin to change my mind as touching your ladyship.'

'Excellent. For indeed I feared you were settling so heavily into one mind on that subject as you should be in danger to become tedious to me.'

'And I do begin to think, madam, that you do think overwell of yourself.' The mere bodily fact of her retorted back the words in his teeth: lily-proud poise of head and neck; smooth sea-waved blackness of parted hair which from under the bediamonded back-turned edge of her riding-bonnet overlay her brow; hands crimson-gloved, resting lightly one on the slacked rein at her horse's withers, the other on the crupper; swell and fall, as upon an undermotion of two silver apples of unvalued price, of the satin bosom of her dress; green eyes full of danger; lips that seemed apt in many a quaint unused way to play at cherry-pit with Satan; all the gems of gentleness and tiger-nursed soft graces of her, each where woman may be kissed. 'I mean,' he said, 'as for leading me in a string. But I,' in a sudden gust of rage, seeing her little silent laugh, 'am not for ever to be fubbed off with lip-work.'

'Pew! What an ungratefulness and unwontness the man is grown unto!'

'Nor keep-your-distance far-away future promises.'

'Which your grace must think very unnatural, and therefore unwholesome, for a prince. Well? Saying is cheap. What will you do, then?'

'And again last night: coming 'pon appointment, and, of all monstrous betrayals, after long attending your leisure in the gallery, to find you private with Morville.'

'With whom shall a careful housewife lawfully be private, then, if not with her lawful husband? To be honest, I was curious to observe you together: how you would behave.'

'A player of mummeries, you think, for your ladyship's entertainment?'

'Why not, if I choose? The better, since you can play the Furioso so lively.'

'Well, good-bye,' said the Duke. He gathered the reins and sat a moment, switching his boot with his riding-whip, his eyes darkling upon her.

'Good-bye,' she said. 'Truth is,' she said, caressing thoughtfully with her right hand her horse about the crupper; and every unheeding motion of her finger seemed as a precious stone, some one of which is of more value than a whole kingdom: 'truth is, I grow tired of the follies of this court.'

Barganax's nostrils tightened.

'Besides, I find I am strangely falling in love with my husband.'

'You think I'll credit that?'

'No,' she said, and her voice lazed itself on the air in a poisony deliciousness that stings, blisters off the skin: 'for indeed you are in case to become blockisher even than he. Blockish in the way you make suit to me: in the presumption of your unmatchableness, chat of love. As if (like as your Bellafronts, Pantasileas, I know not what little loose-legged hens of the game) it should need but a "Madam, undress you and come now to bed."'

Barganax, as struck doubly in the face betwixt such accordances to discord, but caught in his breath and remained staring at her in silence.

'You put me to forget a lady's manners. But indeed and you shall find, my lord Duke (were it to come to that indeed), loving of me is not a play nor a prittle-prattle.'

The fine thread of continual flickering provocations seemed to strain and prevail past all supposed breaking-points between him and that seeming woman: a twine or twist-line, alternate of gold and fire, made fast with little grappling-hooks sharp and harder than diamond-stone to the web, secret within him of blood and spirit. 'Well,' said he. 'When next I see your ladyship I shall look to find you in a more tractable mood.'

'You will not find me. I too purpose to go away.'

'And whither, if it be permissible to inquire?'

'If I answered that, where were the good of going?' The thing that nested by her imperial lips set up its horns at him, special pricks and provokements to ecstasy and anguish.

The blood left his face. 'Go, then,' he said. 'And the Devil tear you in pieces.' He jagged at his mare's mouth, who, uncustomed to such usage, swerved, spun round upon her hindlegs full circle, and bore him away at a gallop.

The lady, for her part, sat on for a minute, watching till the last glimpse of him vanished in trees at a quarter-mile's distance. Mean time the Lord Morville, himself conveniently aspying her from a hiding-place among the alders, had ocular proof how that thing, which had not in all those fourteen weeks of unmatrimonial matrimony so much as cast him a chipping, sat up now to gaze after Barganax in a veiled merriment that seemed to accept as by nature some secret league betwixt them, what unbefits a mind to search into. As amid great fireballs of lightning he sat mute.

But violet-crowned Kythereia, Daughter of Zeus, turned Her thoughts to other things. May be She noted his presence, may be not. Gathering her reins, she turned homeward, guiding her horse not to trample a flower that grew at the shady foot of the bank beside her: a kind of hill poppy, having a saffronish mounded centre and frosty-furred leaves, and the petals of it delicate frills of that pallid yellow that tinges the moon when first it begins to take colour after sunset.

X

The Lieutenant of Reisma

MORVILLE, his lady being gone, fetched his horse that he had tethered in a spinney hard by, and, as best for the unbenumbing of his thoughts, came his way at a slow walking-pace not homeward but north-westward toward Memison. A big man and strong he was and of good carriage, may be five and twenty years of age, proud of eye, clean shaven, with enough of boniness about his features to import masculinity in what had else been almost feminine for its transparency of skin, flaming red now as with furying of inward passions.

Coming upon the highway where it runs north under Memison castle and south toward Zayana, he was met with a courier on horseback who off-capped to him and handed him a letter. 'From my lord High Admiral, my lord, new come up but yestermorn from Sestola to Zayana and expected hourly today in Memison. I have delivered five more at the palace yonder.'

'To whom?' said Morville, undoing the seal.

'Count Medor. The lords Melates, Zapheles, and Barrian. One for his grace of Zayana.'

'Today to ride north,' said Morville in himself, reading Jeronimy's letter, 'for meeting of the King at Rumala, and as guard of honour to conduct him in his progress south to Sestola. That's spend tonight in Rumala.'

'You delivered them all?' he said aloud.

'All save my lord Duke's: he was ridden forth, they said, but expected back within the hour.'

Morville put up the letter, saying in himself, 'The formal phrase of it is invitation; but yet, the requests of King's men can be strong commands. If the Duke must go too, what danger in my going? Besides, 'tis a notable honour.'

'Good,' he said to the messenger: 'here's money. I've saved you your journey to Reisma. I'll attend my lord Admiral.'

The Duchess's use it was to keep late hours in Memison. So it was that few were astir this morning when Morville rode in, save the porter at the gate and some score or so of gardeners and household folk. He gave his horse to a horse-boy and, leaving the Duchess's summer palace on his right, came by way of the great gardens to the colonnade. Here, upon sound of a known voice, rasping and full of mockery, and, most catching of all, his own name striking through his ear, he stopped quickly, stepped aside into the thick leafage of a yew-tree against the north-west corner of the wall, and from that close bushment, listened.

It was Zapheles had spoken. Now Medor: 'Why might not he be called upon as fitly as you or me? He is lieutenant of Reisma.'

'Just: and by what principle of merit?'

'The man is noble: in all kind of civility well brought up.'

'I grant you. And a notable wise fellow until he speaks. This too I have marked: his garments do sit upon him must feater of late, since he is become the great Chancellor's brother-in-law.'

'Beware lest you become a common laughing-stock,' said Melates, making a third: 'wearing your ill will on your sleeve so much, when 'tis known you yourself did put in for that place.'

'What? Of brother-in-law?'

'Of Reisma.'

'I retail you but the ordinary chit-chat in Zayana. Women, Melates, are *mala necessaria*, stepping-stones to fortune in this world. Unless indeed, being well wedded, we be over jealous of 'em: there can be danger in that, a were wise to consider. Our sweet young Duke was not wont of old to dwell weeks together in's mother's court. 'Tis a bye-word now how my lord Chancellor—'

'I'll leave you,' said Medor shortly. Morville, withdrawn his most under the yew-tree, held in his breath while Medor flung out and past him within a yard.

The sound of their talk receded. Morville with stealth and circumspection came out of his hiding-place, and so fetching a circle back through the pleasance and round to the poplar-grove and lily-pond, waited a minute and so came openly over the lawns to the gate-house again: took horse there, and rode for home. Not so skilfully avoiding observation, howsoever, but that Medor, chancing to glance through a window on his way to the Duke's lodging, saw him go and the manner of his going.

Medor being admitted found the Duke his master sitting in his shirt, writing a letter. 'Your grace means to ride to Rumala?'

'No,' answered he, still writing.

Medor raised his eyebrows.

'Stand not on ceremony, good Medor, but sit you down. Eat a peach: peaches of Reisma.' Medor took one from the silver dish. 'They are freestone,' said the Duke, who held one half-eaten in his left hand while he wrote: 'easier to manage one-handed.' He ended his letter: signed it. 'Strike a light: I'll seal it,' he said, taking off his ring. 'You must take this letter, put it into the King's hand (Gods send he live for ever) with my love and duty. He will understand.'

'You will stay behind?' Medor lighted a candle. 'Do not.'

'Reach me the sealing-wax yonder. Why?'

'Tongues are at work already. Heaven forfend I should pry into your grace's secrets; but, if you are bent as they say—'

'"They say?" What say they? They have said. Let them say.'

'I do beseech you, dear my lord Duke, walk warily.'

Barganax with a delicate precision made a round of the melted wax and sealed the letter. He looked up in Medor's eye: a laughing look, but no more than thus far to be played with. He pushed the letter across the table to Medor. 'Well, well,' he said, 'speak on hardly. What's the matter?'

'Morville was here but now.'

The Duke shrugged his shoulders.

'Slinked in a hidden corner whence he overheard Zapheles talk broadly of these conjectures. I, leaving 'em, saw him couched there at eavesdropping. I think he misdoubted not of me, but supposed himself unobserved. Is gone now in a strange haste from Memison, as myself did see by chance from a window. I think a may be expected foully bent.'

'Pish!' said the Duke. 'I regard him not.'

'It is not for me to unease your grace. But if you are set to carry on in this course, as now the text of all talk is both here and in Zayana, I pray you think if it be not better deal with him first ere he in his raging motions let drive at you.'

Barganax said in a scorning, 'An eagle does not quarry upon flies. Moreover,' he said, 'your misgiving falls to nought by what's in that letter in your hand. Neither this nor Rumala sees me tonight. I am for Acrozayana.'

Morville, soon as come down from Memison into the highway that runs here under an overarching of ancient oak-trees, put his horse to a gallop. At the outfields of his own demesne of Reisma he leapt from saddle: tethered his horse: took a turn east-about through the woods, and so to a sunk lane betwixt hedges of hazel and beech and whitehorn and sloe, all overgrown with honeysuckle and that tangling white-starred weed called love-bind: so by a gap in the hedge into the mains, and privily by way of the apple orchard and the stable yard to the back of the house: so in: search the rooms: then up the back stairs, and, with a bounce, into his lady's chamber.

She was sat before her looking-glass, in her hair, and clad but in one under-frock without sleeves, of fine white silk broidered with Meszrian lace. The lieutenant checked for an instant, one hand upon the door-latch, as reft momentarily of thought and sense by the sudden dazzle of her beauty. She looked round at him. 'You might have knocked ere you came in. Leave is light.'

'You are alone, it seems.'

'Is that so strange?'

'I came but to acquaint you, madam, word's come this morning

I must with others north to the Ruyar, to bring the King's highness with a guard of honour down to Sestola. We are to meet him, and your noble brother and the Vicar too besides, it seemeth, tonight at Rumala: tomorrow, 'tis supposed, back to Memison. I'm loth to leave you,' he said, looking narrowly about the chamber. 'We ride an hour before noon.' He waited, then said, 'Are not you glad of this?'

'Why should I be glad or sorry?'

'This is an honour, their sending for me.'

'I'm glad, then.'

'I had rather you said "I care not" than such a poor frosty "I'm glad."'

'Since you prefer it, then, "I care not."'

'Has it ever bethought you,' he said, standing now in the window looking out, face averted, his fingers twisting and untwisting at his belt, 'seeing I love you and dote on you as the apple of my eye, that it were a small favour to wish you take some regard of me and my affairs? Even love me a little in return, perhaps, as honest wives commonly do the husband that so love and dote on them.'

'I see small virtue in that: to be so amorous and besotted on me. It is merely that you cannot otherwise choose.'

'It is a high and pure love,' said Morville, turning with the suddenest movingest strange humility. But Fiorinda but curled her lip, that carried no trace now of that seducing mouth-dweller, keeper of the stings and sweets of darkness, that, under Morville's jealous eye that same morning, had gazed after Barganax. 'A high and pure love? O manifestly so!' she said: 'breeding jealousy, jars, and complaints as a dunghill breeds slugs and flies and maggots.'

'Why will you be so odious and despiteful?'

'I have better cause to ask, why came you so unmannerly sudden but now into my bedchamber?'

'Why came the Duke to Reisma last night?'

'Ask him. How should I know?'

'His fashions displease. I like neither his carriage nor his company.'

'Well, tell him so, if you will. It concerns not me.'

'May fortune one day I will tell him. Mean time, this may concern you: had I found him in my house this morning, I would not a been in his best jerkin for twenty thousand ducats.'

She fell into a laughing. 'O husbands and brothers! The flattering tables of your pricings!' A flight of butterflies passed by the window on the breeze: an ever-changing curling train of seven or eight unstable scraps or motes of whiteness, wreathing and unwreathing and wreathing again on the sunlit air. 'What you have, you bought,' she said. 'Be content with what you paid for. But you bought not me. I am not for sale: least of all to little men. What have you to do with what visits time, but belongs to eternity?'

'You are his strumpet.' As if for the wasting of her heart's blood, Morville whipped out his dagger: then, as she rose up now and faced him, threw it down and stood, his countenance distort. There seemed to be shed suddenly about that lady a chill and a remoteness beside which a statue were companionable human flesh, and the dead marble's stillness kindly and human beside that stillness. He struck her across the mouth with his glove, saying, in that extreme, 'Go your gait, then, you salt bitch.'

Her face, all save the smouldering trail of that blow turned bloodless white. 'This may be your death,' she said.

But Morville went from the room like a man drunk, for the galling and blistering of his eyes with broken tears; and so from the house; and so to horse.

XI

NIGHT-PIECE: APPASSIONATO

DUKE Barganax, while these things were fresh at Reisma, was already gone for Zayana: his folk a mile ahead with the baggage, himself riding alone. Every summer sound as he came on, of wind-stirred leafage, birds singing, becks falling, ran divisions on the tune of *Loth to depart*. He rode at a slowed idle pace, twenty miles south now from Memison and twenty yet before him. Whiles he shifted, as if the saddle chafed him: whiles, cursed aloud; and then, as it were to be spectator, not undergoer, of the comedy, laughed at himself. Here, where the road, high above the head waters of this southernmost arm of Reisma Mere, goes level for at last half mile along the shelf of Kephalanthe and thence rises steeply to the water-shed, he drew to a halt. Betwixt the road and the crag's lip that overhangs the lake, cedar-trees spread a roof, spiss, dense, high-raftered, beneath which the sun's glare entered but as attenuate pale shafts, clear-outlined as glass, motionless to the sight, save for a drowsed motion within them of floating specks which they kindled to dust of gold. The Duke dismounted, loosed girths, let her go graze, and sat down under the trees to rest. It was now the great heat of the day, but the air hung cool under that ceiling of cedar-fronds, and of a spice-laden sweetness. He fell asleep.

It was very still under the trees. A red mouse ran out, sat up to wash his face with his little paws, and went about his affairs unconcerned, scuttering once or twice within an inch of Barganax's boot. A Jennie wren scolded in the brake. As the afternoon wore, a party of long-tailed tits passed through by stages, hanging upside down on the cedar-twigs, filling the air with their tiny pipings. Two young hares came by, and stopped to play. By imperceptible slow degrees the sunbeams took a less steep incline. And now, as it drew on towards evening, two came walking between the trees from the northward as it were two nymphs of the waters and wildernesses, each with her arm about the other's waist. Their dresses, of fine gauzy stuff kilted almost to the knee, shimmered to all greys and greens of distance and whitenesses of snowfield or watersmeet. Light was their tread, scarce bending the grass beneath them; and the little things of the wild, as if knowing them familiarly, took but a hop or step aside as they passed.

'Look, sister,' said she that was little and dark and with beady black eyes: 'a sleeping man.'

'Is it him we were sent after?'

'Are your lynx-eyes become beetle's eyes that you perceive not that?'

'His face is from us,' replied the taller. Slender she was as some cattish creature of the mountains, and the colouring of her deep hair was as fire of gold. 'Besides, I ne'er yet spoke with him face to face. Nor did you neither, sister.'

'No, but I know him by frame and fashion: arms and legs well lengthened and strengthed after the proportions of his body, which is proportioned as a God's. And he is colour-de-roy, too: his hair at least. Come softly till we see his face: I have looked on that Duke, sister, from betwixt the bulrushes, when he little thought 'twas such as me, so innocently beholding him. Come softly. Yes, it is he, it is he.'

They stood a minute looking at Barganax asleep, as reremice at the bright beams of the clear sun. Then Anthea said, 'I'd have known him by his likeness to the Duchess his mother, only with a something straining or biting as ginger: more self-liked and fierce. What was the command to you?'

'When my lady's grace hath dressed this evening, to bring him to come sup at her house.'

'And what to follow? Lie and look babies in one another's eyes? See, he smiles in his sleep. "At pleasure now on stars empireth he"!'

'Sleep is a spying-hole unto man,' said Campaspe. 'Did you hear, sister? he spoke her name in his sleep.'

'Let me consider him in his sleep, sister. You'd have thought there's more than mortal blood swells these veins. And even with the lids closed, as now, there is a somewhat betwixt his eyes, ay, in the whole countenance of him: a somewhat unfaint and durable, such as I ne'er saw till now in mortal man, but in them of our kind is never distracted either from soul or body. And firely and openly he burned with fire of love.'

'See how unsettledly he searches about sideways with his hand. He speaks her name again.'

'I warrant that hand,' said Anthea, 'is a finder of the right way to heaven.'

After a little, Campaspe said, with her liquid naiad voice, 'Whether think you better sport to wake him now, or give him our message while he sleeps? Speak it into his dreams?'

'This is a fine toy: let's try it. We can speak wider so.'

'Which shall speak it?'

'Both, by turns. Then he shall taste in his dreams the true sharps and sweets of it,' said Anthea, and smiled with a white gleam of teeth.

'Which shall begin?'

'I will. Salutation, my lord Duke. We be two waiting-maids unto my Lady Fiorinda in Reisma. And my lady said this morning that, in her seeming, red men be treacherous and full of quaintness and likened to foxes.'

'But then, she said,' said Campaspe, 'your grace was liker a lion than a fox.'

'And sitting so in her starry loveliness, with her breasts unbraced, she said: "That would have stood the Duke of Zayana in far more stead, to have kissed the doggedness out of me, 'stead of, when I bade him go, go indeed. For I already had, truly I think, a certain smackering towards him. And such thing as man's heart is most on," said she, "and that these weeks past he hath made great suit unto me for, indeed I begin to think I'd liever let him have it than any man born."'

'No, no! That was never in the patent.'

Anthea laughed. 'Timorous scrupulosities! 'Twas meant, if it were not said. —"And that," said my lady, "is why tonight I have requested his company at supper. For indeed matters stood altogether unadvanced 'twist me and the Duke, until the jealous ass my husband—'

'—"who is the miserablest young raw puttock that e'er waited slugging on his bed for day—'

'—"this very morning, after many circumstances too long to trattle on now, gave me a smite in the face."'

'Fie, sister! My lady would burst sooner than avouch that fact.'

'I know,' replied Anthea. 'But is a kind of charmed sour mare's-milk very forcible to turn the brain. – "And I told him," says my lady, "that my lord and lover the Duke would doubtless make a capon of him therefor before he had done with him" – Go on, sister.'

'"In token whereof,' said Campaspe, 'I shall wear for the Duke tonight," says she, "my silken gown coloured of red corn-rose."'

'"And for the more conveniency, 'cause I think the night will be close," says she, "I'll wear no undergarment."'

'O sister! We've spoke beyond our licence, and most part, I fear, untrue. This bald unjointed chat of yours! Will you think the Duke heard it indeed in his dream? And will be remember it when he wakes? Truly I hope not.'

''Twill do no hurt, silly flindermouse. What skills it? so only but—

one desire
May both their bloods give an unparted fire!

'Sister, sister! clacketing out this nonsense, we've left the principal errand unsaid.'

'What's that?'

'My lord Duke, in your dreams: we were to inform your grace

directly, my lady sleeps alone tonight, the lieutenant being from home.'

'O my stars, yes! that's more to the purpose than all.'

'Come off, sister, and make an end. I think he's waking.'

'One word of my own then, to bid him adieu. – Wear a good glove, I counsel you, my lord Duke, for your falcon-gentle straineth hard.'

'Away, he opens his eyes.'

Barganax sat up, wide awake on the instant, swiftly looking about him. No living thing was to be seen, save but on a branch close by, touched with the beams of the westering sun, a peggy-whitethroat trilling her sweet unbodied lay with its dying fall; and below her, in an outcropping of grey rock by a cedar's foot, an elegant lynx with speckled fur, tufted ears erect, and eyes that had upright slits for pupils. The Duke leapt to his feet. Every line of his body, and every muscle of his face, seemed to tighten as with some resolve gathering weight from withinwards, unrestrainable as a great tide coming in the high sea-springs of the year. Both creatures, the one with fiery the other with timid bead-like eye, as he stood there motionless, returned him look for look. 'I have dreamed of dream. Unformed stars,' he said. 'Small stake makes cold play. But no more of that.' With a flutter of olive-yellowish breast and wing the little bird flew. The lynx in the same instant bounded away through the undergrowth, graceful in her leap as an oread in the skyish summits at point of day. Barganax whistled his mare: she came, muzzled his neck below the ear. 'Come, child,' he said as he tightened the girths and then jumped into the saddle, 'We must ride: we must ride.'

Day was near spent when the Duke came at a hand-gallop to the ford by the footbridge. Here he halted to let her drink. On the further side the land rises gradually to level stretches wooded with oak and holm-oak, through which the road winds a mile or so, and then, upon a sharp turn south-east, runs straight for a last two hundred yards in a tunnel of these trees and so out again into the open, and so down by gently sloping moory ground to the mains of Reisma. As the Duke rode into that straight, the beams shooting level through the wood from behind him struck red fire-marks on the tree-boles in front. Ahead, the end of the wood was as an arched gateway opening out of gloom upon field and champaign bathed drenched and impregnate with the red sun's glory. And seen full in that archway, in the mid distance as in a picture framed, groves of tall cypresses siding it left and right, stood the house. It shone in the last rays like a casket lifted up against the updrawing curtain of dark night, and lit by the fires of some jewel unprizable cased within it.

As Barganax drew near to that house of Reisma the sun set, and there came upon the land and air a strange uncustomed alteration. For, out of the baked earth of that evening of deep summer, smells of spring began to prick his nostrils as he rode; quinces and cherry-trees showed white through the dusk, under their traceries of pale sweet blossom; and out of short and springy turf young daffodil leaves rose excitedly like fingers, thick stiff and tense with the sap putting upward, and wet with dew. And, as the shadow of approaching night began to creep up the sky behind Reisma and the great snow ranges afar, the heavy obscurities of the strawberry-trees were filled with a passion of nightingales. In this out-of-rule mutation and unfashioning of July to April, only the heavenly bodies were some warrant of constancy, even the unsteadfast moon floating where she ought to do, all rose-colour tonight, low in the southeast among the dim stars of Sagittarius, a day or two short of her full.

The house was silent: not a light showed at door or window. The Duke, making sure of his sword, loosening it in the scabbard, rode into the forecourt past the vine-hung trellis and that bench of asterite. As he passed the empty bench, a taint or perfume as by fine and quick fingering made all his senses stand in a fire-robed expectancy. It was gone the next instant, dissipated and lost on the evening breeze.

The door stood open. He dismounted, ran up the steps, but checked at the threshold. In the profound stillness of the house sat a menace, as if the universal world were become in that sudden a city unsure, not impregnable. It seemed suddenly to be unsufferable cold and he, standing on a bridge of thread precariously above floorless immensities, to look down between his feet to a driving upon noiseless winds, as dead leaves are driven, earthward, skyward, and about, without path or purpose, of half-memories out of the old age of time past, as if from other lives, other worlds. Then natural present cleared itself again; and the Duke, loosing the grip of his strong fingers upon the latch of the silver-studded door by which in that turmoil he had steadied himself, crossed the threshold into the silent house: stood listening: heard only the blood that pounded and pounded in his ears. Then he ransacked the house, room by room in the falling shadows that fell like slowed chords descending of stringed instuments in ever darkening procession, as door after door was flung wide by him and slammed to again. The very kitchens he ransacked, store-rooms, cellars underground, sculleries, buttery, and all. And when all was searched and found void of any living being he began again. And again everywhere, save for the clatter of his heavy riding-boots, was silence: empty all, as last year's nest in November. Only, as it were some intermittent rare flicker kindling ever and again an edge of those shadows falling, came at every while a scarce discernible tang of that most vading perfume. Upon that faint warmth and deliciousness, as though in carnal presence she had brushed by within an inch of him and away again unkissed and unknown, the sense was become to be no more a thing mediate but the unshaled nakedness of the live soul, held quivering like a bird in some titanic hand that was of itself but the bodiment of that world-enfettering sweet hyacinthine smell. As to say: This savour, this thread-like possibility of her, is all that knits the fabric together. Should it depart to come not again, this faint Olympian air which is as from the very mouth of laughter-loving Aphrodite of the flickering eyelids and violet-sweet breast, gone is then all else beside; and you go too, and the world from your hand. Barganax, like now to a man entering in the trembling passage of death, said in himself, 'God keep it!'

Then, in the long upper gallery that opens toward the sunset, he was ware of her in the dusk, standing in the embrasure of a window.

The floor rose by two steps to that embrasure, so that when she turned at the Duke's approaching she looked down on him from above. With her back to the light there was no reading of her face, but she held out her hand to him. It glowed through the half-dusk, a water-chill unsubstanced glow, like the moonstone's; but warm it was to the touch and, as he took and kissed it, redolent, to unseating of the wits, of that ambrosial scent. 'This one too,' she said, and the self-savouring indolent voice of her came like the disclosing of dewy roses, blood-red, underset with thorns, as she held him out the other hand. And while he kissed that, 'So you have come?' she said.

'Yes, my life-blood and my queen,' said the Duke. 'I have come.' Over and over again he kissed the two hands: caught them both together to his lips, to his eyes: fell down upon his knees then before her: seized his arms about her waist that rose slender as neck of a Greek vase above the statuesque smooth languor of her hips and yielding as throat or breast of some sleepy dove. His forearms, crossing each other, were locked now behind her knees so that she stood pinioned, backward-leaning against that window-ledge, breathing fast, limbs unstrung. So for a fire-frozen minute, while the Duke's forehead and eyelids pressing blindly against the folds of her silken gown, here where it covered her flank, here her thigh, here the dream-mounded enchanted mid region between hip and hip.

He bent lower, as if to kiss her foot. 'No.' she said, upon a catch of the breath. 'No. We will wait for that, my friend.'

'Wait? Have I not waited long enough?' and he took her with both hands by the waist again, drawing her down to him. 'By heavens, too long.'

She said, 'No. You must order yourself mannerly with the things are set before you. We will wait till after supper.'

He was on his feet now beside her in the window, gripping with his left hand the window-ledge, searching her face: her colubrine slanting eyes with their lashes now asleep, now a-flicker: eyes enabled, with such a mouth, with such nostrils, to infinite

allurements, confections of sugared gall honeyed with the promise
of unspeakable benedictions, unspeakable delights, or (when the
Devil drives) to the summoning of strange horrors, ice-cruel or
tiger-fanged, out of the deep. 'Foh! I have dreamed dreams,' he said.

She threw up her head in a little laugh, that seemed to take
flesh in her disordinate and unresty beauty. 'Dreams are like an
orange. The rind is hot, and the meat within it is cold. I love a
doer, not a dreamer.'

'Your ladyship sent for me. Is it not so?' He saw how her eyes,
averted now, busied no more with his, were for this once, in the
fast failing light, become softer and stiller than the eyes of a yearling
hind.

'For a wild hart wandering out of order? Well, if I did? In a
dream of my own?'

The Duke looked now where she looked, north-westward to
the lake roughened with wind, a sapphire lit from within, darker
in the distance. A little north of it, Memison showed grey against
cloud-banks of a stronger grey behind it, with a slanting smudge
of pale crimson upon a sky of yellow ochre. To the left, westward,
the cloud-bank was indigo against that yellowishness of the sky,
here smirched with brown. Hesperus, beautifullest of all stars,
burned low in the west. High over all hung that night-hue: that
heaven's-blue which holds depth beyond depth within it, and is
the young unfledged dark. Still the breath of spring persisted on
the air, and the lay, bitter-sweet, of the nightingales.

'Then you sent, and sent not? Good,' he said. Leaning now his
two elbows on the window-sill, he looked up at her sideways. It
was as if the string of a lyre, invisible, unvibrating, strained his
dark eyes to hers and tasted, in some inward contemplation of its
two-fold self, the unboundlessness of music to be. 'Well,' he said,
standing up like a man that shakes himself awake, 'for the present
I am content to unlace no more of these mysteries. Enough that
there is a pair of us.'

'And that it is supper-time.'

Barganax glanced down at his dusty boots. 'First I would lay off
the sweat and dust I have soiled me with, hastening to this place.'

'O, for that, all is laid ready for your grace within there. No, the right-hand door: this left-hand leads, I know not well whither. To heaven, perhaps. Or hell.'

He looked at the doors: then at her. 'Right or left, I saw neither of these two doors till now,' he said. 'And 'tis very certain, madam, that every door in this house I have seen and opened, twice over, before I found you here.'

Surely in that Lady Fiorinda's voice were echoes of the imperishable laughter, as she answered and said, 'Indeed it is true and for every door you shall open in my mansion, my lord Duke, you shall find always another yet that awaits your opening.'

Curtains were drawn and the fire raked up and candles lit and supper set for two in the gallery when the Duke returned. The mistress of the house was already in her place at table. He saw now that she wore a dress of soft scarlet sendaline, flourished with gold and spangles of gold and small bone lace of gold. No jewels she wore, save but only the smaragds and diamonds of her finger-rings and, at her ears, two great escarbuncles, round, smooth-cut, that each tiniest movement set aglow like two coals of fire. He saw on a chair beside her an elegant mountain lynx which she played with and caressed with her white hand luxuriously.

She made sign to him to be seated over against her. There were candles on the table in candlesticks of orichalc, and, in little bowls of Kutarmish glass coloured with rich and cloudy colours like the sunset, odoraments to smell to: rose-water, violet-flowers, balm, rose-cakes, conserves of southernwood and of cowslip. Her face in the candlelight was more beautiful than the evening star when it upsprings as forerider of the night between clouds blackened with thunder.

'I hope your grace will bear with our rude uplandish country manners this evening,' she said. 'Indeed I sent my servants out of the house two hours since, that our converse and business might be more free.'

'But who set the table, then? Your ladyship's self?'

'It amused me.'

'On my account? With such lady-soft a hand? I am ashamed, madam.'

'O but indeed I did it not myself. 'Twas this mountain cat of mine did do it for me. You think that a lie?'

'I think it very like one.'

'How say you to a taste of what she has set before us? What's this: a little sardine, dressed up in love-apple? May I please have that little plate to put this backbone upon.'

'When next you mean to play serving-maid,' said Barganax, reaching her the plate, 'I hope your ladyship will let me be butler.'

'I have told your grace, my creature did it. She is skilled in housewiferies of all kinds fitting.'

The lynx stood up, making an arch of its back, and naughtily with his claws set to work on the edge of the chair: sat down again and, out of the upright slits of its eyes, stared at Barganax. He gave it (as at Kephalanthe) look for look, till it looked away and very coyly fell to licking its fur.

'See what a tiny bird,' Fiorinda said, with a superfine daintiness taking a quail upon her fork. 'A little sparrow, I think. He that shot that must surely have frighted the mother off the nest and then caught it.'

Barganax smiled. 'There be some things ought best to be little. Othersome, best big.'

'As for instance birds,' said she. 'For myself, I would desire always little birds, never big ones. But dogs, always big.'

'And men?'

'Truly that is a kind of cattle I find myself strangely disinclined to overbusy myself with. Of late. In their plurality. Your grace laughs?'

'Some little shrubs of pride and vanity I have in me take comfort at that "plurality".'

'Be not too confident.'

'Faith, I am not. Should a beggar be a jetter? And yet—'

'And yet? it is better kiss a knave than to be troubled with him?'

'Ah, not that. I can tell true coin from false.'

'And yet? in an undue manner the Devil coveted highness that fell not for him?'

'His hopes were dasht, then. And serve him right. Nay but the "and yet" was mine. And, not to fall in open disobedience to your ladyship's command, it shall wait.'

In soft lazy accents that wrought in the blood beyond all love-cups and enchantments, "'Tis a good "and yet",' she said, 'an amiable Devil, to wait so civilly. Let it not be despaired.'

For a while now they ate and drank in such silence as wild hearts' desires will lie joined in, in closer lapped embraces than spoken word could tire them to: Fiorinda at every other while casting her eyes upon him, inscrutable under their curtain of long dark lashes; and he, so tall of his person, of so careless a repose of settled power in his magnificency, and with all his wilfulness and self-liking of ungoverned youth charmed asleep now, under the lynx's hot stare, and under the star of his lady's presence thus goldenly and feelably sitting before him in warrant of what transcendent fare to come.

Presently, 'This is a strange wine, madam,' he said, 'as never in all my days I tasted. Of what sort is it? From the outlands?'

'No, it comes of the grape about Reisma.'

'It is such as might be looked for at your ladyship's table. A moment ago, limpid, transparent, and still: now, restless with bubbles. Blood-red, to suit your lips, if I hold the goblet so. Then, hold it so, snake-green, seaish. Then, against the light, all paly gleams and with changing bands of colour that go and come within it as I let it swirl in the glass. How call you its name?'

'For make-believe,' said she as they pledged each other, 'say it is nectar.'

'I could in sober truth believe that,' he said. Her arm, of a lily-like smoothness and a lily-like paleness, was laid idly across the table, darkly mirrored in the polished surface, idly toying with the cup. 'For make-believe,' he said, sudden out of the silence, 'say you are my Duchess in Zayana. Say you love me.'

Some fire-worm of mockery stirred in her eyes. 'But surely to say that, were a raw weak undurable and soon souring make-believe? My own I am. I stand untied.'

'I too.'

'You too?'

'Yes. And I am an incorrigible person, that will not be ordered.'

She gathered herself sweetly back in her chair, but her eyes were unrelenting flint. 'You think this is a play, then?'

'How can I tell?'

'How can I either?' said she. 'Say it is a play, then; and that, in the play, you and I have forgotten, my friend, that this is the wine we drink always, you and I. And forgotten that he that drinks it with me shall return to me for ever, never altogether finding, but never altogether losing.' She began to fondle the lynx and hold its head in her lap deliciously. 'Is it not a play indeed, my moppet? See: riches come, and the man is not satisfied. Will he expect that freshly roasted larks shall fall into his mouth? Or is it, think you, that he came into the house but an hour ago meaning by force to ravish me, when as prevailed not, these weeks past, his fawning toys and suing tales?'

The beast fuffed at Barganax like a cat.

He laughed. 'When your ladyship speaks to this lapcat it is, I suppose, in some dumb-beast tongue of its own? I understand not a word of it.'

Fiorinda had bent her head, caressing softly with her cheek the lynx's fur. The bloom of her skin had an olive tinge, pallid as fields that spread their night-dews under the morning. And for apparentest outward seal of all perfections was the spider-thread fineness of her hair, seen in the prettily ordered growth of it at the temples, behind the ears, and at the nape of her neck, where it rested? Coiled upon itself, a closely woven knot, superb sleek and disturbing as some sweet black hunting-beast coiled upon itself in sleep. Barganax's eyes were darkened so beholding her and his throat dried.

When she looked up again, he saw her eyes filled with tears. 'There's a blindness upon me,' she said in answer to his look, 'now that I have come so far.'

'A blindness?'

'I know not well whether. Comed so, to the parting of two ways at night. How can I know? Talking, may be, tomorrow with your carousing toss-pot. Meszrian friends: a sweet tale, somewhat hot of the spice too, of the cozening doctor, the crafty Chancellor, and puss his sister. Indeed and indeed I could wish your grace had not gone beside your purpose: were walking even now amongst your orange-trees in Zayana. I wish you'd a stayed there. Wish most, I'd ne'er set eyes on you.'

Barganax said, 'This is damnable false doctrine.' He came and knelt beside her, one hand on the chair-back, but not to touch her.

'Is it?' She was crying now, with little sobs, sometimes held back, sometimes coming miserably in a huddle together. 'My handkerchief.' She found it: a square of cambric edged with bone lace of silver, scarce big enough to cover the width of Barganax's hand. 'I have seen an ugly sight. The ugly face of Nothing,' she said, drying her eyes.

'But when?'

'This morning. This Tuesday morning of this instant July. No, no, no: not when you were there. Without you, I could not, O my friend, I could not, I think go on being.' She avoided his eye: still stifling at every now and again a convulsive sob, while with her left hand she feverishly stroked the lynx's long back. Barganax very gently laid his cheek on her other hand which, resting on the table's edge, held her poor handkerchief, now screwed up in the fist of it like a child's; and very gently, as though it had been a child's indeed, kissed it.

A minute, so. Then she began, still trembling a little, with her finger-ends of the left hand to move caressingly over his short-cut coppery curly hair; then lapped her lovely arms about his head. And Barganax's face, as by star-leap received up into that heaven, rested, unseen, unseeing, where, as it had been two doves, her breasts sat throned, ivory-smooth through the silk, violet-sweet, proud, and Greek.

Without word spoken, they stood up from the table.

The lynx watched them from its chair out of eyes that danced with yellow fires.

That left-hand door opened upon a lobby. Fiorinda locked it behind them. At the end of the lobby they came to another doorway, doorless, curtained with rich and heavy curtains, and so to a room with tall windows at the ends west and east and, at either end between the windows, a fire-place, and the heat and movement and sweetness of fires burning of sweet cedar-logs. Scores of candles stood alight in great branched candlesticks beside the bed, and on tables and mantel-shelves and in golden sconces on the walls. The great canopied bedstead was of pure gold, throwing back fire-glitter and candlebeam, and its hangings and coverings of cramoisie silk were befringed all with gold and worked in gold thread with representations as of gryphons and manti-cores and flying fire-drakes and many unused shapes and semblances besides, but half-divined amid the folds of the costly hangings. The floor was strewn with beast-skins, of wolves, bears, and deep-voiced mountain-lions, upon a carpet honey-coloured, very soft to walk on, silent as sleep. The walls seemed to be of a pale green marble, but with a glistening in the body of it as of gold-dust and dust of silver, and with myriads of little gems inlaid in the veins of the marble like many-coloured sparkles of fire. Betwixt wall and ceiling ran a frieze carved with lotuses, which seemed in the wobbling candlelight and the glow of the logs, now a-smolder, now shooting up tongues of flame, to swing and circle, rise and sink, as upon slumbrous slow eddies and backwashes of their native streams.

But the Duke, little regarding these marvels, regarded but his Fiorinda, standing there so close, into his hand, beautiful as golden flowers. So regarding her, surely his living self was drunk down as into the heat of a pool, deep, black-watered, full of sliding lotus-limbs: of the lotus, which yet floats so virginal-cool on the surface of the surface of the water.

As the turning of the starred sphere of night, that lady turned her head where it lay back now on his shoulder, till his eyes, close-ranged in a nearness of focus that shut out all else, rested upon her green eyes, clear-lidded, stilled, seen a little sideways: upon her nostril, which had transiently now in its cool contours an aspect most arresting, most melting, of undefended innocence: upon her cheek, firm, smooth, delicate-bloomed: last, upon her lips. It was as if, in this slowing of Time upon contemplation, Fiorinda's lips put off all particular characters which in daylight life belonged to them, as to instruments of speech, vehicles of thought, of wit, and of all self-pleasuring fierce subtle colours and musics of their mistress's mind; until, disclothed of all these, the perils and loveliness of her mouth lay naked: a vision not long tolerable in its climacteric. The tickle of her hair against his eyelids stirred his blood to ichor. Her hand, in an unbodiliness fluttering upon his, shepherded it down by small and small till it paused at the tie of her girdle. 'Kiss me again,' she said: 'kiss the strength out of me.' And then, the voice of her speech becoming as the fanning of a moth's wings, felt sooner than heard: 'Unknit me this knot.'

Silence swirled to down-sucking sea-floods of its own extreme, itself into itself. And Barganax, flesh and spirit as by anvil and fire-broil forged to one, beheld how She, tempering first to the capacity of mortal senses the acme and heat of the empyreal light, let slide down rustling to Her ankles Her red corn-rose dress and in the mereness of Her beauty, that wastes not neither waxeth sere, stood naked before him.

At that striking of the hour, Time, with its three-fold frustration of Past which is dead, of Future which is unborn, and of Present which before it can be seized or named is Past, was fallen away. Not as for sleepers, to leave a void: rather, perhaps, as for God and Goddess, to uncover that incandescent reality in which true things consist and have their everlastingness: a kind of flowering in which the bud is neither altered nor gone but endures yet more burningly in the full-blown rose: a kind of action which still sweeping on to new perfections retains yet the prior perfection perfect: an ecstasy that is yet stable in itself: a desire that lives on as form in the material concrete of its fulfilment. And while each

succeeding moment, now as honey-fall, now thunder-shot, folded
in under the hover of its wings the orb of the earth, it was as if
She said:

I am laid for you like starlight.
As white mists
Dispart at morning with touch of the sun,
Look, I wait you:
Look, I am yours:
Secrets before unpublisht.
A God could take no more.

I am a still water:
Come down to me.
I am falling lights that glitter. I am these darknesses
Panther-black,
That scorch and unsight
At the flame of their unspher'd pride.
Make sure of me how you will.

Take me in possession.
First, kiss me, so.
Parting my sea-waved sea-strange sweet-smelling hair
So, left and right.
I am utterly yielded, untiger'd, unqueen'd:
Have I not made me
Softer and tenderer for you than turtle's breast?

Ah, tender well my tenderness:
Life in me
Is a wing'd thing more aery than flies hemerae:
This beauty of me
More fickle and unsure
Than the rainbow'd film of a bubble, hither and gone,
On some tall cataract's lip.

Yet, O God!
Were you God indeed,
Yet, of my unstrength,
Under you, under your lips, under your mastery,
I am Mistress of you and Queen:
I hold you, my king and lord,
The render'd soul of you bar'd in my hand
To spare or kill.
God were ungodded,
The world unworlded,
Were there no Me.

Into the other and may be less perdurable Lotus Room, the
night after that race home from Austria, dawn was already now
beginning to creep between the curtains of the high eastern window,
and the note of a blackbird in Lessingham's garden boded day.
Downstairs in the Armoury the great Italian clock struck four.
And Mary, between sleeping and waking turning again to him,
heard between sleep and waking his voice at her ear:

'O lente, lente, currite noctis equi!
O run slow, run slow, chariot-horses of Night!'

XII

SALUTE TO MORNING

ANTHEA in the mean time, left to follow her devices in that western gallery at Reisma, took her true shape, sat daintily down in her mistress's chair, and began to make her supper of the leavings. Leisurely, delicately, she ate, but playing with the food betweenwhiles after a fashion of her own: now pouring the wine from glass to glass and balancing the glasses perilously one upon another, Ossa upon Olympus, and upon Ossa, Pelion; now chasing a faun hither and thither over the polished table with her finger; again, tearing a quail to pieces and arranging the pieces in little patterns, then a sudden sweeping of them all together again in a heap and begin a new figure. So, with complete contentment, for hours. At length, while she was trying her skill at picking out with her teeth special morsels from the nicely ordered mess she had made, as children play at bob-cherry, her disports were interrupted by the entrance of Doctor Vandermast.

Like a silver birch-tree of the mountains in her kirtle of white satin overlaid with network of black silk, she rose to greet him as with staid philosophic tread he came the length of the long gallery and so to the table. He kissed her brow, white as her own snows of Ramosh Arkab. 'Well, my oread?' he said, touching, as a lapidary might the facets of a noble jewel, with fingers more gentle than a woman's the aureate splendours of her hair which she wore loosely knotted up and tied with a hair-band of yellow topazes. A little shamefaced now she saw his gaze come to rest on the results of her table-work, but, at the twinkle in his eye when he looked from that to her, she sprang laughing to him, hugged him about the neck and kissed him.

'Have you supped, reverend sir?'

Vandermast shook his head. 'It is nearer breakfast-time than supper-time. Where is her ladyship?'

'Where the Duke would have her. In the chamber you made for them.'

'It were best seal the doors,' said Vandermast; and immediately by his art both those doors, the left-hand and the right, were changed to their former state, parts of the panelling of the inner wall. He stood silent a minute, his hawk-nosed face lean in the candlelight 'It is a place of delights,' he said. '*Ex necessitate divinae naturae infinita infinitis modis sequi debent*: out of the necessity of the Divine nature, Her infinite variety. And now he, to the repossession of his kingdom. But let him remember, too, that She is fickle and cannot be holden against Her will.' He stood at the window. 'The moon is set two hours since,' he said. 'The night grows to waste.'

'My lady sent away her servants. Paid 'em all off, every Jack and Jill of 'em.'

'Yes, she intends, I think, for Memison,' said the doctor. 'And the Lord Morville, ridden with the cavalcade to Rumala.'

Anthea bared her teeth. 'Pray Gods he break his neck. There's a lust upon me for a taste of hornified cattle-flesh, after supping on these kickshaws. O I could handle him with rough mittens: leave but guts and sinews for the kites. Can you think of him and not be angry as I am?'

'Yes. For God, according to His impenetrable counsel, hath made it a virtue in you to be angry; but making of me, He cooled that humour with a cooler thing more meet for it in me: I mean with the clear milk of reason which in a philosopher should ever overmaster passion. The unmistrusting man, thinking no evil, a man of common earth and clay, endued with a soul not yet unmortal, how should he wed with a great comet or blazing star, or breathe in Her heights? Doubt not that, from the beginning, he, in the opinion of his own insufficiency, poisoned the very sap should have nourished him at root, and so was become, long ere the Duke took a hand in it, but the simulacrum of a live tree, all dead touchwood or tinder within. And blasted now, under Her devilish effects, with the thunder-stroke of his own jealousy.'

'Why should such dirt live?'

'The egg' answered Doctor Vandermast, 'is a chicken *in potentia*.'

'But this was addled ere it was hatched.'

The learned doctor was sat down now in Barganax's chair. Anthea came and sat sweetly on an arm of it, swinging one foot, her elbow propped on his shoulder, smiling down at him while with immemorial ancient gaze he rested in her cold classic beauty, so strangely sorted with lynx's eyes and lynx's teeth. 'And my Campaspe?' he said, after a little.

'She is yonder in the leas. Some of her rattishnesses tonight, I think. Your eyes grow heavy, reverend master. Why will you sit so late?'

'Ah,' said he, 'in this house nowadays I need not overmuch repose:

Here ripes the rare cheer-cheek Myrobalan,
Mind-gladding fruit, that can unold a man.

And tonight, of all nights, I must not be to seek if her lady-ship haply have need of me, or if he do. What of you, dear snow-maiden?'

'O it is only if I swaddle me in my humanity too thick that I grow sleepy,' said she. 'Besides, my lady bade me watch tonight. How were it if we played primero?'

'Well and excellent,' said the doctor. 'Where are the cards?'

'In the chest yonder.' She fetched them, sat down, and with two sweeps of her hand cleared the remains of supper off the table and onto the floor. 'The bull-fly can pick it up for himself tomorrow,' she said. 'We shall be gone.'

They had scarce got the cards dealt when Morville came into the gallery.

'How, how, who is here?' he said. 'You, old sir?'

The doctor, keeping his seat, looked up at him: saw his face pale as any lead. 'My lord,' he said, 'I came upon urgent summons from her ladyship.'

'What, in this time of night?'

'No. 'Twas about noon-time. She bade me stay.'

'Ha! Did she so? For my own part, I had rather have your room as your company. To speak flatly, I have long doubted whether you wore not your woolly garment upon your wolvy back. And you, madam kiss-i'-the-dark—

> From women light and lickerous
> Good fortune still deliver us—

Why are you not in bed?'

Anthea made no reply: only looked at him, licking her lips.

'You admire the unexpectedness of my return?' said Morville. 'Let the cat wink, and let the mouse run. It is very much if I may not for one short while turn my back, but coming home find all at large and unshut platters, dishes, and other small trashery flung so, o' the floor, with evident signs of surfeit and riot. Must I keep open household, think you, for the disordered resort and haunting of you and your kind? Where's my lady?'

Anthea gave him a bold look. 'She is in bed.'

'You lie, mistress. Her bed is empty. You,' he said to the aged doctor, 'who are in her counsels and, I am let to understand, learned in arts and studies it small befits an honest man to meddle withal, where is she?'

'My Lord Morville,' replied Vandermast, 'it is altogether a cross matter and in itself disagreeing, that you should expect from me an answer to such a question.'

'Say you so? I expect an answer, and by God I'll have it.'

'Where my lady is,' said Vandermast, 'is her affair. I mean you well, my lord, and where in honour I can serve you, serve you I will. But when her ladyship is concerned (even and I knew the answer) it would not be for my honesty to give it even to yourself without I first asked leave of her.'

Morville came a step nearer to him: stood leaning on the table upon his clenched fists that held his riding-whip: clenched till the knuckles showed white as marble. 'You are in a league against me, then? Have a care. I have means to make you tell me. I have a right, too, to know where she is.'

Vandermast said, 'You are master of this house. It is in your lordship's right to search and find what you may find.'

'I have searched every back-nook already. She is fled. Is it not so?'

Vandermast answered never a word. His eyes, holding Morville's, were as pits unplumbed.

'She is fled with the Duke,' said Morville, thrusting his face into his. 'Confess 'tis so. You are his secretary. Confess, and may be I'll spare your life.'

Vandermast said, 'I am an old man. I am not afraid to die. But were it to forfeit my honour, I'd be sore afraid to die after that.'

There was dead silence. Then Morville with a sudden unpremeditated motion swung on his heel and so to the window: stood there with his back to them, elbow crooked upon the window-sill, his forehead pressed into the crook of the arm, while his other hand beat an out-of-joint shapeless tune with his riding-whip against his riding-boot. 'O God!' he said suddenly, aloud, and seemed to choke upon the word: 'why came I not home sooner?' He bit the sleeve of his coat, rolling his head this way and that upon the window-ledge, still beating out the hell-march on his boot-leg, and now with an ugly blubbering sound of unremediable weeping between the bites. Doctor Vandermast, risen from his chair, began to pace with noiseless tread back and forth beside the table. He looked at Anthea. The yellow fires came and went in her strange inhuman eyes.

The Lord Morville, as with sinews righted after that wrestling, stood up now and came to them: sat down in Vandermast's chair.

'I'll put all my cards on the table,' he said, looking at the doctor who, upon the word, staid his haunting walk and came to him. 'There was, and ill it was there was, some semblance of falling out betwixt us this morning, and I spoke a word at her I'm sorry for: hath sticked like a fish-bone across my throat ever since. When it began to be evening, I could not face the night and us not good friends again. Devised some excuse, got leave from my lord Admiral (would to heaven it had been earlier): galloped home. And now,' he said, and his teeth clicked together: 'all's lost.'

'Nay, this is over general,' said the doctor. 'It remaineth with your lordship to save what can yet be saved.'

Morville shook his head. 'I know not what to do. Instruct me.'

'My lord,' said that old man, 'you have not told me the truth.'

'I have told you enough.'

'I can be of little avail to your lordship if you give me unsufficient premises to reason from. But worse than tell it not to me, I fear you tell it not truly to yourself.'

Morville was silent.

'Fall how it may,' said the doctor, 'it is hard to know how I may much avail you. Only this I most dutifully urge upon your lordship: wait. A true saying it is, that that is not to be held for counsel that is taken after supper.'

Morville said, 'I am scalding in a lake of brimstone, and you stand on the edge and bid me wait.'

'With all my heart and for all sakes' sake, yes, I bid you wait. If you fling into action now, in this uncertainty and your blood yet baked with angry passions, there's no help but 'twill be violent action and too little advised. Be you remembered, my lord, 'tis no littler thing than your whole life hangs on it; nay, for beyond the hour-glass of one man's life, your very soul, for being or for not being, is in the balance, and not for this bout only but in *saecula saeculorum*. And that is a matter of far greater moment to you than whether you shall have her or no, whom when you have had you have approved yourself not able nor not worthy of such a mistress: cursed indeed with a destiny too high for you.'

Morville sat still as death and with downcast look while

Vandermast said these things: then jumped up like a raging wild tiger. 'Would to God, then, I'd let her life out!' he said in an ear-deafening voice. 'Do you take me for more than a beast that you dare to speak such words to me? Am I lustless, sexless, tireless, mute? It hath laid up revenue this month past, and I'll now take my interest. She is with her vile leman even now. I know not where; but, if in the bed of Hell, I'll seek 'em out, hew the pair of 'em into collops. For fair beginning, I'll burn this house: a place where no filthy exercise has been left unexercised. Out of my way, bawd.'

He thrust Vandermast aside, so that the old man was like to have fallen. Anthea said in a low voice like the crackling of ice, 'You struck her. You beetle with horns, you struck her, and spat your filth at her.'

'Mew your tongue, mistress, or we'll cut it out. Void the house. You have no business here.'

'I've a good pair of nails to cratch and claw with.'

'Out, both of you, unless you mean to be whipped.'

Anthea rose in her chair. 'Shall I unpaunch him, reverend sir?'

'O be still, I charge you, be still,' said the doctor. 'We will go,' he said to Morville, and in the same nick of time Morville struck Anthea with his riding-whip across the smooth of her neck. Like the opening of the clouds with the levin-flash she leapt into her lynx-shape and upon him: threw him plat under her.

Above the noise of their fighting on the floor, of Morville's pantings and curses, the snarls and spittings of the lynx and the doctor's railing of her off, sounded a battering upon the wall now, and the great voice of Barganax shouting from within, 'Open, or I'll beat down the partition with my heels.' And immediately, by art of Doctor Vandermast, the left-hand door was there, and immediately it was open, and the Duke among them, sword in hand.

That oread lady, still in her lynx-skin, in obedience to Vandermast drew back now, heckles up, still ruffing and growling, ears flattened to her head, claws out, eyes ablaze. Morville was on his feet again, his left cheek scored to the chin with four parallel furrows

from which the blood ran in trickles. 'Where's this whore,' he said
to the Duke: 'this jay of Krestenaya? Your bill I'll clear first, and hers
after, and,' stripping out his sword, 'here's coin shall pay the two
of you.'

'Unmannered dog,' said the Duke, 'fall to. And the foul word
you spoke absolves me utterly.'

'Ay, fall to foinery: your trade, they tell me,' said Morville as they
crossed blades.

They fought in silence: the most desperate foins, cross-blows,
stoccata, imbroccata, rinverso, overthwart pricks, thrusts, breaking
of thrusts: sometimes closes and grips, striking with the hilts. It
was well seen that each was a master in that art: Morville, may
be, of the deeper grounding, but fighting as now with a less cool
resolution than the Duke's and once or twice coming in with so
much madness with his full career upon the body, that past belief
it was how he escaped the Duke's most deadly *montanto*. At last
the Duke, forcing him back against the table, beat him from his
best ward, mastered his weapon and, their hilts being locked now,
by main strength of wrist broke it from his hand. Morville took
a great fall, clean over the table backwards, on his ear and left
shoulder, and lay like one dead. His sword was shot far across
the room: Vandermast picked it up, gave it into the hand of the
Duke. In the same moment they were ware of the Lady Fiorinda
standing in that doorway.

In silence for a breath or two Barganax beheld her so stand,
her nightgown of orange-colour satin fastened about her waist
with a chain of pomanders and ambers and beads of pearl. Her
hair, let down, untressed, freed of pins and fastenings, reached, as
it had been her mantle imperial woven of all mists and stars and
unpathed black darknesses of the heart of night, almost to her
ankle. He said, 'When he comes to, shall it go on till I kill him,
madam? or shall I let him be?'

There was a glitter in her green eyes as if, from behind their
careless outwardness of self-savouring languorous disdain, suddenly
a lion's eyes had glared out, red, fiery, and hollow. 'Your grace
were as good do the one as the other. Commonly, I am told, you

were the death of any that angered you.' The glassy coldness of her face and of her voice was like the ice-sheaths, finger-thick, cold and transparent as glass, that enclose the live twigs and buds after a frozen thaw in winter. 'If his neck be not broke already. It concerns not me,' she said.

'Why, it concerns you solely,' said the Duke. 'Without your ladyship, where were question of choice?' Vandermast watched his master's eagle gaze, fixed upon that lady, a mariner's upon the cynosure, out of mountainous seas: watched her most sphinxian, waiting, ironic, uncommunicative, nothing-answering smile. 'You and I,' said the Duke at last, and fetched a deep breath: 'we are not much unequals.'

'No, my friend. We are not much unequals.'

And now the Lord Morville, coming to, looked at her standing in such sort in that unaccustomed doorway: looked at Duke Barganax. It was as if the injuries he was about to utter shrivelled between his lips. The Duke held Morville's sword in his left hand: offered it him hilt-foremost. 'Were you in my shoes, I make no doubt you'd a finished me on the floor then. May be I had been wiser do the like with you, but my way is not your way. We will now leave you and depart to Memison. Shortly there shall be set on foot a suit for a divorce to be had by the law betwixt you. And remember, I am a sure discharger of my debts to the uttermost. If you shall blab abroad, as vilely you have spoken tonight, one word against her ladyship, by all the great masters of Hell I swear I'll kill you.'

'Keep it,' said Morville, refusing his sword again. 'From you I'll take nothing but your life. And the same of you,' he said to Fiorinda: then, as if afeared of her face, strode hastily from the gallery.

Anthea, yet in her lynx dress, had marked these proceedings from a corner, herself unobserved. She now upon velvet paws, noiseless as a shadow, still unobserved, stole from the gallery on the track of Morville.

Barganax put up his sword. 'O over-dearest Mistress of Mistresses and Queen of Queens,' he said, 'was that rightly handled?' But that Dark Lady but only smiled, as well She knows how to do when She will judge without appeal.

They saw now, through those western windows, how the whole wide champaign and wooded hills and bight of the lake, Memison upon its rock-throne, and the swift-rushing clouds of dawn, threw back the lovely lights and new-washed wide-eyed pure colours of the morning. And the scents and sounds of morning danced through the high gallery from floor to shadowy ceiling: a coolness and a freshness that held intoxications more potent than wine's. From those windows Barganax turned to her: from similitude to the self-substantial reality: her who in her alone unique person, through some uncircumscribable adorableness, seemed to complete and make up morning and evening and night besides and whatsoever is or has been or shall be desirable, were it in earth or heaven. 'It is almost clear dawn,' he said, and her eye-beams answered, 'Almost.'

'And morning,' said Barganax, 'were in proof the sweet of the night, might we but take upon hand to prove it.'

'Your grace's archery,' said that lady, and the mockery in each successive lazy word set on her lips new snares of honey and thorns, 'never, I find, roves far from the mark you should level at. And indeed tonight for the once I truly think you have perhaps deserved to be humoured.'

That learned doctor, alone now at the window, they being departed, abode in his meditation. 'But where have you been?' he said, aware suddenly, after a long time, of Mistress Anthea a little side hand of him, very demure and morning-cool in her birch-tree kirtle. 'I had forgot you, and there's a bad-cat look in your eyes. What have you been eating? What have you done?'

'I've been but gathering news,' answered she, avoiding his gaze. 'Nought seems newer than this of Lord Morville, eat up with wild animals in the west woods they say.'

For a minute Doctor Vandermast regarded her in silence: her Greek features, so passionless, and so chill: her white skin, nails sharpened to claws, strong fierce milk-white teeth; and her yellow eyes, a little horrible now as though fires from the under-skies had but just died down in them. 'Could you not learn by example of the Duke, having beheld him win a man's greatest victory, which is by feeling of his power but not using it?'

'I am not a man,' answered she. 'It was a most needful act. And,' she said, licking her lips and looking at her finger-nails, 'I won't be blamed.'

Vandermast was silent. 'Well.' he said at length, 'I, for one at least, will not blame you over much.'

XIII

SHORT CIRCUIT

IT was Easter in England, the fifth year after, as in this world we reckon them: nineteen hundred and nineteen. The sun's limb, flashing suddenly from behind the shoulder of Illgill Head, shot a dazzle of white light through the french window of the breakfast-room at Nether Wastdale and into Lessingham's eyes as, porridge-plate in hand, he came from the sideboard to his place at the table. Patterned to squares by the window-panes the light flooded the white table-cloth: danced upon silver, glowed warm through translucent yellow trumpets and green leaves of the wild daffodils which filled a great Venetian bowl in the table's centre. On the left, windows, with their lower sashes thrown up, widely let in the morning air and the view up the lake north-eastwards, of Gable, with outlines as of a wave-crest in the instant of breaking struck to stone, framed between severities of headlong scree-clad mountain sides. White clouds, blown to spidery streaks and flying dappled flecks, radiated, like the ribs and feathers of a fan, upwards from the sun against the stainless blue. Country noises, bleating of lambs, a cock crowing, a dog's bark, a cock pheasant's raucous rattling squawk, broke now and again the stillness which listened to, was never a silence but a stream of subdued sound: thin bird-voices, under-tones of water running over stones. Here in the room the fire crackled merrily with a smell of wood burning. Breakfast-smells, moving in a free fugato of fried Cumberland ham, kidneys, buttered eggs, devilled chicken-legs, steaming hot milk and the fragrancies of tea and coffee and new-made toast, came from the sideboard, where two yard-long 'sluggard's friends' of burnished copper kept warm these things and the piles of hot plates for helping them.

No one else was down yet. Lessingham added first the salt then the sugar to his porridge, and was now drowning all with a rising ocean of cream, when Mary, still in her dark-green riding-habit, pattered on the glass of the garden door to be let in. 'Though why all round the house and in at the window,' he said, unbolting, opening, and standing aside to let her by, 'when nature provided a door from the hall—'

'Hungry. Want feeding.' The Terpsichorean lilt in her step as she crossed the threshold smoothed itself to a more level, more swan-maiden motion. 'Look at the sun on those daffies!' she said, pausing over them a moment on her way to the sideboard. 'And I saw the tree-creeper out there on the big ash. It doesn't ever go up and down the tree without little screams.' As if in such mirrors the springs should be looked for of such an April morning and its pied and airy loveliness: a loveliness unfolding of itself from within, radiant ever outwards, with clear morning lids uplifted upon all but itself alone, and all eyes drawn to it, taking light from its light. As if in such broken mirrors, sooner than in Mary.

'I suppose it's the touchstone of genius,' Lessingham said, while he lifted the covers one by one to show her what was underneath.

'A scrappet of ham: just half of that littlest slab,' she said, pointing with her finger. 'And scrambled eggs. – What is?'

He helped the dishes while Mary held out her plate. To do what no normal person ever dreamed of doing, but do it just so; so that, soon as see it, they think: How on earth could anyone have dreamt of doing it differently!'

'Wanted just to see,' she said: 'see how you look from outside. Where are the others?'

'Like Sardanapalus, in bed I suppose.'

'Bed! How people can! this time of year.'

'I'm not so sure about that. I seem to remember occasions—'

'O well, that's different. – What are you thinking about?' she said, watching him with eyes in which the question reposed itself like the shimmer of the sun on rippled water, half bantering half serene, as they took their seats at the table.

'Memories. And you, Señorita?'

'Thinking.' The diamonds and emeralds blazed and slept again on her ring as she transfixed with her fork a little piece of buttered egg, applying to the action as much deliberation of raised eyebrows and exquisite precision of touch as an artist might bring to bear upon some last and crucial detail. 'Thinking of you and your methods.'

They went on with their breakfasts in silence. After a while Lessingham said, out of the blue, 'Are you coming abroad with me?'

'Abroad?'

'Get away from it all for six months. Get into step again.'

Mary opened her eyes wide and nodded three times. 'Yes, I am. When?'

'The sooner the better. Tomorrow. Tuesday. Wednesday.'

'Very well.'

'Where shall we go?' he said, keeping up the game. 'South America? Glow-worm caves I'd like to have a look for, somewhere at the back of beyond in New Zealand? Iceland? a bit too early in the year, perhaps, for Iceland. What would you like? The world's free again, and we're free. Better choose. Anywhere except German East or France.'

'Some island?'

The Marquesas? We might found a kingdom in the Marquesas. I dare say the French Government are fond enough of me to stretch a point. Freehold, with powers of life and death. I king: you queen. Jim might be lord chamberlain: Anne second lady in the land, with title of princess in her own right: Charles, lord high admiral. I'll put Milcrest on to dig out the details after breakfast'

'Better be quick, or someone will find another job for you before we can get off. We've got to make up for these missed years.'

'I was thinking just now,' said Lessingham: 'glad my dear knew the Dolomites before the rot set in. Five years ago this summer, that last time. One moment it seems a generation: another way about five minutes.'

'And you've only been home about five days. And tomorrow, it's Rob's fourth birthday.'

Lady Bremmerdale came in from the hall. 'Good morning, Mary,' kissing her from behind: 'good morning, Edward. No, no, don't bother: I'll help myself. How long have you folks been up?'

'Sunrise,' said Mary.

'O come.'

'Pretty nearly.'

'Rode over to Wastdale Head,' said Lessingham.

'Early service?'

'Back to traditions.'

Anne sat down. 'And here's my god-daughter.'

Janet, on her best behaviour, embraced each in turn, and ensconced herself upon Anne's knee. 'I had scrambly eggs for my breakfast too. Do you know, auntie, I'd a most nasty dream. All about the most horrible, but alive, sort of wuffy snakes. And a huge great dragon: much bigger nor a house. And it had a face rather like a camel.'

'Had it a long neck?' said Anne.

'No. It was much more thick. A 'normous great green thing.'

Lessingham said, 'What did you do with it?'

'Tried to eat it up.'

'And what did it do with you?'

Janet was silent.

'Anyhow, you did quite right. Always eat them up. I always do. They can't possibly hurt you then.'

'Good morning everybody,' said Fanny Chedisford, very smart in her new grey tweed. 'Last as usual? No! No Charles yet. Saved again.'

'By a short length,' said Charles Bremmerdale. 'My dear Mary, I apologize.'

'But you know Jim's poem: "Late for breakfast: shows your sense", and so on? a strict rule in this household.'

Janet had a piece of paper which all the time she kept on folding and unfolding. 'Muvvie, I've writed a story,' she said. 'It's for Rob's happy birthday present. Shall I show it Father first?'

'Yes, I should,' said Mary.

Janet got down: brought it to Lessingham. 'Would you like to read me my story, Father? Will you read it aloud to me, please? Just you and me?'

He received it, very conspiratorially, and read it in a whisper, his cheek against hers:

'*The Kitchen*. – The cat has a baby kitten and the kitten is three weeks old. The parrot is grey with a red tail. "Oh dear" said the parrot. "I do wish cook wasn't out. "We are not sorry" said the cat and the kitten. – Tramp! Tramp! Tramp! "The cook" whispered the cat. "Bother" said the kitten. In came the cook. She had a large bundle in her hand. Suddenly, the cat got her temper up. She rushed at the parrots cage and tried to hurt the cook. At last she managed to drive the cook out of the kitchen. "Thank goodness" said the kitten. "Last year" said the cat. "I had six kittens, but the fool of a cook drowned them." "She really is the limit" said the kitten. "I tell you what" said the cat. "I'll eat the parrot of I can get him. Then the cat prounced on the parrot's cage got the door open and eat it. – *The End*.

That's the stuff,' he said.

'Do you like it? Really?'

'Yes, I like it,' he said, going over it again as if enjoying the after-taste of some nice dish.

'Do you truly, Father? Really and truly you do?'

'I like it. There's style about it.'

She laughed with pleasure. 'What's that mean?'

'Never you mind.' He rang the bell with his foot. 'I like the way they talk and the way they do things. And I like the finish. You go on writing like that, and you'll end somewhere between Emily Brontë and Joseph Conrad when you're grown up: a twentieth century Sappho.'

'Who's Emily?'

'Tell Mr Milcrest I want to see him,' he said to the servant:

then to Janet, 'No, not that Emily. A girl who wrote a story; and poems. Go on now, and read that to Sheila while we finish breakfast. Nothing from the post office, I suppose?' he said to the secretary.

'No, sir, nothing.'

'You're satisfied your arrangements will work properly in case anything should come?'

'Absolutely.'

'Good. Easter Day, just the moment they'd choose for some hurroosh. I'll be about the grounds all day, in case. Any word from Snittlegarth?'

'Yes, sir, I've just been on the phone. Mr Eric got your letter last night. There are some matters he's anxious to talk over with you. He's riding over: started six o'clock this morning, and hoped to be with you before noon.'

It'll certainly have to be the Marquesas, at this rate,' Lessingham said, with a comic look at Mary. Then to Milcrest, 'Come in to the library, Jack: one or two things I want seen to.' He left the room, Milcrest following.

'Eric. O my God,' said Bremmerdale *sotto voce*. His wife smiled at this undisguised feeling on the subject of her eldest brother.

Mary smiled too. 'Never mind, Charles. You and I will flee together. – Dear, will you feed these creatures and yourself,' she said to Anne. 'Ring for anything you want.' She collected Janet from the hearthrug and departed.

Charles shook his head. 'Edward never seems to get a "let-up": how he goes on at this rate heaven knows. I don't believe, until now, he's had four days together to call his own since the war started.'

Anne said, 'Quite sure he hasn't. But Edward is Edward.'

'I shouldn't be surprised if they sent him off to be the military governor again of one of these comic countries somewhere, before long. He'd like that.'

'I never remember names,' said Fanny. 'Where was it he issued stamps with his own head on them, and the Foreign Office recalled him for exceeding his instructions?'

'He always will exceed instructions,' said Charles. 'And the more honour to him for that. I only hope he won't kill himself with overwork before he's done.'

Anne said, 'We Lessinghams take quite a lot of killing.'

The world, at three hundred yards' range in all directions, was apprised of Eric Lessingham's arrival by the carrying-power of his voice. Not that it was a specially loud voice, but there was in it the timbre of sounding brass; so that his inquiry, in ordinary tones at the front door, for Lady Mary, reverberated past the long west wing round to the terraces above the river, causing a thrush there to drop her worm and take to flight. Despite crooked passages and double doors, Lessingham heard it plainly in the library. At the home farm the geese screamed in the paddock. Eastward in the water-gardens where, amid drifts of wild daffodil and water-blobs, the lake gives birth to the river Irt, Mary's eyebrows lifted in faint amusement and Charles Bremmerdale invoked his Maker.

'Is it really to be a holiday this time?' Anne was saying.

Mary graciously accepted a bunch of flowers presented by Lessingham's son and heir. 'I don't know. I don't know. I don't know. I've learnt not to count on anything. Make no plans, and you won't have to change them. – Yes, Rob, Muvvie does like primmy-roses.'

'Anyhow, brother Eric won't upset anything?'

'O dear no.'

Rob said, 'We put some on the grave too, like those. The bat's grave what Ruth killed in the nursery last night. I cried when it was deaded. Father buried it. We put an emptaph on the grave. Father wrote it. I tolded Father what to write: "This bat was small."'

'Poor little bat.' said Mary.

'I'd like to have had-ed it.'

'Take care. We mustn't walk on those daffodils.'

'No, no, no, we mustn't, must we. Mustn't walk on those,' he said, with great satisfaction and conviction.

'But how the devil, my dear fellow,' Lessingham was saying to his brother as they came to the top of the three flights of steps that led down to the wild water-gardens, 'Was I to be expected to throw over my military and diplomatic responsibilities and come home to embark on a damned election campaign to please you? Be sensible.'

'It's your duty: with all the money you've got and the brains you've got in a generation of fools.'

'So you said before the war. And I told you then, that the only use of money as I conceive it is not to be a slave. And I'm not so innocent about modern politics as to want to go and get bogged in them.'

Eric pushed back his hat from his broad and bony forehead and twirled his mustachios which he wore long like a viking's. For the rest, he was clean shaven. His face showed, in nose and brow and cheekbone and jawbone, a crag-like strength, and under the tan the colour came and went with every sway of his mood. His hair, darkish brown flecked with grey, was rather long at the back and about the ears: a vigorous curling growth: his ears rough and hairy. There was a demoniac twist in his eyebrows. A big man and a strong he was, of an easy six foot tall, heavy and somewhat clumsy of build, yet, for all his forty-seven years, with little sign of corpulence. He said again, 'It's your duty. If everyone with your abilities took up the attitude you do, where would the country come to?'

Lessingham paused half-way down the second flight and laughed. 'I don't know anyone with exactly my abilities, so your Kantian principle of the universal doesn't work very well here. As for my duty, I do it according to my lights. And I think, with respect, I'm rather a better judge of it than you are.'

'Well and I think, with respect, you're a damned unsatisfactory hound.'

Lessingham said nothing, but his nostrils hardened. Presently, as they walked on, he said quietly, with a tang of raillery in his voice that lightened the sting of the words, 'I thought you'd something important to talk about. If you've only come over to quarrel with me you'd better go home again. I've enough eggs on the spit without a dog-fight with you into the bargain.'

They were on the grass now, and the others coming up from

the waterside to meet them. With the magnificence of a caballero
Eric swept off his hat to his sister-in-law, bent to kiss her hand,
then kiss her on both cheeks. 'Bless you, dear Mary,' he said. 'Make
him do something. I can't. If he'd gone into politics when I told
him to, in 'fourteen, might have got some of our troubles straight-
ened out before this. If he'd do it now (Hullo, Anne. Hullo, Charles,
haven't seen you for years: Taverford still standing? Going to have
any pheasants this autumn? I'll come and shoot 'em for you: if
I'm invited, of course) – if he'd do it now,' he turned to Mary
again, 'he'd be Prime Minister before he's many years older, damn
him. Would myself, if I'd a wife like you.'

'That's the essential qualification, is it? Really, where to hide
my blushes, the way you flatter me.'

'Pity is,' Eric said, 'I had been married three times already
before you and I met. And if I hadn't, he'd have cut me out all
the same, before I'd a chance to start the siege. That's the trick
of these younger brothers. And he's youngest, and the worst. Look
at the state of the country today,' he said: 'strikes all over the
place, mines, railways, the Devil knows what. Damn the lot of
'em. They want a master.'

'Why don't you give them one?' said Lessingham dryly.

'It's what I'm trying to do. The trouble with your husband,' he
took Mary's arm, 'you can take it from me, is that he was born
about three hundred years too late.'

Lessingham said, 'Three hundred and sixty, I've always thought.
Get out before the Stuarts came in: I prefer that Tudor atmosphere.
Or be born, say, six hundred years ago: have a dukedom in Italy:
arts of peace and art of war, both *in excelsis*. War was part of the
humanities as the condottieri waged it, until the French and the
Spaniards came down over the Alps and showed them what. I
should have enjoyed myself in the skin of our maternal ancestor,
Frederick II of Hohenstaufen. Or go back a thousand years, to
the days of our ancestor on the other side and your namesake:
Eric Bloodaxe. Or the Persian wars. Or Troy. But what does it
matter, the time one is born in? A man can build his freedom in
any age, any land. I can live as well today as I could have in Egil

Skallagrimson's time, or Sir Walter Ralegh's. If I couldn't, I'd be a failure then too.'

Eric snorted like a bull. 'I can't understand chaps like you. Hankering already for the next war, or a revolution.'

'You certainly don't understand me,' said Lessingham very quietly.

Charles shook his head. '"There ain't going to be no" next war.'

'Isn't there?' said Lessingham. 'Who's going to stop it?'

'I don't know. But it's got to be stopped. Or alternatively, the whole show goes west. Don't you agree, Edward? What did you and I fight for?'

Lessingham made no reply for a moment: only a myriad most slight and subtle alterations charactered the eagle in him against mountain and sky. 'Fight for?' he said at last. 'The motive, you mean? or the accomplished fact? I suppose we went into it because we were fighting men, and had a mind to defend what we cared for. And in the event I think we'll find we've preserved England as a land for eunuchs to dwell in, and made the world safe for short-haired females.'

'That's only superficial,' said Charles.

Eric gave a great guffaw. 'Two distinct operations, ladies and gents; and yet, you observe, the product identical in both cases – Now I've shocked you, Mary. I do beg your pardon.'

'Not in the least. I'm not shocked. It's simply that that sort of witticism doesn't frightfully amuse me. Shall we leave them to their argy-bargyings?' she said to Anne, and walked away with her toward the house.

'Superficial, my dear Charles? May be,' said Lessingham. 'So too is the surface of the grass-growth, seen from an aeroplane, superficial; but yet you can tell by it where the buried cities lie, accurately, street by street, feet-deep under the earth, in Mesopotamia.'

These are things that will pass. All part of the mess-up. But if they are to pass – then, no "next war". Another war would put the lid on it.'

'I see no early prospect of their passing,' said Lessingham. 'They have hardly begun. There's a promising future for them and for what they stand for.'

Charles Bremmerdale grunted. 'I don't deny the danger,' he said, very quiet and serious. 'I think nothing will do but a real change of heart. We've said that about the enemy till one's nauseated. Got to say it now to ourselves, and do it – or else. I do what I can. I think one's got to.'

Lessingham looked at him with a queer and uncustomed tenderness in his speckled grey eyes. 'Forty-five million hearts to change over?' he said. 'And that's only a beginning. My dear Charles, what we're really up to is – if we can – to make the world safe for big business: for a new kind of slave state: that's the first deep current under the surface, evolution towards Hobbes's Leviathan and away from the individual. And your unhaired woman (they'll be as common as the cartway soon) and your unmasculated man, are part of the engine, worker ants, worker termites, neuters: worthless lives to themselves, which only exist to run the engine, which itself exists only to run. Until it runs down. And then sink with stink *ad Tartara Termagorum*.'

Eric's laugh came short, sharp, and harsh, like an eagle's bark. 'The only true word Plato ever said,' said he, the brass tenor of his voice contrasting with his brother's basso profondo, 'was that the world will never go right till philosophers are kings.'

'He said one or two true things besides that,' said Lessingham. 'What? O yes, I can think of one: about the high-hearted man, the μεγαλόψυχος.'

'That such kind of men have wrought the greatest evils both upon cities and upon private persons, and also the greatest benefits, according to their bent of mind? Yes, and then he says a weak nature can be cause of no great thing, neither of a good thing nor of an evil. Well, that's not true. Many weak natures together can be cause of the greatest evils: most of all if they are used by a scoundrel of genius as his instruments. And that is the rock on which all revolutions run to wreck.'

Charles said, 'Why not a man of genius to use them for good ends?'

'Because smallness of spirit,' answered Lessingham, 'is an apt instrument for evil: an unhandy one for good. And yet all the chat today is, that democratic institutions are somehow going to be the salvation of the civilized world.'

'Well,' said Charles, 'what's your alternative?'

'I see none, on the grand scale. The folly lies not in supporting democracy as a *pis aller*, but in singing hymns to it, treating it as something fundamentally good. No hard thinking, no resolute policy, even when our foot is on their neck: instead, a reiteration (like a bunch of superannuated school-ma'ams) of comfortable platitudes, with our eyes on the ballot-box. We have defeated "Prussianism". Have we so? I thought the object in war was to defeat your enemy, not defeat some absurd abstraction. We gave him an armistice when, at the last gasp, he asked for it. Now we're going to dictate terms of peace, in Paris apparently. I'd rather have carried the war to destruction clean through Germany, defeated him bloodily beyond cavil or equivocation, let him taste it at his own fire side, and dictated peace in Berlin. If we'd lost a hundred thousand lives by doing it (and we shouldn't have: nothing like it), it would have been worth the price.'

'And you one of them, perhaps?' said Charles.

'Certainly: gladly: and I one of them. For if we'd done it we could now be generous without risk of misunderstanding. As it is, I fancy we're going to be rather less than generous. And a load of mischief to come of it. Even if it doesn't cost us all the fruits of these past four years, and leave us the job to do all over again.'

Eric said, 'I dislike talking to you, Edward, on world politics. You depress me.'

'You shouldn't be so easily depressed.'

'I always remember what you said before the war, about modern war between Great Powers in Europe: what it would mean. Do you remember? Knock two chestnuts together on strings (game of conquerors): no harm done. But try that game with two expensive gold watches, and see what happens.'

'The event hasn't proved that the analogy works, though,' said Charles.

'Hasn't yet,' said Eric. 'But don't you go imagining we're out of the wood yet, my boy. Not by the hell of a long way. Edward's a cynical dog, damn him. But he talks sense.'

'Edward's not a cynic,' said Charles. 'He's a philosopher. And a poet.'

'And a painter. And a man of affairs. And a cantankerous devil. And (to give him his due), a damn good soldier,' said Eric.

Lessingham laughed. 'If I'm a philosopher, I love England, and you, brother, as my real Englishman. But this is the time for looking at ourselves in foreign looking-glasses. Scaliger said, four centuries ago, "The English are proud, savage, insolent, untruthful, lazy, inhospitable, ungainly, stupid, and perfidious."'

'Good God,' said Eric. 'And there's a Japanese proverb: "When a fool spits at Heaven, the spittle falls back in his own face."'

'Well?' said Lessingham. 'Do you want to have a look at the new mistals we're building at the farm?'

As they came up upon the terrace Mary met them, with Anne Bremmerdale. She said, 'Have you seen Mr Milcrest?'

'No,' said Lessingham. 'And I don't desperately want to.'

'He's hunting for you with some things from the post office.'

'Confound them.'

'Here he comes.'

'What's the use of you as a secretary?' said Lessingham, as Milcrest, heated with the chase, handed him two terracotta envelopes. 'Couldn't you burn the beastly things, or drown them, or lose them till tomorrow?'

'If you'll give me an indemnity in advance, sir.'

'What's that you say?' Lessingham was undoing the envelope marked *Priority*: he read it through swiftly, then again slowly, then, upon a salvo of damns, began striding up and down oblivious of his company, hands in his pockets, brow black as thunder. After two or three turns, so, he opened the second telegram and, having read it, stood for perhaps twenty seconds as if withdrawn into himself. 'Bad news for you, old man,' he said, turning to his brother. 'And for me, and the dear girl': he looked at Anne, whose grey eyes, very like his own, waited on his words. He handed Eric the telegram. 'There'll be one for you, no doubt, at Snittlegarth.' Anne came and read it over Eric's shoulder: with difficulty, for his big hand shook and made the words run together. 'Didn't live long to enjoy his K.C.B.,' he said gruffly, almost brutally; but Mary thought she saw in the hard blue eyes of him, as he turned away, something incongruously like a tear.

Fanny Chedisford was writing letters in the drawing-room. Mary came and said to her, 'You and I will have to keep each other company tomorrow.' Fanny looked up brightly, but her expression changed. 'We've just heard,' Mary said: 'my youngest brother-in-law, Will Lessingham, died suddenly in London last night. Rather a favourite.'

'O Mary, I am so terribly sorry.'

'Edward has to go up by the night train tomorrow in any case: some important conference suddenly called at the Foreign Office. Anne and Charles are off at once, after lunch, by car. He was a bachelor, as you know, and Anne always rather the one in the family for him. We've no details: only that he collapsed in his consulting-room in Harley Street.'

'You're not going yourself?'

'No. Couldn't do anything. I don't like funerals, and Edward doesn't like them for me. I don't like them for him either. However.'

Fanny was prodding at the blotting-paper with her pen. 'A terrible loss to his profession. I remember him so well in the old days: always coming to stay with Anne. How old was he?'

'Eric, Frederick, Antony and Margaret, William, Anne – he came between the twins and Anne: forty-one this year, I think.'

'Young.'

'One used not to think forty young. Too young, certainly.'

'I can't get hold of Edward,' said Eric, coming in from the hall. 'Seems to have locked himself into the library, and told the servants he's not to be disturbed.'

'You know each other, don't you?' said Mary. 'My brother-in-law—'

'Mrs Chedisford? I should think we do!' They shook hands. Fanny looked uncomfortable.

'Edward has shut himself up to work,' Mary said. 'Got to get something ready for one of his hush-hush meetings on Tuesday.'

'O. Well, I'll catch him at lunch. Several things I want to suck his brains about.'

'I doubt whether you'll get him at lunch. Possibly not at dinner even. You'd much better stay the night: we can fit you out. Lovely silk pyjamas. Brand new toothbrush. Everything you want. Do. To please me.'

'Most awfully nice of you, Mary. Upon my word, I think I will.'

'O good. We'll telephone to Jacqueline, so that she needn't be anxious about you.'

'Not she. She's too well trained after fourteen years of me, to worry about where I have got to. Tell me, do you think Edward's got one of his berserk rages on him?'

'I shouldn't be surprised, from the way he got down to this job, whatever it is, in the library.'

'Rolling his eyes, biting on the rim of his shield, bellowing like a bull?'

'Figuratively, yes.'

'Gad. I'd have liked to have seen it. Does it often happen nowadays?'

'Well, we haven't seen such a great deal of each other during these nightmare years. No oftener, so far as I know, than it used to do. It's a family trait, isn't it? I've always understood you had those times of, shall we say, violent inspiration followed by flop like a wrung-out dishcloth, yourself?'

'Who told you that, my dear Mary? Jacqueline?'

'Perhaps.'

'Secrets of the nuptial chamber: by Jove, it's monstrous. Well, I can promise you my goes are as Mother Siegel's soothing syrup compared with Edward's. Do you remember that famous occasion at Avignon, summer before the war?'

'Do I not!'

'Yes, but you only saw the working-up. I had a ring seat for the grand main act.'

'What was all this?' said Fanny.

'O, that's a great story.'

'Tell Miss Chedisford.'

'A great story. I and my wife, Edward and Mary, all sitting enjoying ourselves in one of those open-air café places: warm summer night, lovely moon and all that, lots of chairs and tables, folks gossiping away, band playing. Table near us, pretty girl – French – and her young man: nice quiet inoffensive-looking people. Presently, hulking great rascal, looking like one of those Yankee prize-ring johnnies, lounges up, takes a good look at the young lady, then planks himself down at their table. Well, they don't seem to value him: move away. Chap follows them: sized 'em up, apparently: got a bit of liquor on board: anyway, roots himself down on a chair and starts making up to the girl. Young man a bit rabbitish by the look of him: doesn't seem to know quite what to do. Well, Edward watches this for a minute, and his heckles begin to rise. "Damn it all," he says, "I'm going to put a stop to this." I tried to stop him: none of our business: don't want a scene. Not a bit of it. Up he gets, strolls over in that quiet devil-may-care way of his, stands over this tough and, I suppose, tells him to behave himself. Too far off for us to hear what they said, but evidently some back-chat. At last, man ups with his arm, glass in hand, as if he meant to shy it in Edward's face: however, seems to think better of it. – You remember, Mary?'

'O dear, O dear! Go on. It all comes back to me so perfectly.'

'This is fun,' said Fanny. 'I like this.'

'Next thing, both standing up; then walk away together, the fellow damned angry, blustering away, but as if under marching orders, in front, scowling and snapping over his shoulder: Edward as if treading on his heels to make him go a bit faster. By God, I said, I'm going to see this through. Left the women, and tooled along behind, keeping out of sight not to annoy Edward; but just in case. They went straight through a kind of passage there is, direction of the Palace of the Popes, till they land up at that hotel – what was it? Silver Eagle or something – and a porter in uniform standing at the door: quiet street, no one about. Poor old bruiser chap hurrying along as if he didn't know why, and didn't quite like it, but just had to: marched off like a pickpocket. Then Edward says to the porter, "You know me?" "Oui, monsieur." "Do you see this man?" he says. "Oui, monsieur." "Very well. You're a witness." And he says to the chappie, "You insulted a lady in my presence," he says, "and you insulted me. And when I told you to apologize, you insulted me again. Is that true?" That gets the fellow's rag out proper: wakes him out of his trance. "Yes it is," he says, making a face at him like a hydrophobic pig, "yes it is, you blanky blanking blanker, and I'll blanky well blank you up the blanking blank blank": rush at him, try to kick him, the way those blackguards do; but before you could say knife, Edward grabs him somehow – too quick to see; too dark – but in about one second he has him off his feet, throws him bodily against the wall – plonk! And there he dropped.'

'Threw him? Do you mean threw him through the air?' said Fanny incredulously.

'Yes, like a cat. Chap weighed twelve stone if he weighed an ounce. For a minute I thought he was dead: looked damned like it. Nasty mess—'

'O thank you,' Mary said, 'we can leave out the decorations.'

Five minutes later, showing Eric his room, she said, 'I ought to have told you about Fanny. She's dropped the *Mrs.*'

'What do you say? Dropped? O Lord, I made a gaff, did I? Can't be helped. What happened?'

'A great many things that had better not.'

'Fellow turn out bad hat?'

'About as bad as they make them.'

'Marriage of first cousins, wasn't it? and parents disapproved. Quite right too. Divorce, or what?'

'Yes.'

'Quite in the fashion. Damned fool. She's a fine woman. Most people are damned fools, one way or another. I wonder what's become of that nice brother of hers, Tom Chedisford?'

Mary was silent.

'Look here, my dear Mary,' he said suddenly: 'you see a lot more of Anne these days than I do. Is everything going as it should there? You know what I mean.'

'Absolutely, I should have said. Why?'

'That fellow Charles. Does he treat her properly?'

'Dotes on her. Always has.'

'He's a dull dog. You think they're happy together?'

Mary laughed. 'Good heavens, I don't know why you ask me these things. Of course they are.'

'A bit hum-drum.'

'Most of us get a bit hum-drum as the years go by.'

'Most of us may, but some of us don't.'

'Perhaps some people get on better that way. One can't lay down a *Code Napoléon* for happy marriages.'

'You think she's got what she wants?'

'I certainly think so. If she hadn't we certainly couldn't give it her.'

Eric wrinkled up his nose and shot out his lips. 'What I don't like to see is the dear girl getting to look more and more like a spinster: kind of unattached look. Better never have married the fellow if the effect of him is to turn her into a maiden aunt. Edward hasn't done that to you. Nor I to Jacqueline.'

'O dear, we're getting painfully personal. Hadn't we better stop?'

'Just as you like, my dear. But before we leave the subject I may as well tell you that you and Edward are the only married people I've ever known who always seem as if you weren't married at all, but were carrying on some clandestine affair that nobody was supposed to have wind of but yourselves. And you keep young and full of beans on it, as if you would always go on growing up, but never grow old. And if you ask me which of you deserves the honours for that, I'm inclined to think it's honours easy: between the two of you. And you can tell him from me, if you like, that that's my opinion.'

It was past eleven o'clock, the same night. Lessingham was in the library among a mass of papers, books, maps, statistics, and cigar-smoke. 'You'd better turn in now, Jack: be fresh for the morning. We've got most of the stuff taped and sorted now. I'll go on for a bit: get my covering memorandum into shape: that's the ticklish part of it, what the whole thing stands or falls by, and I can do it best by myself. You've got the annexes all off the roneo now, have you?'

'All but Annex V,' said Milcrest.

'You'll have lots of time to finish up before lunch. You're certain they're not going to let us down about that aeroplane?'

'Certain, sir. I got the general's promise from his own mouth. Confirmation in writing too: he rummaged among the papers on the table and produced it.

'Capital. David will run you over to the aerodrome. He'll have to be back in good time to go with me to Carlisle: I start at seven o'clock sharp. All right about my sleeper?'

'Yes.'

'And they know at Carlton House Terrace to expect me for bath and breakfast on Tuesday morning, and that you sleep there Monday night?'

'Yes.'

'I may have to go straight on to Paris: can't tell till after Tuesday's meeting. If so, I'll want you with me. Make all arrangements on that assumption.'

'Right, sir.'

'Off you go to bed, then. We've done a rattling good day's work. Good night.'

Lessingham, left to himself, lighted a cigar, threw up his legs on the sofa, and for a quarter of an hour sat thinking. Then he sprang up, went to the writing-table, and set to work. Two o'clock struck, and still he wrote, tossing each sheet as it was finished onto the floor beside him. At three he put down his pen, stretched his arms, went over to the side-table where, under white napkins, cold supper was appetizingly set out: chicken in aspic, green salad with radishes, and things ready for making coffee. By twenty past he was back again at work. Day began to filter through the curtains. It struck five. He drew the curtains: ate a sandwich: opened a bottle of Clicquot: collected the sheets off the floor, and sat down to go through them: checking, condensing, a rider here, a rider there, here three pages reduced to one, there an annex brought up into the body of the memorandum, or a section of the memorandum itself turned into an annex, this transposed, that deleted, the whole by pruning and compression brought down from about seven thousand words to three. Eight or nine pages, perhaps, of open-spaced typing: three foolscap pages, three and a half at most, the Foreign Office printer would make of it; apart from the annexes, which contained the real meat, the factual and logical foundation upon which the whole proposal rested. But which nobody would read, he said in himself as he snapped to the self-locking lid of the dispatch-box over the completed whole. What are the facts and what is logic? Things to play with: make a demonstration: dress your shop window with. Facts and logic can make a case for what you please. The vast majority of civilized mankind are, politically, a mongrel breed of sheep and monkey: the timidity, the herded idiocy, of the sheep: the cunning, the dissimulation, the ferocity, of the great ape. These facts are omitted in the annexes, but they are the governing facts; and policy will still be based upon them, and justified before the world as embodying the benevolent aspirations of the woolly flock together with the cleverness of the bandarlog. And the offspring of such a policy will be such as such a world deserves, that was mid-wife to it: a kind of bastard Egyptian beast-god incarnate, all ewe-lamb in the hinder parts with a gorilla's head and the sphinx's claws of brass; likely to pass away in an ungainly and displeasing hara-kiri: head and claws making a bloody havoc of their own backside and puddings, and themselves by natural consequence perishing for lack of essential organs thus unintelligently disposed of.

It was nearly half past nine when he rang the bell for Milcrest. 'There it is, in the box. I don't want to see it again. Pull off copies for circulation: I rely on you to check it: wake me if there's any real doubt on any point, otherwise don't. Leave me two copies in my pouch: take the rest personally to 2 Whitehall Gardens without fail this evening. The sooner the better.' He yawned and stretched. 'I'm a fool,' he said: 'kicking against the hard wall.'

Dog-tired suddenly, he went upstairs and, without enough energy to undress, flung himself on his bed just as he was. His brain had been working at full pressure for twenty-two hours on end. In less than a minute he was fast asleep. Mary peeped in at the door: came in softly: put an eider-down over him, and went out again, closing the door soundlessly behind her.

He woke late in the afternoon, had a bath, came down to tea, settled Eric's problems for him, and by seven o'clock was well on the way to Carlisle. Old David's heart was in his mouth, between the terrifying speed and the cool control of Lessingham's driving.

Summer night wheeled slowly above the out-terraces of Memison: the moon up: Venus in her splendour like a young moon high in the west. The King said, 'He is returned to Acrozayana, to hold tomorrow his weekly presence. That is well done. And you shall see there is a back-bias shall bring him swiftly here again.'

Vandermast stroked his beard.

The King said, 'I am troubled in a question about God. Omnipotence, omnipresence, omniscience: having these three, what hath He left to hope for? By my soul, did I find in myself these swelling members grown out of form – to do all, to know all, to be all – I swear I'd die of their tediousness.'

Vandermast said, 'Your serene highness may yet consider that the greater the power, or the pleasure, the greater needeth to be the ἄσκησις or discipline.'

The King said, 'You mean that the Omniscient and Omnipotent must discipline Himself and His own power and His own knowledge, treading, as upon a bridge of two strained ropes above the abysses, at once the way of reason and the way of sensuality?'

Vandermast said, 'Yes. Within which two ways and their permutations shall be found two million ways wherein a man may live perfectly, or a God. Or two million million ways. Or what more you will. For who shall limit God's power, or who Her beguiling, Her δολοπλοκία?

The king said, 'What is τό τέλος, then? What is the end and aim of life in this world we live in?'

Vandermast said. 'She is the end. Though the heaven perish,

She shall endure. A man is unmanned if he level at any lower mark. God can reach no higher.'

The King said, 'But what of that dictum of the sage, *Deus se ipsum amore intellectuali infinite amat*: God loves His own Self with an infinite intellectual love? And is not that a higher mark?'

Vandermast said, 'It is a good point of philosophy: but your serenity hath left out of the reckoning the ultimate Duality in Oneness of the nature of God. The Self hath its being – its cause material, its cause formal, its cause efficient and its cause final – wholly in that which it loves. And yet, by unresolvable antinomy, remains it of necessity other than that which it loves. For in love there must needs be ever both a selfsameness and an otherness.'

The King said, 'Who are you, old man? Winding up stars to me out of the unbottomed well of truth, as it were myself speaking to myself, and yet they are mysteries I never scarce cast a thought upon until now?'

Vandermast said, 'The self, as we have said, hath its being wholly in that which it loves.'

And the King said, under stars in Memison, 'And She too, by like argument, awful, gold-crowned, beautiful Aphrodite, loving Herself and Her own perfectnesses, loves them, I suppose, not for their own sake but because of Him that loves Her and by Her is loved.'

Vandermast said, 'That is undoubtable. And it is the twofold anchor-cable of truth and truth. And thus in Her and because of Her, is the supreme ἄσκησις: an infinitude of formal limits whereby the dead unformed infinite of being and becoming is made to live.'

The King said, slowly, as out of a slow deep study, 'So that, were it to be God: then, may be, through the mind of this horse, this fish, this slave, this sage, this queen, this conqueror, this poet, this lover, this albatross, as He or She, to open Our eyes here and there: see what manner of world this is, from inside it. And, for interest of the game, drink Lethe before so looking: be forgetful awhile of Our Olympian home and breeding. Even to look,' he said after a minute's silence, 'through many windows at once, many pairs of eyes. As, spill quicksilver: many shining bodies, every one outwardly reflecting all other but shut off by its own skin from all other, inwardly secret to itself: yet will join together again at the full close.'

Vandermast held his peace. The King, gazing into the eyes of that old man, gazed into profundities of night: of Night, that is sister to death, but mother also of desire and mother of dreams, and between the pillars of her bed are the untravelled immensities of the interstellar spaces.

It was nineteen twenty-three, the first week in February, a gloomy sodden-souled day colourless with east wind. Mary reined up her horse at the edge of Kelling Heath. 'We'd better keep to the road,' she said over her shoulder to Anne Bremmerdale, who had halted a yard or two behind her. 'Rather dangerous, with all these old trenches. They ought to fill them up.'

'Useful for the next war,' Anne said.

They waited a minute, looking northwards and seawards over the heath. Mary turned in the saddle for a sweep of the eye over the country inland. All was brown and bare now and the trees unleaved; but near at hand the may-bushes were beginning to show signs of waking with their dark intricacy of thorns and their myriad tiny stars: green little balls, the first swelling of the buds, in a criss-cross twiggy heaven. No buttercups this time of year, no meadowsweet, dew-pearled, creamy and heavy-scented, no lovely falling note of the peggy-whitethroat nor lark's song mounting and mounting more golden than gold to salute the lady dawn; and yet, in this wide heathland and the turbulent sky above it, a fifteen-year-old echo of these things, and of those galloping hooves that had been as flying darkness under the morning, with muffled rollings in the heart of darkness like distant drums. 'Do you think we get older?' Mary said, as they drew back into the road and at a walking-pace turned inland. 'Or do you think we are like the audience at a cinema, and sit still and watch the thing go by?'

The proud lines of Anne's face hardened to a yet closer likeness to her brother Edward's. 'I think we grow older,' she said. 'Most of us.'

The wind seemed to think so too. Grow older and die. Sometimes die first. Mary said, 'I think we get more awake.'

And yet: to untell the days and redeem those hours? Ah, if it were possible. That had been the day of the last of those cricket matches that there used to be every year for so many years, against Hyrnbastwick. Poor Hugh, blinded in the war: at least he had his wife: probably the right one. And Lady Southmere was there, did Anne remember? Of course she did: gone long ago, both those old people. And Mr Romer, whom Jim admired so and was so fond of up at Trinity: a great favourite of Edward's too: a man eminent in spheres usually incompatible, both as don and as man of the world: an education in itself to have known him. He died in 'fifteen. So many of those people caught by the war: Jack Bailey, killed: Major Rustham, Hesper Dagworth, Captain Feveringhay, killed, killed, killed: Norman Rustham, that delightful little boy, gone down with the Hawke. Nigel Howard, killed: poor Lucy. And her brother married to that – well, we won't use Edward's word for her. And Tom Chedisford, of all people, drinking himself to death, it seems: incredible: appalling. 'What does Janet Rustham do nowadays?' said Mary.

'Good works.'

'And those awful Playter girls?'

Anne smiled. 'One turned nun: the other's in some government job. Cuthbert Margesson captained your side that year, didn't he? I can't bear to think of Nell's never to this day knowing what became of him: too ghastly, that "reported missing".'

'It was worse for Amabel,' Mary said, 'having Nicholas murdered under her nose by those brutes in Kieff. They let her go, because she was English. But you're being dreadfully gloomy: almost making me cry, with this ugly wind and all. Remember, there have been some happy things: Tom Appleyard, an Admiral now and quite undamaged: Rosamund a full-blown marchioness: you and Charles: Edward and me: dear Jim, the salt of the earth, I don't think doomsday could change him; and Uncle Everard and Aunt Bella: and Father, so hale and hearty, though he is getting on for seventy.'

'Getting on for seventy. And lonely,' Anne said in her own mind.

'Lonely.' To some unclothing quality in that word, the rude wind seemed to leap as to a huntsman's call, taking her breath, striking through her thick winter clothes to raise gooseflesh on her skin. She shivered and put her horse to a trot. For a while they rode in silence, each, for friendship, with the other's private ghosts for company: for Mary, Anne's dead brothers, Fred and Will Lessingham, and the only other sister, Margaret, who married that eccentric explorer man and died of yellow fever in the basin of the Orinoco; and for Anne, all Mary's three brothers, all gone: eldest and youngest killed in the war, and Maxwell, the middle one, years before that in a hunting accident. Ghosts of the past, dank and chilling. But not actively menacing as was this secret one, present to Lady Bremmerdale alone, which all the time held its ground undisturbed by her other thoughts that came and went. It held its ground with a kind of mock obsequiousness and paraded its obedience to her will: an incipient ghost, grey, obscuring with its breath the windows of the future: a ghost without distinct form, except that, like the comic man in old-fashioned pantomimes, it seemed to be perpetually removing yet another waistcoat. And at each removal, the effect was not a revealing, but an effect of ever more unmistakable and ever bleaker emptiness.

As they walked their horses up out of the dip towards Salt-house Common, she said, 'Here's a general knowledge question for you, Mary dear: a point that's been teasing me a good deal lately. Would you say it was possible for two people to live successfully simply as friends? Married people, I mean: so to say, a Platonic marriage?'

Mary inclined her head as if weighing the matter before she answered. 'I think I would apply there Dr Johnson's saying about the dog walking on its hind legs: it is not done well, but you are surprised to find it done at all.'

'I doubt, myself, whether it is possible,' said Anne. 'Surely it ought to be. Not that there's any particular virtue in it: it's so obviously a matter of taste. But tastes count for a good deal when you're considering a pair of Siamese twins. I fancy differences of taste on a point like that can be unsurmountable barriers, don't you?'

Mary looked at her, but Anne's face was averted. 'I don't think I ever really thought about it. Unsurmountable is a big word. I should have thought if they were fond of each other they might hit upon some *modus vivendi*.'

'But there might be people, of course, with such poles-asunder ideas.'

'If they really cared,' said Mary, 'I shouldn't think ideas ought to matter much.'

'Ideas about love, I meant. What it is.'

'Well, if they loved each other?'

'But might it not be that, just because they do love each other, and their ideas are so different (or ideals), they settle down to a *modus vivendi* that evades these controversial ideas? And will not that lead to living on the surface: shirking the deep relationships? If you're colourblind you can't expect to be very amusing company for someone whose whole interest is taken up with colour schemes based on red and green.'

Mary said, 'I wonder? Surely, when one marries one undertakes to play the game according to certain rules. Both do. It seems a bit feeble to give it up because, for one or other or for both, the rules happen to make it specially difficult.'

Anne was silent for a while. Then she said, 'You speak as a born mistress of the game, my beloved. I was thinking of less gifted, less fortunate, bunglers.'

'Perhaps it's hard for you and me to put ourselves in their shoes,' said Mary.

'Perhaps it is.'

'What I'm quite sure of,' said Mary, 'is that if there is friction of that sort, it's much better that, of the two, the woman should be the less deeply in love.'

Anne said, after a pause, 'You don't believe in cutting Gordian knots, then?'

'No. I don't.'

'Never?'

'Never for people in the particular kind of muddle we're thinking of.'

'But why never? I'd like to know why you think that.'

Mary seemed to ponder a minute, stroking her horse's neck. 'I expect really it is because I believe we are put into this world simply and solely to practise undoing Gordian knots.' She looked at Anne, then away again: concluded very gently, 'To practise undoing them: not sit down on them and pretend they aren't there.'

Lady Bremmerdale sighed. 'I should imagine the real trouble comes in a case where the players have themselves made the game about ten times more unplayable than it ever need have been: spoilt it, perhaps, right at the beginning, by pulling the knot into a jam there's no undoing. And then, if there is no undoing, the choice is to sit tight on the tangle and pretend it isn't there (which I think dishonest and destructive of one's self-respect), or else be honest and cut it. Or chuck it away and have done with it.'

'I certainly shouldn't sit on it, myself,' said Mary. 'Very galling, I should think, to the sitting apparatus! But as for cutting, or throwing away,' she said with a deeper seriousness, '– well, my darlin', that's against the rules.' Anne said nothing: looked steadily before her. 'Besides,' said Mary, 'I don't see how you can ever, in real life, say in advance: Here's a tangle there's no undoing.'

After a long pause Anne said, 'Jim takes exactly the same line as you do.' She looked round, into a pair of eyes so easy to rest in, it might have been her own eyes regarding themselves from a mirror.

'O, Jim has been tried on the general knowledge paper, has he?'

'The two people I know in the world fit to be asked their opinion on such a subject.'

'People talk to Jim, because he talks to nobody. I'm glad he agrees with me. Leaving out present company, I think Edward qualifies for third on your list.'

'I don't count him,' said Anne. 'He hardly counts as another person.'

Mary's silence, clearer and gentler than words could have said it, said, 'I understand.'

'Edward says cut it and be damned to it.'

'I would agree with that,' said Mary, 'if there were a *tertium quid*: the vulgar triangle. There usually turns out to be, of course.

Practically always. But in this hypothetical case, I gathered there
was not?'

'In this hypothetical case I can promise you there isn't'

'Well then—'

It was getting late. They had fetched a circle round by Glandford
and the Downs and so through Wiveton and Cley with its great
church and windmill and up onto the common again and were
now riding down the hill above Salthouse. The broad was alive
with water-fowl. Beyond the bank they saw the North Sea like
roughened lead and all the sky dark and leaden with the dusk
coming on and a great curtain of cloud to northward and a sleet-
storm driving over from the sea. Mary said, 'I should think Charles's
view might be valuable.'

Lady Bremmerdale's handsome face darkened. 'I haven't
consulted Charles,' she said, after a pause.

They came riding into Salthouse now, level with the bank. They
saw how a flight of brent geese, a score or more, swept suddenly
down steeply from that louring sky like a flight of arrows, to
take the water: a rushing of wings, black heads and necks arrow-
like pointing their path, and white sterns vivid as lightning against
that murk and beginnings of winter night.

Anne said slowly, 'But I think I'm inclined to agree with you
and Jim.'

'And we, madonna, are we not exiles still?
When first we met
Some shadowy door swung wide.
Some faint voice cried,
– Not heeded then
For clack of drawing-room chit-chat, fiddles, glittering lights,
Waltzes, dim stairs, scents, smiles of other women – yet,
'Twas so: that night of nights.
Behind the hill
Some light that does not set
Had stirr'd, bringing again
New earth, new morning-tide.

'I didn't mean that seriously, years ago when I wrote it,' Lessingham said: 'that night you were such a naughty girl at Wolkenstein.' He was working on a life-size portrait of Mary in an emerald-green dress of singular but beautiful design, by artificial light, between tea and dinner that same afternoon, in the old original Refuge at Anmering Blunds. 'I mean, I felt it but I hadn't the intellectual courage of my feelings. Strange how the words can come before the thought,' he talked as if half to her, half to himself, while he worked: 'certainly before the conscious thought. As if one stuck down words on paper, or paint on canvas, and afterwards these symbols in some obscure way have a power of coming to life and telling you (who made them) what was in fact at the back of your mind when you did it; though you never suspected it was there, and would have repudiated it if you had.'

Mary said, 'It opens up fascinating possibilities. On that principle you might have an unconscious Almighty, saying, as He creates the universe, *Moi, je ne crois pas en Dieu.*'

'I know. I can't see why not. An atheistical Creator is a contradiction. But is not reality, the nearer you get to the heart of it, framed of contradictions? I'm quite sure our deepest desires are.'

'I'm sure they are.' A comic light began to play almost imperceptibly about the corners of Mary's lips. 'Really, I think I should find an atheistical Almighty much more amusing to meet than an Almighty who solemnly believed in Himself. Can you imagine anything more pompous and boring?'

Lessingham was silent a minute, painting with concentrated care and intention. Then he stopped, met her eye, and laughed. 'Like an inflated Wordsworth, or Shelley, or Napoleon: prize bores all of them, for all their genius. You can't imagine Homer, or the man who was responsible for *Njal's Saga*, or Shakespeare, or Webster, or Marlowe, thinking like that of themselves.'

Mary smiled. 'Marlowe,' she said: 'when he was like to die, "being persuaded to make himself ready to God for his soul, he answered that he would carry his soul up to the top of a hill, and run God, run devil, fetch it that will have it." I could hug him for that.'

'So could I. They were far too deep in love with their job to bother about themselves as doers of it. They knew the stature of their own works, of course: Beethoven's saying of the *cavatina* (wasn't it?) in Op. 130, "It will please them someday"; but that is worlds apart from the solemn self-satisfaction of these one-sided freaks, not men but sports of nature. How would you like Shelley for your *inamorato*?'

'I think I should bite his nose,' Mary said.

Something danced in Lessingham's eye. He painted swiftly for a minute in silence. 'Just as I know,' he said, taking up the thread of his thought again '(better than I know any of your what people call accepted scientific facts) whether a picture of mine is right when I've finished it, or whether it's worthless. It's one or the other: there's no third condition. When I've finished it. Till then, one knows nothing. This one, for instance: heaven knows whether it will come off or not. My God, I want it to.'

'Yes. You used to slash them into pieces or smudge them over when they were half finished. Till you learnt better.'

'Till you taught me better. You, by being Mary.' He stood quickly back, to see sitter and portrait together. 'You are the most intolerable and hopeless person to paint I should think since man was man. Why do I go on trying?'

'You succeeded once. Perhaps that is why. The appetite grows with feeding.'

'*The Vision of Zimiamvia* portrait? Yes. It caught a moment, out of your unnumerable moments: a perfect moment: I think it did. But what is one among the hundreds of millions? Besides, I want a perfect one of you that the world can see. That one is only for you and me and the Gods. O, the Devil's in it,' he said, changing his brush: 'it's a lunacy, a madness, this painting. And writing is as bad. And action is as bad, or worse.' He stepped forward to put a careful touch on the mouth: stepped back, considered, and corrected it 'Est-ce que vous pouvez me dire, madame, quelle est la différence entre une brosse à dents et un écureuil?'

Mary's response was the curiousiest of little inarticulate sounds, lazy, mocking, deprecatory, that seemed, as a sleepy child might if you stroked it, or a sleepy puppy, to stretch itself luxuriously and turn over again, hiding its nose in the downy deep contentment of many beloved absurdities: how stupid you are, and yet how dear you are to be so stupid, and how cosy us two together, and how absurd indeed the world is, and how amusing to be you and me.

'Do you know the answer? His eyes were busy.

'No,' she said, in a voice that seemed to snuggle deeper yet into that downiness of honey-scented pillows.

'Quand on les mit tous les deux en dessous d'un arbre, c'est celui qui le grimpe qui est l'écureuil.'

'O silly riddle!'

'Do you know what you did then?' said Lessingham, painting with sudden extreme precision and certitude. 'You did a kind of pussy-cat movement with your chin, as though you were smoothing it against a ruff. I know now what this picture wants. Have you got a ruffle? Can't we make one? I can see it: I could do it out of my head. But I'd like to have it in the flesh, all the same.'

'Angier can make one by tomorrow. I can show her.'

'Tired?'

'No.'

He put down palette and brushes. 'Anyhow, let's knock off and have a rest. Come and look at it. There. Aren't I right?'

Mary, standing beside him, looked at it awhile in silence. 'Not one of those enormous ones,' she said, 'like a peacock's tail.'

'Good heavens, no.'

'Nor the kind that swaddles one up to the chin in a sort of white concertina, as if one hadn't any neck.'

'No, no. I want it quite narrow: not more than two inches deep, like Isabella d'Este's in our Titian in the music-room at home. But much longer, of course, following the opening of your dress.'

'When you designed this dress,' said Mary, 'did you mean it to be a Zimiamvian dress?'

'Pure Zimiamvian. It clothes, but does not unduly conceal:

adorns, but is not silly enough to try to emulate: displays, but
does not distort.'

'On the principle of Herrick's *Lily in Crystal*.'

'Exactly. It's a Zimiamvian principle, isn't it? Up to a point.'

'Or rather down.'

'I should have said, down. There again: another of these anti-
nomies at the heart of things. Every experience of pure beauty is
climacteric; which means it gathers into its own being everything
that has led on to it, and, conversely, all that leads on to it has
value only because of that leading on. You can't live on climaxes
alone.'

'Words!'

He was busy selecting new brushes and setting his palette
for the green. 'I stand rebuked. A concrete parallel, then. Think
of the climax, like all the morning stars singing together, worked
up in those terrific tremolo passages towards the end of the *Arietta*
in Op. 111. Played by itself, what is it but just a brilliant and
extraordinarily difficult display of technique? But play it in its
context, coming after the self-destroying Armageddon and
Ragnarok of the *Allegro con brio ed appassionato*, and after those
early unfoldings of the *Arietta* itself—'

'Ah, that little simple beginning,' said Mary, 'like little farms all
undesecrated, and over there the sea without a blemish; and all
the fields full of tiny speckets, lambs in spring.'

'And so gradually, gradually, to the empyrean. Which is itself
simply the ultimate essence crammed with the implications of all
these things. White hot with them.'

'Or a great mountain,' she said. 'Ushba, as we first saw him
from those slopes of the Gul glen above Betsho, facing the dawn.
Take away the sky: take away the roots of the mountain: the
Suanetian forest about the roots – crab-apples, thorns, rowan,
sweet brier and rhododendron, hornbeam and aspen and beech
and oak, those monkshoods higher than your head as you rode
by on horseback, and great yellow scabious eight feet tall, and
further up, that riot of poppies and anemones, gentian, speedwell
and ranunculus, forget-me-not geraniums, and huge Caucasian

snowdrops: take these trimmings away, you lose the size and the wonderfulness and the living glory of it, and have nothing left but a lump of ice and stone.'

'The unrelated climax. Dead. Nothing.'

Mary was studying the picture on the easel. 'You've started the hair, I see.'

'Just roughed it in.'

'It ought to be black. Jet-black.'

'Ought it?'

'Oughtn't it? And scarlet dress?'

'Because I've captured the Queen of Spades mood about the mouth?'

'Well, of course. Why should she be tied down to red-gold and green? She doesn't like it. Has to put up with it in this stodgy world; but, when you can paint like that, it's most unkind not to give her her own outsides sometimes. After all, she is me, just as much as I am myself. You painted her in your Valkyrie picture, but I've always felt that as fancy dress. I can't wear poppy-red, or yellow or even honey-colour. But I itch to wear them: will, too, someday. For (you and I know) there will be days there, won't there?'

'Days. And nights. How could you and I get along without them?'

'Why should we be expected to? – Well,' she said, 'I'm ready. An hour yet before it will be time to change for dinner.'

'Head's free now,' said Lessingham as he settled her pose again: 'I'm only on the dress. I can't alter this now,' he said, returning to his easel. 'And the truth is, I couldn't bear to. But I'll do the spit image of it, if you like – same pose, same everything, but in Dark Lady form – as soon as this is finished.'

'And a self-portrait too, perhaps,' said Mary, 'on the same principle?'

'Very well.'

'She'd like it. Personally, of course, I prefer my King suited in black rather than red. But when she gets the upper hand – and remember, she is me—'

Lessingham laughed. 'It's a mercy that these Jekyll–Hyde pre-
dilections of ours don't lead to promiscuity on both sides. How
is it they don't?'

'Because when longing aches you for *La Rose Noire*, it is still
me you ache for. The empty body, or with someone not me behind
it: what would you give for that?'

'*O madonna mia*, who sent you into this world, I wonder?'

'Who sent us?'

Lessingham painted for a while without speaking. The clock
ticked, while slowly on the canvas inert pigments ground in oil
gradually, through innumerable subtle relationships of form and
colour, took life: gradually and painfully, like the upthrusting of
daffodil blades through the hard earth in spring, became to be the
material witness to the vision, seen through Lessingham's eyes, of
Mary's warm and breathing body clothed in that dress which from
throat to hips, like a fifteenth-century coat-hardy, fitted like a skin.
Still painting, he began to say, 'What happens when we get old:
twenty, thirty, forty years hence? To lovers, I mean. Get old, and
powers fail: blind, deaf, impotent, paralysed? Is memory enough?
Even that fails. Bad to think of: a going down into fog and obscurity.
All the things of the spirit belong so entirely to the body. And the
body is (in our experience) matter. Time dissolves it away. What
remains?'

Mary made no answer: only sat there, breathing, beautiful,
desirable, while the clock ticked on.

'Some Absolute? Some universalized Being? The Self resumed
like a drop of water into a river, or like the electric lamplight into
the general supply of electrical energy, to be switched on again,
perhaps, in new lamp-bulbs? Surely all these conceptions are
pompous toys of the imagination, meaning the same thing – Death
– from the point of view of the Me and You: from the point of
view, that is to say, of the only things that have ultimate value.
Futile toys, too. Abstractions. Unrealities.'

'Futile toys,' Mary said, under her breath.

'"Love is stronger than Death,"' Lessingham said. 'How glibly
people trot out these facile optimisms, till the brutal fact pashes

them to pieces. "The spirit lives on": orthodox Christian ideals of love. Well,' he said, 'goodness counts.' He painted in silence for a time. 'And, in this world, goodness fails.'

Mary half opened her lips. 'Yes. It does,' she said at last, in a voice that seemed to go sorrowful over sea-streams to oblivion.

Lessingham's words came slower as the tempo of his painting became faster, his brushwork surer and more triumphant. 'The tragedy,' he said, 'is in the failure of other people's goodness: to see someone you love suffer unjustly. No good man cares a snap about his own goodness' failing. Probably because, seen from inside, it is not such a good goodness after all.'

Mary said, 'I think we all see truest from outside.'

'I hope we do.'

After a silence, while the splendour of the picture grew together swiftlier and swiftlier on the canvas, he began to say, 'The ideal of the non-attached. It's a compromise ideal. A sour-grapes ideal. A spiritless weak negation, to reject the goods of this world, the heaven of the senses. Sensual delight by itself is an abstraction, therefore worthless. But in its just context, it folds in the whole orb of the world: it becomes the life-blood, the beatific vision.'

Mary said, 'That is pure truth, *mon ami*.'

'It is the arch-truth,' he said; 'and of it is born the great truth of conflict and contradiction. But it is not a truth of this life. Look at the two good characters of perfection: the static and the dynamic. You must have both. But, in this life, that is just what you can't have. Evanescence in itself; the sunrise, a sheet of trembling shell-pink blossom at midday, bare twigs and fallen petals by evening: sunset light on the Sella (do you remember?): human birth, flowering time, decay, and death: the kitten becoming a cat: night giving place to day, day to night: all the uncertainnesses and unknownness of the future. Are not all these part of the very being of perfection? The Ever-Changing: the γλυκύπικρος, bitter-sweet: that which cannot be reversed: that which will never come back: that which says "never again". But so also, the imperishable laughter: the sun that never sets: the night that stands still for lovers: the eternal eyes of the Gods: the Never-Changing.'

Mary said, 'Ever-Changing: Never-Changing. You had it engraved in my alexandrite ring.'

'But how reconcile them?' He squeezed out more paint. 'Can you and I?'

'Only Omnipotence can do it.'

'And Omnipotence is a fraud if it doesn't?'

'Dare we say that?'

'With our last breath, we must. Or be blasphemers.'

After a moment's silence, 'Where does that come,' Mary said: '*God's adversaries are some way His own; and that ownness works patience?*' Then, after another silence, 'I am sometimes so taken with astonishment,' she said, 'at the unspeakable blessedness of some passing minute, that I could not have the heart to be unthankful even if I knew for certain there was nothing besides: nothing before that minute and nothing after it, for ever and ever and ever. And that minute, nothing too, as soon as it was over.'

'And my answer to that,' said Lessingham, very slowly, 'is that in the pure goodness and perfectness that bred those words out of your mouth this moment, burns a reality that blows to the wind in ashes the doubt those words plead for.'

She watched him painting while he spoke. 'And so, you believe it?' she said at last.

Lessingham said, 'Because of you.'

'Literally believe it, as sober matter of fact? So firmly as to be able to die in that belief?'

'Yes,' he said: 'as firmly as that.'

'Even at the risk of its being a false belief? And (as you used so often to say to me) how can we tell?'

'Don't you think a belief so strong that you can die in it is too strong to be false? Must it not, of its mere strength, be true?'

'I would say yes. But if it were the other to die. If you had me here dead this minute. What then?'

Lessingham painted swiftly. 'Compromise,' he said, 'is a virtue in an imperfect world: it is the virtue of statesmanship. But in philosophy, compromise is abdication of the sovereign mind within us, and a fogging of the issue. Our love, yours and mine, is native to a perfect world, where spirit and flesh are one: where you can both eat your cake and have it. Isn't that true?' After a pause he said, very low, 'And when it comes to dying, I had actually rather you went first. Not long first, I should hope; but first.'

Their eyes met.

Mary said, 'I know. And I know why. And, for the very same "why" I had rather, myself, have it the other way.'

She watched him awhile in silence: the Olympian grace and strength of him, the singular marriage of his bodily frame of north with south, the gyr-falcon lights in his eyes, the sensitive powerful hand that guided the brush as he painted, the great black beard. Presently he stepped back to survey his work. From half-finished portrait to original his eyes leapt, and there stayed held. Utterly unselfconscious Mary seemed, sitting there, all turned outward to the world; yet with that unselfconsciousness that accepts admiration, which is its natural atmosphere, as a flower accepts sunshine; as of course. Her hair was done low on the back of her neck, plaited so that the plaits gave a tesselated effect with ever varying shades of gold and copper and red in the tight-wound gleaming surfaces; and at the side, upon the neck behind the ear, the growth of the extreme hairs, delicate as single threads of the silkworm, rose exquisite in intricate variety of upward curve, as the lines of fire or of a fountain's upward jet blown sideways in the wind. 'You say it is credible because of me,' she said softly. 'I suppose that must always be so: easy to see the Divine shine through in the person one loves: quite impossible to see or imagine it in oneself.'

Suddenly, by a short-circuiting of the electric current, the light went out. Neither he nor she moved.

'That was a strange effect,' Lessingham said out of the blackness. 'My eyes were filled, I suppose, with the green of your dress, so that when the light went I still saw, for a flash, clear cut on the darkness, that dress, but flaming scarlet.'

He struck a match.

'Well, here I am,' Mary said, 'still in my right complexion. But why scarlet?'

'The complementary colour.'

'Very appropriate too, *mon ami*, after what we were talking about?'

XIV

THE FISH DINNER: PRAELUDIUM

MEAN time in lovely Memison (if indeed, betwixt here and yonder, there could be other than mean time), the Lady Fiorinda, pleasuring her senses with the balm-sweet breathings of the air in that Zimiamvian garden, walked, with none but her own most unexperimented thoughts for company, in the tented glory, wide-rayed, cloudless, golden, serene, of the slow July sun descending. Here, upon the Duchess's birthday, but a month ago, had she lazed herself, beneath these poplars, beside this lily-pond, but then under heat of noon: a month ago only and a day. And now, like a refrain to bring back with its presence the preluding music of that midsummer night, there came through the trees the lord Chancellor Beroald, gorgeously apparelled in doublet and hose of gold-broidered brocade.

'Good evening, good brother. Are these your mourning weeds, for your late brother-in-law?'

'No,' he said. 'Are these yours, for your late husband?'

'Now I think on't, they will serve.' She looked down at her coat-hardy, woven of thousands of tiny margery-pearls and yellow sapphires, skin-close, clinging like a glove, and her velvet skin, black as the raven, fastened low about the hips with a broad girdle laid over with branches of honeysuckles of fine flat gold and cloudy strawberry-coloured tourmalines. 'I have evened accounts with you now,' she said, meeting with mockery in her eyes his haughty outwardness of ironic calm. 'You put on your ruffians to ease me from the first bad card you dealt me: not out of any undue study of my convenience, but because you thought you knew a likelier to serve your purpose. And now I have turned your likelier second (almost of the same suit) with the deuces and treys out of the deck.'

'What course took you to destroy him?' asked Beroald equably, as it had been to ask 'rode he on Tuesday to Rumala?' or such ordinary matter.

Fiorinda laughed. 'And your intelligencers have not told you that? You, who keep a servant fee'd in every man's house from Sestola to Rialmar?'

'He was found torn in pieces in the woods hereabout,' said the Chancellor. 'This is the bruit in this countryside. I know no more.'

'Suffice it, he had me wronged. May be that is enough for your lordship to know. I did not dive into your profundities in that matter of Krestenaya, thinking your most ingenious policies your affair. You may justly use a like discretion when (as now) my private matter is in question.'

'Sometimes, my lady sister,' he said, 'I am almost a little afeared of you.'

Fiorinda looked at him through her fingers. 'I know you are. It is wholesome for us both you should treat me with respect. If I am minded to lend you a hand in the otherwhile vacations of your graver businesses, be thankful. But forget not, sweet brother, I am not to be used for ends outside myself: not by any man: not were he my lover even: much less by a politician such as you.'

The Lord Beroald's lean lips under his short clipped mustachios stirred upon a sardonic smile. 'You are all firishness and summer lightnings this afternoon. There's something unovercomable underlies it,' he said. 'Howsoever, I think we have the wit to understand each other. Enough, then. I came not to speak on these trifles, but to let you know her grace hath bid me to supper tonight, private, a fish dinner, at the summer palace. Know you who shall be there?'

'The King. The Duke. The Parry. You. My lord Admiral (Gods be gentle to his harmless soul). There's the sum, I think.'

'No ladies?'

'Myself.' All delicious pleasures and delectations worldly respired about that word as she spoke it.

'No more?'

'O a one or two, for form sake.' She looked at him a moment, then said: 'I will tell you a thing, now I remember me. I have been honoured with a new proposal of marriage.'

'Ha?' The Chancellor's cold eye sparkled. 'I know from whence.'

'You know?'

'All Meszria knows.'

'Indeed? Well, and I have refused it.'

'Nay, I am put from shore then. Who was it?'

'Ask not overcuriously.'

'Not the Duke of Zayana.'

'The Duke of Zayana.'

'But I thought so. But you jest, sister. You have refused the Duke?'

'I have refused him once, twice.'

'But third time?'

'And he come to me a hundred times with such a suit, he shall have No for every time he shall ask me.'

'But wherefore so? Duke Barganax?'

'I know not,' said she. 'Perhaps for because that I grow out of liking of this vain custom, whereby husbands have been sessed and laid upon me, as soldiers are upon subjects, against my will.'

Like wind on clear water, ruffling the surface that none may see what rests below, a kind of laughter hid the deeps of her unblemishable green eyes. Beroald shrugged his shoulders. 'I would know some more weighty and more serious reason why you refused so great a match.'

'For a reason too nice for a man of law to unravel,' she said. 'Because truly and undissemblingly I wonder, sometimes, if I be not fallen, may be, a little in love with him.'

Beroald looked her in the eye. 'In love with him? And therefore would strain him fast and sure? And therefore not minded to dwindle into his Duchess?'

'Why truly and indeed you are my brother!' she said, and very sisterly kissed him.

The Chancellor being departed, Fiorinda resumed her walk, to and fro under the trees, from splendour to shadow and from shadow to splendour again as the arrows of gold found or missed her as she passed. There alighted upon pebbles at the pond's further brink a water ousel and began to regard her, with much dipping and bobbing of his body and much rolling up of the whites of his eyes. Whether because of her being alone, without so much as a brother's unenchanted eye to rest upon her, or for whatever cause, Her presence, in this hour of but natural beauties' composing of themselves for slumber, seemed to unsubstantiate all that was not Her. Black velvet's self and this milky way of seed-pearls and yellow sapphires: close-bodied coat, gown, and girdle: seemed as if fined to tissue of night made palpable, unveiling more than they clothed. Slowly some perfection, opening its heart like evening, began to enfold air, sky, and shadowy earth.

Presently came two little yellow wagtails to play in the air like butterflies, up and down, back and across, above the water. She held out a hand: they left playing, to perch upon her fingers, and there fell to billing and kissing of one another.

'The little silly birds too!' said Barganax, as, suddenly aware of his presence behind her, she shook them off.

'And will your grace think there is anything new in that?' said she, looking at him over her shoulder through the curtained fringes of her lids. There was something questionable, coloured her mood, this evening. Her lips, where but a moment since, like the dog-star's frosted sparkle of winter-nights, the colours of her thought seemed to dance, settled suddenly to the appearance as of lips carved out of sard or cornelian: so stone-like, so suddenly unmerciful in the harsh upward curling of them, like fish-hooks at her mouth's corners. 'Will you think there is anything new in that? They are grateful, I suppose, for the tricks I teach them.'

'Ingenuities beyond Aretine's', he said.

She flamed crimson, cheek and neck.

'Forgive that,' said the Duke. 'I forgot myself. And small marvel: I find all infirm and unstable whatever I behold out of you. But I forget not—'

Very delicately she bent, upon that hesitation and with widened nostrils, to a yellow lily that she wore pinned at the bosom of her dress. Then, with questioning eyebrows: 'And what will your grace's untamed thoughts forget not?'

'Tuesday night,' answered he; and watched the fires of her eyes curdle to some impenetrability of flint or ironstone.

'Well? And what will your grace wish me to say to that?'

'What you will. Worst woe in the world to me, were you ever act or speak upon order.' He paused: then, 'Nor, I think, need your ladyship forget it neither,' he said.

The sphinxian hooks unmild hardened in the corners of her mouth. 'I am yet to learn but that a night is a night, and one night as another.' In the stilled silence, the blades of their eye-glances engaged: as in sword-play, feeling one another's temper.

'Shall I, for my turn,' said Barganax, 'to match the honesty of your conversation, madam, tell you, then, a like truth?'

'As you will. An unlawful and useless game, this truth-telling. Remember, too, you did not desire me to say truth, but say what I would.'

'Know you what the wild unwise tongue of them blabbeth abroad about you, that I have it thrice in one day 'twixt here and Zayana?'

'I can conceive.'

'What? That you do rustle in unpaid-for silks? live so disorderly? marry but to unmarry yourself by running away? Or, the better to uncumber you of your husband, take a resolution to have him murdered.'

'Fair words and good semblant.'

'And fitly paid for. I'm sorry, madam, that the last, and the most mouthiest, speaker of these things—'

'A duello?'

'It was somewhat too sudden, overhearing him speak so buggishly of your ladyship: took him neck and breech, and threw him against the wall.'

'And so?'

'And so.' The Duke shrugged, looking at his fingernails. 'Well,' he said, after a moment, looking up: 'that was the third. You perceive how effectual and operative your ladyship's last dealings with me were: three men's blood,' he tapped his sword-hilt, 'for washing out this slander-work.'

She smelled once more to the lily, all the while looking up at him with a smoulder of eyes from under delicate-arching eyebrows: very slowly smiling. It was as if some string had been plucked. All little evening noises of that garden, stir of leaf, babble of running water, winding of tiny horn of gnat, beetle, or bee, seemed to put on a kind of tumultuous enormity.

'O You, unmedicinable,' he said, and his voice caught: 'unparagoned: ineffable: unnameable.' And he said, very deep and low:

> 'Nightshaded moon-still'd meadow-close,
> Where the Black Iris grows:
> The Black Musk Rose:
>
> Musk-breathing, deadly sweet,
> Setting the veins a-beat
> Till eyes fail and the sense founder and fleet:
>
> Imperial petals curl'd,
> Sable falls and wings deep-furl'd—
> You have drunk up the World.
>
> Flow'r of unsounded Night:
> Black fire over-bright:
> Blinder of sight—
>
> So, the supreme full close.
> So, drink up me, my Rose.'

With unreadable grave eyes still holding his, she listened, her
face still inclining above the sulphur-coloured scarlet-anthered
lily-flower, where it bedded so softly, there at the sweet dividing
of her breasts. Surely all the pleasures of irresolution and uncer-
tainness, all disordinate appetites of the body and unlawful desires
of the soul, the very deepest secretaries of nature, unnaturalizing
itself, took flesh in their most unshelled shining mother-of-pearled
proportions, in that lady's most slow and covert smile. At length
she spoke:

> *'Si tu m'aimes dix fois*
>   *Qu'une nuit de mal,*
> *Onziesme j'y croys*
>   *Que ton amour soit vrai—*

And remember, I will be wooed afresh *chaque fois, mon ami: mais
chaque fois.'*

The voice of her speech trailed under-tones as of ankle-rings
a-clink, or as the playing of idle polished fingernails upon hanging
mirrors, or the drawing of curtains to shut in the warmth and the
things of heart's desire and shut out the dark. Then, like some
day-drowsy sweet beast that wakes, stretches, and rises for night
and action, she faced him at her full stature. 'Some cannot do',
she said, 'but they overdo. Or did I wish your impudent grace,
indeed, to meet me here tonight?'

'Chaque fois?' said the Duke, gazing at her between half-closed
lids. 'It has been so, and it ever shall be so, and the better so shall
our tastes run in harness. I hold, not as the poet, but thus:

> Love given unsought is good, but sought is better.'

'"Ce que femme veut, Dieu le veut"? Well?' said she. 'But "our
tastes" you said? As for Meszrian grandeur, will you think, and
well-shapen mustachios?'

'O and in very particular matters I have studied your ladyship's
taste too.'

She turned from him: then, after a step or two, upon a lazing motion full of languishing luxuriousness, paused at the pond's brim, to look down, hands lightly clasped behind her, to her own counter-shape in the cool of the water. Her hair was dressed for tonight to a new fashion of hers, close-braided in two thick tresses which, coiling each twice about her head and interwoven with strings of honey-coloured cat's-eye chrysoberyls, made her a kind of crown in the likeness of two hearts bound together; all setting back, like an aureole of polished jet, from her beautiful white brow and from the parting above it, where the black hair, albeit drawn never so demurely backward on either side, carried even so some untameable note of its own free natural habit of smooth-running waves of ocean beneath midnight unstarred. The Duke, as a man that draws tight the curb on some unrulable thing within him, stayed himself for a minute, overlooking her from that distance, twice and again, from head to foot. Without further word spoken, he came over to stand beside her, so that they looked down to their two selves, mirrored there side by side.

'I find,' he said presently, 'that I do begin, in you, to know my own self. My way it hath long been, born bastard and unlegitimate, to have what I have a mind to, as the whirlwind, suddenly, unresistably. But you shall find I am not a man quickly fired and quickly laid down with satisfaction.' He paused. It was as if his heart's pounding were become a thing outwardly audible. 'These four days,' he said: 'Tuesday, and now it is Saturday: back to Zayana and back again: the unfillable desire of you. Take away you out of the world,' he said, 'and it unworlds all.'

As if bodied out of that appassionate quietude, a little owl settled on Fiorinda's shoulder. Barganax, looking round at her, met its eyes, sharp, inscrutable, staring into his. The lovely face of that lady, and lovely head inclining forward a little, showed clear, side-face in the light that began to be crimsoned now toward sun-setting: clear of the small feathered thing that perched bolt upright upon her shoulder. The whole unseizable beauty of her seemed moment by moment to suffer alteration, waxing, waning, blazing anew, as now some Greek purity of feature, now some passing favour of an unassayed sensual sweetness or, in cheekbone or nostril, some old Tartarean fierceness untreatable in the blood, wore for the instant her beauty as its own. 'Another taste in common,' he said: 'for that fire that burneth eternally without feeding.'

Utterly still she abode, save for the upward mounting of her bosom and deep fall and swell again, like the unquiet sea remembering.

Barganax said: 'You are unattainable. I have proved it. The sun rising, a roundel of copper incandescent against purple cloud: you'd swear – upon witness of your senses – 'tis come near, divinely come down to earth 'twixt us and that cloudbank; and yet, with the drifting of some thicker fold of that cloud 'twixt us and the sun's face – suddenly we know. So you. Even in the extreme having of you, I had you not. The knownest and unknownest thing in the world.'

'And that,' said she: 'is it not in the essence and very perfect nature of love?' Her words were as the plumed silence of the owl's flight that, sudden as it came, now departed, sudden from her shoulder on noiseless wing. The plague that sat dozing in her mouth's corner proked at him swiftly, an unslockened burning merry look, as she turned to him, hands behind her head, settling the plaits of her hair. 'I hope it remains not unkindly with your grace that I am not one that will eat a pear unpared? Nor that there's more than but make me dress and undress because you find me pliant?'

'You and I!' said the Duke. In their stilled eye-parley, darkness trembled upon darkness. 'And I think I shall carry to my grave,' here he touched his left shoulder, 'the print of your most eloquent teeth, madam!'

As golden bells pealing down star-lit sleep-muffled corridors of all dreaming worlds, Fiorinda laughed. 'Come,' she held out her hand. 'Your grace may take your revenge upon this.'

He took the divine white daisy-hand: took the little finger: delicately, his eyes on hers, as might a cat in play, to let feel the teeth but not to hurt, bit it.

'Your ladyship smiles.'

'Perhaps. At my thought.'

The hand rested soft in his. He turned it up slowly: the under-part of the wrist: that place where hand joins arm, and the bluish tracings of veins but enhance the immaculation of skin, beneath which, a bird in prison, the pulse flutters or quiets. He kissed the hand suddenly, full in the warm palm of it: then, very formally, gave it back. 'At your thought? And it is – if one may know?'

'That your grace is an artist.'

'You like an artist?'

'I am hard to please. I like a good servant.'

'And, for you, the better artist the better servant?'

Her eyelids flickered.

'Enough. Your ladyship shall take me as servant.'

''Las, my unpatient lord, and have I not taken,' said she, and the sidelong downward halcyon-dart of her eyes was a caress, secret, precise, butterfly-fingered, mind-unthroning, 'all eleven-tenths of the journey toward that consummation already?'

Barganax's glance flashed and darkened. 'Ah,' he said: 'but I look to perpetuity. I mean, 'pon indenture.'

'O no indentures. I keep my servant so long as he please me.'

'And I my mistress, 'pon like terms: so unsure, both of us, what manner mind we will have tomorrow. To avoid which, madam, no remedy but we must instantly be married.'

'Never. I have twice answered that.'

'With answers which are not worth an egg.'

'I have answered unanswerably.'

'To be Duchess of mine? Your ladyship is the first woman was e'er so stubborn set as say no to that offer.'

'And the first, I dare say, e'er had the offer, to say yea to or nay to?'

'Instance again, we be like-minded.'

'You mean, you to offer *in extremis* a bond you'd hate to be tied withal? While I, in sheer discerning bounty, please my own self – and you – by refusing of it?'

'My life's-queen, once more your hand,' said the Duke. 'As for this suit, the court's up: stands adjourned – till tomorrow. But,' he said, 'there's measure in all things. Summer nights are but half-length. I hold me bound for tonight.'

'Well, and for tonight, then,' said she, letting him by her hands in his, draw her: letting herself be drawn so, from arm's-length, in a slow and level gradualness of air-light sailing motion, nearer and nearer, as a swan descending calm streams in windless July weather: 'for tonight, may be, I'll not tie up all refusals fast beyond untying.'

'Then, to seal the title': for all the supple strength of her striving and eluding, he kissed her in the mouth. '*Copula spiritualis*. And, 'cause One is naught: 'cause all university's reckoned in Two alone: therefore' – and again, deep and long, he kissed her, pasturing his eyes, in that close-ranged nearness, on hers which, open-lidded, impersonal as a dove's eyes, still avoiding his, seemed as in soft amazement all unperceiving of outward things, their sight turned inward. 'And the third: nay, then, by heaven! But 'cause I will!' From her quickened breaths new intoxications disclosed themselves and spread abroad, and from that lily, crushed in the straining of her sweet body to his, and, in that crushing, yielding up its deliciousness. ''Cause must be must be. 'Cause blind men go by feeling. 'Cause – What's here?'

'Girls,' she said, coolly disembroiling herself. 'Had your grace not seen such a beast before? Mistress Anthea: Mistress Campaspe: a kind of servants too of mine.' With all demureness, they made their courtesies to the Duke. 'They grow,' said the Lady Fiorinda, 'like rosemary, in any air: despatched now with commends, most like, from her grace, to desire us go in to supper. Nay, misdoubt them not: of a most exquisite tried discretion. Will you think her grace would employ 'em else? or that I would?'

'I wager no wagers upon that,' replied he. 'Enough that I ne'er beheld them till now; nor e'er heard tell of 'em neither.'

'And yet, since they first could prattle, have been of our lady Duchess's household. There yet remain matters hid from you, there, my lord.'

Barganax looked at them. 'If I should hear a cat low like an ox,' he said, 'that should surprise me. And so now, if I should see a pretty mountain lynx wear partlets of cobweb lawn and go gowned in peach-coloured chamlet; or see a peggy-white-throat,' here he changed glances with Campaspe's shy black bead-like eyes, 'with red Tyrian hair-lace, and dressed in velvet the hue of the coat of a water-rat, and with little brown musky gloves—'

Anthea laughed behind her fan. Her eyes, looking at him over the edge of it, were yellow, with upright fiery slits for pupils.

XV

THE FISH DINNER: SYMPOSIUM

IT was in her asphodel garden, under the south wall of the old keep, overlooking Reisma Mere, that the Duchess of Memison gave supper that night to guests select and few. The table was ring-shaped, eleven or twelve foot across by outside measurement breadthways, and nine from back to front, and its top about two foot wide. Where the bezel of the ring should be, where the two ends of the table curved round to meet each other, was a gap, may be of some four-foot width, for the coming and going of serving-maids to serve the company where they sat ranged in order round about the outer side of the table. 'A fish dinner,' the Duchess said as they took their places: 'sea-fare, in Her praise that is bred of the sea foam.' Lower, for the King's ear beside her, she said, *L'absente de tous bouquets*. You remember, my Lord?'

The great King said, 'I remember.'

They sat them down now: in the midst, the King in his majesty, and the Duchess at his right hand, in high-seats of sweet-smelling sandalwood cushioned with rough-plumed silver plush and inlaid with gold and ivory and all kinds of precious stones. Next to the King, Duke Barganax had his place; next to the Duke, the Vicar of Rerek; next, the lord Admiral Jeronimy; and so at the end upon that side the lord High Chancellor Beroald. Upon the other side, looking across to these, sat first, on the Duchess's right, the Princess Zenianthe, niece to King Mezentius and guesting as now with her grace in Memison; on Zenianthe's right, my Lady Fiorinda; and beyond her again, making ten in all, Anthea and Campaspe.

The legs of the table were of all kinds and colours of marble, massive and curiously carved, and the table top of figured yew and elm and cedarwood and its edges filleted with inlay-work of silver and lapis lazuli and panteron stone and pale mountain-gold. A lofty arbour with squared pillars of rose-pink clouded quartz partly shut out the sky above the table. From its trellised roof, over-run with ancient vines whose boles were big at the base as a man's thigh, grapes depended in a hundred clusters, barely beginning at this season of the year to turn colour: heavy sleepy-hued bunches of globed jewels hanging high on the confines of the candle-light. Three-score candles and more burned upon the table, of a warm-coloured sweet-scented wax in branched candlesticks of glittering gold. So still hung the air of the summer night, the flames of the candles were steady as sleeping crocuses: save but only for a little swaying of them now and again to some such light stirring of the air as speech or laughter made, or the passing of serving-damsels in their sleeveless Grecian gowns, some green, some sky-colour, some saffron yellow, to and fro for changing of the plates or filling out of fresh wines. Pomegranates, lemons, oranges, love-apples, peaches of the sun, made an ordered show, heaped high upon mighty dishes of silver or of alabaster at set intervals along that table. Smaller dishes held dry and wet sweetmeats; and there was store of olives, soused haberdine, cavier on toast, anchovies, botargoes, pilchards, almonds, red herrings, parmesan cheese, red and green peppers: things in their kind to sharpen the stomach against luxurious feasting, and prepare the palate for noble wines. Cream wafers there were besides, and cream cheese; but, for the body and substance of their feasting, no meat save fish-meat alone, dressed in innumerable delicious ways and of all sorts of fishes, borne in upon great platters and chargers by turns continually: eels, lampreys, and crayfish: pickerells, salt salmon, fry of tunny; gurnards and thornbacks in muscadine sauce; barbels great and small, silver eels, basses, loaches, hen lobsters, eel-pouts, mussels, frogs, cockles, crabfish, snails and whilks; great prawns, a turtle; a sturgeon; skate, mackerel, turbot, and delicate firm-fleshed speckled trouts.

All the company were in holiday attire. The King wore a rich doublet of cloth of gold, with wine-dark velvet slashes. The linked belt about his middle was of massive gold set with emeralds and night-dark sapphires, every stone big as a thrush's egg: the buckle of the belt in the likeness of two hippogriffs wrought in gold; with wings expansed, and between the hippogriffs a lion's face, garnished with sparks of rubies, and for its eyes two escarbuncles that glowed like hot burning coals. The Duke, upon his left, was clad from throat to toe in soft-woven dark-brown satin, cut about and bepinked with broidery of silken and silver thread: close-fitting, moulding itself to his lithe strong body's grace, upon such under-rhythms as, when a panther moves or a wakening python, with sleek-gliding ripple and swell inform the smooth outward skin. His ruff and wrist-ruffs were stiffened with saffron, and his sword-belt of bull's-hide edged above and below with beads of opal and fire-opal and balas ruby: its clasps, two dark hyacinth stones cabochon, of the colour of peat-water when the sun wades deep in it. The Vicar, sitting next to him, was all in scarlet, with a gorget of dull gold about his neck. There was, when he moved, a hard look about his chest and large broad belly, witness that beneath that peaceful outward covering of weak silk he carried a privy coat, against stabbers at unawares; having, indeed, many unlovers in the land, and especially here in Meszria, and of all estates. His beard, clipped and bristly, showed red as Thor's in the candlelight. For the rest, the Chancellor went in gold-broidered brocade the colour of a moonless night in summer where the blue shows blackest: the Admiral in a loose-sleeved coat of unshorn velvet of sober green, with black brocaded cloak and white trunk hose. But as for the costly gorgeous apparel of those ladies, hardly should a man have marked it, dazzling as it was, were he come suddenly to that board, but should have stood mute amazed by their first countenance, so untranspassably lovely of themselves – breathing, moving, discoursing – without need of all adornments in this flattering candlelight: each in herself a natural heaven in which, unmanured, all pleasure lies.

Malmsey presently and muscatel, being strong sweet wines, began to circle sunwise about the board; and now free ranged their discourse, with bandyings to and fro of the ball of wit, and with disputation, and laughter, and with sparkles struck, as from flint, out of thought by thought. King Mezentius, taking, for the while, little part in the game of words, yet of his only mere presence seemed to rule it. Almost it was as if this one man sat hooded, and unbeknown looker-on at a scene of his devising, and the players thereof but creatures engendered of his hid and deep judgements out of his own secretness. In whose free persons he seemed to call into being each particularly of speech or look or thought itself, when, how, in whom and from whom, he would.

'So silent, madonna?'

The Duchess dimpled her cheek. 'I was but considering how good a gift that were, to be able to stay Time, make it stand still.'

'To taste the perfect moment?'

'What else?'

'But how? when Time is put to a stop and no time left to taste it in?'

'I would taste it, I think,' said she, 'in a kind of timeless contemplation.'

'Timeless?' said the Princess Zenianthe.

'Why not?'

'Contemplation. 'Tis a long word. To say it takes time. To do it, more, I'd have thought.'

'Ah, cut Time's claws, then,' said the Duchess. 'Let him be, for me, so he snatch not things away.'

Barganax smiled. 'Say I were a squirrel, sat in the fork of a nut-tree, pleasantly eating a nut. At first bite, Time stands still. Where's my second?'

The Duchess wrinkled up her nose. 'Why, just! Into what distemper have the Gods let decline this sweet world of ours! It is so. But need it be so in a perfect world?'

'A perfect?' said the King.

'Now and then I have conceived of it.'

'Was it like to this world?'

She nodded. 'Most strangely like.' And now, while the sturgeon was ushered in with music in a golden dish, she said privately, 'Are you remembered, dear my Lord, of a thing I asked you: the night you rode north alone with Beroald and left me, good as fresh wed and fresh bereaved? – If we were Gods, able to make worlds and unmake 'em as we list, what world would we have?'

'Yes, I remember.'

'And your answer? You remember that?'

'May be I could and I would. But natural present, *madonna mia*, should better best rememberings?'

'Your very answer!' she said. 'Not word for word; but the mind behind the word.' She paused. 'Makes me frightened sometimes,' she said, in a yet lower voice, looking down.

'Frighted?'

'When I'm alone.'

'We are as the Gods fashioned us.' Unseen, beneath the table, his hand closed for a moment over hers: Amalie's hand, mistress and outward symbol of so unconsumable store and incorruptible of shyest and tenderest particular wisdoms and goodnesses and nobilities of the heart, heaped through slow generations to that dear abundance, yet outwardly of so lamb-like an unprovidedness against the crude nude gluttony of the world and iniquities of time and change and death.

'There's wits enough about this table, could we unmuzzle them,' he said aloud, after a moment's silence, 'enough to pick the world to pieces and devise it again span new. My Lord Horius Parry: what world will you make us, say, when we shall have granted you patent to be God Almighty?'

'Go, some have called me ere now,' answered he, 'and not always out of pure love of me, a man of high-vaulting ambitions. But, Satan shield us! here is a new puzzle. I ne'er looked above the moon. I can not know how to answer.'

'Answer, cousin, without these protestations,' said the King;

'which be stale as sea-beef. I and you do know one another by this time.'

'Your highness knoweth me. Would God I were sure I as thoroughly knew your highness.' He guzzled down his wine, carouse: stayed toying a minute with the empty cup. 'Why, as for worlds,' he said, 'this world fits: I ask no other. A world where the best man' – here his eye, enduring the King's, had a look less unsearchable in its depths, belike, than the looker reckoned – 'a world where the best man beareth away the victory. Wine, women, war: nay, I rate it fit enough. And, upon conditions,' he swept a hot bold stare round the table, 'even peace,' he said, 'can be tolerable.'

'*Pax Mezentiana*,' said the Duke to himself.

'But peace,' said the Vicar, 'softeneth, womanizeth a man'; and his stare, to the disembarrassing of the ladies, singled in turn the Chancellor, the Admiral, and the Duke. Fiorinda, catching the Duke's eye, did no more but act him again a gesture of his, of an hour since in the garden: look at her finger-nails.

'In sum, my Lord the King,' said the Vicar, 'I am a plain man. Know my trade. Know myself. Obey my master. And, for the rest (saving present company):' he glowered, right and left, upon Duke, Admiral, and Chancellor: '*nemo me impune lacessit*.'

'In sum,' said the King, 'you like well this world and would let well alone?'

'Humbly, it is my judgement.'

'Which,' said the King, 'your excellency may very wisely and wholesomely act upon.'

It was as if, for a freezing instant, an axe had shown its mouth. The lean lines of the Chancellor's lip and nostril hardened to a sardonic smile.

'You and I,' said the King, turning to the Lord Jeronimy, 'are oldest here. What say you?'

'My Lord the King,' answered he, 'I am five years older, I think, than your serene highness. And the older I grow the more, I think, I trust my judgement, the less my knowledge. Things I thought I knew,' he said, leaning an elbow on the table, finger and thumb drawing down over his forehead one strand of his lank pale hair, while he cast about the company a very kindly, very tolerant, very philosophic look, 'I find I was mistaken. What in a manner were certainties, turn to doubt. In fine—' he fell silent.

'There you have, charactered in speech, the very inwardness of our noble Admiral,' whispered the Duchess in Zenianthe's ear: 'a man wise and good, yet in discretive niceness so over-abounding that oft when it comes to action he but runneth into a palsy, from unability to choose 'twixt two most balanced but irreconcilable alternatives.'

Eyes were gentle, resting on the lord Admiral. A humorousness sweetened even Beroald's satirical smile as he said, answering the King's look, 'I, too, hold by the material condition. This world will serve. I'd be loth to hazard it by meddling with the works.'

The Duke shrugged his shoulders. 'Unless thus far only, perhaps,' he said, eyeing that Lady Fiorinda across the table: 'seeing that a world should be, to say, a garment, should it not be – to fit the wearer 'twas made for—' and something momentarily ruffled the level line of her underlids as the sun's limb at point of day cuts suddenly the level horizon of the sea, 'everchanging, never-changing?'

'And is this of ours not so?' said the King, his eyes too on that lady.

'Ever-changing,' the Duke said: 'yes. But as for never-changing,' Campaspe heard the alteration in his voice! as the nightbreeze sudden among sallows by the margin of some forsaken lake, 'I know not. Best, may be, not to know.' Anthea, too, pricked ears at the alteration: scurry of sleet betwixt moraine and ice-cave when all the inside voices of the glacier are stilled by reason of the cold.

'Yes, even and were we Gods,' said the King, and the stillness seemed to wait upon his words: 'best, may be, not to know. Best not to know our own changelessness, our own eternal power and unspeakable majesty altogether uncircumscriptible. For there is, may be, in doubts and uncertainties a salt or savour, without which, all should be turned at last unto weariness and no zest remain. Even in that Olympus.'

'Time,' said the Duchess, breaking the silence. 'And Change. Time, as a river: and each of us chained like Andromeda upon the bank, to behold thence the ever-changing treasure or mischief of our days borne past us upon the flood: things never to be seized by us till they be here: never tarrying to be enjoyed: never, for all our striving, to be eluded, neither for our longing, once gone to be had again. And, last mischief, Death.'

'A just image,' said the Admiral. 'And, as with the falling waters of the river, no stay: no turn back.'

'Yes. We may see it is so,' Zenianthe said. 'But how and it were other than as we see it? We on the bank, moveless at our window: Time and the world stream by. But how if the window be (though we knew it not) the windows of a caroche or litter, wherein we are borne onward with so smooth, soft, and imperceptible a motion, as floating in air, morning mists are carried beside some lake—?'

'So that we could not tell, but by descending from our chariot, whether, in a manner, the motion were in us or in the scene we look out on? 'Tis all a matter, howsoever: the masque, howsoever, of our life-days goeth by.'

'Ah, but is it all a matter, my lord Admiral?' said the Duchess. 'For, upon this supposition, there is not but one river only and the floating burden upon its waters: there is the wide world to move in, forth back and about, could we but command the charioteer—'

'Or but leap from chariot and walk, as a man should, in freedom of the world,' said the Duke.

The King said, 'Or as God and Goddess should, in freedom of all the university of all possible worlds.'

'As to say,' said Barganax, '*I will that it be now last Tuesday night, midnight*; and, at a word, at a thought, make it so.' His eye waited on Fiorinda's, which, as in some overcast night at sea the lode-star, opened upon him momentarily green fires.

'Should need a God, I should think,' said she, and some bell of mockery chimed in her lazy accents, 'to devise wisely, with such infinite choice. New singular judgement, I should think, to fit your times to the high of their perfection.'

The King turned to her. 'Your ladyship thinks, then, 'tis as well that all is done ready to our hand, without all power whether to tarry or go back, or choose another road: much less, have done with all roads and chariots and be free?'

"Tis as well, I should say,' the idle self-preening glance of her hovered about the Vicar: 'for some of us. Your serene highness will call to mind the old tale of the goodman and his wife and the three wishes.' Her brother, the Lord Beroald, stiffened: shifted in his chair. 'O, ne'er imagine I'd tell it, sweet brother: plain naked words stript from their shirts – foh! Yet holdeth as excellent a lesson as a man shall read any. I mean when, at their third wishing, so as to rid 'em out of the nasty pickle whereinto they had brought themselves with the two former, they were fain but to unwish those, and so have all back again as *in statu quo prius*. And here was but question of three plain wishes: not of the myriads upon myriads you should need, I suppose, for devising a world.'

The King laughed in his beard. 'Which is as much as to say,' he looked over his left shoulder into the face of Barganax, 'that a God, if He will dabble in world-making, had best not be God only but artist?'

'Because both create?' said Amalie.

Barganax smiled: shook his head. 'Your artist creates not. Say I paint your grace a picture: make you a poem: that is not create. I but find, choose, set in order.'

'Yet we say God created the world? Is that wrong then?' She looked from father to son. 'How came the world, then?'

There fell a silence: in the midst of it, the Vicar with his teeth cracking of a lobster's claw. Amalie looked on the King, within hand's-reach upon her left. She said, as resolving her own question: 'I suppose it lay in glory in His mind.'

Barganax seemed to pause upon his mother's words. 'And yet, so lying,' he said, 'is not a world yet. To be that, it must lie outside. Nor it cannot, surely, lie whole in his mind afore it be first laid also outside. So here's need to create, afore e'er you think of a world.' He paused: looked at Fiorinda. 'And even a God,' he said, 'cannot create beauty: can but discover.'

'Disputing of these things,' the King said, 'what are we but children, who, playing on the shore, chart in childish fancy the unharvested sea? Even so, sweet is divine philosophy and a pastime at the feast.

'But to play primero you must have cards first. Grant, then, the eternity of the World (not this world: I mean all the whole university of things and beings and times). Grant God is omnipotent. Then must not that universal World be infinite, by reason of the omnipotence of God? It is the body; and the soul thereof, that omnipotence. And so, to create that universality, that infinite World, is no great matter, nor worth divinity: 'tis but the unwilled natural breath-take or blood-beat, of His omnipotence. But to make a particular several world, like this of ours: to carve that ὕλη, that *prima materia*, that gross body of chaos, and shape it to make you your World of Heart's Desire – why, here's work for God indeed!'

'Ἐμὴν δ'ἔντυνον ἀοίδην,' said Fiorinda slowly, as if savouring the words upon her tongue: '"*and do You attune my song*,' said Fiorinda slowly, as if savouring the words upon her tongue: '*and do You attune my song*. – I was but remembering,' she said as in answer to the King's swift look.

But Anthea, scanning, as shepherds will some red April sunrise, the shadow-play of that lady's lip and eyelash, said, for Campaspe's private ear. 'Honey-dew: a certain spittle of the stars. We shall see dog-tricks tonight.'

'Have I your highness' drift?' said the Duke: 'that when Truth's unhusked to the kernel, every imaginable thing is real as any other? And every one of them imperishable and eternal?'

'Ay,' said the King: 'things past, things present, and things to come. And alike things not to come. And things imaginable and unimaginable alike.'

'So that a God, walking where He will (as you, madam,' to his lady mother, 'In your garden, making a bunch of flowers), may gather, or note, this or this: make Him so His own particular world at choice.'

The King nodded.

'And soon as made, fling it away, if not to His mind, as you your nosegay. Yet this difference: rose-bud or canker-bud, His flowers are immortal. Worlds He may create and destroy again: but not the stuff of worlds.'

'Nay, there,' said the King, 'you go beyond me. No matter. Proceed.'

'I go beyond your highness? But did not you say 'tis eternal, this stuff worlds are made of?'

'True: but who are you, to hobble the omnipotency of the most Highest? Will you deny the capacity to Almighty God with one breath to uncreate all Being, and, next breath, bring all back again pat as before?'

'To uncreate?' said the Lord Beroald: 'and Himself along with it?'

'And Himself along with it. Why not, if 'tis His whim?'

'Omnipotency is able, then, on your highness's showing, to be, by very virtue of its omnipotency, also impotence? *Quod est absurdum.*'

'Be it absurd: yet what more is it than to say He is able to create chaos? Chaos is a thing absurd. The condition of its existence is unreasonable. Yet it can exist.'

Beroald smiled his cold smile. 'Your serene highness will bear with me. In this empyreal light I am grown so owly-eyed as see but reason set to unthrone reason, and all confounded to confusion.'

'You must consider of it less narrowly: *sub specie aeternitatis.* Supposition is, every conceivable bunch of circumstances, that is to say, every conceivable world, exists: but unworlded, unbunched: to our more mean capacities an unpassable bog or flux of seas, cities, rivers, lakes, wolds and deserts and mountain ranges, all with their plants, forests, mosses, water-weeds, what you will; and all manner of peoples, beasts, birds, fishes, creeping things, climes, dreams, loves, loathings, abominations, ecstasies, dissolutions, hopes, fears, forgetfulnesses, infinite in variety, infinite in number, fantasies beyond nightmare or madness. All this *in potentia.* All are there, even just as are all the particulars in a landscape: He, like as the landscape-painter, selects and orders. The one paints a picture, the Other creates a world.'

'A task to decay the patience of a God!'

'No, Beroald: easy, soon done, if you be Almighty and All-knowing.'

'As the poet hath it,' said the Duke, and his eyes narrowed as a man's that stares up-wind searching yet more remote horizons:

> 'To an unfettered soules quick nimble hast
> Are falling stars, and hearts thoughts, but slow pac'd.'

'What of Time, then?' said the Duchess.

'That is easy,' said Barganax: 'a separate Time for each separate world – call't earth, heaven, what you will – that He creates.'

The Duchess mused. 'While Himself, will you think? so dealing, moveth not in these lower, cribbed, successions which we call Time, but in a more diviner Time which we call Eternity. It must be so,' she said, sitting back, gazing, herself too, as into unseen distances. 'And these worlds must exist, full and actual, as the God chooses them, remaining or going back, as He neglects or destroys them, to that more dim estate which we call possibility – *These flowers, as in their causes, sleepe.*'

'All which possible worlds,' said the King, 'infinitely many, infinitely diverse, are one as another, being they are every one available alike to His choice.'

'Except that a God,' said the Duchess, 'will choose the Best.'

'Of an infinite number perfect, each bearing its singular and unique perfection, what is best?'

'And an infinite number imperfect?'

'How otherwise? And infinitely various and innumerable heavens. And infinitely various and innumerable hells.'

'But a God,' Amalie said, 'will never choose one of the hells to dwell in.'

'He is God, remember,' said the Duke, 'and can rid it away again when as the fancy takes Him.'

The Vicar gave a brutal laugh. 'I cannot speak as a God. But I'll stake my soul there's no man born will choose to be in the shoes of one judged to die some ill death, as (saving your presence) be flayed alive; and there's he, stripped to's buff, strapped convenient on a plank, and the hangman with's knife, split, nick, splay, roll back the skin from's belly as you'd roll up a blanket.'

Zenianthe bit her knuckles. 'No, no.'

The King spoke, and his words came as a darkness. 'As His rule is infinite, His knowing is unconfined.'

'To look on at it: enough knowing so, I'd a thought,' said the Parry. 'Or do it. Not be done by.'

'Even that,' said the King, as it were thick darkness turned to speech. The eagless looked forth in Fiorinda's eyes.

'Go,' said the Vicar: 'I hold it plain blasphemy.' Fiorinda, with unreadable gaze beholding him, drew her tongue along her lips with a strange and covert smile.

'Come, we have fallen into unhappy talk,' said the King. 'But I'll not disthrone and dissceptre God of His omniscience: not abridge His choice: no, not were it to become of Himself a little stinking muck of dirt that is swept out of unclean corners. For a moment. To know.'

But the Duchess Amalie shivered. 'Not that – that filthiness the man spoke on. God is good: will not behold evil.'

'Ah, madam,' the King said, 'here, where this lower Time determines all our instants, and where is no turning back: here indeed is good and evil. But *sub specie aeternitatis*, all that IS is good. For how shall God, having supreme and uncontrollable authority to come and go in those infinite successions of eternity, be subject unto time, change, or death? His toys they are, not conditions of His being.'

There was a pause. Then said the Duke, thoughtfully dividing with his silver fork the flesh from the bones of a red mullet, 'Needs must then (so reasoneth at least my unexpert youth) that death and annihilation be real: the circle squared: square root of minus one, a real number. Needs must all particular beings, nay, spirits (if there be) unmade, without beginning or ending in time, be brought to not-being; and with these, the One unical, the only-being Being, be obliterate, put out of memory, *vox inanis*, Nothing.'

The Vicar, upon a swig of wine, here bedravelled both beard and cheek with his too swift up-tipping of the cup. The Lord Jeronimy, as grown suddenly a very old man, stared, slackmouthed, hollow-eyed, into vacancy, fingering tremulously the while the jewel of the kingly order of the hippogriff that hung about his neck. Zenianthe, herself too at gaze, yet bore not, as the Admiral, aught of human terror in her eye: only the loveliness of her youth seemed to settle deeper, as if rooted in the right and unjarring harmonies of some great oak-tree's being, when the rust of its leaves is melted in the incandescence of a still November sunset which feeds on summer and shines towards spring. Anthea whispered Campaspe: their nymphish glances darted from the Duchess's face to the face of her lady of honour: so, and back: so, again.

After a little, the Duchess began to say, resting her eyes the while on that Lady Fiorinda: 'But there is, I think, a dweller in the innermost which yet IS, even when that immeasurable death shall have disrobed it of all being. There is that which made death, and can unmake. And that dweller, I think, is love. Nay, I question if there truly BE, in the end, aught but love and lovers; and God is the Love that unites them.'

There fell a stillness. Out of which stillness, the Duke was ware of the King his Father saying, 'Well? But what world, then, for us, my Amalie?'

'Answer me first,' said she, 'why will God this world and not that? Out of this infinity of choice?'

The King answered, 'For Her 'tis wrought.'

'So Her choice it is?'

'Must we not think so?'

'But how is She to choose?'

'How can She choose amiss? Seeing that every choice of Hers is, of Her very nature, a kind of beauty.'

'But if He may so lightly and so unthriftily make and unmake, can He not make and unmake Her?'

'We must think so,' said the King. 'But only at cost of making and unmaking of Himself.'

'My lord Chancellor smiles.'

'But to observe,' said the Chancellor, 'How his serene highness, spite of that conclusion he hath driven upon so many reasonable principles, is enforced at last to say No to the Most Highest.'

'It is Himself hast said it, not I. There is this No in His very nature, I should say,' said the King. 'The most single and alonely One, abiding still one in itself, though it be possible, is not a thing to be dreamed of by a God: it is poverty, parsimony, an imagination not tolerable save to unbloody and insectile creatures as far removed below men's natures as men's below Gods'.'

'As the philosopher hath it,' said Barganax: '*lnfinitus Amor potestate infinitâ Pulchritudinem infinitam in infinitâ perfectione creatur et conservatur*: infinite Love, of His infinite power, createth and conserveth infinite Beauty in Her infinite perfection. You see, I have sat at the feet of Doctor Vandermast.'

Fiorinda's uncomparable lips chilled again to the contours of the sphinx's, as she said, with accents where the bee's sting stabbed through the honey to the shuddering sense, 'But whether it be more than windy words, which of us can know?'

'Which of us indeed, dear Lady of Sakes?' said the King. 'And what need we care?'

Anthea, upon a touch, feather-light, tremulous as a willow-wren's fluttered wing, of Campaspe's hand against her arm, looked round at her: with eyes feral and tawny, into eyes black and bead-like as a little water-rat's: exchanging with these a most strange, discharmed, unweariable look. And that was a look most unaccordant with the wont of human eyes: beasts' eyes, rather, wherein played bo-peep and hid themselves sudden profundities, proceeding, a learned man might have guessed, from near copulation with deity.

Amalie spoke: 'It was in my mouth to answer, dear my Lord (but I've changed my mind): "Ah, what world if not this? But this made sure of, secured. Roses, but no thorns. Change, but no growing old. Transfiguration, but no death."'

'A world without stoat or weasel?' cried Anthea, laughing a little wild-cat laugh, very outlandish and strange.

'I note in such a world,' said the Admiral, 'some breath of an overweeningness apt to tempt in a manner the jealousy of the Gods.'

'I hold it flat impiety, such talk,' said the Vicar, scarlet with furious feasting, and emptied his brimming cup of muscadine.

'Nay, you ought not so ungroundably,' said the Chancellor, 'my good lord Admiral, to imagine Gods distrained with such meaner passions as do most disbeautify mankind. Yet I see in such a world an unleefulness, and a want of logic.'

'A pool without a ripple?' said Campaspe. 'A sky with never at any time a hawk in it? Day, but no night?'

Again Anthea flashed lynx-like teeth. 'Because She is turned virtuous, shall there be no more blood to suck?'

The Duke tightened his lips.

'I could teach stoat and weasel to be gentle,' the Duchess said, very low; slowly with her fan tracing little pictures on the table. 'But I changed my mind.'

The King waited. 'What then, *madonna mia*?' he said, and opened his hand, palm upwards, on the table. The Duchess's came: daintily under its shimmer of rings touched with its middle finger the centre of his open palm: escaped before it could be caught.'

'For I bethought me a little,' said she, 'of your highness' words awhile since, that there's a blessedness in not knowing – yes, were we God and Goddess in very deed; and a zest, and a savour. So that this world will I choose, dear my Lord, and choose it not caponed but entire. Who e'er could abide a capon unless to eat? And, for a world, 'tis not eat but live withal. And be in love withal. And time hath an art, and change too, like as the lantern of the moon, to make lovely and lovable. Beyond that, I think it best not to know.'

While she so spoke, Barganax's gaze, chancing upwards, was caught by the sapphired gleam of Vega shining down through vine-leaves overhead: some purer unfadable eye, joining with the common and unevitable mortality of these candleflames to survey the things which these surveyed and, albeit more distantly and with less flattering beams, caress them, pronounce them good. In that star's light he followed his mother's words: the honeyed accents, the owl-winged thought, the rainbow-shot web of memories, the unheard inwardness of laughter under all, as a night's dewing of grace and sweetness. Then his eye, coming down again, met with that Dark Lady's. There shone a fire there starrier than that natural star's, greener than the glow-worm's lamp, speaking, too, in articulate shudders down the spine. As to say: Yes, My friend. These words are My words: Mine to You, even just as they are Hers to Him.

'Time. And Change. But the last change,' said the King: 'your own word, madonna: "last mischief, Death."'

For a minute, the Duchess held her peace. Then she said: 'I will remember you, dear my Lord, of the tragical story of the Volsungs and the Niblungs, after the battle in King Atli's hall, and they had fallen on Hogni and cut the heart out of him; but he laughed while he abode that torment. And they showed it to Gunnar, his brother, and he said, "The mighty heart of Hogni, little like the faint heart of Hjalli, for little as it trembleth now, less it trembled whenas in his breast it lay." And Death we know not: but without that unknown, to look it in the eye, even as did Hogni, and even as did Gunnar after, when he was cast into the worm-close: without that, I wonder, could there be greatness of heart and courage in the world? No: we will have this world, and Death itself. For we will choose no world that shall not be noble.'

XVI

THE FISH DINNER: CAVIAR

'So you and I,' said the King, 'will have this world? Well, I am answered. But the game's ended ere well begun; for this world's ready made to our hand.'

'If we must try tricks elsewhere, let her choose,' said Amalie, looking at Fiorinda. 'She is too silent. Let her speak and decide.'

'Better not,' he said. 'She is in a contrary mood tonight. A world of her choosing, as now she is, should be a strange unlucky world indeed.'

'Nay, but I am curious,' said the Duchess. 'Nay, I will choose her world for tonight, whatever it be. Come, you promised me.'

'Well?' said the King.

In Fiorinda's eyes sat the smile, unrelentless, Olympian, fancy-free, of Her that leads at Her train the ancient golden world. 'The choice is easy,' she said. 'I choose *That which is*.' There was a discordancy betwixt her words, so plain and so simple, and the manner of their speaking, as from an imperial lust that, being unreined, should hardly be resisted anywhere.

The King held his peace. The Duchess looked round at him, sitting so close at her left hand that sleeve brushed sleeve, yet to look on as some watch-tower removed, black and tremendous among hills: as Our Father Zeus, watching out of Ida. '*That which is*?' he said at last. 'Out of your ladyship's mouth we look for meanings in such simplicities, as for colours in those shining exhalations that appear in tempests. Come, is't but this world again you mean?'

'I speak,' answered she, 'in honest plainness. I would wish your serene highness to receive it so.'

Campaspe and Anthea laughed with one another in secret way behind their fans.

'*That which is*, then: in honest plainness what can that be,' said the King, 'but the ultimate Two alone? They, and the blessed Gods and Goddesses Who keep the wide heaven, of a lower reality, may be, than His and Hers, yet themselves more real than such summer-worms as men? Is this your choice, then, and the golden mansions of the Father? If: then picture it to me. Let me perceive it.'

That lady smoothed her cheek, cat-like, against her ruff. To look in her eyes now was to see strange matter, as of something dancing a dance untowardly about a pit's brink. 'No. No,' said she. 'Like as her grace, I also will change my mind too: look lower.

'Well,' she said after a minute, 'I have thought of a world. Will your highness create it indeed for me, as I shall specificate?' The dying fall of her voice, so languefied in its melodious faint discords, held in the very sloth of it some menace, as of one in her affections unbitted, intemperable by her estate, raging by her power.

The King beheld her so an instant in silence; then said, 'I'll do my endeavour.'

Fiorinda lifted her head, as a she-panther that takes the wind. 'Good,' she said; and her eyes, leaving the King's, rested now constantly on Duke Barganax's who gazed upon her as a man carved in stone. 'And ere we begin upon our world for tonight's disport,' she said, 'I, as so peerlessly to be doted upon, will lay you down your terms of service, as master-builder of my worlds. Seeing I am She, I will be content with no outward shows. The wine of our loving-cup shall be the chosen butt of the chosen vintage. The very cobblers of my shoes shall be the wittiest and honestest and goodliest to look on in the world, and the best at their trade. One world shall not be enough for me. Nor one in a life-time. No, nor one a day. Aeons of unremembered ages, shall go to the making of the crumb I brush from my dress upon rising from board. Generations of mankind, innumerable as the generations of the may-fly through a hundred years, shall live and die to no purpose but to merry my senses for five minutes, if I affect for pastime before my looking-glass to untwine my tressed hair. The slow mutations of the immemorial rocks of the ancient earth shall be but for the making ready of a soft cushion of turf for me upon some hillside, in case the fancy should one day take me there to recline myself after my walking in the mountains. Upon millions of trees millions of millions of leaves shall sprout, open, turn colour, and begin to fall, only but to give me a sweet prospect from my window some sunshiny November morning. Because of me, not Troy nor not this world only, but even the whole wide universe and giant mass of things to come at large, shall be cast away, abolished, and forgot.'

Amalie's eyes, resting in the King's, read there, clear as if his lips had spoken: Yes, madonna. These words are your words: Yours to Me, even just as they are Hers to Him.

But the Duke, paler now than grass in summer, rose up, thrust back his chair; taking his stand now a little behind the King his father and his lady mother, he leaned against the bole of a strawberry-tree. Here, out of the lights, himself but hardly to be seen, he could sideways over their shoulders behold her: that mouth unparagoned, the unhealable plague of it, dark characters which who can uncypher? that moon-chilled imperial pallour of cheek and brow: all those provocations, heats, enlurings, and countermatchings, tiger's milk and enlacements of black water-snakes, which (when she turned her head) nakedly and feelingly before his eyes lay bound where, in the nape of her delicate neck, the black braids crossed and gleamed and coiled upwards: last (and unspeakable uniting together of all these), ever and again an unmasking of her eyes to meet, conscient, the burning gaze of his, constant upon her out of the shadow of darkness.

'Speak on,' said the King, to Fiorinda, but his eyes always with Amalie. 'All this is true and just and condition absolute of all conceivable worlds. Now to particulars.'

'I will desire of you, here and now,' replied that lady, 'such a world as never yet was nor was thought of. And for first principle of its foundation, it shall be a world perfect and sufficient unto itself.'

'Well,' said the King. 'What shall we frame it of?'

'You shall frame it,' answered she, 'of the infinities: of Time without beginning and without ending; and of Space without centre and without bourne.'

'Of what fashion shall it be?'

'O I will have it of infinite fashions. But all by rule.'

'But how, if you will have it of these infinities, shall it be perfect? Perfection reasoneth a limit and a bourne.'

'That is easily answered. It shall be of Time and in Time: not Time in it. And in Space and of Space: not Space in it.'

'So that these infinities stand not part of your world,' said the King, 'but it, part of them: as this bread was made of wheaten flour, yet there's wheaten flour enough and to spare, and was and shall be, other than what this bread containeth, and of other shapes too?' He dipped a piece in the gravy, and gave it to his great dog to eat that sat beside him. 'Well, I have it so far,' he said: 'but is, so far, yet but the shadow of a world: but empty space and time.'

She said, 'I will desire your serene highness fill it for me.'

'And what to fill it withal?'

'O, with an infinity of little entities, if you please: so tiny, a thousand at once shall dance upon the point of a needle. And even so, betwixt and between them where they dance, shall be room and to spare for another thousand.'

'Another thousand? No more than so?'

'Oh, if you will, infinitely more: until you, that are tireless, tire. Crowd, if you will, infinities betwixt infinities till thought swoon at it.'

Presently, 'It is done,' said he. 'And yet remaineth, spite all this multitudinousness, a dull uniformity of a world. What then?'

'Then (with humility) is't not for you, Lord, to lay to your hand: devise, continue? Have not I required it to be of infinite fashions? And must I instruct you, the great Artificer, what way you shall do your trade?'

'You must. Nay, mistress, what is the whole matter but some upstart fancy of your own? Nay, I'll read you your mind, then. You would have me set 'em infinite dances, infinite steps and figures. Behold, then: though every dancer be like as every other, the figures or patterns of their dancing are infinitely various. Of a pavane, look, I make you gold: of a coranto, air: of a bourree, granite: brimstone, quicksilver, lead, copper, antimony, proceed but each out of his several figure of this universal dance, yes, and the very elements of fire and water, and all minerals that compose the earth's natural body; even to this, which I have made for you of the allemande: this iron, which is the archaean dreamless soul of the world. Well?' he looked piercingly at her.

She, superciliously smiling, and with a faint delicate upward backward motion of her head, answered him, 'So far, I'll allow, Lord, 'tis not so greatly amiss.'

'Pshaw! It is a dead world,' he said. 'A dead soul.'

'Nay, then, let it teem with life,' said she, 'if needs must. And that horribly.'

'And what,' said the Duchess, 'is life?'

Bending with a fastidious daintiness above her plate, Fiorinda selected and held up to view upon her fork a single globule of the caviar. 'In such a world,' she answered, offering to her nearer inspection upon the fork's prong the little jellied fish-egg, 'what else would your grace desire it to be, if not some such trash as this?'

'A fish-like world!' said the King.

'Nay, but here's a most God-given exquisite precision in it,' Fiorinda said. 'Life! But a new dance only, but in more complicated figures, enacted by your same little simplicities. Sort but the numbers aright, time but their steps aright, their moppings and mowings, their twirlings, curvets and caprioles – 'tis done. Out of dead substance, living substance: even such a little nasty bit of sour jelly as this is. And, for the more mockery, let it arise from the sea: a very neoterical Anadyomene, worthy the world it riseth on.'

The King's hands, beautiful to watch in the play of their able subtle strength, were busied before him on the table. Presently he opened them slowly apart. Slowly, in even measure with their parting, the world of his making grew between them: a thing of most aery seeming substance, ensphered, glimmering of a myriad colours where the eye rested oblique on it, but, being looked to more directly, all mirk, darkling, and unsure. And within it, depth beneath depth: wherein appeared as if a seething and a churning together and apart continual of the dark and the bright. 'Well, I have given it life, as you bade. Life only. Not living beings.'

Fiorinda, considering it awhile in silence, nodded a soft assent. All else gazed upon it with eyes expressionless, unseeing, as though encountered, sudden out of light, with a void or a darkness: all save the Duchess only. Her eyes, beholding this toy, were wide with the innocent wonder of a child's.

'Well?' said the King of Fiorinda. 'Is your ladyship content, then?'

'Your highness hath been sadly badly served of your intelligencers if you conceive I should ever be content. Generality of life, thus as you present me withal, is life indeed, but 'tis not enough.'

The Duchess looked at it closely. 'You have given it life, you think?' she said very softly. 'What is life?'

'It is,' answered he, 'as you may perceive, in this world of our devising, a thing compact but of three ingredients: as, first, to feel, to wince, to answer to each intrusive touch of the outward world: second, to grow: third, to engender and give birth, like from like.' His gaze, unfastening itself from her, came back to that Dark Lady, and so again to Amalie. 'You,' he said to both: 'You, that wast with Me in the beginning of My way, before My works of old: what next?'

Fiorinda, still curiously beholding it, gave a little silent laugh. But the Duchess, shivering suddenly in the warm night air, leant back against King Mezentius as for warmth.

'I will,' said the Lady Fiorinda, and each honeyed word seemed as a kissing or a handling lickerously of some new-discovered particularity of her thought: 'I will that you so proceed with it, now from this beginning, as that even out of such contemptible slime as this is, shall be engendered all myriads of living creatures after their kind: little slimy polyps in the warm seas: little sea-anemones, jellyfishes, worms, slugs, sand-hoppers, water-fleas, toadstools, grass and all manner of herbs and trees which grow. Run through all the lewd forms of them: fishes, birds, beasts even to human kind.'

'Even to human kind? what, men and women, as we be?' said the Duchess.

Fiorinda, as not having marked the question, but continued; but slowlier: 'I will,' said she, 'that this shall be the life of them, of every thing that breatheth the breath of life in this new world of ours: to be put part of the waters as it were of a whirlpool, wherein is everything for ever neither produced nor destroyed, but for ever transformed: the living substance for ever drawn in, moulded to some shape of life, and voided again as dead substance, having for that span of time yielded its strength and purpose to that common sink or cesspool of Being. So in this, my world, shall all proceed, self-made, self-sought, out of one only original: this little spittly jelly.'

'A world,' said the King, 'of most infinite complication.'

'Nay, but I give it simple laws to work by, for makeweight.'

'What laws, then?'

'First (to order perfectly my perfect world, as perfect in action), this law: that at each succeeding moment of its existence the sum and totality of my world, and all that in it is, shall be determined reasonably and inevitably by that which was the moment before.'

'Sensible chaos, yet grounded in an infinite order.'

'Which is,' said that lady, 'the strainable force of destiny. No chanceableness. Nor no meddling finger of God neither, to ruffle the serenity of my world's unfolding. As a rose-bud discloseth itself and spreadeth abroad, so shall its processions be: as inevitable as one and one is two, one and two is three, and so on for ever, *ad infinitum*. The general forms, constant, unchangeable, untransformable; but all else changing as oft as weathercock in wind. Truly a world most exquisitely well fitted to be comprehended by a man of law?' She glanced at the Lord Beroald, who, for answer, but smiled his unbelieving smile.

'But no world, sure,' said the lord Admiral, 'for the living beings that must live in it. What manner freedom have they, where all must be predetermined and like a clock-work?'

There was a cruel look of that lady's lips and teeth, daintily eating up the little piece of caviar. She turned upon the King eyes over the balls of which suddenly a film seemed to be drawn, as they had been the eyes of an empoisoned serpent. 'I think,' she said, 'I will tease them a little with my laws. They shall seem indeed to themselves to have freedom; yet we, who look on, know 'tis no such matter. And they shall seem to themselves to live; yet if, 'tis a life not their own. And they shall die. Every one that knoweth life in my world shall know also death. The little simplicities, indeed, shall not die. But the living creatures shall. Die, and dissipate as children's castles in sand when the tide takes them, but the sand-grains abide. Is it not a just and equal choice? either be a little senseless lump of jelly or of dead matter, and subsist for ever; or else be a bird, a fish, a rose, a woman, 'pon condition to fade, wax old, waste at last to carrion and corruption?'

'Men and women, as we be?' said the Duchess. 'O, you have answered me! Or is it,' she said under her breath, 'that Myself hath answered Myself?' And again the King's gaze, unfastening itself from Fiorinda's, rested curiously on his Amalie. She was staring, as fascinated, into the teeming inwardness of the sphered thing which, motionless save for a scarce perceptible rhythmic expanding and contracting of its translucent envelope from within-inward, remained balanced as it had been some heavy bubble, a foot, may be, in diameter, upon the table betwixt her and the King. There was silence for a minute, while, under the eyes of those feasters, miniature aeons trained their untermed texture of death and birth within the artificial confines of that cosmos.

Presently Fiorinda spoke, 'As we be? I question that (saving your grace). How were that possible, out of this? Is there mind in this?' Lovelier than the argent limb of the cold moon, the curve showed of that lady's arm as, chin propped on hand, she leaned pensive over the table. 'Unless, indeed,' she said, and the slowed music of her voice sounded to new deeps: 'unless, indeed, We Ourselves will go in and enter it. Know it so. Go down—'

'Undergrope it so from within,' said the King. 'For a moment, We might. To know.'

The Duchess trembled. It was as if, in the stillness, she had suffered his mind and thought to enter so deep into her own, that she tasted, in her inmost being and without necessity of communication, the inwardness of his: tasted how, as one awakening in a strange bed sinks back into sleep again and the place of visions, he beheld now in the baseless clearness of a dream, a meadow grey with the rime of hoar-frost that sparkled with many colours as the sun made and unmade stars of the tiny crystals. A sycamore-tree was shedding its golden leaves in a slow shower in the nearly windless air: two or three at a time it shed them, translucent gold against the rising sun, and at the foot of the tree they made a carpet of darker gold where they fell. And in that necessity of dreams, that binds together as of course things which in waking life are severed and unrelated, he perceived, in the falling of each particular leaf in that bounteousness and Danaë's shower of beauty, the falling away of something that had been his. His ancient royal palace and seat-town on two-horned Rialmar, his fleets, armies, great vassals, princes and counsellors and lords of the Three Kingdoms, his queens, mistresses, children, alive or dead, they of his courts and households afar or near, under his hands: all his wide dominions welded and shaped to his will, of Meszria, Rerek, and Fingiswold: lovely Memison itself, whose balm was in his nostrils, the turf of whose garden was soft here beneath his feet: very Amalie herself, sitting and breathing now beside him: the whole of his life, this actual world he lived in, fluttered downward, unregarded, severed, golden, through that cold still air in the bright beams of the clear sun: floating scraps of memory, every one of which, even while the mind strove to grasp it, was dissipated and gone to spread deeper the bed of gold at that tree's foot.

Fiorinda but flickered an eyelid. 'It moves,' she said presently. 'It amuses me. Always it moves. Always it – changes. Yet, for all its changing, is never much the better. Nor much the worse.' She paused.

In the beholding of her face, thus pensive and stilled, was such unquiet pleasures as the sight of the stars gives. Then, 'This amuses me, too,' she began to say again: 'to note how, by merest clockwork, is a kind of perfection created, brought to maturity, maintained in being.' The scaled familiar gathered itself at her mouth's corner, intent, like as a lizard that espies a fly. 'Amuses me to regard, as in some crooked mirror, this perfection which wanteth but one jot to be a master-work, and that jot—'

'That it be truth,' said Barganax, out of the thick shadow.

It was as if a frozen blast went suddenly about that garden, come and gone in a moment of time behind the flower-sweet darknesses and the candles' soft and comfortable radiance.

Barganax and Fiorinda beheld the Duchess Amalie's hand fasten over the King's hand at her side upon the table: beheld her beauty gather itself like a serpent coiled, as she sat, level-browed, level-eyed, some high-descended Queen dreadless on the brink of fate. 'The game's too much in earnest,' she whispered in the King's ear. 'Stay for me. You and I,' she whispered: 'we are noosed: we are limed. We are in it.'

XVII

IN WHAT A SHADOW

IT was October now, of that same year nineteen hundred and twenty-three: the nineteenth of October. Night shut down on Nether Wastdale in a great rain without wind: rain steadily falling out of the premature darkness of rain-cloud that covered the sky without a gap. There was nothing to hear but the rain: nothing to see but the appearance of trunks and leafage picked out, chalky and unsubstantial, where the glare of headlights struck the holm-oaks west of the house; these, and the rain that the cold twin beams made visible, and a feebler, more distant, luminosity as of another car waiting in the road below the drive gates.

Jim Scarnside pressed the door-bell and waited. He pressed it again: waited again: then set his thumb hard upon it and kept it there, may be for thirty seconds, while he listened to the shrill metallic whirr far away within. Then lights went up in the porch: steps sounded in the hall: turn of a key, drawing of bolts, and the door stood ajar on the chain, with old Ruth's face peering through the opening. With a little inarticulate apology, she closed the door to shoot the chain, then opened it wide. They stood silent a moment, she in the doorway, Jim over against her on the doorstep. Her face showed a death-like pallour: eyes dull and puffy.

'Master at home?' he said. He saw that her cheeks were stained with the lashing of tears.

'We don't expect him till tomorrow, at earliest.'

'Nonsense. What's the car doing at the drive gates, then?'

She looked helplessly at Jim's own car, her hands, with their swollen joints and wrinkled skin, twitching at her apron.

'At the drive gates. Out in the road. It's his car. Empty, and lights on.'

She brought her hand up to her mouth. 'O, not that too. Please dear God, not that. And yet,' she said, with a kind of sob—

'All right,' said Jim. 'I expect he made better time than he expected.' He pulled up the collar of his mackintosh: began to run down the steps. At first step he turned. 'Any man in the house?'

She shook her head: 'No but me and the girls. We were shutting up for the winter, when Mr Edward comes back all sudden-like (you know his ways, sir), and starts to, packing up and I don't know what; and then, Tuesday it was: that telegram—' she choked. 'And then. Then he went,' she said. 'No, no man in the house. Only old David, sir, and he took David, so as he was to wait, mind the car at Dover, while the master went across to—' she broke down. 'O, Mr James, sir. Her ladyship: that telegram: it can't be true, sir: not killed: God couldn't permit it. And my Miss Janet and all. God couldn't—'

'Look here, Ruth,' he said, very kind but firmly, taking her by the arms, 'you and I have got to see about this: no good crying. Is the master's room ready? Fires? He'll want some dinner. You get on with it: I'll be back in a few minutes.'

'Yes, Mr James, sir. That's right, sir,' she said with a gulp: 'that's right.' Both her hands fastened on Jim's right, squeezing it. Suddenly the squeeze became tighter. He turned, looking where she looked. Their hands disengaged. Lessingham was in the porch beside them: bareheaded, in his travelling-clothes, seemingly soaked to the skin with rain.

'Jim. Good. Wait while I get the car in.'

Jim, noting the steady ring of Lessingham's voice, noted too, for all the uncertain light, as it were some glint, some poise of sinew or of lineament, in the iron-seeming face of Lessingham, that stayed the impulse to offer to go too: kept him obedient in the porch. After a few minutes they saw the lights stir and creep round at the foot of the drive; then presently met the full glare of them as the car rounded the last sweep past the strawberry-trees and swung out of sight behind the house towards the garage.

'You'll be staying to dinner, sir?'

Jim shrugged his shoulders. 'I don't know.'

'You'd better, sir. It isn't good for Mr Edward to be too much by his self, sir. Not just now it isn't.'

'We'll see.'

Lessingham's step returning, elastic and firm, crunched the gravel. 'Put your car in there if you like. Ruth will get us something to eat presently. I wish I could put you up, but I may not be staying myself tonight.'

Jim checked himself. 'Right,' he said, and got into his car.

'Well, Ruth,' said Lessingham. Their eyes met for a moment. 'I'm wet through, I think.' He looked down at his rain-sodden coat and trousers and muddy waterlogged shoes as if he had but just discovered it.

'The luggage, sir? If you'll let me have the keys, Sally will put out your things in the dressing-room and get the bath ready and I'll be seeing about your dinner. I'll just unlock the lobby door for her, upstairs.'

'No. Put the things in the Trellis Room. Here's the key of the suitcase': he took it off his chain. 'Lay for two.'

'You'll have it in the dining-room?'

'No. Lay it in the Armoury. A couple of bottles of the Lafite. Careful how you decant it.'

'And letters, please, sir.' She handed them on the silver tray from the hall table. The tray shook a little in her hand as Lessingham rapidly went over the envelopes, took a particular one (her eye was on it, too) and put it unopened in his pocket. 'Let them wait.'

The old woman put them back on the table. She hesitated for a moment, looking up at him with sad eyes like a dog's. 'Nothing fresh, I suppose, sir? Over there? I suppose—?'

'Nothing.'

'Hope?' the word was almost inaudible.

'Nothing. Except,' he said, 'I've seen—' his voice hardened, 'what there is to see. And that's enough for the purpose.'

The hall door stood wide, lighting Jim up the steps as he returned: lighting the thin curtain of the rain. He could hear Lessingham's measured tread pacing the uncarpeted floor in the hall, the squelch of water at every foot-step. As he shut the door behind him, Ruth bustled in from the kitchen quarters with a tray: set it down on the table: tumblers, a syphon, and the curious purple bottle of Bristol glass that served as whisky-decanter. 'Bath ready in ten minutes, sir. You'd better have something to warm you inside, sir: that soaked as you are.'

Lessingham poured out for both. His face was unreadable: like the great rock faces, lean north crags of Mickledore, two or three miles away, three thousand feet up, alone now in the lampless darkness and the rain that turned, up there, no doubt to sleet.

As they drained the glasses, the emptiness of the house chilled Jim Scarnside's members: took hold as with claws at the pit of his stomach.

They ate at first in silence made audible by the click of knife and fork, Ruth's quiet footsteps on the parquet floor, the faint rustle of her black dress as she came and went, the steadfast tick-tack of the great Italian clock above the door, and the crackle and hiss of the logs whenever a scutter of rain came down the chimney. Unshaded candles in Venetian silver candlesticks of the cinquecento lighted the table, and candles in sconces on the walls gleamed with sometimes a windy light on the arms and armour. Ugly shadows lengthened, shortened, trembled, or stilled themselves: shadows of these things on the walls: the pig-faced basinet dating from 1400 with its camail of chain mail: the Italian armet, late fifteenth century, an heirloom come down to Lessingham through his mother along with that morning-star beside it, plated and exquisitely damascened in gold and silver, which family tradition traced back to the Prince Pier Luigi, bastard of Pope Paul III and Cellini's best-hated oppressor – Signor Pier Luigi Farnese, whose portrait by Titian, in black armour, black-bearded, with a wolf in each eye and bearing on his forehead and in every line of his face the brand of archangel ruined, hung over the fire-place, frighteningly like (as Jim with a new vividness of perception saw now) to Lessingham. And here were maces, war-hammers etched and gilt, pole-axes, swords by the dozen – German, Italian, French, English, Spanish: pistols, arquebuses richly wrought, a dagger of russet steel (supposed François Premier's) with gold inlaid and mother-of-pearl: the complete suit of war-harness for man and horse, a thing unique, given to Lessingham by that Arab sultan somewhere in the Middle East two or three years since, in memory of service rendered: and there, in a glass case, dark with age, notched and grown lean like a mummy, the viking sword dug up twelve years ago by Lessingham that summer they had spent carrying out excavations in Alstenö, far up the coast of Norway off Halogaland: Thorolf Kveldulfson's 'Alost'. Dug up, at the very spot which expert conjecture pointed to as the site of the old hall at Sandness: Thorolf's house, where more than ten centuries ago he fell defending his life at hopeless odds against the great King he deserved well of. It might, for all anyone knew, have been Thorolf Kveldulfson's sword: the date was near enough: his, or one of theirs that fought beside him while the burning house scorched them from behind and King Harald Hairfair and his three hundred men set on them from before. She had loved the slow sunshiny Arctic summer: the open-air life, the far-ranging mountains, the Norse country-folk and their ways of life (so effortless, her mastery of the language), the sailing, the long drawn out processions of sunset and sunrise, the unearthly sense as of Time's clock run down. But she – Jim swallowed his second glass at a draught: the fine claret, tasteless in his mouth, at least prevented the dryness of his throat from strangling him. He saw that though Lessingham ate, his glass stood untasted. Six weeks ago they had danced in this hall; a dozen couples, in the family mostly: the old Blunds tradition. Time never touched her: that divine and lovely gift of abiding youth, no older, only maturer; a little deepening and sweetening. Six weeks: what did it mean? Dead. Killed in that railway smash in France. He looked at Lessingham who, as if unconscious of his presence, was staring before him with a stare that seemed to be blunted and forced back upon itself: turned inward.

Lessingham spoke. 'Well, Jim, how do you like our post-war politics?'

'What, in this country?'

'Europe. The world.'

'The Ruhr, you mean? This morning's papers? I don't like them at all.'

'Are you surprised at the way things are shaping?'

'Not much surprised. But sorry.'

'Fear, and stupidity. The two universal counsellors and path-finders of mankind. There's really nothing singular about it.'

'I remember you saw it coming long since.'

'So did you.'

'When you pointed it out to me. But I don't think I honestly believed it. Just as nobody believed what you said a year ago, when a hundred marks were worth about two-pence.'

'What was it I said?'

'That you wouldn't discount a million of them for sixpence on twelve months' credit.'

'Too optimistic, as things have turned out.'

'What is it today? a hundred million or so to the dollar?'

'You and I have to remember,' Lessingham said, 'that we were born and bred up in our early youth in reposed and peaceful times almost, I suppose, without example. That led us by the sleeve: showed us but a back-eddy only in the great stream of things. Made us apt to imagine that the war was something remarkable, when it was truly no more but a ripple on the stream. You remember James Bryce's saying about the Middle Ages: that never at any other time has theory, professing all the while to control practice, been so utterly divorced from it: an age ferocious and sensual, that yet worshipped humility and asceticism: never a purer ideal of love nor a grosser profligacy of life. It is a great untruth. The description is just, but it fits all human history, not merely a particular age. And as for those unhappy five years, there was nothing new in them: unless, possibly, an unusual babblery of self-righteousness.'

'I'm not sure,' said Jim. 'Possibly there might be something a little bit new underlying just that.'

'What? "War to end war?" "World safe for democracy"? "A land fit for heroes to live in"? I wonder. I've more respect for old Clemenceau. He, at any rate, realized what company he was in in nineteen-nineteen, sitting between his "sham Napoleon and sham Christ".'

'You're unfair to them. Even the catchwords do stand for something. That they should be said at all, is something.'

'I agree. And to say "Liberté, Egalité, Fraternité" was something.' Lessingham toyed with his untasted glass, his hand closing round the stem of the delicate Murano goblet, between the body of it and the foot. 'A quite unimpeachable copy-book text. But (very amusingly) it turned in practice to the cutting off of people's heads with a mechanical slicer. You remember that wire puzzle made in Germany I used to bring out in school sometimes, when we were up to old Harry Broadbent in Middle Division? called *The Merry Decapitation without Trousers*?' He was smiling; but from under the smile suddenly came a sound of teeth gritted together. Jim averted his eyes: heard, as though across some solution of continuity, the ticking of the clock: then Lessingham's voice, toneless, even, and detached, resuming, as if upon an after-thought: 'Women's heads, in considerable numbers.' Then the clock again, intolerably loud and clear: once: twice. Then a crack, and something falling. Jim looked up quickly. The stem of the glass had snapped in Lessingham's grip and the great red stain spread wet and slow-oozing over the white cloth.

'Careless of me. Never mind. Leave it. For my own inclinations,' he said after a pause, wiping his hand carefully on his dinner-napkin, 'I infinitely prefer Jenghiz Khan. But then I have always favored the great carnivora rather than the monkey tribe.'

They were silent. Then Jim said, 'I wish you'd ring for Ruth to get a bandage or something. Your hand—'

Lessingham examined it. 'It's nothing.' He took out a clean handkerchief. 'Give me a hand with this: that'll stop it. I'm sorry,' he said, as Jim, finishing off the knot, sat back, very white. 'Go on: you must finish it up.' He pushed the decanter across. Jim filled, drank, and sat back once more, passing his hand with a light stroking movement from brows upwards over his forehead to the hair and so over to the back of his head. 'It's purely physical,' Lessingham said: 'like sea-sickness, or a bad head on mountains. My father, for instance: the toughest sailor you'd find in all England; and yet, stand him on a height, he'd feel nausea: vertigo: catch behind the knees. It's the same thing.'

'I suppose it is.' Jim finished his glass: forced a smile. 'Makes one feel a damned fool, all the same. You, of course—' he stopped.

'Yes,' said Lessingham, his voice quiet and level, while Jim watched frame and feature gather by some indefinable transmutations to a yet closer likeness to the Titian on the wall: 'I have. And enough, at any rate, to deaden the spice of novelty.'

'You're a comfort to me, Jim,' he said after a moment's silence. 'You are the most perfect Tory I ever met.'

'And you, the most complete and absolute Whig.'

'I? I have no politics.'

'You are a Whig of the Whigs. Consequently (as I've told you before) your politics are (a) damnable, and (b) completely out of date.'

'I have, it is true,' said Lessingham, 'an interest in politics: to observe them, survey them back again: note how, under every new suit of clothes, the same body, the same soul, live on unchanged. Apparently unchangeable. An amusing study, my dear Signor Giacomo. And Machiavelli is the one philosopher who had the genius and the honesty to write down the truth about politics.'

'I know what you mean. It is a limited truth, though.'

'Limited to this world. I hope so.'

'I limit it more narrowly than that. Besides, I've never heard you applaud our modern practitioners who live by the gospel according to Machiavelli.'

'As an artist, I have a certain regard for one or two of them: always (curiously, you may think) where the field of action has been comparatively small. In the Middle East I've come across it: in the Balkans: among the Arabs, here and there.'

'Yes, and you've practised it.'

'Well, I have ruled 'em for their own good now and then. On the right, small, human scale.'

'But the real Machiavelli: on the grand scale. You haven't much regard for him in Russia, for instance.'

'The fox in the lion's skin,' replied Lessingham, 'is admirable up to a point. But in the bellwether's skin, uncured and beginning to putrefy, he is no longer an impressive sight; while the mixture of stinking fox and stinking carrion—' He stopped as if he had bitten on his tongue. Jim felt his own teeth click together and a chill steal from the back of his throat down his spine: a shivering-fit blown from France.

'Mussolini?' he said quickly.

Lessingham answered with a shrug: 'There is the better always, and there is the worse. But the mischief is more in the game than in the player. In mankind, not in particular men. The field, and the apparatus, are too much overgrown and sprawling.'

'You know I don't wholly agree there,' said Jim. 'You and I never do wholly agree when it comes to fundamentals. I say the fault is in the players.'

'I know you do. So do I. But not quite in the same way.' He pushed back his chair. 'Have some more wine? No? Come along then, we'll smoke in the library.'

'Not in the Refuge,' Jim said in himself, rising to follow him. 'Thank God for that, at any rate.'

Lessingham, as if retired on the sudden into some secret workings of his brain, stood motionless at the table, hands in pockets, head bent on his chest, but back and shoulders straight free and majestical as some Olympian God's. Presently he began to pace slowly towards the door, pausing here and again at a weapon or a piece of harness as he passed, inspecting it narrowly, tapping it with his fingernail. With a hand upon the door-knob, he turned, head erect now, to overrun with swift, searching gaze all four walls of that armoury. Opening the door, he laid a hand on Jim's shoulder, swinging him round so that he too might survey these things. 'There's one example,' he said: 'death of all this. Gunpowder, the first mighty leveller.' He laughed in his great black beard, while the strength of his fingers, like an iron clamp, bit into Jim's shoulder. Jim sucked from the sheer pain of it a kind of comfort; as though such vicarious hurting should be able in some faint degree to ease Lessingham's own torment: in some faint degree dilute it (as ordinary communications could not) by sharing.

'Letting go your orthodoxies and my Pyrrhonism,' Lessingham said, as they passed into the library, 'there does seem to be a kind of blindness or curse, endemic in all human affairs. A slow death. Never mind about the explanation: the facts are there, observable. After a certain stage, you see it begin: thenceforward technique, step by step as it advances, so correspondingly step by step you see it stultify itself. After a certain stage, you see dominion, as if by some inward necessity at each extension of its field, forced to take to itself more and more of what is not worth the having. So that the game becomes not worth playing. Not for a man.'

'The machine age.'

'It goes to more than that. The fallacy of material size and extent. Man is as unteachable a beast as can be. Take it in grand outline, the whole of human endeavour in this game of life as we know it – What will you have with your coffee, Jim? Old brandy? Grand Marnier? Kümmel?'

'Nothing, thanks.'

'You must. Come: good for your digestion. Able to make exhalation, too, or smoke up into your brain. Distilled perfections of the orange: blossom and fruit.' Lessingham filled a glass for him. 'It used to be a ritual of ours, every time we dined on the train in France. Ever since the first: fifteen years ago.'

Jim stared: durst not meet his gaze.

'Come.'

'Well, if you'll join me. You've drunk nothing yourself, the whole evening.'

Lessingham filled the other glass, then offered his cigar-case. 'They're Partagas: your old friends. They go on, you see.'

'I see they do.'

There was silence while they lighted their cigars. Lessingham rose from his armchair. Jim watched him go to the writing-table, take up, without looking at it, Mary's photograph, rip it from its frame, tear it twice across, pitch it into the fire. As he sat down again, their eyes met. 'I have an objection,' Lessingham said, 'to what the Germans call *ersatz*.'

Jim swallowed the Grand Marnier at a gulp: poured himself out a second glass: drank that. His face was expressionless as wax.

'What were we talking about?' said Lessingham. 'O yes: the grand fallacy of progress. The cold lechery of more and more. All human endeavour, as if to play cricket, so to speak, on a pitch a hundred yards long: with a ball the size of a football: a bat to hit it with as big as a Thames punt. Good. Then, one of two things: we must either alter the whole nature of the game, or else become giants. We cannot make ourselves giants (and if we could, we should soon wish it undone again; unless indeed at the same time we altered the whole material universe – organic and inorganic, macrocosm and microcosm and all – to fit our new proportions. And then, that done, we should be precisely *in statu quo prius*: indeed, being merely bigger creatures in a bigger world, I suppose we should be quite unconscious of any change at all.) And so, that door being locked, here we are busy altering, instead, the nature of the game. And in its altered nature, the game of life, the game of war, the game of politics, the game of ruling and being ruled, of merely subsisting, the whole material appurtenance and engine of our daily existence, becomes more and more a game not for men but for termites.'

Jim's eyes began to smart, staring into the fire, where the last incandescent shreds of her photograph had finally disappeared. The silence hung heavy and bad-boding. 'What would you have?' he said at length.

'The Greek city. I speak from experience, of course: have had it, and mean to again. Perhaps a little more; but that for the centre of your state. City and countryside: a polity the size of England – less, perhaps. And a population measured by a few tens of thousands. Beyond that, all becomes skimble-skamble.'

'The Greeks made a nice mess of it.'

'Because they choked themselves trying to swallow a cherry, seems a poor reason why we must guzzle down the whole pie-dish at a mouthful.'

'It is an infinitely finer achievement to govern a modern state.'

'I do not think so. It is not practicable, on any self-respecting interpretation of the word "govern". You might as well call it a finer achievement—'

'I said "nobler",' said Jim.

'—to skate on a pond when the ice doesn't bear than when it does. It is not more difficult: it is not an "achievement" at all. It is merely impossible. Humans affairs conducted on the basis of megalopolitan civilization are simply not susceptible of good government. You have two choices: tyranny and mob-rule.'

Jim held his tongue.

Presently Lessingham resumed, as if following some elusive thought through the floating trails of cigar-smoke: '*Wein, Weib, und Gesang*: after all, what other thing is needful? I hate the folly, the false ends, the will-o'-the-wisps. Samuel Butler knew better: said the three most important things a man has are briefly, his (very well, my dear Jim. I'll spare your blushes), and his money, and his religious opinions.'

'Yes. Like all true Whigs, you are fundamentally immoral. And unreligious.'

'I have never professed to have any morals whatsoever. As for religion—'

Jim Scarnside ground his partly-smoked cigar into the ash-tray. 'What I want to know,' he said violently, 'is why you tore that up and threw it into the fire.' And, without looking for an answer, he buried his face in his hands.

Lessingham made no sign, save for, on brow and cheekbones, a sudden paleness or discolour. Jim jumped up: met in Lessingham's eyes a flash of red-looked anger: swung away from them to lean, elbows and forehead, against the high mantelpiece. 'I can bear it no more: hide and seek in the dark. I don't know what you're thinking about. Don't know what you're feeling – if you do feel. I'd better go,' he said. 'Only for God's sake—'

Lessingham rose. His grey eagly eyes, when Jim faced them, seemed dulled now, unproachable. However, he held out a hand: the left hand: Jim saw, as in the bright clarity of a tempera painting, the blood on the handkerchief that bandaged the right. Jim's ring, in the grip of their handshake, was driven into the flesh of his fingers like a tooth.

'It was good of you to come to me, Jim. I think you had better go now.'

'I'm not sure. Not sure I ought to.'

Lessingham's mustachios stirred with a sardonic smile. 'You can set your mind at rest for that, my dear keeper. And in any case, I do as I please. And not all the great masters of Hell – much less you – are ever going to stop that.' The cold words seemed to thin themselves on the air to a great still miasma of unfortunateness, in a loneliness of night unhandsome to work in, and (for his taking) no through-path. 'I've been glad to have you,' he said as, coming to the hall now, he helped Jim on with his coat.

'I wasn't much use to you.'

'A little. Chiefly because you, too—'

'O, my God!'

'And yet, another ingenious device that amuses Them, I suppose (if there is any "Them"), Who look on at it all from above,' said Lessingham, 'is that each of us, and every living creature in the world, has to suffer alone. In the flesh, alone.'

XVIII

DEEP PIT OF DARKNESS

LESSINGHAM went back to the library: rang the bell. 'Take these things, Ruth. I shan't want anything else tonight. Better all get to bed early. Call me at half past five: breakfast, six fifteen sharp: I want to be off by seven. Funeral is at Anmering on Sunday. I shall come straight back. Get on with shutting up the house while I'm away. I shall only come back to finish packing: then straight abroad. Good night.'

'Good night, sir. And asking your pardon for your old servant, Mr Edward, sir, we know we are in His hand, sir; and it is written, *Our Saviour Jesus Christ hath abolished death.*'

'Yes, yes. I know. Good night, Ruth. Good night.'

She had brought a pile of letters from the hall. He now sat down to them at the table and for a couple of hours dealt with them, pushing some aside to be attended to later on by Milcrest, crumpling up others and throwing them into the waste-paper basket, writing answers to some two dozen in his own hand. That done, he opened a drawer or two, burnt one or two more photographs, and so went through the hall and along the passage to the Refuge.

There was no fire here. There was her hunting-crop, on the sofa: her book-case, Meredith, Jane Austen, the Alice books, Edward Lear, Ethel Sidgwick's *Lady of Leisure* and *Duke Jones*,

half a dozen Conrads, Keats, Sappho, Homer: *Peter Ibbetson* – his
nostrils stiffened:

> Death said, I gather, and pursued his way.

Here in this drawer, her account books: sweets in a tin box: sewing
things, little reels of cotton and silk thread of all kinds of colours,
and these little balls of wool that Mischi liked to scrabble with
his white hind paws: Mischi's toy bird, with two real feathers for
wings: everything in the drawer so beautifully arranged and
smelling of that special French scent of hers. He shut the drawer
gently: crossed over to the mantelpiece: several more photographs
to burn, of various dates. He tore them up without looking at
them: took from its frame and tore up also, after a moment of
hesitation, that pencil drawing he had done in 1907.

It wanted a bare half-hour of midnight when he came up the
leisured ascent of the great staircase, turned right, along the gallery,
and stood, his back to the old oak balustrade, and before him the
lobby door. Behind and beneath, in the square well of the hall, as
he glanced down over his shoulder, all showed warmthless and
lifeless. Against the gilded sconces unlighted candles pointed up:
stiff, like dead women's fingers. The hearth stood swept and empty.
A circlet of electric bulbs, high in the seven-sided lantern of the
skylight – things meant but as for occasional convenience, not, as
the candlelight and the lamplight, to live with – shed an unquali-
fied strengthless glare. He had his key in the door. A step sounded
behind him: Ruth in a grey flannel dressing-gown, her hair down
in plaits, a candle in her hand.

She had a scared look. 'O I'm sorry, sir. I thought I heard
something. Thought happen you might be wanting something, sir.'

'No, thank you. I shall be turning in soon. One or two things
I've got to get together in here, ready for the morning. You get
along back to bed.'

'Can I put a match to the fire in there? It'll be fair perishing,
Mr Edward, sir.'

'I'll light it if I want it.'

It's all ready, sir, same as always at all times it was, in case—'

'I know. You go to bed, Ruth. I'll see to it.'

'Very well, sir.' She looked at him, and her face took on something of reassurance.

Lessingham went in and locked the door behind him. It was dark in the lobby. On the deep carpet his footfall made no sound. In half a dozen paces he came to the inner doorway leading to the Lotus Room. It had no door, but was closed with rich curtains, coloured dusky green of the moss agate, but, in this invisibility, black of the all-pervading black darkness.

At the touch of the unseen curtains, heavy, silken, smooth to the hand, and at the invading of his senses by a most faint but precise perfume which preserved within itself (as perfumes will) memories, as ephemeral winged creatures are preserved even to each tiniest particularity, unique, apparent, eternized in amber: at that touch, at the inhaling of that perfume, a memory warmed the darkness, and suddenly flamed through it to the point of hallucination. It was as if his hands, motionless in fact on the mid division of those curtains, had thrown them apart: as if the moment that was actual ten years ago were by miracle restored, and Mary, caught between the warm firelight and the glitter of the candles, sat at her dressing-table before her tortoise-shell looking-glass: her dress of sea-blue silk, webbed over with seed-pearls, as with streaks and flowers of sea-foam, fallen down billowy about her hips. It was as if she turned: gave him her face: gave him also, shadowy in the looking-glass where the candles wove ever dissolving nets of radiance, the adorable back-view: the line of her cheek, seen from behind a little to one side; and the braided coils of all hues from dark chestnut through tawny Sicilian wine-gleams to hues of gold burning to redness. It was as if all the whole university of times and things sat ready in Mary's eyes. Her lips parted, but no word came.

He opened the curtains: switched on the electric light.

It was as if, than this stillness, than the houselessness of this suddenly unrelated room, nothing other remained: only here, for yet a little while, the hideous bottom of the world unworlded,

bearing but this last fading character – of the irrefragable irreversibility
of death.

For a minute he paused there in the threshold, like a man that
maintains his footing against battering great gusts of wind. Then
he thrust his way into the emptiness as into some resisting
substance: a substance heavy against all senses, penetrable, breathable as common air is breathable, yet too still. In a strange violent
haste, he lighted the lamps now: lighted scores of candles that
stood waiting on dressing-table, writing-tables, mantelpieces, walls,
and beside the great canopied bed: kindled the fires of cedar-wood,
in both fireplaces: then switched off the hard electric glare. Still
in a deep drunkenness of the outward senses, he unlocked that
cabinet that held his picture of pictures. Without looking at the
picture, he cut it from the frame, rolled it up, and put it on his
writing-table. Then he unlocked and threw wide the ponderous
steel door of the fire-proof safe that was built into the wall behind
a panel to the left of the further fireplace, pulled out of it two
deed-boxes, banged the door of the safe and locked it up again,
put the boxes on his writing-table, and sat down. First he unlocked
the box covered with pale blue morocco leather: it was full of
letters, arranged in bundles by years: hundreds, all of them of her
writing, each in its original envelope, with sometimes a mark or
a note on the envelope in Lessingham's own hand. He added two
letters from the letter-case in his pocket to the collection in the
box: locked it again. The second box, the black one, held docu-
ments. He went through them rapidly: deeds of title, his will,
Mary's will, a score perhaps in all. He tore across and across and
threw into the fire the fire-insurance policy for the manor house
of Nether Wastdale: tossed the rest back in the box: locked it.
Last, pausing a moment as to bethink him whether anything were
forgotten, he took his keys once more: opened the drawer under
his right hand: took out a bunch of notes, cheque-book, pass-book,
one or two Greek gems. His heavy Service revolver, box of
cartridges beside it, lay in this drawer. He regarded it for a moment
with a curious twitching of the nostrils, as a man might stand

looking in readiness at a snarling poison-toothed jackal, then slammed the drawer and locked it.

And now, still standing at his writing-table, he began slowly and meditatively to arrange the things upon it: boxes, rolled-up canvas, tortoiseshell paper-knife, chequebook, silver ink-stand, pass-book, rings: all to lie true with the edges of the gold-cornered black seal-skin blotter. So will a man, waiting for the next course, adjust (with his thoughts elsewhere) knife or spoon to a tangential correctitude in relation to the empty plate beside it. Suddenly he sat down in the chair, lurching forward, in a dumb beast-like extremity grinding his forehead against the table-top.

He stood up again: waited a minute, his hands flat-palmed upon the table. Slowly at last he turned: began pacing with measured steps to and about from end to end of that room, as of his cage or prison: lotus frieze, precious tapestries and hangings, carpets, priceless Eastern rugs, huge deep-reflecting mirrors, and that great bed with its carved and inlaid pillars, its golden and silken luxury. All these had a ghastliness as of things cut off, wreckage, obscene mutilations, without root or cause in reason.

He stopped presently at the far window, opened the curtains, and threw up the lower sash. Rain had long set in for the night: October downpour, that filthily, with no wind to deflect or vary it, fell out of pitch darkness into pitch darkness: gurgle of rain-gutters, intermittent plash upon soaked earth of water from some overcharged gully clogged with leaves. 'What I saw at Amiens,' he said in himself: 'meaningless: like a dead bird: without any—' There was a horrible sudden sucking in of his breath through the nostrils '—O my queen, my heart's dear, my beautiful – thank God if that meant too quick to hurt' – He stood staring where the light from behind him was cast back in weak reflections from the face of the rain. Then, as if shaking his senses awake again, resumed his ranging walk.

'She: self-conscious as I am self-conscious.' Then suddenly, out loud: 'O speak to me, my dear, my dear—' and his teeth ground together.

'No,' after the two or three hundredth to-and-about in that

cage or room (in himself again). 'No. Because this is the true material Hell. Because the imagination or illusion of her which I have conceived, to my own eternal ruin, has'— Something as it had been a scorpion sitting in his brain began to speak abominations to the profanation and unhallowing both of life and death, both of body and soul, till past and present and future loomed now as transformed to tinselled tattered trappings of their own inanity, to flicker momentally between corpse-fire and charnel-house, turning the sweet air poisonous as with the sickening smell of blood.

'Alone. Punishment of the damned: an outmoded foolishness not worthy the confutation. Yet it is here. Unless,' and he flung a look at the writing table, 'unless that could end it. But I do not choose that.'

He threw more wood on the fire near her dressing-table. 'I knew. Know now. The scientific fact. Truth, like enough. But it means nothing. It may be the explanation of Edward Lessingham and Mary Scarnside: of Edward Lessingham and Mary Lessingham. No explanation whatever of Me and She.' As if in utter weariness of body and mind, he flung himself into the deep armchair and sat watching the bark curl, twist, and burst into flame: the sparks fly up: disappear.

After a long time, the workings in his brain began to say: 'But here: – what to bank on? Empirical evidence of fact? Or the knowledge inside you that cuts and burns? Knowledge of what is perfect: of what is the unique thing desirable for itself alone. Which I have loved, had, lived with. Thought the thoughts of. Breathed the breath of. Naked in bed with.' He sprang up.

'And I will make no compromise.'

He began walking again, twice, three times, back and again betwixt outmost and inmost wall. Then, as upon a sudden reminder, he took from his pocket Mary's unopened letter. It was not very long: dated from that hotel in the Champs-Elysées, Sunday, the fourteenth of October. He scanned it swiftly, sometimes skipping a line or two, sometimes stopping, as if the reading of it scalded him behind the eyeballs. He was standing at the bed's foot, the letter in his left hand. He reached out the right to take hold of the massive satinwood pillar of the bed, and so read on to the end.

As the letter fluttered from his hand onto the bed, the thin chime and answering deeper-throated strokes of the great Italian clock told four. Unstirrable as a stone he listened, bolt upright, gripping now with both hands against his chest that pillar of the wide bed, staring down at its coverlet of silk, dark green of the bay-leaf and fringed with gold:

O lente, lente, currite noctis equi!

O run slow, run slow, chariot-horses of Night! – The memory that belonged to those words stole with a quickening and down-searching of roots, lithe warm and alert, swift among secretest blood-reservoirs of the under darkness, changing suddenly to a huge unbearable pain as with the opening of him by slow incision from the roots of his belly upwards.

XIX

TEN YEARS: TEN MILLION YEARS: TEN MINUTES

'BUT you've got to move with the times,' said the little man with a square jaw. He was polishing with his handkerchief the lenses of his imitation tortoise-shell spectacles, surveying meanwhile, with that myopic blurred look common to the temporarily unspectacled, the scene before him: this spacious Piazza Brà, little white tables under the sky, music playing, laughter, people sitting, people promenading, tourists, Veronese townsfolk, habitués, birds of passage, old and young, men and women, with a good sprinkling of military uniforms here and there and the sweeping feathers of the bersaglieri: smoking, drinking, in motion or at rest, grave or gay, always talking: always the persistent rhythm of the Italian tongue running like a warp through the shifting patterns of sound; and the Roman arena rearing its curved façade, huge and blind, over all. And over all was a cold illumination shed of the electric arc-lights, mundane and harsh compared with the moonlight, yet stirring to the animal spirits and the busy fancies of the mind.

'I say, Frank, what a profound observation!' said the youngest of them at the table. He had black hair, and a voice suggestive of the ping of a mosquito.

'Anyhow it's true. Ronald'll tell you that.'

The eldest (by looks, perhaps five-and-thirty), was carefully rolling a cigarette. 'O, it's God's truth, no doubt, my dear Michael. *Vox populi, vox Dei*. And "move with the times" has been the parrot-word of the L.C.M. of popular unintelligence since history started.'

'What we were talking about was modern art,' said the man with little whiskers, brown hair brushed back, and eyes like a gannet's. 'I'm a modern artist myself; at any rate Willie's called me that in print, so it must be true. But I agree with Ronald that ninety-nine hundredths of it is simply fodder for engineers or eunuchs.'

'Don't go away, Willie.'

'I'm not going to listen to any more. It's so boring. It really is, Ronald, old man. We disagree on most things and I enjoy arguing; but on this question of art – really, I don't want to be offensive, but you don't begin to understand it and your views don't interest me.'

'He's gone! Never mind,' said the painter.

'I'm going to take a stroll round with Willie.'

'Right O, Frank. Talk to him about "Mr Jones". Not too loud, or you'll both be arrested. And that would be hard luck on you, in such company: such a good little proselyte as you are of the regime. – Well, Peter. Perhaps Willie's right. Perhaps I don't understand it.'

The painter shrugged his shoulders. 'Wants a psychoanalyst to understand it.'

'A kind of sublimation?'

'A kind of excrement.'

'Of the mind? That's an attractive idea.'

'By the Lord, I'm not sure it isn't true. Aristotle's *katharsis*. Always thought it rather an inadequate account of the *Agamemnon*, to compare it to a dose of calomel. But our friend Daldy Roome's abortions you were talking of—'

'I'm convinced it's true,' said Ronald Carwell. 'Not the effect on the audience though (which Aristotle meant when he talked about purging the emotions): the effect on Roome.'

'Well; I don't see he need hire a gallery to inflict them on the public, then.'

'Nor I, Michael. Except that the public will every time and all the time admire what they're told they ought to admire. So that there's money in it. And we artists have to earn our living.'

'So he prostitutes his art because that's what the public wants – or what Willie and the rest of 'em teach them they ought to want?'

'Not a bit of it. Roome's an artist. He hasn't the ghostliest idea why he does it. O yes, he's a very fine artist, Ronald, I assure you, as far as that goes. He's done one or two lovely things.'

'Then why doesn't he do them always, instead of this pathological stuff?'

'I don't know. No more does he.'

'Doesn't know himself?'

'Not a bit,' said the painter. 'Look at Matisse, now: the nude's rather a test case, I think. Exquisite line in the abstract. But trouble is, art isn't abstract: it's concrete. Take a hundred of Matisse's nudes: I should say you'd find twenty from that point of view very much in the same boat as Roome's: another seventy, say, suffering in some degree from inappropriate distortion. Then, in the remaining ten, you'll find one or two masterpieces. As good as the best. As good as Lessingham's.'

'Human form divine. If divine, why distort it?'

'To show we're cleverer than God Almighty.'

The painter shook his head. 'It isn't always "divine", you know. Even Phryne, probably, if you'd seen her in the flesh, wasn't quite as divine as the Aphrodite of Knidos.'

'"Divine"? What's the standard? A female woodlouse would be diviner than either, to a woodlouse.'

'There is no standard – of beauty.'

'Then,' said Carwell, 'what do you judge by? For, by saying what you said about the Aphrodite of Knidos, you admit distortion of some kind (meaning by distortion, variation from the norm). Take your Lessingham, or take your Matisse.'

'When I come to the word "beauty",' said Otterdale, 'I put down the book. It's a perfectly infallible symptom.'

'Of what?'

'Tosh. Tripe. Absence of grey matter.'

'How engagingly juvenile you are, to be so frightened by a word.'

'Well, it's true I'm two years younger in sin than you, Peter; but even my dawning intelligence of twenty-three summers can tell the difference between words that mean something and words that are just hot air. They don't frighten me: merely give me a pain in the tummy.'

'"*Crede experto* – trust one who has tried,"' said the painter, 'one word goes about as near as another to explaining this business of beauty. Beauty in nature: beauty in art. It's magic. Pure magic, like the witch-doctor's. And that's all there is to it.'

'So that's that.'

'Hullo, Willie, back again?'

'Quite a galaxy of the great and good exercising their parasitical functions here tonight. Biggest noise, that – what's-his-name? – Lessingham. We saw him, didn't we, Frank? A few minutes ago, stalking about by himself: larger than life and about half as natural: typical nose-in-air haw-dammy look about him—'

'Shut up, Willie. There he is.'

They watched. When he had passed there was a curious silence, perhaps for half a minute.

Michael Otterdale broke it, like a mosquito. 'That was a good close-up. Never seen him before, not to get a proper look at him. What is he really, Willie?'

'An aristocratical plutocratical self-obtruding dilettante.'

'He's a bit more than that,' said Ronald Carwell, still chain-smoking with cigarettes.

'How do you account for all the experts accepting him as master in their own particular line? Soldiers, as a top-notch fighting man – I heard General Sterramore at dinner only the other night letting himself go on that subject: called Lessingham the finest tactician in irregular warfare since Montrose. Your artist cracks him up as an artist, your writer as a writer. And so on. It's a fact. And it's extraordinary.'

'And what good has he ever done? Damn all.'

'A damned sight more than you ever will.'

'Depends on what you call good.'

'I suppose you know he had more than any other living soul to do, behind the scenes, with the busting up of Bela Kun's tyranny in August 'nineteen? I know. I was correspondent in Buda-Pesth at the time.'

'The East African campaign, too: that fastened his reputation as a soldier.'

'And what about that amazing guerilla fighting, only two years ago, in the Rif?'

'O, an adventurer. No one denies he's a big man in a way.'

'And all the while, for years, as a kind of sparetime recreation I suppose, that colossal work on the Emperor Frederick II: out last spring. The Cambridge pundits will tell you there's been nothing in the same street with it since Gibbon. And a kind of philosophy of history in itself, too, into the bargain.'

'There was some sort of a romance, wasn't there? I seem to remember—'

'Yes. Before the war. Almost before you were born, Willie. Married Anmering's daughter: a famous beauty. She died, some accident I think: that must have been ten or twelve years ago. Burnt his house down after her death: never settled down anywhere permanently ever since.'

'Burnt his house? A bit of Hollywoodish, what?'

'Great house up in Cumberland: full of treasures. The kind of man you can't predict his acts.'

'They say he destroyed all his wife's pictures after that,' said the painter: 'every likeness of her he could get hold of. Masterpieces of his own among them: the famous *Green Dress* and all. Ten years ago: nineteen twenty-three: I was a student in Paris a year or two later: remember the sensation it made even then. A wicked thing to do.'

'Couldn't stick her, I suppose?'

'I don't know at all, my dear Michael.'

There was a pause. Carwell resumed: 'Funny: I can't have been more than ten: nineteen-eight, it was. This'll interest you as a Freudian, Willie. First time I consciously realized what was meant by – well, by *beauty* – in a woman—'

'Look out! you've shocked me and you've shocked our Willie. Don't use that word. You must say sex-appeal.'

'I shall say Beauty. The illustrated papers were full of her at the time; and people talking, you know. Lady Mary Scarnside, she was then. Something about the name, seemed extraordinarily lovely: God knows why – Virgin Mary, Our Lady, I don't know if it's anything to do with that kind of association. Any way, I remember surreptitiously cutting out a full-page picture of her, in her riding-habit, out of the *Illustrated London News* and keeping it for months hidden away somewhere: I'd have died with shame if anyone had—'

'Dear me, Ronald! what a precocious little lounge lizard you must have been!'

'Be quiet, Michael. I want to hear this.'

'Well then at Lords – I was taken because I'd a brother in the Eton Eleven that year – I saw her: quite close, in the tea tent. And, my God, Peter, I knew it was her from the pictures and I can tell you I've never seen from that day to this – All your Venuses: any other woman I've ever seen: simply not to be spoken of beside it. And, so charming too. So lovely. Classic if you like, but not cold. A kind of wildness. A kind of Ἀρτέμιδος κελαδεινῆς – swift-rushing Artemis. I never saw her again, but the impression was terrific. And permanent. Like branding. Shut my eyes, I can see her again today. Every detail.'

'Sounds an unusual experience.'

'A propitious start for you, Ronald. No. I'm not ragging.'

'Extraordinarily interesting. At that age.'

'It's a possession I wouldn't willingly give up,' Carwell said simply.

'And the celebrated Mr Lessingham, sitting at his table over there, looking like Sir Richard Grenville—'

'Or like an up-to-date Sicilian brigand—'

'Like a God exiled from wide Heaven,' said the painter.

'How bloody romantic!'

'I'm quoting his own book.'

'And all the time, quite conceivably the identical same image in his mind as in yours, Ronald.'

'And much more likely, quite a different one. They say he's a regular sailor. Wife in every port.'

'Blast the fellow! He looks it. Must admit, takes the gilt off the romance a bit!'

'Who knows?'

A long pause: nearly a minute.

'Look there—'

With a lovely swift swaying walk, a lady was threading her way towards Lessingham's table. She was tall: black hair, slanty eyes, white fox-fur stole or collar, black hat, black dress: exquisite, vital, strong, and with a strange infection of excitement in her every motion as though she trailed like a comet, behind her as she walked, a train of fire.

Lessingham rose to greet her: kissed her hand. They sat down at his table.

'You had given me up?'

'No, signora, I knew you would come.'

'How did you know, when I did not myself even?'

'I wanted you.'

She looked swiftly in his face, then as swiftly away again. 'Your words are suited to your eyes,' she said, out of a tense little hushed silence.

'Words should say what they mean, neither less nor more. I have trained mine: good hounds: open not but where they find. You prefer vino rosso? or bianco?' He signalled to the waiter.

'The crimson rose or the gold one? O I think the crimson for tonight.'

'I had thought so too, as you observe,' Lessingham said as he ordered it, taking for her at the same time from a jar on the table a rose, dark as blood, that bowed down its head as with the very weight of its own sweetness. 'Do you, in addition to your other accomplishments, read the Greek, signora?—

ἦρος ἀνθεμόεντος ἐπάϊον ἀρχομένοιο.'

'I heard the flowery spring beginning.' – So softly she echoed the words, it might have been the red rose that spoke, not her red lips as she scented it. 'But this is autumn with us, not spring,' she said, pinning it to her dress. 'Or do you as a great man of authority command the seasons as your subjects? A forcer of them to your pleasure?'

The two tables were out of ear-shot, but within easy eye-reach. Peter Sherrill was watching that lady with his gannet-like eyes: As, upon a movement, her fur stole fell open, unapparelling the beauties of her neck and hair, he snatched the menu-card and, from his pocket, a piece of chalk: began swiftly to draw. Carwell, for his part, had all this while been staring at her as if he had forgotten where he was: like a man in a dream.

'But the advantage of complete scepticism,' Lessingham was saying, as he lighted a fresh cigar, 'is that, having once reached that position, one is free: free to believe or unbelieve exactly what one pleases.'

'As for example?'

'As for example, madame, that you and I were sitting in this piazza twenty-five years ago – here, in Verona, almost this very table, I think – criticizing the ways of God with men.'

'Twenty-five years ago! That is not a very charmant compliment to me?'

'Private heavens are the only solution.'

She was silent.

'You are not yourself yet twenty-five?'

'I am nineteen, signor.'

'You are immeasurably older. You are older than the world. Older, I think, than Time.'

'A strange fancy.'

'Is it not true?'

'It does not sound to me very like a truth.'

Lessingham watched her for a minute, in profile: this unregarding, unattached, contemplative pose: these beauties beyond the Greek, yet, in high cheek-bone and in modelling of eyelash and lip, and in the wing of the nose, something of a more rough and sharp taste, to strain the tongue; and the turning up of her hair at the nape of her neck, like a smooth beast of night coiling itself, fold

upon fold, self-lovingly upon some hidden privity and unbounded-
ness of its own desires and somnolent luxury of its own secretness.
'I am not a commodity,' she said, very low: 'not for any man.'

'I regard women,' said he, 'not as commodities, but as dresses
of Hers.'

'And who is "She"?'

'Never mind. I have known Her. Intimately. For years and years.
If you were She, signora, would you visit this earth?'

He saw something twist and elongate itself like a self-pleasing
cat, in the region of her mouth and nostrils, as she replied, 'Perhaps.
Sometimes. If it amused me. Not often.'

'And does it amuse you? "*Ça m'amuse*": did you not say that?
Twenty-five years ago?—'

'How should I know if I said it before I was born?'

'—This clockwork world, this mockshow, operated by Time
and the endless chain of cause and effect? And the second law of
thermodynamics to assure us that in time, a few million or billion
years, may be, but still in time, the whole thing will have come
to an end. Not dead; for to be dead implies a condition called
Death, and Death itself will have ceased to be. Not forgotten
either; for there will be nobody to do the forgetting. Neither
forgotten nor remembered. The end laid down by the great law
of entropy: the impregnable vacuity of ultimate Nothing. – Ça
vous amuse, madame?'

With an almost imperceptible, half-mocking, half-listening,
inclination of her head she answered, 'Pour le moment – oui,
monsieur. Ça m'amuse.'

'Pour le moment? And next moment, drop it: bored with it:
away with it and try something else. Ah, if we could.'

'It is easy.'

'Pistol, or over-dose of veronal?'

'But I think that way too easy.'

'Needs courage. Courage of a gambler. Perhaps if people knew,
beyond quibble or doubt, what was through the Door the world
would be depopulated? Death, so easy, so familiar and dreadless,
to a believer?'

'Does anyone, to say, know?'

'What is "know"? Do I know whether my hotel is still where I left it after dinner?'

'Have you sometimes thought, we may have forgotten?'

'I have thought many things. Tell me, signora: when all this becomes boring, have you never thought suicide might be commendable?'

She looked at him with her green eyes: slowly smiled her secular smile. 'God is not like a bee, which when she has stung cannot sting again. Also I think, Signor Lessingham (in my present mood), that I would desire you to play the game according to its strict rules.'

'And we can take nothing out of the world. Is not that true?'

'Is it not rather that we can take everything worth the taking?'

'I wonder. For me, what was most worth taking is gone already. And yet, how shall I unlove this world, that has been my bosom-darling so long? And yet – this is talk, signora. Who are we, to talk? What am I? You cannot answer; if indeed you are really there to answer. For all I know, you are not there. I am, myself: but you – why, like all this, these people, this place, the times: you fly through my hands like wind ungropable, or dreams.'

'Perhaps, signor, we do not sufficiently, and as much as we ought, trust the heavens with ourselves.'

'You have forgotten,' said Lessingham. 'Then must I remember you of what you forget: how, when long ago I told you "Je ne crois pas en Dieu", you approved of that: called it a regrettable defect of character (in a young man) to believe in God. I am not yet an old man, signora: but I know more than in those days I did. And have borne more.

'Does that, too, amuse you?' he said suddenly: 'You that go still tripping through the world in your proper form, armed and unguled?'

'Yes. Very much,' she said, lifting up her chin and steadily meeting his gaze. The unfillable desire of Her, with the force as of some wind and sea-gate, seemed to set the body of night athrob.

'It is past ten o'clock,' said Lessingham, after a minute, leaning nearer across the table. 'Will you do me the honour, signora, to take supper with me in my rooms at the hotel that overlooks the river and the Ponte Vecchio? We can review better there the details of the portrait I am to paint of you.'

May be it was not, for that moment, the eagly eyes, steel-grey and speckled, of Lessingham that she looked in; but more troublous, more faunish eyes, brown, talking directlier to the blood: eyes of Zayana. Slowly, unsmilingly, her eyes yet staring into his, she bent her head. 'Yes,' she answered. 'Yes.'

Dawn was on Verona. Lessingham, in his dressing-gown of wine-dark brocaded silk, watched from his balcony the pink glow along the brickwork of those eared battlements of the Ponte Vecchio: watched, beneath him, the tumbled waters of the Adige ceaselessly hastening from the mountains to the sea. A long while he remained there with the dewy morning lapped in the lap unspeakable of memories of the forenight: latest of all, of her sleeping face and body, as in the morning of life: of the unmasked miracle, for ever new, of he and she: the impersonality, the innocence, and the wonder, of a sleeping woman: and, as the reed-like music of swans' wings, flown high, unseen in the mist, the old riddles of sleep and death.

But She, when the time came, departed at but one step from Italian autumn to summer in Zimiamvia: from this room that looked upon the Ponte Vecchio and the golden-slippered dawn, to the star-proof shade of strawberry-trees where Duke Barganax, still a silent spectator at that now silent supper-party, waited alone.

The Duke did not move: did not look at her: said but, under his breath, 'Is this the dream? Or was that?'

'What will you think, my friend?' The faint mockery that undersung the accents of that lady's voice seemed as a forewalker of things not of this earth.

'What will you suppose I should think of?' answered he. He felt for her in the dark: found her: drew her close.

'κάλθ' ὅσα μαίνης μ' ἄδεα καλλόνα—
Come – sweet with all that beauty you mad me with!'

Her waist yielded to his arm as the young night yields, drawn by sunset down to that western couch, and opens her beauties with the evening star. 'You burn me,' he said, 'O you of many gifts.'

She laughed, so, under Her servant's lips. And he, as She laughed, became aware of the music in Her laughter, that the hush of it seemed to darken sight, as with the lifting of some coverlet that had covered till now the unknowable inner things of darkness; and he was alone with those things, through Her and through that music, in their unspeakable blessedness. And, while he so held Her, the blessedness seemed to spread from the nadir up to the sightless zenith, and the heart of darkness seemed to beat faster, as, in an earthly night, the east pales in expectation of the unrisen moon; until, high beyond the dimmest ultimate scarce suspected star, the strains of that unaltering, unhastening, secret music flew and shone as sounds made visible in their white ecstasy of fire. With that, a crash went from darkness to darkness like the trumpet of God, as if the foundations of hell and heaven thundered together to fling down the shadows and blow away the times. So the eternal moment contemplates itself anew beside the eternal sea that sleeps about the heavenly Paphos.

There was silence, save for Campaspe's whisper, as the trembling of tiny waves among rushes in a windless autumn midnight: 'The King of Worlds, undeadly and unsightable.'

But the King, elbow on the table still, looking still from above on this curious world of his creation, waited with the pleasant idleness of one content to drowse on in that borderland where the changing of the grey light is the only reality, and that less substantial than the elusive perfume of a forgotten dream. His mustachios stirred with the flicker of a smile, as he realized how long he must have stood with his hand upon the door-handle while his mind, in the timelessness of contemplation, had been riding with that music. With an art to refine to the delicatest half-retracted touch the dawning and unveiling of an expected joy, he let go the handle, stepped backwards a pace or two, and, with his back to the old oak balustrade, stood looking at that door. Behind and beneath him, in the square well of the hall, warm gleams and warm stirring shadows pulsed and wandered, here and there a spear of radiance shooting as high as the door's dark panels, with the spurting of fresh flame as the logs settled together. He glanced down, over his shoulder. Against golden sconces a score of candles burned on the walls. On a chair was her hunting-crop thrown by: on another, things for sewing, and packets of flower-seeds (he could see the coloured pictures on the backs); and on the table in the middle of the hall were letters addressed and stamped ready for posting, and her account book and little golden pencil. On the great white bear-skin rug before the fire her Sheila, a little flat dog without much legs, iron grey and hairy and with feathery bat-like ears laid back, was stretched asleep: now and then with twitchings in her sleep, and half-smothered excited little dream-cries. Daffodils in a silver bowl in the middle of the table mixed with the candle scent and the wood scent their scent of spring.

He went to the bay-window at the end of the gallery on his left and, for a last deep draught of those airs of promise, opened it wide and stood for a minute out on the balcony. Dusk was on the garden and on the river. There were quiet noises of blackbirds and thrushes settling down to roost. The Copeland hills to the west were hard-outlined against the sky which low down glowed still with a waterish orange-coloured light. Higher, the bosom of the sky was neither blue nor grey nor green nor rosy but all of these at once, and yet far too pale for any of these, as if the illimitable spaces of heaven had been laid bare and found pure and perfect with the promise of alternate night and day. Across that purity, two or three vast smoky clouds drifted sea-wards; others, banked in flaky darkness, rested on the horizon south of the going down of the sun. The wind was falling to sleep among the apple-trees. Night, beginning to make up her jewels, set upon her forehead the evening star.

He came back, turned the handle, went in, and locked the door

behind him. Before him, the lobby opened shadowy, with night-
lights burning of scented wax in the embrasures of the walls to
left and right. On the deep carpet his footfall made no sound; in
half a dozen paces he came to the inner doorway; it had no door,
but was closed with rich curtains coloured dusky green of the
moss agate. Two blows of amethyst, upon tables of gold, right
and left of that doorway, held immortal flowers: quiet dusky
blooms of Elysian nepenthe, drenching the air with their fragrancy.

He parted the curtains and stood on the threshold. Mary, caught
between the warm firelight and the glitter of the candles, sat at
her dressing-table before her tortoise-shell looking-glass.

Through a glamour blinding the eyes he beheld her stand up
now: beheld her turn to him, and that sea-foam dress slide down
to foam about her feet. Like the wind on the mountains falling
upon the oaks, Her beauty fell upon him, intolerable, that no eye
can bear. And there was a shout, terrible, all-pervading, as of a
voice crying and saying that all Gods, and men, and beasts, and
fowls, and fishes, and creeping things, should bow down and give
praise because of Her; and that the sun and the moon should be
glad, and the stars sing, and the winds and the mountains laugh
because of Her, and the golden mansions of the Father and the
desirable concourse of the Gods be open unto Her, as it was and
is and ever shall be. Surely he was become as one dead, covering
his face before Her on that timeless shore: he that, a mortal man,
not once but ten thousand times, but ten thousand times—

ἀθανάτῃ παρέλεκτο Θεᾷ βροτός, οὐ σάφα εἰδώς·

—with an immortal Goddess: not clearly knowing. At that thought,
as the heart of Her doves turns cold and they drop their wings,
so he.

The King, shaking himself awake out of that study he had for
these past minutes seemed lost in, sat back in his golden chair.
Sidelong he regarded Her for a minute, sitting there beside him,
wearing that downward inward-listening look; upper lids level and
still, under lids still and wide: mouth lightly closed in a secretness

cool and virginal as the inward throat of a white lily, yet with the faint flicker of some tigerness, alive but sleeping, at Her mouth's corner. He said, very low, 'Well, Señorita Maria?'

With a motion scarce to be seen, she leaned nearer. The moth-like touch of her arm against his sleeve let him know she was trembling. His hand found hers, in her lap beneath the table. She said in a whisper, 'It did not hurt, did it? – The coming out?'

'Not the coming out,' he answered, 'but the not knowing.'

'The not knowing? You, that do know all? Things past, present, and to come, and alike things not to come?'

'The not knowing – there – that, for you, it did not hurt. Fifty more years I endured it there, remember, wanting you.'

'But surely you knew, even in there, my friend?—

And we, madonna, are we not exiles still—

Surely you remember that?'

'Some things we knew, even in there. Some things we will remember.'

'But what need to remember things true and perfect? When all of them are ours. What need to remember present good?'

The King smiled. 'It is but a name, this "remember".'

They looked for a minute at the unsure thing on the table before them. 'Fifty more years, afterwards, I wrought there,' said the King: 'yet here, what was it? the winking of an eyelid. And you see, it hath in itself, that world, the seeds of its own decay. Its way is not onward, but all turns in upon itself, so that every kind of being becomes there, as Time wears, ever more mongreled with the corruption of other kind. As at night all cats are grey: and as the dust of all right living things turns, mixed with bright water, to a grey mud.'

'It is, what you said it should be, a strange unlucky word,' he said. 'Much like this real world, but crooked. The same canvas, same silks, same pattern, same colours; and yet something amiss in the working. As if a naughty child had unpicked it here and there, cut the threads, played the mischief with it.' Her hand was still in the King's under the table. 'You and I dreamed it: that dream. – I'm frighted,' she said suddenly, and buried her face on his shoulder beside her. Under the comfort of the King's hand which tenderly, as things too dear for hand to touch, touched now her bended neck, now the up-piled red magnificences of her hair, she was ware of Zenianthe's voice: the voice of a hamadryad, as out of the stillness of the heart of some great oak-forest:

> It was no dream; or say a dream it was,
> Real are the dreams of Gods, and smoothly pass
> Their pleasures in one long immortal dream.

'Was it a dream?' the Duchess whispered, 'or is this the dream? What is true?'

'That I love you,' he said, 'beyond dream or waking. Further than that, it is best not to know.'

She raised her head. 'But you. I believe you know.'

'I know,' he answered. 'But I can forget, as you forget. It is necessary to forget.'

'It is but a name, you say, this "remember". Shall you and I remember—?'

The King drew her closer, to say in her ear, '—the Lotus Room, tonight?'

'Yes, my dear, my lover, and my friend: the Lotus Room.'

'And for us, madonna,' said the Duke privately to that Dark Lady, from behind, in the dark: 'our Lotus Room?' As the white of her neck where her jewelled hand stroked it, smooth sleek and tender below the sleek close-wound tresses of her jet-black hair, untrodden snow is not so spotless.

'Your grace,' she replied, without looking round, 'may wisely unlearn to use this cast.'

'What cast, dear Lady Unpeace?'

'As though you were my husband.'

'Would heaven I were.'

'And so foreknowledged to the estate of becco or cornuto?'

'I will not hear you, wasp. He that would unwive me – well,

your ladyship hath had example: he should ne'er come home uncut.'

She laughed: a sweeping of lute-strings to set all the velvet night suddenly awhirl with fire-flies. 'O your grace hath a tongue to outcharm the nightingale: unsinews all my powers: is a key to unshut me quite, and leave me a poor lady uncounsellable, all o'ermastered with strawberry-water and bull-beef.' Lithe as a she-leopard she eluded him, and, stepping out of the shadow, indolently approached the table. Her beauty, to the unquiet eye beholding her, seemed, spite bodice and gown's close veiling, to shine through with such pure bounty as in Titian's Venus is, naked upon her couch in that sunlit palace in Urbino: a body in its most yielding swan-soft and aching loveliness more ethereal, more aery-tender, than other women's souls.

'Your promise given, you shall not unpromise it again,' said the Duke at her ear, following her.

'I have not yet made up my mind. And indeed,' she said, 'I think, when 'tis well made up, I'll change it.'

The King stood up in his majesty, the Duchess Amalie with him. All, at that, stood up from the table: all save the Vicar only, who, being untraded in philosophy, and having wisely drowned in wine the tedium of a discourse little to his taste, now slept drunk in his chair. And the King, with his Amalie's hand in his, spoke and said: 'It is high time to say goodnight. For, as the poet hath sung—

Sleep folds mountain and precipic'd ridge and steep abysm,
Wave-worn headland and deep chasm;
Creeping creatures as many as dark earth doth harbour;
Beasts too that live in the hills, and all the bee-folk;
And monsters in gulfs of the purple ocean;
Sleep folds all: folds
The tribes of the wide-wing'd birds.

And, because tomorrow the great stage of the world waits my action, and because not many such nights may we enjoy in lovely Memison, therefore we will for this night, to all who have sat at your board, madonna, wish (as Sappho of Lesbos wished) the length of our night doubled. And why we wish it,' he said, secret to Amalie, 'we know full well, you and I; for Night that hath the many ears calls it to us across the dividing sea.'

But now, as a score of little boys, for torch-bearers, formed two lines to light them to bedward and the guests began two by two to take their stations for departing, the Lord Beroald, marking where this ensphered creation rested yet where the King had left it, said, 'What of that new world there your serenity was pleased to make us?'

The King half looked round. 'I had forgot it. No matter. Leave it. It will ungo of itself. For indeed,' he said, with a back-cast look at Fiorinda, 'rightly reading, I hope, the picture in your mind, madam, I took occasion to give it for all your little entities that compose it, this crowning law: – that at every change in the figures of their dances they shall by an uneschewable destiny conform themselves more and more nearly to that figure which is, in the nature of things, their likeliest; which when they shall reach it at last, you shall find dance no more, but immobility: not Being any more, but Not-Being: end of the world and desistency of all things.'

The Duchess's arm twined itself tighter in his. Fiorinda said, 'I had noted that pretty kind of strategematical invention in it. And I humbly thank the King's highness and excellency for taking this pains to pleasure me.'

'O, we have done with it, surely?' said the Duchess. 'What began it but an unfledged fancy of hers?' Her eye-glance and Fiorinda's, like a pair of fire-flies, darted and parted: a secret dance in the air together. 'Her fault it ever was made.'

'For myself,' said that lady. 'I do begin to find no great sweetness in it. It has served its turn. And were ever occasion to arise, doubtless his serene highness could lightly make a better.'

The King laughed in his black beard. 'Doubtless I could. Doubtless, another day, I will. And,' he said, under his breath and for that lady's ear alone, looking her sudden in the eye, 'doubtless I have already. Else, O Beguiler of Guiles, how came We here?'

Anthea whispered something, inaudible save to Campaspe. Their dryad eyes, and that Princess Zenianthe's, rested now on the King, now on Barganax, now once more on the King.

And now, as the company began again to take their departure towards the Duchess's summer palace, my Lady Fiorinda, in her most languefied luxuriousness lazying on Barganax's arm, idly drew from her back hair a hair-pin all aglitter with tiny anachite diamonds and idly with it pricked the thing. With a nearly noise-less fuff it burst, leaving, upon the table where it had rested, a little wet mark the size of her fingernail. The Duke might behold now how she wore glow-worms in her hair. His eyes and hers met, as in a mutual for ever untongued understanding of his own wild unlikely surmise of Who in very truth She was: Who, for the untractable profoundness' sake of his own nature and his unsatiable desires' and untamed passions' sake, which safety and certitude but unhappieth, could so unheaven Herself too with dangerous elysiums, of so great frailty, such hope unsure: unmeasurable joys, may be undecayable, yet mercifully, if so, not known to be so. – Her gift: the bitter-sweet:

γλυκύπικρος ἔρώς.

'Well?' she said, slowly fanning herself as they walked away, slowly turning to him once more, with flickering eyelids, Her face which is the beginning and the ending, from all unbegun eternity, of all conceivable worlds: 'Well? – And what follows next, My Friend?'

NOTE

In Doctor Vandermast's aphorisms students of Spinoza may often recognize their master's words, charged, no doubt, with implications which go beyond his meaning. Lovers of the supreme poetess will note that, apart from quotations, I have not scrupled to enrich my pages with echoes of her: this for the sufficient reason that Sappho, above all others, is the poet not of 'that obscure Venus of the hollow hill' but of 'awful, gold-crowned, beautiful Aphrodite'.

As for the verses, all originals (except as noted below) are mine, as also (except where noted) are all translations. For Sappho's *Ode to Anaktoria* I follow the text of H. T. Wharton's edition (John Lane, 1898); references to 'Loeb' are to *Lyra Graeca* Vol. I, of the *Loeb Classical Library*. I have lost the references for the two verse quotations in Chapter XII.

I thank those who have helped and inspired me with their criticisms, notably George Rostrevor Hamilton and Kenneth Hesketh Higson: also Gerald Ravenscourt Hayes for his excellent map, which should help readers in picturing to themselves the country where the action takes place; and I thank Edward Abbe Niles, for nearly twenty years friend and supporter of my work in our great sister-country the United States of America.

CH. I	'Mighty, mightily fallen'	Homer, *Iliad*, xvi, 775.
	'With the Gods' will, or if not, against'	Aeschylos, *Seven against Thebes*.
CH. IV	'He's tell'd her father	Old Ballad: *Katharine Jaffray*: Herd's MSS. I, 61; II, 56.
	'Awful, gold-crowned, Beautiful Aphrodite'	Homer, *Hymn to Aphrodite*.
CH. V	'Who, on the high-running ranges'	Homer, *Hymn to Aphrodite*.
CH. VI	'Tho' wisdom oft hath sought me'	Thomas Moore, *Irish Melodies*: 'The Time I've lost in wooing'.
	'Like is he, I think, to a God immortal'	Sappho, *Ode to Anaktoria*.
CH. VIII	'The day shall be when holy Ilios'	Homer, *Iliad*, vi, 448.
	'A quiet woman'	Webster, *The White Devil*, iv, 2.
CH. IX	'Injoy'd no sooner but dispised straight'	Shakespeare *Sonnet* CXXIX.
CH. XI	'One desire may both their bloods'	Chapman.
	'O lente, lente'	Marlowe, *Doctor Faustus* (after Ovid, *Amores*, i, 13, II.39-40): transl. George Rostrevor Hamilton.
CH. XII	'Here ripes the rare cheer-cheek Myrobalan'	
	'From women light and lickerous'	
CH. XIII	'God's adversaries are some way his own'	Robert Harris, *Sermon* (1642).

Ch. xv	'To an unfettered soules quick nimble hast'	Donne, *Progress of the Soul* (First Song, xviii).
Ch. xviii	'Death said, I gather'	George Meredith, *A Ballad of Postmeridian*.
Ch. xix	'I heard the flowery spring beginning'	Alkaios (Loeb, 166).
	'Come – sweet with all that beauty you mad me with'	Sappho, *To Atthis* (Loeb, 82).
	'With an immortal Goddess, clearly knowing'	Homer, *Hymn to Aphrodite*.
	'It was no dream: or say a dream it was'	Keats, *Lamia*.
	'Sleep folds mountain and precipic'd ridge and steep abysm'	Alkman (Loeb, 36).

E. R. E.

DRAMATIS PERSONAE

THE ACTION begins on 24th June, *Anno Zayanae Conditae* 775. In this list the number of the chapter where each person is *first* mentioned is given in parenthesis after his or her name.

B.R.E.

KING MEZENTIUS	(II)	tyrant of Fingiswold, Meszria and Rerek.
BARGANAX	(V)	Duke of Zayana, bastard son to King Mezentius.
DUCHESS OF MEMISON	(II)	mother to Barganax.
FIORINDA	(II)	young sister to the Chancellor, and lady of the bedchamber to the Duchess.
STYLLIS	(VII)	son to King Mezentius.
HORIUS PARRY	(II)	lord of Laimak, and Vicar of the King in Rerek.
JERONIMY	(II)	High Admiral of Fingiswold.
BEROALD	(II)	Chancellor of Fingiswold.
RODER	(II)	an Earl in Fingiswold.
BODENAY	(II)	Knight Marshal of Fingiswold.

ERCLES	(VI)	
ARAMONE	(VII)	Princes in Rerek
GILMANES	(VII)	
VALERO	(II)	
MEDOR	(VI)	a Count in Meszria, captain of Barganax's bodyguard.
BARRIAN	(X)	
IBIAN	(VI)	
MELATES	(VI)	lords and gentlemen of Meszria.
MORVILLE	(II)	
ZAPHELES	(VI)	

ARQUEZ		
CLAVIUS		
MANDRICARD		
OLPMAN	(VII)	lords and gentlemen of Rerek.
ROSSILION		
SORMS		
STATHMAR		
VANDERMAST	(VI)	a learned man, secretary to Barganax.
GABRIEL FLORES	(VII)	secretary to the Vicar.
ZENIANTHE	(XV)	a princess of Fingiswold, niece to King Mezentius.

BELLAFRONT	(VI)	ladies at the ducal court of Zayana.
PANTASILEA	(VI)	

ANTHEA	(VIII)	
CAMPASPE	(VIII)	
LYDIA	(VI)	
MYRRHA	(VI)	ladies at the ducal court of Memison.
NINETTA	(VI)	
VIOLANTE	(VI)	

FERGUS	(vi)	
AKMONE	(vii)	Princes in Rerek
GILMANES	(vii)	
VALLPO	(iii)	
MEDOR	(vi)	a Count in Meszria, captain of Barganax's bodyguard
BARRIAN	(x)	
IRIAN	(iv)	
MELATES	(iv)	lords and gentlemen of Meszria
MORVILLE	(iv)	
ZAPHELES	(vi)	
ARQUEZ		
CLAVIUS		
MANDRICARD		
OLPMAN	(iii)	lords and gentlemen of Rerek
ROYSTION		
SORMS		
STATHMAR		
VANDERMAST	(vii)	a learned man, secretary to Barganax
GABRIEL FLORES	(vii)	secretary to the Vicar
ZENIANTHE	(xv)	a princess of Fingiswold, niece to King Mezentius
BELLAFRONT	(vi)	ladies at the ducal court of Zayana
ANTHEA	(vi)	
ANTHEA	(viii)	
CAMPASPE	(viii)	
LYDIA	(vi)	ladies at the ducal court of Memison
MYRRHA	(xv)	
NINETTA	(vi)	
VIOLANTA	(vi)	

MAP OF THE THREE KINGDOMS

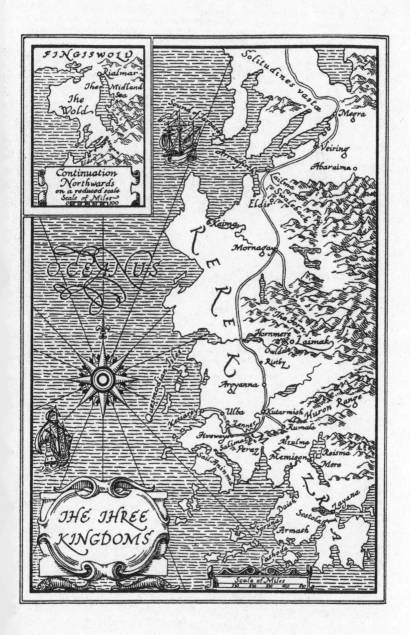

FINGISWOLD

Rialmar
The Midland Sea
The Wold
Eldir

Continuation
Northwards
on a reduced scale
Scale of Miles
0   100

Solitudines vasta

Sound of
Megra
Chrono
Veiring
Abaraima o
Leisma
Swaleback
Eldir

RERE K

Kaima
Mornagay
OCEANUS
The Forn
Hornmere
o Laimak
Owldale
Ristby

Argyanna

Ulba
Kutarmish
Zenner
Rumala
Fiveways
Azuma
Reisma
Salimat
Perax
Memison
Mere
Ril Armun

Huron Range

MEZENTIA

Sound
Zayana
Daish
Sestola
Armash
Fasheda

THE THREE
KINGDOMS

Scale of Miles
100   200   300   400   500